Praise for Sherryl Woods and the Sweet Magnolias

"Woods begins the Sweet Magnolias series with a focus on the unsettling effects of divorce and infidelity on the children of broken marriages, a theme that adds depth and emotional intensity to the romantic relationship."

—*Booklist* on *Stealing Home*

"Woods continues her Sweet Magnolias trilogy with this topical, interesting story. The characters are nicely layered, and the conflict is believable."

—*RT Book Reviews* on *A Slice of Heaven*

"Woods updates her readers on the continuing antics of the Sweet Magnolias in her holiday-themed, heartwarming contemporary romance, paving the way for even more stories set in this charming South Carolina town only a short drive from Charleston."

—*Booklist* on *Welcome to Serenity*

"Woods's readers will eagerly anticipate her trademark small-town setting, loyal friendships, and honorable mentors as they meet new characters and reconnect with familiar ones in this heartwarming tale."

—*Booklist* on *Home in Carolina*

"Woods never fails to come back to the romantic point."

—*Publishers Weekly* on *Sweet Tea at Sunrise*

SHERRYL WOODS

HONEYSUCKLE SUMMER

mira

mira

ISBN-13: 978-0-7783-1996-2

Honeysuckle Summer

Dear Friends,

Setting out to write a book with an agoraphobic heroine was probably pure foolishness. And yet those of you who've been keeping up with the Sweet Magnolias know that nothing is impossible when it comes to these incomparable women. Raylene Hammond simply had to have her own story.

For a victim of domestic violence, any future can be filled with uncertainty and fear, but for Raylene, the fear is so overwhelming that she's retreated to the home she shares with her friend Sarah and simply hasn't left. Add in the threat that her ex-husband could once again come after her when he's released from prison, and there's a very real chance that she will never conquer those fears.

It would take an amazing man to walk into such a situation and put his heart on the line. Carter Rollins is such a man. Though they get off to a terrible beginning, he quickly becomes Raylene's staunchest supporter. He's kind, patient and, most of all, determined. He offers her hope for a brighter future than she'd imagined possible.

I hope you'll enjoy this story about the Sweet Magnolias. I wish each of you loyal and lasting friendships to get you through the tough times and to fill your lives with laughter…and maybe the occasional margarita!

All best,

Sheryl Woods

HONEYSUCKLE SUMMER

CHAPTER ONE

Raylene stood in the kitchen doorway on a day that was surprisingly cool for the first of June. She stared in dismay at the backyard where Sarah's children, Tommy and Libby, had been playing not two minutes before. Now only two-year-old Libby was in sight. She was standing next to the open gate of the fenced-in yard.

Tommy's absence immediately set off panic in Raylene. "Libby," she called. "Sweetie, come here. Where's Tommy?"

Toddling to Raylene, her big eyes filled with tears, Libby pointed in the direction of the street.

"Come inside," Raylene commanded. She could only deal with one missing child at a time. Raylene scooped up Libby, then raced toward the front door and flung it open to peer up and down the block. Tommy was nowhere in sight. Barely five, he couldn't have gone too far in the time she'd been in the kitchen, she assured herself. She'd turned away just long enough to put a few cookies on a plate and pour three glasses of lemonade. Two minutes, maybe three.

Normally she would have brought the kids inside when the sitter left to run an errand, but it had been such a beautiful day, she'd decided to let them continue playing in the yard. What had she been thinking? She'd been terrified ever since she'd moved in with Sarah and her family that something like this would happen on her watch. She'd taken every precaution she could think of to avoid it. Now, just one slip and all her worst fears were coming true.

Opening the door, she shouted at the top of her lungs. "Tommy!" She managed to inch over the threshold, but just barely. The panic she'd felt upon discovering Tommy was gone multiplied a thousandfold as she tried to force herself to take the next step and then the next. It took every bit of willpower she possessed not to scramble right back inside. She clutched Libby so tightly that the little girl whimpered in protest.

"Sorry, baby," Raylene soothed.

Again, she shouted for Tommy, but there was no response. Frustration warred with terror.

Tommy knew the rules. He knew, even if he didn't understand, that she couldn't leave the house to go chasing after him. He was also an adventurous preschooler for whom rules meant very little. He couldn't possibly comprehend that the thought of leaving the safe haven of their home terrified her. Sometimes it was beyond her understanding, too.

Ever since Raylene had run from her abusive husband, she'd grown increasingly housebound, scared of everything beyond the boundaries of these walls. It didn't seem to matter that Paul Hammond was safely locked behind bars, at least for a few more months. She couldn't make herself leave the house. If anything, she'd been getting worse, not better.

She forced herself to inch down the last step and onto the sidewalk, fought the fear clawing its way up the back of her throat, the trembling in her limbs. Unable to take one more step, she shouted again and again.

"Tommy Price! You get back in this yard right this minute!"

She scanned the street in every direction, fully expecting him to pop out from behind a bush, a lopsided grin on his face at having won some misguided game of hide-and-seek.

Instead, there was no sign of movement on the quiet, tree-lined street. Any teens were inside playing video games or doing homework. The younger children on the block were probably indoors having an after-school snack. An hour from now, more than likely there would be a dozen kids who could tell her in which direction Tommy had gone, but for now there was no one in sight.

Raylene tried to calm herself with the reminder that Serenity was a safe town, and small enough that almost anyone would recognize Tommy and bring him straight home. Unfortunately, those thoughts warred with too many dangerous possibilities.

She tried telling herself that if a stranger had approached, one or both of the kids would have screamed. They'd been drilled often enough to be alert to that kind of danger. Even Libby was old enough to be wary of anyone she didn't know. That Raylene hadn't heard any fearful shouts was some consolation.

All of this went spinning through her head in what seemed like an eternity, but was probably no more than a couple of minutes. She had a choice to make. She could fight her fears and try to go farther than the front steps, or she could call for help. Given her inability to leave the house for so long, she opted for being smart over saving her pride. Not wanting to waste another precious second, she punched in 911 on the portable phone.

Her second call was to the Serenity radio station where Sarah had a morning show of talk and music. She often stayed after the show ended to book future guests. It was the station owner and Sarah's soon-to-be husband, Travis McDonald, who took the call.

"I'm so sorry," Raylene kept telling him, trying not to break down in tears as she rambled through the story. "I swear I only looked away for a few minutes, and I tried to go searching for him, Travis. I really tried. I'm standing on the sidewalk now, and you know how long it's been since I've come even this far. I've called the sheriff's office. They're sending a deputy right away."

"It's okay, Raylene. Everything's going to be fine," he reassured her, though she could hear the underlying tension in his normally laid-back tone. "I'll tell Sarah what's going on and we'll be there in five minutes. No need to panic. Tommy's probably playing next door. Give Lynn a call."

"But surely she would have heard me shouting for him," Raylene protested. "Hurry, Travis, please. I'll try to go looking myself, but I don't know if I can."

Travis, bless him, didn't criticize her for this phobia that had taken over her life. He just reassured her that he was on his way. "Call next door," he repeated. "The number's on the bulletin board by the phone in the kitchen. Lynn will help until we get there."

"Of course," she said, furious with herself for not thinking of that sooner.

But when she reached Lynn, the neighbor reminded Raylene that her daughter was in a playgroup this afternoon.

"I haven't seen Tommy, but I'll be right over to help with the search," Lynn said at once.

"Don't bother coming here," Raylene told her. "If you could just look up and down the street toward town and maybe alert some more of the neighbors, I'll send Travis in the other direction as soon as he gets here. Surely Tommy can't be more than a few blocks away."

"Will do," Lynn promised, then hesitated. "Are you okay? Anything you need before I start hunting?"

"No, I'm fine." In fact, finding herself with an actual role—acting as command central for news from those actually out searching—finally began to steady her nerves. This was something she could do. She could keep Libby close and safe, make calls, coordinate efforts, even wait for Tommy to wander back from whatever adventure he'd gone on. Shaking with relief that others were now doing what she couldn't, she sat down on the top step to watch and wait.

Sitting there on the front stoop, phone and lemonade in hand, Libby in her arms, Raylene peered up and down the street for some sign of Tommy, or at least of Travis or the deputy that the sheriff's department had promised to send.

When the wait began to seem endless, she once again tried to venture back down the sidewalk. Even though she took a deep breath and told herself she'd already done this once today, her palms began to sweat. Her heartbeat accelerated, and her breath seemed to lodge in her throat. Tears of frustration filled her eyes. She ought to be able to take this one short step, dammit! There was a crisis, and she was absolutely useless.

For the first time since she'd given in to her fears and settled for such a limited existence, she realized just how much might be at stake. Though the kids were the sitter's responsibility at this time of day, Sarah had depended on Raylene to be her backup, to keep her children safe if she ever happened to be left in charge, even for a brief time. She'd let Sarah down, let Tommy down.

Consumed with self-derision, Raylene realized they all should have known better. Any length of time with her was too long, especially for Tommy, who had his daddy's stubbornness and tenacity along with the conviction that he was now a big boy. He was growing more independent by the day.

Raylene should have put her foot down and refused to look after the kids at all, not for an hour, not even for five minutes. She knew Sarah was determined to convince her that she was still normal, instead of some basket case, but Raylene should have insisted that the risks were too great. If anything happened to that little boy, she'd never be able to forgive herself.

When Travis's car squealed into the driveway and Sarah jumped out practically before he hit the brakes, Raylene nearly collapsed with relief.

"I'm sorry. I'm so, so sorry," she said as Sarah hugged her fiercely and told her not to worry. It was ironic really to have Tommy's mom consoling *her,* when it should have been the other way around.

Libby took one look at Travis and held out her arms. There was no question that she adored her prospective stepdaddy. Travis took Libby from Raylene's arms and held her close.

"It's going to be fine," Sarah said, though her confident words were belied by the fear shadowing her eyes. "Tommy can't possibly have gone far. What happened, anyway? Travis tried to tell me, but all I could hear was blah-blah-blah through the haze of terror that rushed through me."

Raylene repeated the story she'd told Travis on the phone. "The sitter went to pick up a few things we needed for supper." She glanced at her watch and saw that even after all the commotion, less than a half hour had passed. "She should be back here any second. I swear, Tommy and Libby weren't out of my sight more than a couple of minutes. When I looked back, the gate was open and Tommy was gone. I couldn't believe my eyes."

"Well, I can believe it," Sarah said. "He's as slippery as

a little eel. He's constantly escaping, you know that, even when Travis and I think we're watching him like hawks. He's figured out where his friends live and likes to go visit. He doesn't grasp the concept of getting permission. That's probably what happened today."

"Lynn's out knocking on doors," Raylene said. "If that's what happened, she should have news soon." She met Sarah's gaze, reluctant to stir the distrust that still existed between Sarah and her ex-husband. "I hate to bring this up, but you don't suppose Walter stopped by and picked him up without coming inside to let me know?"

Sarah shook her head. "I've already called him, just to let him know what's happening, and, to be honest, to make sure he's making a sales call at the business where he said he'd be this afternoon. I phoned him at the business, rather than on his cell, just to be sure."

"Thank God for that, at least," Raylene said, just as the sheriff's car rolled to a stop out front.

Expecting to see the familiar face of one of the long-time deputies or the paunchy form of the sheriff himself, she was stunned to see a tall, lean specimen of pure masculinity emerge from behind the wheel. He had chiseled cheekbones, thick brown hair and, when he removed his aviator sunglasses, a penetrating gaze that could spin a thousand feminine fantasies.

Furious with herself for ogling the man like a lovesick idiot despite being in the middle of a crisis, Raylene took a gulp of ice-cold lemonade to soothe her suddenly parched throat.

Anticipating a cross-examination, she steadied herself to wait, but instead, he reached out and opened the passenger door to the police cruiser. Tommy emerged, wearing an excited little-boy's grin over the adventure he'd apparently had.

"I got to ride in a police car," Tommy announced unnecessarily. "And I got to turn on the siren."

Sarah knelt down and pulled Tommy into her arms. Her tears were openly flowing now. Then she held him at arm's length and her expression turned stern. "Young man, do you have any idea how much trouble you're in? What were you thinking, leaving this yard without permission? You know you're not allowed to go anywhere that Raylene can't see you."

Tommy's chin wobbled precariously. He cast a guilty look in Raylene's direction. "I heard the ice-cream truck, and I had my money in my pocket 'cause we knew Freddie'd be coming soon. I thought I could find him."

Raylene nearly groaned. Of course he'd go chasing after ice cream, though Freddie Wilson usually didn't make his rounds until late afternoon, and normally he stopped right in front of their house so Raylene or the sitter could watch as Tommy made his purchase.

"I looked and looked, but I couldn't find Freddie," Tommy said sorrowfully. "And then I got lost. The policeman found me. He knew my name." He regarded his mom worriedly. "That's okay, right? Policemen are our friends, not strangers."

Sarah nodded. "That's exactly right."

"I found him over on Oak Street," the deputy said, still eyeing Raylene with disapproval. "He took himself quite a walk."

"It's hot and I'm thirsty," Tommy said. "Can Libby and me have lemonade and cookies now?"

"Lemonade, but no cookies," Sarah told him firmly. "Then you're going to your room so Travis and I can have a talk with you about leaving here without an adult. I suspect your daddy will have a few things to say to you, too, when he gets here."

Sarah turned to the deputy. "Thank you so much for finding him and bringing him home."

"No problem," he said, then focused on Raylene. "Ma'am, if you're in charge, you're going to need to keep a closer eye on the children. If something like this happens again, there could be serious consequences."

Raylene flinched at his judgmental tone, though she could hardly argue with the message. "Believe me, it won't happen again," she assured him.

Because as soon as she got back inside, she intended to go through the classified ads and find another place to live. She'd imposed on Sarah long enough. She'd always intended to offer to buy this house from Sarah when she and Travis were married and living at his place, but staying here until then was now out of the question. Surely Sarah would see that after what had happened this afternoon, and if she didn't, then Raylene would enlist Travis, their friend Annie or anyone else she could think of to make sure that Sarah saw reason. After all, where her kids were concerned, Sarah couldn't justify taking chances, not even to protect her best friend.

Unfortunately, Sarah wasn't being reasonable. Just after dinner, Raylene had announced her plans to move out, but Sarah was having none of it. To Raylene's surprise, Travis was on her side. Even Annie had come over toting her new baby to offer her two cents'. Raylene fully expected the entire contingent of Sweet Magnolias to turn up any second to provide backup. When they united in solidarity, they were a force to be reckoned with. Everyone in Serenity knew that.

"Just because a man none of us had ever set eyes on before this afternoon criticized you without knowing all the facts does not mean you're going to move out," Sarah told Raylene. "And you can just take those bags you've packed right back to your room and unpack them."

"I agree," Travis said. "What happened today could have happened to any one of us."

"But it happened to *me*," Raylene protested, "and there wasn't anything I could do except scream for Tommy and then make phone calls. You would have been outside chasing after him. He'd never have made it all the way to Oak Street if you'd been here."

"You did exactly what needed to be done," Sarah argued. "You called the sheriff."

"It wasn't enough," Raylene countered. "I love you for taking me in and putting up with my craziness for all this time, but it needs to stop now. I will not put your children at risk."

Sarah frowned at her determined tone. "What I know is that my children love you. You're one of my two best friends and right now this is your home. It's where you feel safe. Until you feel stronger and really, really want to move out on your own, you're staying right here with us, and that's final."

Raylene regarded her with a mix of frustration and amazement. "How can you want that after what happened?"

"Because I love you, you dope. And like Travis said, what happened with the kids today could just as easily have happened to me or to him."

"Listen to her," Annie said, cradling Meg in her arms. "Trevor gets away from me in the blink of an eye. I swear one of these days I'm going to put that boy on a leash when I take him to the mall. Who knew kids that size could move so fast? Their legs are short, for goodness' sake. Of course, Ty has a conniption when I say that, but he's not the one standing in a crowded mall trying to spot a kid in a sea of legs."

She met Raylene's gaze. "And another thing, since Trevor's my stepson, I feel an even greater sense of responsibility in a way. If anything ever happened to him on my watch, I don't know if Ty would ever forgive me. So you see, I do understand how you feel, Raylene. I know exactly how terrifying this must have been."

"So do I," Travis said, his gaze on Sarah. "Don't you think I feel a huge weight of responsibility every time I take Libby and Tommy out with me? Sure, I'd feel that if I were their biological dad, but, like Annie said, somehow I think it's harder being their stepparent or, in your case, the friend who's been left in charge."

They were wearing away at all of Raylene's arguments. She did have one more, though. "Okay, what about Walter?" she asked Sarah. "I'm sure he has an opinion about all this. Do you want to give him the perfect excuse to file for custody?"

Right after her own divorce, any mention of a custody suit would have scared Sarah to death, but now she waved it off. "I anticipated something like this, so I asked Walter flat out if he intended to make an issue of what happened today. He told me no, and he meant it. I could tell."

She reached over and squeezed Raylene's hand. "He likes you, sweetie. How you've pulled it off is beyond me, but he considers you a friend. He acted like I was nuts when I suggested he might use this to seek custody. He told me we were past all that a long time ago, he agreed it was better for the kids to live mainly with me and he had no intention of dragging you into that kind of fight. I'll call him right now, and he can tell you that himself, if you need to hear it from the horse's mouth."

"No," Raylene said. "But you all are being entirely too understanding, Walter included. The important thing is to keep the kids safe. They're obviously not safe with me."

"Okay, we can deal with that," Sarah said decisively. "From now on, you won't stay here alone with them, not even for a few minutes, but that's the only thing that's going to change. This is your home, period. Don't waste your breath trying to make me change my mind."

Raylene sighed with frustration and, if she were being honest, a hint of relief. "I appreciate this, I really do, but I just don't see how you can be so generous after the way I let Tommy get away from me. Anything could have happened."

"But it didn't," Sarah said emphatically. "And I said it because it's how I feel. You're a Sweet Magnolia, just like me and Annie, Maddie, Helen, Dana Sue and Jeanette. That makes you the next best thing to a sister, okay? And families stick together." She regarded Raylene slyly. "There is one thing you could do for me in return, though."

Raylene braced herself. She already knew what was coming. They'd had the conversation before. "You want me to see Dr. McDaniels." The psychologist had treated Annie years ago for an eating disorder and continued to monitor her progress whenever Annie felt herself slipping. After well over a year of watching Raylene get worse, Annie and Sarah had started pushing Raylene to consult her. Their pleas had become increasingly forceful lately. Now, understandably, they were bound to be amped up even more.

Sarah nodded. "I do. Whether you just have a panic disorder or full-blown agoraphobia, it's time to face it, Raylene. Not just because of what happened today, but so you can get your life back. Maybe this incident today happened for a reason, to make you finally get the help you need."

Raylene had been waging an internal battle against seeking help from the moment her friends had first mentioned it. It had probably been a ridiculous point of pride that she conquer this problem on her own. The truth was, though, that she obviously couldn't. Whatever was going on was bigger than she was.

When she remained silent, trying to work up the courage to concede defeat and ask for help, Annie stepped in.

"Raylene, this is treatable," Annie assured her. "You know that. I've shown you all the research I could find on the Internet. There's a very good chance Dr. McDaniels can work with a physician to get you on the right combination of medicine to help, and maybe teach you some calming and relaxation techniques. Don't let that horrific ex-husband of yours rob you of the rest of your life. Now that you're free of him, you need to live every second to the absolute fullest. You need to meet someone new, someone who's kind and gentle and treats you with the respect you deserve. We all want that for you."

"And you think I'll meet that kind of man in Serenity?" Raylene scoffed with some of the leftover snobbishness she'd been taught by her mother, a Charleston socialite who'd married a local man, then found herself stuck in Serenity and had chafed at every minute of her life here.

"I have," Sarah reminded her, glancing over at Travis, who gave her a wink. "So have Annie and Jeanette. And look at the men in Maddie, Dana Sue and Helen's lives. They're all amazing. And, if you don't mind my saying so, that highly educated blueblooded doctor you met in Charleston wasn't exactly a catch, now was he?"

Raylene's lips quirked despite the reminder of just how awful Paul Hammond had been.

"You have me there," she admitted. "Although a man is the last thing on my mind at the moment, I will call Dr. McDaniels." Because she'd made the promise at least a dozen times before, she knew it probably sounded empty now. "I mean it. I'll do it this time, first thing in the morning. You can stand right by the phone and listen in, if you want to. I owe you that much for sticking by me despite what happened."

"You're not doing it for me," Sarah corrected. "You're doing it for yourself. You need to concentrate on that. And I don't need to listen to the call, Raylene. If you make a promise, you'll keep it."

Raylene was grateful for the trust Sarah had in her word. She just wasn't so sure she deserved either the trust or a future. That was one more aftereffect of living with a man who'd literally and figuratively beaten her into submission for way too long before she'd wised up and left. That it had taken her years, rather than minutes, would shame her forever. That it had cost her the baby she'd been carrying had left her with the kind of gut-wrenching guilt from which she couldn't imagine ever recovering.

Even she recognized that she'd been punishing herself by locking herself away in this house. Paul might be serving his time in prison, but she'd been serving her self-imposed sentence right here. Even now, she wasn't a hundred percent certain she deserved to have it end, but today the stakes of doing nothing had increased to a level she could no longer ignore.

CHAPTER TWO

Carter Rollins had taken one look at the woman standing on the front stoop at Sarah Price's house the day before and labeled her some kind of expensively clad snob who thought she was too good to get her hands dirty. The fact that she'd been standing around, rather than looking for the missing boy, had grated on him. It had cemented his first impression that she was a selfish, overindulged, irresponsible female. If it had been up to him, he'd have found some way to charge her with child neglect on the spot.

Unfortunately, he'd learned a few things since moving to Serenity. It was a tight-knit, friendly community that stuck together. Unless he had the law very firmly on his side, it was best to handle things with that in mind.

WSER might not be the most powerful radio station in the state, or even in the region, but its owner, Travis McDonald, and star personality, Sarah Price, were local celebrities. He'd heard about their very public romance when he'd first arrived in town. Everybody in Serenity, it seemed, loved a love story. If Travis and Sarah intended to back up this woman, then there was very little Carter could do about it. And their protective attitude toward her yesterday had been as unmistakable as it was unfathomable.

The next time, though—if there was one—he wouldn't hesitate to handle things differently, local politics be damned. He'd involve the child protective authorities in a heartbeat.

It was his job to protect people, especially innocent kids. Finding Tommy Price wandering alone several blocks from home had stirred his anger, so he didn't much care who was on that babysitter's side. Next time, he'd haul her in.

"Why do you look so grim?" his sister Carrie asked, eyeing him warily as he set an assortment of take-out boxes from the local Chinese restaurant on the kitchen table.

"Just a bad day," he told his fifteen-year-old sister. One of these days, one of them—he, Carrie or his other sister, Mandy—was going to have to learn to cook. Beyond throwing meat, chicken or fish on a grill, he was pretty useless in the kitchen. Carrie had once excelled at baking chocolate-chip cookies from a package, though lately she'd refused to bake them for reasons beyond him. Mandy could make popcorn in the microwave and scramble eggs. When they'd moved and his hours had become more predictable, he'd vowed to change their pitiful culinary ineptitude, but so far, they mostly existed on takeout. Sadly, the variety in Serenity was pretty slim.

"You've had a lot of bad days since we moved to Serenity," Mandy noted. She was the younger of the girls for whom he'd had full responsibility since their parents' deaths two years ago. "Wasn't that the whole point of moving here, so you'd be in a better mood? I have to tell you, big brother, I don't think it's working."

Carter frowned at her interpretation of the decision he'd made to leave his police job in Columbia for a smaller community. "We're here because this is a better environment for the two of you."

"In other words, because it's totally boring," Carrie said,

disdain in her voice. "You didn't want us to have fun ever again."

"No, I wanted you to be safe," Carter countered, passing the kung pao chicken.

"Then how come you had a bad day?" Carrie persisted, scooping a tiny spoonful of rice onto her plate and adding a few of the vegetables from another container. It was barely enough to feed a bird, but Carter resisted pointing that out. His comments inevitably led to an argument.

"If it's so safe, your days should be dull as dirt," she added, her expression challenging.

He shook his head at her logic. "A little boy went missing this afternoon."

Carrie immediately looked chagrined. "But you found him, right? And he was okay?"

"He was fine. He'd gone looking for the ice-cream truck."

Carrie looked relieved. "So it all turned out okay," she concluded. "You should be happy."

"I'm just irritated that he got away from the woman who was supposed to be watching him in the first place," he admitted.

Mandy gave him an incredulous look. "Oh, come on! You used to run away from home all the time. Mom and Dad told us. Mom said it's why her hair turned gray."

Carter winced. They were enough younger that he hadn't realized they would know about his own adventures on the wild side when he was only a few years older than Tommy Price. "That was different," he claimed.

"How?" Carrie asked. "You scared Mom and Dad to death, and you did it deliberately. It sounds as if this little boy just went on an innocent search for ice cream."

"You're missing the point. Anything could have happened to him."

"Anything could have happened to you, too," Carrie said. "Do you blame Mom and Dad for letting you sneak away?"

He saw he wasn't going to win this argument. Truthfully, he very rarely came out on top with these two. They could twist him in knots faster than anyone else in his life. Worse, now that they were both in their teens, the dangers were even greater and his influence on them was still shaky. They were all still getting used to the idea that he was in charge, and not just a bossy big brother anymore.

"It was different," he repeated. "I was older than this little boy. I could take care of myself."

"You were six the first time you ran away," Mandy corrected. "Dad said he followed you until it got dark. You finally got scared at some noise or a shadow or something and ran home."

Carter scowled. "Did they tell you every stupid thing I ever did?"

Carrie grinned impudently. "No, they pretty much glossed over all the stuff you did with girls. We just know there were a lot of them."

"Ancient history," Carter said. And given how much trouble these two were likely to be, he couldn't imagine having time for any kind of relationship of his own in the near future.

"Too bad," Mandy commented, her expression thoughtful. "You might mellow out if you had a girlfriend. I hear not having sex is tough on guys."

"We are *so* not discussing my sex life," he declared emphatically, feeling heat climb into his cheeks. He supposed he should be grateful that the girls still thought they could say anything to him, but not if one of those topics was going to be his personal relationships...or lack thereof.

Carrie's eyes brightened. "Hey, we could work on finding someone for you," she suggested eagerly.

"I do not need you to pick out a woman for me," he said, horrified by the thought. "I have enough on my plate right now, anyway, so just forget it, okay?"

Both girls shrugged.

"Whatever you say," Mandy said. "But if you're cranky all the time, don't blame us."

Carter shook his head. "Give it a rest. I am not cranky all the time."

Carrie gave him a disbelieving look, then turned to her sister. "He's in denial, right?"

"Lives there," Mandy confirmed.

And then they were gone, leaving him to clean up their take-out meal and to wrestle with the possibility that his overall mood these days was less than cheery. Thinking about this afternoon's events certainly wasn't doing a thing to improve that, and something told him he was going to be lying awake all night wondering why that was. Was it really about what might have happened to Tommy Price? Or was it about the woman to whom he'd taken an instant dislike?

When morning rolled around and the girls had left for school, Carter reported for duty at the sheriff's department, then told the dispatcher he was going to patrol in Serenity unless a call came in and he was needed elsewhere.

"You're not doing a drive-by in Tommy Price's neighborhood, are you?" Gayle Kincaid asked.

Carter frowned at her astute guesswork. "What makes you think that's where I'm headed?"

"Because I've been in this job for thirty years, and I saw the way you looked when you got back here yesterday afternoon," she told him. "Your eyes were as dark as any storm cloud I ever saw. Spotted a few flashes of lightning in there, too."

"What did you expect? I found that boy blocks from home," he said in his own defense. "Why wouldn't I check to make sure someone's keeping a closer eye on him today?"

"I'm not saying you shouldn't, but if you take every case to heart like this, you'll burn out before you turn thirty, which as I recall is only a few months from now."

"I'm just riding around a neighborhood," he told her. "I don't think we need to worry about my mental health just yet. Call me if you need me."

"Will do," she said. "By the way, Sarah Price has been singing your praises on the air this morning. I imagine you're a real hero around town by now."

Carter wondered how she'd feel about him if he decided he had to take some kind of action against her babysitter, but he left that unsaid.

A few minutes later, he was cruising past the little bungalow looking for any sign that something might be amiss this morning. He heard kids squealing with glee in the backyard and caught a glimpse of Tommy and his younger sister—Libby, as he recalled—swinging on a swing set, being pushed by someone unfamiliar. Not much more than a teenager, from the looks of it, but still it had to be an improvement over the alternative. For an instant, relief washed over him. Maybe Sarah Price had fired the irresponsible woman and hired someone new already. If so, his worries were over.

Just as that thought crossed his mind, though, the back door swung open and the other woman called out, "Breakfast's ready." She turned her head, spotted him, and Carter swore he saw the blood drain out of her face. The screen door immediately slammed shut.

He waited until the kids and the other woman went inside before driving off. He was more confused than ever now. The woman from the day before was still there, but what was her role beyond dressing up the scenery?

Once again, she'd been wearing a pair of slacks and a blouse that he'd bet his entire month's salary had cost a fortune. Thanks to Carrie and Mandy, who were obsessed with designer fashion, he recognized pricey clothes when he saw them. He'd spent too many hours listening to tearful pleas from his sisters for the latest jeans or fancy shoes. They didn't seem to understand just how tight money was since their parents had died with little savings and only a minimum amount of life insurance. Added together, it had been barely enough to cover funeral expenses. He refused to touch the money they'd put aside for the girls' college education. Instead, he tried to add a little to it each month, which further eroded the amount he had for basic expenses.

Nor did Carrie or Mandy seem to care that he was woefully inept at the whole parenting role that had been thrust upon him at the age of twenty-seven. They rarely cut him a break of any kind, but that was another issue.

Thinking about the boatload of responsibility that he'd struggled with for the past couple of years made him even more annoyed at how the babysitter had just let Tommy take off yesterday afternoon. If someone was going to take on the job of looking after someone else's kids, then by gosh, they ought to be focused on it and not sitting around in the kitchen reading fashion magazines, or whatever, while the kids ran wild and put themselves in danger. He'd turned his life upside down to take care of Carrie and Mandy, hadn't he?

He still had half a mind to park the cruiser, barge inside and warn her that if her friend hadn't been so nice, a child-negligence charge could have been brought against her. Maybe that would get her attention so she'd take the job seriously. Then, again, maybe watching the kids wasn't her job. Maybe she was some flighty relative who was visiting temporarily. He realized he needed more evidence—scratch that, more *information*—before he put his job on the line by stirring up a ruckus.

He decided to give the matter some more thought over an early lunch at Wharton's, which made the only decent burger in town, and at a price he could afford on his paltry deputy's salary. Most days, he made himself peanut butter and jelly or bologna sandwiches, same as he did for the girls.

Half a dozen locals greeted him as he slid into the red vinyl booth. Mayor Lewis, whom he'd met making the rounds of local officials after taking the job, stopped by the table before he could even place his order.

"Heard what happened with Sarah's boy yesterday. Glad it turned out okay," the mayor said. "Nice work."

"I got lucky. I spotted Tommy on the second street I canvassed," Carter told him. He hesitated, then asked, "Mind telling me what you know about the woman who was supposed to be watching him?"

The mayor blinked in apparent confusion, then nodded. "Oh, right. The babysitter's just out of high school and working for Sarah until she goes off to college. Laurie Jenkins. She's a good girl."

Carter shook his head. That must have been the woman he'd seen in the backyard this morning. "This was someone older, mid-twenties, I'd say, about the same age as Sarah."

Howard's expression brightened. "Ah, you must mean Raylene."

"We didn't meet, but I suppose that's who it was. Tall, too thin, dark hair. Looks like she belongs in a fashion magazine."

"That's Raylene, all right," the mayor confirmed. "She and Sarah Price go way back. She's tight with Annie Townsend, too. Have you met her? She's married to Ty Townsend, a local boy who pitches for the Braves."

This wasn't the first time Carter had noticed how much the mayor liked to talk once he got wound up. Usually the meandering chitchat got on his last nerve, but this time he found the topic fascinating. He waited for more, and Howard didn't disappoint him.

"Those three girls—Raylene, Annie and Sarah, that is—were best friends from about the time they could walk," the mayor continued. "Never saw one without the other. Raylene was living over in Charleston for a while. Married a highfalutin doctor, as I recall. Then there was trouble of some kind and she came back here. She's been stayin' with Sarah ever since. Doesn't get out much from what I hear."

"Is she actually living with them, then?" Carter asked, wondering why a woman who could afford that expensive wardrobe would be living in a little bungalow with a family that wasn't her own. Maybe it had something to do with that trouble she'd been running from.

"Far as I know, she's there permanently." Howard Lewis regarded him with curiosity. "Haven't seen much of her, but she used to be a pretty little thing. You interested?"

"Not a chance," Carter said fiercely. "The only thing I care about is making sure she doesn't let those kids go roaming around on their own again. Next time, things could turn out a whole lot worse."

Howard frowned at his somber tone. "You feel that strongly about it, maybe you should have a talk with Travis. He's about to become their stepdad, and he just now walked in the door." He beckoned the man in question over to the booth. "You two musta met yesterday. Travis McDonald, Carter Rollins." He stepped aside and gestured for Travis to sit. "I'll leave you both to your meals."

Presented with the opportunity, Carter laid out his concerns for the man seated opposite him. As he talked, though, Travis's expression turned increasingly indignant.

"Nobody loves those kids or is more protective of them than Raylene," he told Carter. "You don't know what the hell you're talking about."

"She didn't do much to keep Tommy safe yesterday afternoon, now, did she?" Carter said. "I didn't see her combing the streets to find him. No, indeed, she stood right there on the front steps and waited for everyone else to get the job done."

Travis leveled a hard look at him that gave him pause. "I thought folks in police work were supposed to wait till the evidence was in before jumping to conclusions."

"I saw all the evidence I needed to see," Carter insisted, refusing to back down. "It was plain as day what happened. She didn't take her responsibility seriously, and Tommy wandered off and could have gotten himself run over or kidnapped or who knows what. I'd think you'd be as concerned about that as I am."

Despite the dire picture Carter painted, Travis didn't back down. "Did you notice that even after Tommy came home, Raylene never left that front stoop?"

"Probably too guilt-ridden," Carter assessed, dismissing the odd behavior that, frankly, hadn't struck him at the time as anything other than a complete lack of caring. "Or scared I was going to arrest her on the spot."

"No, it's because she *couldn't*," Travis said, heat in his voice. "She has something called agoraphobia, at least that's what Sarah and Annie think. Hasn't left the house but once or twice since she moved in and that was well over a year ago, after she arrived here all battered and bruised from her abusive husband. Just think about that for a minute, why don't you?"

He leaned in closer to hammer his point home without raising his voice. "That front stoop is as far as Raylene can make herself go without having a full-blown panic attack. When she phoned me yesterday, right after calling the sheriff's office, she'd made it to the sidewalk and was beside herself that she couldn't take another step. In fact, she was so guilt-ridden, she wanted to move out so the kids would never be at risk again."

"Maybe she should," Carter said, though he was beginning to see another side to the story, one he wasn't quite ready to believe.

Travis's scowl deepened. "Not happening," he said emphatically. "For the record, she's not the babysitter. In fact, she's the one who insisted we hire someone else to look after the kids because of her panic attacks. She was only alone with them yesterday because Laurie ran to the store for a few minutes."

Carter had heard of that kind of phobia, but he'd never run across anyone who suffered from it. Agoraphobia had always struck him as some sort of psychobabble explanation people used as an excuse to avoid things they didn't want to do. Given how seriously Travis seemed to be taking it in Raylene's case, maybe he'd been wrong.

Still regarding Travis with skepticism, he said, "Honest to God? You're sure she's got a real problem?"

Travis nodded, then slid out of the booth, leaving his menu untouched. Apparently he'd lost his appetite.

"Next time you might want to do a little more investigating before making judgments," Travis suggested mildly. "People in this town don't take kindly to newcomers talking trash about one of our own. If you're going to do any good in this community, you'd do well to remember that."

He walked away and left Carter feeling like a jerk. Okay,

maybe he'd been well intentioned, but he sure as hell hadn't been fully informed, just the way Travis said. It was a good lesson for him. To his surprise, he realized that even though he hadn't made a single accusation to Raylene's face, he felt as if he owed her an apology.

And one of these days, when he'd managed to swallow his pride, he'd have to deliver it in person.

Walter dropped by Sarah's house on his lunch hour. He'd seen the guilt in Raylene's eyes the day before, and it had gotten to him. He might not be the most sensitive guy on the face of the earth, but somehow he felt connected to her. They'd both been down some bumpy roads and were still struggling to find their way.

During all the time his relationship with Sarah and his kids had been on shaky ground, Raylene had bridged the gap. She'd talked to him in her frank, uncensored way and made him see his own flaws. If things were better now between him and his ex-wife, it was at least in part due to Raylene. He didn't want to see her worrying herself sick over what had happened, and he knew, without a doubt, that she would be.

"Did you stop by to make sure the kids are safe?" she asked when he walked into the kitchen.

Walter frowned at her. "Never any question about that, and you know it. Now stop beating yourself up over what happened."

She regarded him with surprise. "Sarah told me you weren't mad at me, but I didn't entirely believe her."

"Didn't I tell you the same thing when I was here last night?"

"I thought maybe you'd have second thoughts once you'd had time to reflect about what happened."

"Well, I didn't, which is exactly why I'm here again today.

I wanted to be sure you knew I don't blame you." He grinned at her. "And since I'm giving up my lunch break to come over here, how about fixing me one of those fancy salads of yours? I'm gaining too much weight living on burgers from Wharton's and pizza from Rosalina's."

"Isn't it way past time for you to find your own place and fix your own lunches?" Raylene said, though she immediately pulled lettuce, tomatoes and other ingredients from the refrigerator. "Now that you know it's going to work out selling ads for the radio station, it's time, Walter. The kids need a real bedroom so they can spend the night with you. Nice as it is, the inn's no place for them for more than an hour or two."

He shrugged. "I've gotten used to the inn. They've given me a decent monthly rate, and there's no housekeeping or upkeep."

Raylene shook her head. "You are downright pitiful. You spent way too many years being waited on, didn't you?"

He grinned unrepentantly. "Probably. The truth is, though, that I haven't had ten minutes to string together to go house hunting, much less enough money put aside for a down payment," he said. "The house in Alabama still hasn't sold because the real estate market over there sucks. It's a mill town and people are losing their jobs. Their homes are going into foreclosure. The market's glutted, but I did finally get a solid lead on a buyer last week."

"Well, then, it's time to start looking here," Raylene said optimistically.

"Not until the deal's closed," Walter insisted. "Too many things could go wrong. I can't just rely on what I'm making at the station. The pay's not that great. Travis is working on getting approval for a stronger signal for the station. If that comes through, then I'm going to be on the road even more driving to all the new towns our signal will reach. It'll mean more money, though."

"You're just full of excuses, aren't you?" Raylene commented. "Think about this. Being on the road more is all the more reason to find a comfortable home to come back to." She set a bowl in front of him, then handed him a light dressing. Her expression dared him to ask for his preferred blue cheese.

Walter took the vinaigrette with a sigh. "You can be such a nag. Worse, you don't even have to say a word."

"You're the one who was complaining about gaining weight," she reminded him. "Now, about the house. Why don't you call Rory Sue Lewis. She's working with her mother now. Tell her what you want and let her do all the legwork. Then give her an hour and see what she's come up with. I'll bet she can help you figure out financing, too. At the least she can make the sale contingent on selling the house in Alabama, so you won't have that worry hanging over you. You won't be on the hook unless the money's there."

"You honestly think it will be that easy?" he asked skeptically. "Rory Sue's new at the real estate business from what I hear. Her mama's the expert."

Raylene got a wicked gleam in her eye. "But Rory Sue's an expert at figuring out what men want. I'll put money on her finding a way to satisfy you."

Walter paused, his fork in midair, and studied Raylene's suddenly innocent expression. "Are you matchmaking?" he asked warily.

"What if I am? You're a free man."

"With no spare time," he corrected. "Between work and the kids, I have no time. I just told you that."

"Every man will make time for women and sex," she countered. "It's a law of nature."

"And women?" he queried, tossing the ball right back into her court. "You've been shut away in here for the better part of a year. How's your love life?"

Rather than taking offense, as he'd half expected, she merely laughed. "Hey, I'm willing. The men just have to find me."

Walter regarded her soberly. Despite her laughter, he found the response unbearably sad. "That's no way to live, Raylene, and you know it."

She sobered at once. "Not the first time you've mentioned that. Just so you know, I called Dr. McDaniels this morning. She's coming here tomorrow. I guess we'll finally get to the bottom of my problem."

"About time," Walter said, relieved for her.

She regarded him wearily. "That's what all of you think," she said. "But no one seems to be thinking about what happens if there's no way to fix me."

Walter heard the genuine fear behind her lightly spoken words and reached for her hand. "Then you'll handle that," he said confidently. "But I believe you're strong enough to deal with anything, Raylene. I mean that. You just may be the strongest woman I know."

Uncomfortable with the unexpected, if heartfelt, emotion, he stood up and backed away. "Now I've got to get back to work before Travis finds out I'm over here instead of selling airtime. You need anything after you see the doctor tomorrow, you call me, you hear? I may be a poor substitute for a Sweet Magnolia, but I am your friend, and I've got a broad shoulder you can lean on."

Raylene's eyes filled with tears. "Sure," she said. "Thanks."

As Walter got in his car, he thought about what had just happened. If anyone had ever told him he could have deep feelings for a woman without wanting to get her into bed, he'd have sworn they were nuts. That was the way it was be-tween him and Raylene, though. They were friends, the kind who backed each other up, and he'd meant what he said. If she needed him, he would be here.

Of course, knowing Raylene, it would be a cold day in hell before she ever admitted needing anyone.

CHAPTER THREE

Raylene wasn't entirely shocked when she saw Helen Decatur coming up the walk after dinner on the night after Tommy's adventure. She'd half expected the attorney to stop by and warn her about possible charges that could be filed against her if she wasn't more careful in the future.

When she opened the door, though, Helen merely held out a bottle of tequila, a bag of limes and a can of frozen limeade.

"Time for a margarita night," Helen declared.

"Just you and me?" Raylene queried.

Helen grinned. "Are you kidding me? Sweet Magnolias do not get to drink alone, or even in pairs. The others will be here soon."

"Did Sarah know about this?"

Helen nodded. "She's the one who made the calls," she revealed as she headed for the kitchen to start making a batch of her lethal margaritas. "She thought you needed a boost to your spirits. She also said she had the Triple Sec. Any idea where I'd find it?"

As Raylene retrieved the bottle from the pantry, Helen found the blender without asking and then, with the skill of many years of practice, she put the ingredients for the frozen drinks in and turned it on. A moment later, she added crushed ice and ran the mixture through another cycle until she had an innocent-looking concoction that could fell a lumberjack.

"Sarah also thought you might want to talk about what that deputy implied when he was here," Helen added casually, glancing at Raylene as she handed her a drink.

"You mean the implication that there would be legal consequences if Tommy ever slipped away from me again?"

Helen nodded. "If the man wants to be a hard-ass, he could probably stir up some trouble, but I'll handle it." She grinned and lifted a glass filled with a frothy, icy drink. "It's taken me a little longer than expected to hit my stride again after maternity leave and my mom's broken hip, but I'm back now. No one is tougher in court than I am."

"I know you might relish the idea of going toe-to-toe with the deputy in court, but I think it might be wiser if I'm not in a position for anything like this to happen again," Raylene told her. "Sarah, Travis and I are agreed, I will never be alone with the kids, not even for a few minutes. We were lucky this time, but I'm not taking any more chances."

"Still, things can happen," Helen said. "I'm just saying you don't need to worry. I have your back."

"Thank you. You came through for me with my divorce from Paul. I have enough financial resources that I haven't had to think about trying to work. And you gave me great advice when I had to give my deposition against him for assault and abuse. I trust you implicitly, but I'm also determined that your help won't be needed with this."

Helen studied her intently, then nodded. "Okay, then," she said. "Let's get this party started."

As if her words had been carefully timed, Sarah suddenly came into the kitchen. Annie appeared at the back door, followed by her mother, Dana Sue Sullivan, the owner of Sullivan's restaurant, as well as Maddie Maddox, who ran The Corner Spa—which was owned by Dana Sue, Maddie and Helen—and Jeanette McDonald, who ran the day-spa services and was married to Travis's cousin. Years ago as teenagers, Dana Sue, Maddie and Helen had formed the Sweet Magnolias, a tight circle of friends. Then they'd drawn in Jeanette, and now the new generation, which included Annie, Sarah and Raylene.

The margarita-night gatherings had become a tradition years ago, a time for the women to share their problems, their successes and a whole lot of laughter. That they'd come together for her touched Raylene in unexpected ways. She couldn't seem to stop the tears that welled up.

"Hey, are you about to cry?" Sarah asked her.

Raylene nodded. "Afraid so. I can't believe everyone is here just to cheer me up, especially when I'm the one who messed up."

"Hey, little princess, it's not *all* about cheering you up," Annie said, nudging her in the side. "Some of it's about the margaritas and Mom's guacamole. Not that *I* get to drink a margarita. I'm still nursing the baby."

"It's a small sacrifice to make to have a healthy baby," Raylene scolded. "And by the way, I am so not a princess."

"Did you or did you not have a debutante ball in Charleston?" Sarah asked. "I seem to recall you looking like a princess in a fairy tale that night. You showed us the pictures often enough."

Raylene winced. It seemed like a million years ago when her grandparents had talked her into that. That she'd gotten all caught up in the social whirl and lost focus about what really mattered in life still amazed her. She'd been persuaded to go to private school for her senior year and had lost contact with her friends.

Recently, the best part of coming back to Serenity had been finding herself surrounded by people who didn't put on airs, live by a calendar of parties and fund-raisers, and who were totally grounded. Her friends here—Sweet Magnolias and beyond—were real. She understood the difference now and valued it.

"To my very deep regret, I did have a coming out season," she conceded.

"There's nothing wrong with having a big, fancy party," Helen soothed. "In my day, I loved any chance to get dressed up and put on a pair of kick-ass shoes." Her expression turned mournful as she held out feet clad in expensive flats. "These days I can't stand up for more than two seconds in the kind of high heels I always loved."

"Tonight is not about how much you miss your Manolos and Jimmy Choos," Maddie teased.

"I was just trying to point out to Raylene that parties aren't necessarily bad," Helen countered.

"They are if you start thinking those kinds of events are the most important things in life," Raylene said. "I was so determined to make my mother and grandparents happy, I forgot what mattered to me. And let's not forget that was the night I met Paul Hammond and sealed my fate with that louse."

Paul had been older, a medical student, in fact, but he'd come to the party as a date for a plain Jane cousin whose partner had bailed on her. He'd spent the entire evening flirting with Raylene, whose own dull date was the grandson of friends of her grandparents.

By the end of the evening she'd been smitten, and despite the difference in ages, her grandparents and even her mother had encouraged the match. Her father had clearly disapproved, but he hadn't gone against his wife's wishes. She and Paul had married soon after she turned eighteen, while he was serving his medical internship.

The stress of his demanding training had been the excuse for all the times he'd lost his temper with her. After a while he hadn't bothered with excuses for what began as verbal attacks and escalated over time into more violent behavior.

The marriage had been a horror show, all the more terrifying because on the few occasions when she'd tried to tell her mother what was happening, her fears had been dismissed. She'd been told she was overreacting, and that all marriages hit rough patches. Too many times she'd been reminded of all the advantages that would come with being married to a successful doctor from a prominent Charleston family. Her relationship with her mother had been permanently damaged by Raylene's discovery that she couldn't count on her mother when it mattered.

Not wanting to dwell in the past, Raylene shook off the memories and took another sip of her margarita. "Let's not go there," she said as the others nodded readily and lifted their glasses.

"I propose a toast to Raylene and a brighter future," Sarah said. "Do you mind if I tell them about tomorrow?"

"What's happening tomorrow?" Helen asked.

"Dr. McDaniels is coming here to determine if I have a panic disorder of some kind that keeps me from leaving the house," Raylene told them. "I guess we'll find out if I'm nuts or just lazy."

"You're not either one," Sarah said fiercely. "Stop saying things like that."

"I agree," Dana Sue said, crossing the room to give Raylene a hug. "I'm so glad you're finally seeing her. She was a godsend to Annie, wasn't she, sweetie?"

Annie nodded. "I'd probably be dead if not for her. I still

rely on her guidance from time to time when I get scared that I'm falling into my old eating pattern. Fortunately, right now, I seem to be eating all the time. And nursing Meg seems to keep me from gaining an ounce."

Any mention of Annie's baby was enough to make Raylene feel a deep sense of sorrow for the baby she'd lost. Even though she'd only been in her first trimester, the baby had already been real to her. When she'd started bleeding and had miscarried just days after one of Paul's beatings, it had been worse than anything else she'd suffered at his hands. The only blessing that had come from that awful tragedy was that she'd finally found the strength to leave him and end her marriage.

Annie gave her hand a squeeze, her expression sympathetic. Though Raylene had never mentioned losing her child to Annie, she knew Sarah had probably told her. It was one secret she was relieved not to have to talk about herself.

"Your turn will come," Annie whispered. "I know it."

Raylene regarded her sadly. "I'm just glad to be here with friends. I don't need miracles."

"But you deserve one," Annie insisted. "And something tells me one is just around the corner."

When Raylene saw the sheriff's cruiser pull to a stop in front of the house, her heart climbed into her throat. She thought of Annie's words the night before and had to choke back a laugh. Surely this wasn't the miracle Annie had had in mind for her. She knew what the man now identified as Carter Rollins thought of her. Travis had told Sarah of their conversation, and Sarah, fit to be tied, had told Raylene after last night's Sweet Magnolias gathering.

She watched as he crossed the front lawn with long strides and a look of purpose on his face. Was it possible he'd found some crime with which to charge her? Could he do that without Travis and Sarah wanting him to? She barely resisted the desire to grab the phone and call Helen for advice before opening the door to him.

Instead, though, she stood tall and waited. One thing she knew all too well was how to put on a facade when she was feeling scared or out of her element. She'd put on more shows in public during her pitiful marriage than any actress in a Broadway production. The minute the doorbell rang, she swung open the door and offered him her brightest smile.

"Deputy Rollins, I wasn't expecting to see you again so soon. Did you stop by to check on Tommy and Libby?" she asked, seizing the initiative. "They're taking their naps right now. I can assure you they're in their beds, right where they belong. Laurie, the babysitter, is in the den." She leveled a knowing look directly into his eyes. "Feel free to check if you don't believe me."

To his credit, he flushed ever so slightly. He removed his sunglasses, revealing hazel eyes with emerald flecks. He fiddled nervously with the glasses. "Actually I was around the corner on a call and thought I'd come by to offer you the apology I think I owe you."

"Oh?"

"I misjudged you the other day," he admitted, looking uncomfortable.

"Did you really?"

His lips twitched a little at her response. "I'm sure you know all about it, because Mr. McDonald was pretty indignant on your behalf."

"He might have mentioned something about a conversation the two of you had, though he told his wife, not me," she admitted. "Sarah filled me in."

He nodded. "I had a feeling it would work something like

that, Serenity being the kind of town it is. As Mr. McDonald informed me, folks here look after their own."

"We certainly try to," she agreed. She decided he'd squirmed enough and let her ingrained manners kick in. Southern women were always ready to offer a cool drink, if not an entire spread of food, at a moment's notice. "Could I offer you some coffee? Maybe a glass of lemonade or some sweet tea? It's another scorcher out there today. There are cookies, too, if the kids haven't gotten to them today."

He looked a bit startled by the invitation. "You sure?"

She gave him a thoughtful survey that brought more color to his cheeks. "Well, despite the fact that you're wearing a gun, you don't look all that dangerous to me, so yes, I'm sure."

"I just thought maybe me being a stranger would make you nervous."

"It's not people who terrify me," she found herself saying. "It's everything outside this house." She gave him a wry look. "Crazy, isn't it, since I grew up in this town and all my problems were over in Charleston."

"What kind of problems, if you don't mind me asking? Travis said something about domestic violence."

Raylene hesitated. Her disastrous marriage wasn't something she liked to talk about to anyone, much less a stranger. If he knew about the abuse, he knew more than enough.

"It's in the past, and I don't like to talk about it," she said. "Now, about that coffee, are you interested?"

"The lemonade sounds better," he said, then followed her inside.

In the kitchen, she gestured for him to take a seat, then poured two tall glasses of lemonade over ice and handed one to him. She put an assortment of chocolate-chip and oatmeal cookies on a plate and set it on the table, then took a seat herself. Only a trained observer might notice that she sat on the edge of the chair and a safe distance away, rather than relaxing. She had a hunch that Carter noticed.

Calling on her once-instinctive social graces, she said, "Are you new to Serenity? I know you weren't in school with us, and you seem to be about the same age."

"I moved here a few months ago when I hired on as a deputy. It seemed like a good place to raise kids."

His response surprised her. She'd automatically checked for a wedding band and there hadn't been one. Of course, as she knew all too well from her philandering ex-husband, some men were adept at hiding rings when it suited their purposes. Or he could be divorced or even a widower.

"How many children do you have?" she asked.

"None of my own, but my two younger sisters are living with me. They're fourteen and almost sixteen. Our parents died a couple of years back. We stuck it out in Columbia for a while, but I liked the idea of a small town. When a job opened up here this spring, I grabbed it. I'm hoping they'll get in less trouble here than they might have in the city."

Raylene chuckled, thinking of some of the mischief she, Annie and Sarah had gotten into as teenagers. "Trust me, if girls want to get into trouble, they can do it anywhere."

He regarded her with an impudent grin. "Do tell. Just what kind of trouble did you get yourself into? If I go into the computer, will I find a dark criminal past?"

"Hardly," she said, then grinned. "We were far too clever to get caught."

"Really?"

She thought back over her high school years and chose one of many incidents. "Really. For instance, there was one memorable slumber party when we let boys sneak in," she confided. "Annie's mom, Dana Sue Sullivan..." Her voice trailed off.

"The owner of the restaurant," he guessed.

"Exactly. She about had a fit over that one. Of course, the fact that Annie collapsed that night and wound up in the hospital pretty much trumped whatever trouble we probably would have gotten in over inviting the boys to the party."

"What happened to Annie?"

She hesitated at talking about Annie's personal business, but then everyone in town already knew the story. "She had anorexia. It nearly killed her." She waved off the subject and grinned. "As for the mischief we got ourselves into, I'm sure I could tell a few other stories, if I racked my brain. And most of the teachers at the high school could probably add a dozen or more."

He looked a little pale as he shook his head. "I'll definitely keep that slumber party scam in mind when Carrie—she's the fifteen-year-old—tells me she wants to spend the night with a friend. I had no idea teenage girls were so sneaky."

"The ones I knew certainly were," she told him.

He smiled, causing an unexpected bump in her heart rate. Then his expression sobered.

"May I ask you a personal question?" he said.

"Sure."

"Travis mentioned something about you not being able to leave the house. Is that true?"

She nodded. Whatever embarrassment she'd once felt over her problem had faded as people in town had come to accept that if they wanted to spend time with her, they had to do it here.

"When I first came back to town, I was able to sit on the back patio. I was so relieved to be someplace safe that I didn't realize at first that leaving here was even an issue."

"Makes sense," he said.

"Then, after a couple of months of healing physically and mentally, I tried going out with Sarah and Annie," she said ruefully. "I never made it past the driveway before I'd break out in a cold sweat. My heart would start racing so fast, I was sure I was going to pass out. After that happened a few times, well, I hate to admit it, but I just stopped trying. Eventually it got so bad, I couldn't even take a step outside."

"Why'd you give up?"

The question was simple, but the answer was complicated. Raylene wasn't sure she could explain it. "I suppose it just seemed easier," she said eventually. She shrugged. "And there was no place I really needed to be, nothing I really wanted to do."

Carter looked unconvinced. "You're content to make this house enough for the rest of your life?" he asked incredulously.

"I suppose I haven't let myself think long term. Right now, when I consider leaving here, the fear outweighs the joy of whatever might be out there. Forever's not a concept I can grapple with."

"What about the yard, at least? Can you go outside that far?"

"You know that I can't," she responded, meeting his gaze. "You saw me frozen in place on the top step the other day. If I could have gone farther, believe me, I would have. Knowing Tommy was somewhere out there and I couldn't look for him was horrible. I've never felt so helpless in my life." She regarded him with curiosity. "Why does this matter to you? Are you that worried about the kids? Because if that's it, you can stop. I will never have the responsibility for looking after them again."

"For their sake, I'm relieved to hear that," he admitted

candidly. "But it strikes me as sad that you might not get to experience all that life has to offer. You're a young, beautiful woman. You're smart and funny. Seems to me it's a waste to stay hidden away here." He frowned. "Don't you even want to get better?"

"I doubt you can understand this, but getting better, leaving this house, seems to mean more to other people right now than it does to me. I feel safe here. I love being with Sarah's kids. People come and go all the time, and that's what matters. I'm not alone or lonely."

"There must have been things you enjoyed before the panic attacks started," he protested. "Don't you miss at least some of them?"

Raylene thought about it. She wondered if maybe this whole cycle of fear and panic hadn't started even while she'd been married. It wasn't that her home had been a safe haven. Far from it, in fact. But in it, she had been free of the speculation that would have spread had people in her social circle ever spotted her with the kind of bruises that had been inflicted too many times to count.

Back then she'd lived a solitary life in many ways, living for quiet moments in the garden, where she'd nurtured her fragile plants the way she'd longed for someone to nurture her. Thinking about that brought on an overwhelming sense of nostalgia.

"I miss my garden," she said softly, closing her eyes as she remembered it—purple, white and magenta azaleas in spring, a sea of tulips, then hollyhocks, summer phlox, golden lilies, shaded beds of impatiens and a tinkling waterfall amid a fragrant collection of rosebushes.

"Planting flowers, watching the yard fill with color, even pulling the weeds. The doggone honeysuckle nearly drove me mad, but it smelled so sweet, I even loved that. And I loved the way the sun felt on my shoulders."

In the year before she'd finally ended her marriage, she'd stopped gardening. Even now she shuddered at the memory of the rampage her husband had gone on, destroying all her hard work, leaving the rosebushes ruined, the flowers wilted and dying in a chaotic heap before he was done. In some ways, his savage attack on her garden had hurt as much as any of the physical attacks she'd endured.

Even after all this time tears filled her eyes at the memory. Suddenly she felt a warm, solid hand covering hers.

"I'm sorry," Carter said, his expression apologetic. "I shouldn't have pushed you. This is really none of my business."

She forced a smile. "It's okay. I'm fine."

She said the words, maybe even managed to sound convincing, but the truth was, she was anything but fine. The memories had touched a place deep inside that she'd almost buried and left her filled with longing.

The minute Carter Rollins left, she sank down on the sofa to await the arrival of Dr. McDaniels, relieved that she'd finally made the call, even as she was dreading what the psychologist might tell her.

Because if Carter Rollins had done nothing else with his well-timed visit and probing questions, he'd reminded her that there was a life outside these four walls—even if only as far as the backyard—that truly might be worth fighting for.

CHAPTER FOUR

Dr. McDaniels was a thin woman in her fifties with a hint of gray threading through her short dark hair. She had the kind of reassuring smile that invited confidences and a warmth in her eyes that suggested compassion. Though Raylene had only crossed paths with her casually years ago during Annie's hospitalization, she immediately felt comfortable with her.

"Thank you for agreeing to come here," Raylene said as she led the way into the living room. "The sitter's taken the kids to the park, so we won't be interrupted."

"Under the circumstances, I'm happy to come here," Dr. McDaniels said. "Hopefully we can figure out what's going on and determine the right treatment. If we can accomplish that, it won't be long before you can come to me."

"I don't know," Raylene said skeptically. "I haven't left this house in a very long time."

"How long?"

"I first moved in here right after I left Charleston. Back then, I could at least sit out back in the evening, but eventually even that got to be too much. I suppose it's been a year or more since I've left at all."

"Have you tried?"

Raylene shook her head. "Once I was back in Serenity and inside this house, it was like I'd used up every bit of bravery I had. I saw this as my safe haven. Thankfully I didn't have to go back for my husband's sentencing. He'd pleaded no contest once the D.A. showed him my deposition, along with the medical records that documented how many times I'd been to various emergency rooms, plus the condition I was in the night I lost my baby. Though the prosecutor opted not to charge him in the baby's death, Paul didn't want the whole messy incident coming out in court and causing an even bigger scandal for his family. The plea bargain lessened his sentence, as well."

There was no visible reaction on the doctor's face as Raylene reported the abuse that had driven her home to Serenity. "How long were you married?" she asked.

"Too long," Raylene said fervently.

"And you were abused throughout the marriage?"

Humiliated, Raylene nodded. "It was mostly verbal at first, temper tantrums from the stress he was under as an intern."

"And you thought it was your fault for triggering these bursts of anger," the psychologist said.

Something in her matter-of-fact approach and her obvious understanding made Raylene feel less ashamed. "You've heard this before," she guessed.

"Too many times," Dr. McDaniels said. "You do know it wasn't your fault."

"I do now. I think I even understood that on an intellectual level back then, but when the man you love keeps hammering it home that you're responsible if he gets angry, on some level you start to think it must be true. I was too young— barely eighteen when we married—to know better."

"Did you consider leaving him?"

"I did leave once. I went to my mother and told her what

was happening. She thought I was exaggerating. She convinced me to go back and work on my marriage, on making Paul happy. She honestly believed, I think, that I must have been doing something wrong for him to act that way."

"How'd that make you feel?"

Tears streamed down Raylene's face at the memory of walking away from her parents' house that day, her suitcase in hand, what she'd seen as her only hope for an escape dashed. "Alone," she said at once. "I'd never felt more alone in my life."

"Couldn't you have called someone else, Sarah or Annie, perhaps?"

"I'd lost touch with them, and I was too embarrassed, anyway. I hadn't made any real friends in Charleston. Most were the wives of Paul's friends, and I didn't dare go to them."

"So you were scared and isolated," the psychologist concluded.

"Pretty much."

"What finally changed to get you out of the house for good?"

Raylene swallowed hard. "We fought," she said, not wanting to remember.

"But you'd fought before."

"This was worse. I...was pregnant. Just a couple of months along." Paul hadn't been happy about the baby, but she had been. She'd wanted someone she could love unconditionally, someone to protect the way no one had protected her. In a way, she'd convinced herself that the baby would give her the strength to leave. Ironically, that's exactly what had happened, though not in the way she'd envisioned.

Raylene buried her face in her hands and wept as she thought about that night, about the punches deliberately aimed at her stomach, the blows that had brought on a miscarriage days later. Paul hadn't wanted her to go to the emergency room when the bleeding started, but for once she'd defied him, threatening to run screaming from the house if he didn't let her go quietly. Naturally the threat of exposure in his own neighborhood had given him pause.

She hadn't gone to the hospital where Paul had privileges. She'd feared his associates would help Paul to cover up the abuse. Instead, she went across town. The doctors there had been horrified. They'd known at a glance what had happened and taken enough pictures to guarantee that Paul would be convicted of a crime, even though sentencing guidelines for a first offense, even of aggravated felony abuse, were next to nothing.

When she'd declared she was leaving him, two doctors at the hospital had physically restrained Paul to keep him from following her. The moment they'd released her, she'd driven straight to Serenity and walked into The Corner Spa to see Annie.

"You'd been living in Charleston?" Dr. McDaniels said, glancing at her notes. "Is that right?"

Raylene nodded.

"How did you get over here? Did you drive yourself?"

She nodded. "I think I was in a state of shock. I barely remember making it to The Corner Spa. Then Annie brought me here."

"And you literally haven't left since?"

"I tried a couple of times. It was horrible. I'd get to the car and start shaking so badly that Sarah and Annie practically had to carry me back inside."

"What do you think is going to happen if you leave the house?"

"I know it's irrational since my ex-husband is still in jail, but I think he's going to be there, waiting. I tell myself over and over that there's nothing to be afraid of anymore, but I still can't take that next step. I always thought I was pretty strong, but this has me beat."

"Why haven't you asked for help before?"

"I guess I felt ashamed because I couldn't conquer this on my own. Like I said, I knew my reaction was irrational, but the fear was there just the same." She took a deep breath, then admitted what she'd never told Sarah or Annie. "And I think I was punishing myself."

"Because you hadn't protected your baby?" Dr. McDaniels said at once.

Raylene nodded.

"If you can see that much, then you've made more progress than you realize. You understand the underlying causes of your problem. Now we just have to get busy and see what works so we can fix it."

She said it so optimistically that Raylene took heart. "You make it sound so simple."

"I didn't say it was going to be simple or easy," Dr. McDaniels cautioned. "There could be a lot of trial and error and a lot of setbacks before we get it right. Have you tried any medications?"

"None. I thought I could figure it out, you know, with some kind of mind-over-matter thing."

"But you weren't figuring it out."

"I gave up," she admitted. "I felt safe here."

"And now? What's changed?"

"I told you on the phone about letting Tommy slip away from the house. Not being able to go after him was the final straw. Even though Sarah and Travis said they understood and forgave me, I haven't been able to shake the image of what could have happened."

"So, you want to change to protect the kids?"

Raylene heard a faint hint of criticism in the question. "You think I should want it for myself."

"Yes, I do," Dr. McDaniels said, though not unkindly. "Despite what your ex-husband tried to make you believe, you deserve to have a full life. You have to want that for yourself. I won't kid you, you're not going to conquer this overnight. You'll need a powerful motivation to deal with all the setbacks that might happen along the way."

"Do you think the medication will help?"

"It may. I'll consult with your physician—"

"I don't have one here," Raylene told her.

"Then I'll call a colleague of mine. We'll give medication a try. Even so, I have to be realistic. I can't promise you a quick fix, Raylene, not to correct a pattern that's gone on this long. Panic disorder can be complicated, especially when the fear is grounded in a traumatic incident. In your case, it's not even one incident, but years of living in fear."

Even though she'd expected that, Raylene felt a fresh batch of tears welling up. On some level she'd hoped Dr. McDaniels could snap her fingers, give her a few pills and the whole problem would vanish. She'd be able to live a normal life again.

"What if nothing works?" she asked, swiping angrily at the tears. It was as if she'd had a fresh start dangled in front of her then snatched away. Even though she told herself that fighting to get better was important, no matter how long it took, she'd obviously hoped for a miracle.

"Don't be discouraged," the psychologist said, correctly gauging her mood. "Something will work. I'm not a quitter, and something tells me you aren't, either."

"I don't know how you can say that. I gave up a long time ago."

"No, you didn't seek help, and now you have. It's always

better late than never." She pulled out her cell phone and
made a call, apparently to the colleague she'd mentioned.
After consulting for a couple of minutes, she nodded and
thanked him. "He's going to call a prescription in to Wharton's. Someone will deliver it this afternoon. It's an anti-
anxiety medication, a relatively mild dose. We'll give it a
couple of days, then I'll come back and we'll try a few experiments."

Raylene regarded her with suspicion. "Experiments?"

"See if we can get you down those front steps. If you can,
so much the better. If you can't, I'll have an even better idea
of what we're dealing with."

Raylene couldn't imagine a drug on earth powerful enough
to accomplish that. "I don't know——" she began, only to have
the doctor cut her off.

"It's just the beginning, Raylene. We'll pray for an instant
cure, but we'll work however long it takes to make it happen. The good news is that we know what's behind the fear.
For some people we don't even have that as a starting point."

"Okay, then," Raylene said, her spirits bolstered slightly
by the doctor's quiet confidence.

Dr. McDaniels gave her hand a squeeze. "I'll say it again,
as often as you need to hear it—don't be discouraged. Every
recovery starts with a single step. Just look at Annie and
how well she's doing these days, then think about where we
began with her. Today, you've taken your first step. On Friday, you'll take your next one." She consulted her appointment book. "Is this same time okay for you?"

"It's fine." Raylene chuckled. "It's not as if I'm going anywhere."

"But you will be," Dr. McDaniels said. "I promise."

When she was gone, Raylene stared after her, surprised
by the sensation spreading through her. It felt a lot like hope.

She hadn't felt anything like it since the day she'd shown up in Annie's office and her friend had told her everything was going to be okay. After years of distrusting the person closest to her, it had been a wonder to finally believe in someone again.

Walter had his notes from the day's sales calls spread out on a table at Rosalina's. A half-eaten pepperoni pizza, which he'd pay for with indigestion in a couple of hours, was pushed to one side, and his second beer sat on the table untouched. He didn't even know why he'd ordered it beyond wanting an excuse not to head back to his room at the Serenity Inn just yet.

When a shadow fell across the table, he glanced up expecting to see the waitress with his check. Instead, he found a woman wearing a halter top, short shorts and a friendly grin. She didn't wait for an invitation, but slid into the booth opposite him.

"You're Walter Price, right?" she said.

"I am."

"Raylene nailed the description," she said, looking impressed. "For a woman who doesn't get out, she sure does know the hottest men in town."

Walter held back a sigh of resignation. "You must be Rory Sue Lewis."

She looked surprised. "How'd you know?"

"Raylene mentioned you. I figured sooner or later you'd turn up, whether I came looking for you or not."

"Yeah, she's matchmaking," Rory Sue said without a hint of dismay. "But she also said you might be looking for a house or a condo. I could probably live without the meddling, but I never turn my back on a solid real estate lead. That's one thing I learned from my mom." She studied him intently. "So, are you? Looking for some property, I mean?"

"First tell me how you knew I'd be here tonight. I assume this isn't a chance encounter."

"Raylene said you always eat either here or at Wharton's around six-thirty. Since I was in the mood for pizza myself, I started here."

Walter chuckled at Raylene's audacity in setting this up without clearing it with him, and in her apt description of Rory Sue's methodology. "Okay, yes, I'd like to find a place to buy. I don't have time to do a lot of looking, but if the right thing came along, I'd be interested," he admitted. "Did she explain that I'm waiting for a deal to come through on my house in Alabama?"

"She filled me in. We can work around that. If you can spare a few minutes now to tell me what you'd like, I'll line up the perfect places and have you all moved in by this time next month." She eyed the remaining pizza. "Hey, are you going to eat the rest of this?"

"Help yourself." He beckoned the waitress, then asked Rory Sue, "What would you like to drink?"

"A diet cola will do," she said, already biting into the first slice of pizza. She sighed with undisguised pleasure. "I only allow myself to eat this once a month. It's way too fattening otherwise."

"I've noticed," Walter said, thinking of his own expanding waistline. Maybe he would take Ronnie Sullivan up on his invitation to join him, Cal Maddox, Tom McDonald and some of the other men in town to shoot hoops sometime.

"Hey, there's nothing wrong with your body," she said, giving him a frank survey. "I did mention you're hot, didn't I?"

Walter had been hearing some variation of that since high school. It no longer had the power to seduce him. He'd realized how little looks mattered. He'd prefer it these days if someone told him he was living his life with integrity.

"Is that part of your sales spiel?" he asked Rory Sue.

"Nope, just an observation. I pretty much say what's on my mind."

"I imagine that gets you into trouble from time to time."

"Not so much with men," she said candidly. "They seem to appreciate knowing where they stand with me. I don't have a lot of women friends, though."

"Not even Raylene?"

"Not really. She, Annie and Sarah are tight, but I'm a couple of years younger." She gave him a chagrined look. "And then there was a bit of a misunderstanding when Sarah thought I was after Travis."

Walter was finding the conversation more intriguing by the minute. "Were you?"

"Sure," she said with a shrug. "What woman with a libido wouldn't have been, but he only had eyes for Sarah." She winced, then added, "Sorry. See what I mean? I say whatever comes into my head. I didn't think about the fact that Sarah's your ex-wife. Does it bother you that she and Travis are together?"

Walter didn't think the situation called for an in-depth discussion of his very complicated feelings on that subject. "My marriage was over a long time ago," he said, and left it at that.

She regarded him skeptically. "There's an edge in your voice that tells me you're not as happy about that as you'd like everyone to believe."

Surprised that she was that astute, he decided he shouldn't sell her short again. "The situation is what it is. I thought we were going to talk about real estate."

Rory Sue immediately sat up straighter, displaying an intriguing amount of cleavage, especially when she leaned forward and reached for a piece of paper from his notepad. "You mind?" she asked, also borrowing his pen. "Okay, let's get started. Describe the perfect house."

Walter thought of the large colonial he and Sarah had lived in back in Alabama. It had been chosen by his mother, mostly because it was the largest house in the most impressive neighborhood in town. He'd never felt comfortable there. Nor had Sarah, though she'd done her best to make the echoing, too-large rooms seem cozy and inviting.

"Something small," he said at once. "Three bedrooms, a couple of baths, maybe a patio out back. A nice yard for the kids. Nothing fancy."

"You need a gourmet kitchen?"

"I need a functioning kitchen."

"You know the house you just described, don't you? The one Sarah's living in right now. Maybe you could buy it when she and Travis get married."

Walter shook his head. "Right style, but I want something I can move into now. Besides, I think Raylene's planning to buy it." They'd talked about that on several occasions. He'd tried telling her it would be a mistake, that she was getting entirely too comfortable in her hideout. Maybe, though, Dr. McDaniels would get through to her and she'd move on, find her own home and her own life.

"Do you prefer a house or a condo?" Rory Sue asked. "Something brand new or older?"

"A house," he said at once, wanting something that would feel at least marginally like a home, rather than a bachelor pad. "And older, with full-grown trees and a lawn, not a patch of bare ground with no shade."

She nodded. "Got it. When are you free? Can you give me an hour tomorrow?"

Walter was startled by the hint of efficiency. He'd labeled

her more of a scatterbrain, which just proved his instincts about women were no better than they use to be. Heaven knew, he'd misjudged Sarah often enough.

"That soon?" he asked.

She shrugged. "You said you wanted to move in now. Why mess around? I'll go through my listings tonight and be ready to show you three or four things tomorrow. You tell me when."

"Five o'clock?" he suggested.

"Works for me," she said, then gave him a look that was more impish than come-hither. "And if I've found the perfect place, you can buy me dinner to celebrate. How's that for a deal?"

Regarding her with bemusement, Walter nodded. "I can't recall a better one."

She slid out of the booth. "Then I'd better get busy, if I'm going to prove that I'm as good as my mom in this real estate gig. Thanks for the pizza, Walter. We'll chalk this up as our first date." She winked. "Just so you know, with me things usually start to get really interesting by the end of the second date."

"I'll keep that in mind," he said. "Just one thing."

"Yes?"

"In my world, for them to count as dates, I need to do the asking, so let's think of tonight and tomorrow as all business, okay?"

For a moment, she looked startled, but then she tossed her mane of chestnut hair and laughed. "An old-fashioned guy! Who'd have thought it? Okay, Walter, we'll play this your way. I'll see you tomorrow at five. And since dinner's business, I'll buy."

"Do you always have to have the last word?"

"I don't have to," she told him, "but it usually works out that way."

She sashayed off before he could respond, giving him an excellent view of a backside that would make most men weep. She left Walter wondering just what in heaven's name Raylene had been thinking.

He pulled his cell phone out of his pocket and punched in the number at Sarah's. Raylene picked up.

"I've just had a very interesting, supposedly chance encounter with Rory Sue Lewis," he told her. "What do you know about that?"

"I might have mentioned your real estate needs to her," she said, a barely contained hint of laughter threading through her voice. "Does she think she can find you a house?"

"That's the least of what she thinks she can do for me," he said.

"I thought the two of you might hit it off."

"Hit it off? She scares me to death."

Raylene did laugh then. "Walter Price, you did not just say that."

"I mean it. She's pushy and blatantly sexual."

"Isn't that every man's dream?"

"I suppose some men fantasize about women chasing them, but personally I prefer a more demure, traditional type."

"Because your marriage to a woman like that worked out so well?" Raylene taunted.

Walter faltered at that. When he remained silent, Raylene added, "You need a woman who'll stand up to you and give you a run for your money, Walter. Admit it, once Sarah left you and started doing that, you found her a lot more fascinating."

"True, but there's no comparison between Sarah, even now with her newfound self-confidence, and Rory Sue. Sarah would kill you if she heard you trying to make one. Rory Sue's like some kind of barracuda-in-training."

"An apt description," Raylene agreed. "You don't have to date Rory Sue, you know. Just let her find you someplace to live and enjoy the sparks along the way. There were sparks at least, right?"

"Oh, there were sparks," he conceded reluctantly. "The kind that could burn a man if he's not careful."

"Then be careful."

"Oh, I will be," he assured her. "And next time you get any crazy ideas about matchmaking, my friend, see if you can't find someone who'll put some roses in your cheeks and leave me alone."

Raylene didn't respond. Walter pounced on her silence.

"Raylene Hammond, have you already found that someone?"

"Don't be silly. Where would I find someone?" she asked. "Men don't just appear magically outside my door. Isn't that what you're always telling me?"

"But one has. I can hear it in your voice."

"You're imagining things," she said.

Walter let it drop. If there was something going on in her life, God bless her, he'd find out about it soon enough. Tommy, for example, was a little blabbermouth when it came to anything going on at home.

"Tell me how things went with Dr. McDaniels," he said instead.

As she filled him in, Walter heard a familiar note of defeat in her voice.

"You didn't expect to run out of the first session and go skipping down the block, did you?"

"Not really, but it's clearly going to be hard work. She managed to drag out a lot of bad memories and insisted on dissecting them. I think it's going to get worse before it gets better."

"You're not scared of hard work, are you?"

"No," she said with a hint of indignation, but then her bravado failed her. "I'm scared of failing."

"You are not going to fail," he said adamantly. "There's too much at stake—your entire future, in case you need reminding. Besides, you have this huge support system in place. We'll all be right beside you every step of the way."

His words were greeted by silence and then she asked, "Walter, back when I was on your case every ten seconds for the way you were treating Sarah, did you ever think we'd wind up being friends?"

"To be honest, I never thought much about being friends with any woman," he said.

She laughed. "Exactly as I thought, which is why Rory Sue is perfect for you. You can thank me later. Good night."

"Good night."

"Oh, Walter, wait," she said, a teasing note in her voice. "Pleasant dreams!"

He bit off the retort that came to mind. With an image of Rory Sue's scantily clad body firmly implanted in his head, he doubted there was much sleep in his immediate future, anyway.

CHAPTER FIVE

Carter had no idea why Raylene got to him the way she did. She was obviously going through a tough time and it was just as plain her problems were more than he had any idea how to handle. He was barely coping with his own life these days. Trying to keep two strong-willed teenagers on the straight and narrow had turned out to be a challenge beyond his wildest expectations.

Still, despite all of his own worries, he couldn't seem to shake that nostalgic, tearful expression on Raylene's face when she'd mentioned gardening. That hint of vulnerability from a woman who was otherwise strong enough to accept her own limitations—self-imposed though they might be—nagged at him for several days.

On Saturday morning, done with fretting and ready to take action, he dragged the girls out of bed at what they considered the unholy hour of ten, and told them to be dressed and in the car in thirty minutes.

"Why?" Carrie asked with a moan. "It's Saturday."

"And you don't want to waste a minute of it," he said cheerfully.

Unimpressed by his good mood, she scowled back at him. "What's the big hurry?"

"We have places to go, things to do, people to see," he declared, using something their mother had frequently cited when she wanted them to get moving. She'd also said that getting everyone into the car was a little like herding cats, something he was just beginning to understand as his sisters grew increasingly stubborn and independent.

Carrie eyed him suspiciously. "What places? What things? What people?"

"You'll see," he told her. "Now, hustle."

Mandy was marginally more upbeat and cooperative. Always eager for something new, she was downstairs shoveling Cheerios into her mouth in ten minutes.

"Can we drive over to McDonald's for lunch?" she asked, even as she consumed enough cereal for five normal kids.

"We'll see," he told her.

"I don't want fast food," Carrie said, overhearing the end of the conversation as she wandered into the kitchen, still in her pj's. "It's too fattening."

This was a recent refrain, he'd noticed. It had started when she turned fifteen and gotten worse as she approached her sixteenth birthday. He found it worrisome, since she weighed next to nothing as it was. "You don't need to worry about that," he told her emphatically. "Now, eat something, and let's hit the road."

Carrie rolled her eyes. "Unlike *some* people, I don't have to eat my weight in cereal first thing in the morning."

Carter frowned at her. "And unlike *some* people, you don't have nearly as much energy. Eat! Do I need to remind you—"

"That breakfast is the most important meal of the day," she said sourly. "Okay, fine."

He stood there until she'd finished at least a token serving of cereal, then rinsed the dishes and put them into the dishwasher.

As soon as the girls were buckled into the car, he pulled out of the driveway and turned toward the nursery he'd spotted outside of town.

"Where are we going?" Carrie asked again. "There's nothing out here. Why can't we go to Columbia? At least there, we lived in civilization. There were actually movies in town, and stores. You promised when we moved here we could go back to visit, but you hardly ever take us."

Carter had heard it all before. "I took you two weeks ago," he reminded her. "We went to the mall, where you spent an hour calling your friends from your cell phone, instead of doing the shopping you'd told me was so vital to your very existence. Today we're doing something different."

"I know," Mandy said excitedly. "We're going to get plants for the garden, aren't we? There's a nursery out here."

"You got it, kid," he confirmed, only to see Carrie roll her eyes in disgust.

"I want tomatoes and squash and corn and maybe even watermelon, okay?" Mandy said. "I think there's enough room in the backyard. And it's really sunny back there, so everything should grow great."

"We'll ask at the nursery," Carter said. "How about you, Carrie? What do you want in the garden this year?"

She was silent until he sent a warning look in her direction.

"Some lettuce and yellow peppers, I guess," she said without much enthusiasm. "At least I can make a salad."

"Good idea. I think we'll get some flowers, too," Carter said, his tone deliberately nonchalant. "They'd look nice out front, don't you think?"

Next to him, Carrie made a face. "Who's going to plant them and take care of them? Not me."

"I will," Mandy offered. "Flowers will look pretty by the front door." She frowned. "But we've never grown them before. Mom always took care of the flowers. What if they die?"

An idea had been blossoming in Carter's mind for a few days now. "I know someone who might be able to give us some advice," he said.

"Who?" Carrie asked, instantly suspicious.

"A woman I met the other day."

His sister gave him a knowing look. "So what? You're using us and the whole flower thing to get a date or something?"

He shook his head at once. "It's not like that," he insisted, then fell silent, because the truth was, it might be exactly like that. If this worked out the way he hoped, he might be spending a whole lot more time with Raylene.

When an unfamiliar truck turned into the driveway at Sarah's, Raylene checked to make sure the kids were still watching a video in the den with Laurie. They'd both fallen asleep on the sofa, and Laurie was looking through a teen magazine of some kind. Raylene left them and went to the door.

When Carter Rollins emerged from the truck, wearing a pair of faded jeans and a T-shirt rather than his deputy uniform, she felt a little *zing* of anticipation. The sensation stunned her. Because of her marriage, she'd assumed there'd never be another man in her life she'd trust, much less be happy to see. That it happened to be this particular man was even more of a surprise.

Of course, she reminded herself, sexual attraction didn't necessarily go hand in hand with trust. Carter might appeal to her on some purely sensual level, but that didn't mean she intended to let him into her life. In a way, though, it was nice to know she could still appreciate a fine specimen of manhood when one happened to cross her path.

She opened the door, but remained safely inside. "You must be off duty," she said as he approached. "What brings you by?"

"I came by to ask a favor," he said, regarding her with a sheepish expression. "And I'll do something for you in return, if you agree."

She regarded him warily. When strong men got that helpless look, they were usually up to something. When they started talking about mysterious favors, alarm bells went off.

"Oh?" she said. "What exactly is this favor?"

"You mentioned something the other day about gardening, and I was hoping you could give me some tips."

She frowned. "I'm not an expert. You could talk to Doug at the nursery just west of town and get better advice. His family's owned it forever. I think they're all master gardeners."

He shook his head sorrowfully. "You must not know much about men. We hate admitting to other men that there are things we don't know."

She regarded him doubtfully. "But it's okay to admit it to me?"

"Sure. You'll just think I'm charmingly inept. Don't all women love feeling superior to the men in their lives?"

"To be honest, I've never had that experience," she said. "That certainly wasn't the way the balance of power worked in my marriage."

He gave her a questioning look, but didn't pry. She gave him points for that.

"Will you at least think about giving me some advice?" he asked.

"And what do I get in return?"

"I bought a lot more plants than we'll ever find room for in my yard. I thought you might want some for here."

A tiny spark of forgotten excitement stirred to life inside her, and then reality hit. "I can't accept them," she said, unable to hide her disappointment.

"Why?"

She scrambled for an excuse, rather than admitting that it would be impossible for her to plant the garden, no matter how badly she might want to. "This isn't my house. I'm not sure Sarah would appreciate it if I suddenly started landscaping around here." The excuse sounded hollow to her ears, especially since she knew that as soon as Sarah and Travis set their wedding date, this house was likely to become hers. Hopefully Carter knew nothing of that plan.

His gaze met hers and he waited, clearly anticipating more.

Raylene sighed. "I thought you understood. I can't leave the house, and I can't expect Sarah to plant a garden to indulge some whim of mine."

"But I could do it," he said. "You could tell me what to do and I'll provide the labor. You'd probably enjoy bossing me around. My sisters certainly do."

She considered the possibility. Even if she let him do all the planting, who would care for the garden? In this heat, it would need frequent watering, to say nothing of weeding.

"It's a lovely offer, but I don't think so," she said with real regret.

He studied her intently, then muttered what sounded like a curse under his breath. "It's about the upkeep, too, isn't it? Don't worry about that. I'll come by. So will my sisters. Let us do this for you."

Pleased by his determination and too delighted with the idea to keep coming up with excuses, valid or otherwise, Raylene slowly nodded. "Are you sure you want to do this?"

"I wouldn't have suggested it if I weren't. Do we have a deal?"

She couldn't help the rush of excitement that stirred when she imagined having a garden again. If she closed her eyes, she could even imagine a time when she'd be able to sit outside and enjoy it.

"I would love it," she admitted eventually, "if you're sure you don't mind doing all the work."

"I don't mind," he confirmed. "You can pay me back with advice and lemonade. Shall we give it a try? I have the plants in the truck."

She regarded him with amusement. "You were awfully confident you could talk me into this, weren't you?"

He grinned. "Pretty much. Something told me you'd be a pushover if I dangled the promise of a few flowers in front of you."

"Don't get the idea I'm a pushover, Deputy Rollins," she said with mock severity. "You'd be wrong."

"Every woman has a few weaknesses," he commented with a wink. "I just happened to figure out one of yours."

He walked toward the truck and left her wondering why he'd even given the matter so much thought. Most men, knowing her circumstances and the unlikelihood of anything approaching a normal relationship, wouldn't have bothered. Rather than worrying about his motives, though, she told herself to be grateful for this impulsive, sweet gesture of his.

While Carter unloaded the plants and carried them around back, she woke the kids and brought them into the kitchen. "You want to help Deputy Rollins with the garden?" she asked, knowing they'd be safe with him and would enjoy the freedom of being outside. It would also give Laurie time to run to the store to look for the dress she wanted for her date tonight.

Tommy immediately raced for the kitchen door, but Libby hung back. Rebuffed once too often by her own father, whose entire focus seemed to be on her big brother, she'd only recently begun to feel more comfortable around men. Thankfully, Walter himself was responsible for the change. He'd finally realized what a treasure she was and started giving her a fair share of his attention. That, plus undisguised adoration from Travis, had been a huge boost to Libby's confidence, but she still hung back around other men until she was sure of her welcome.

Raylene pulled a chair over to the doorway and lifted Libby into her lap. "You and I get to supervise," she told her, loudly enough to be overheard by Carter. He cast a grin in her direction.

"Oh, great! Now I have two women bossing me around," he grumbled with mock dismay. "Tommy, you're going to have to help me stand up to them."

"Okay," Tommy agreed at once, eager to please. "What do we do?"

Carter shrugged. "Beats me." He turned to Raylene. "Any ideas?"

For the next two hours, he and Tommy dug where she told them to and trimmed the yard with tall sunflowers and vibrant hollyhocks, patches of bright impatiens in partially shaded areas and even two fragrant rosebushes for either side of the kitchen doorway. The result was a far cry from the carefully tended garden at her home in Charleston, but it was bright and cheery and brought a smile to her face. Looking at the results, she had to blink back tears.

Standing in front of her, Carter seemed shaken by her display of emotion. "This was supposed to be a good thing."

"It's a wonderful thing," she said, impulsively reaching out to give his hand a squeeze. "Thank you. It was wonderful of you to think of doing this. Even if I can't take a single step outside, I'll be able to smell the roses from right here."

"No big deal," he insisted, looking uncomfortable with her gratitude.

"Now, what can I do in return? Of course, I want to pay you for the plants."

"Absolutely not," he said indignantly. "I told you I bought too many."

"I can believe you bought too many flats of annuals, but extra rosebushes? I doubt that."

"Really, no. I can't take your money. It was my pleasure."

"It was more like a backbreaking couple of hours."

"I enjoyed every minute," he said, meeting her gaze with a steady look. "Really."

Raylene shuddered under the intensity of that gaze. "Okay, then, what advice do you need for your garden?"

"Actually, you've already helped out. I'll just try to re-create what we've done here." He frowned. "Of course, we don't have much shade."

"Then you're really going to have to keep an eye on the impatiens. They need a lot of water if they're in bright sunlight. Otherwise they'll wilt. And the sunflowers and hollyhocks will do best either against a fence or with stakes. Once they're in full bloom, they'll tend to fall over without some kind of support."

"Got it," he said. He gave her an appealing look. "Maybe one of these days, when you know me better and feel safe with me, you'll come over and take a look and see if there's any other advice I need to follow."

She regarded him with frustration. "It doesn't work that way, Carter. I'm plenty comfortable with Sarah and Annie, but I can't leave here with them, either. Don't take it personally."

He backed down at once. "You're right," he said, looking flustered. "I'm sorry. I don't totally understand how something like this works. Worse, I'm the kind of guy who automatically wants to make things better. I shouldn't have pushed."

"It's okay," she said, not wanting to ruin his lovely gesture. "But I do think you should go now. I need to fix the kids a snack and then get started on supper before Sarah and Travis get home. They were doing some kind of remote for the radio station today."

"And they're not back yet? Where's the sitter?" His worried expression was far more telling than the simple question.

Under other circumstances, she would have found his attitude insulting, but she understood why he was concerned. It just grated that it had to be that way. "She came back a while ago. Want me to call her in here so you can see for yourself that the kids are in good hands?"

He winced at her sarcasm. "Sorry."

"Don't be," she said with a resigned sigh. "I understand why you felt the need to ask. I really do."

"Okay, then, I'll see you soon. Maybe next time I drop by, I'll bring the girls over. Would that be okay? I know Mandy would love to see the garden. She's not going to believe I actually pulled off an actual flower garden. Up until this year I've stuck to vegetables."

Raylene regarded him with a penetrating look. "Carter, what's going on here? Are you still trying to make up for accusing me of being negligent with the kids? Or am I your pet charity case?"

He looked annoyed by the question. He took a step closer, but something in her expression must have warned him away, because he immediately backed off. Oddly, she felt suddenly bereft, as if she'd missed an important opportunity to feel alive again.

Holding her gaze, he said quietly, "If you don't see what's going on here, then I'll have to figure out some way to make it plain." For the second time he looked deep into her eyes, his gaze steady. "I like you. I enjoy your company. And one of these days, I have a hunch I'm going to kiss you, Raylene." He grinned. "By then, you're going to be ready for it."

She trembled at the warning and the promise. She just doubted that such a day would ever come. Because no matter how attracted they might be to each other, a relationship simply wasn't in the cards.

"I have a garden in my backyard," Sarah announced with wonder that evening. She turned to stare at Raylene. "How'd that happen?"

"Carter Rollins," Raylene said, her voice tight.

Sarah frowned. "Okay, let me see if I can figure this out. Carter Rollins made what seems to me to be an incredibly sweet gesture, and somehow that's annoyed you."

"It's not the gesture that annoyed me," Raylene insisted. "It's what he wants in return."

"Which is?"

"Me," Raylene said, still not able to get over her shock that a man as sexy and appealing as Carter would want someone with her emotional baggage. "He obviously has some knight-in-shining-armor complex or something."

"He's a cop. Don't they all want to save the world?"

"Well, I don't want to be his project."

"But you do want him," Sarah guessed. "I can see it in your eyes. The guy turns you on."

Sarah was the second person to suggest such a thing. Even

Walter had figured it out, and he hadn't even had to see her face to do it. Obviously there was no point in faking a denial. "Well, if you weren't madly in love with Travis, Carter would probably turn you on, too. He'd turn on any woman with a functioning libido."

"But your libido has been in hibernation," Sarah said, fighting a grin. "Is that what you find so annoying? You're suddenly faced with the fact that you're still alive?"

Raylene scowled at her, but Sarah merely waited her out. "Okay, yes," she said finally. "I don't want to feel anything for him or anyone else because there's not a damn thing I can do about it. No man is ever going to want to be tied to a woman who can't leave the house."

"If I recall, most bedrooms are *inside* houses," Sarah teased.

"You know what I mean," Raylene said. "My situation isn't normal. It may never be normal."

"Didn't you tell me after your second appointment with Dr. McDaniels yesterday that she's optimistic?"

"Of course she's optimistic. Do you think she's going to come in here, throw up her hands and tell me I'm beyond hope? Shrinks don't like to admit defeat."

"Or maybe she really believes you're going to get better," Sarah countered. Her gaze narrowed. "Or did I miss something? Did something happen on Friday to leave you sounding so discouraged? Now that I think about it, you've been in this weird mood ever since that session."

"I'm just facing reality," Raylene said.

"Meaning?"

"The medication didn't do a thing to help. I felt so good, too. I was calm and relaxed. Dr. McDaniels had this really soothing tone that helped me. I was so ready to walk out of the house. I just knew I could do it." She sighed. "And then, the second I tried to step outside, I nearly came unglued. It was bizarre. I had absolutely no control over it. Talk about a reality check."

"Gee, and you'd been on the medication and in treatment for how long? Two whole days? I'm shocked," Sarah said with exaggerated disbelief.

"It's not funny," Raylene said. "There should have been some sign of change."

"Was Dr. McDaniels expecting a miraculous change?" Sarah asked.

"No."

"What exactly did she say?"

"Not to be discouraged, that it could take a while for the medication to kick in, that I might need a stronger dose or a different medication, blah-blah-blah."

"Oh, sweetie, I know it must have been frustrating, but she's right. You've been suffering with this disorder, phobia or whatever it is for a couple of years now. It's not going to vanish overnight."

"It might never go away," Raylene said. "I need to accept that."

"Don't you dare give in to such a defeatist attitude!" Sarah said heatedly. "I will not allow you to give up, especially after just two sessions with Dr. McDaniels. Do I have to call the rest of the Sweet Magnolias and stage an intervention? Because I will, if that's what you need. You are better than this, Raylene Hammond. You are not a quitter. And, frankly, if a man as sexy as you seem to think Carter Rollins is suddenly wants to hang around, I'd think that would be motivation enough to keep you fighting to get better."

"I never said I was going to quit," Raylene said. "You don't need to resort to an intervention. I just said I need to accept reality."

"Accepting is barely one step away from giving up," Sarah said, obviously still agitated. "Not an option, is that clear?"

Raylene regarded her with amusement. "If Walter could only see you now. You're definitely not the meek little woman who let him and his parents get away with bullying her."

Sarah blinked at the comment. "You know, you're right. I have changed. And while we're on the subject of Walter, what's this I hear about you trying to fix him up with Rory Sue? The word is out the two of them were at Rosalina's the other night."

Relieved to have the focus off her mental state and off Carter, Raylene merely grinned. "I thought it might be fun."

"Are you crazy? Rory Sue and Walter?" She shook her head. "If he ever took her home to Alabama, both his parents would wind up in the cardiac-care unit of the local hospital."

"Like I said, fun," Raylene repeated. "You can't possibly expect me to believe you actually care about what those two awful people think."

"No, but I don't necessarily want them dead."

"Well, their state of mind and health are no longer your concern, and Walter's life needs shaking up. It's time he stops pining for what he lost when the two of you got divorced."

"Walter has hardly been pining for me."

"Of course he has. He just knows he doesn't stand a chance now that you have Travis in your life, though frankly, the fact that you haven't set a wedding date yet must be giving him hope."

Sarah regarded her indignantly. "You know perfectly well that there are a lot of reasons we haven't set a date yet. Getting the station up and running has been a lot of work. With such a small staff, we couldn't both be gone for even a brief honeymoon, and we agreed we want a big wedding. That takes time to plan. And then there are my folks. My dad's health hasn't been good, so he hasn't been up to traveling."

"Okay, I get it," Raylene said. "But does Walter?"

"He certainly ought to by now," Sarah said. "The two of us were always a terrible match, anyway."

"True enough," Raylene said. "He fed your insecurities. Not intentionally, maybe. It's just the way things were as long as you were living under his parents' thumb."

"Let's get back to Rory Sue," Sarah said, once again looking bewildered. "Seriously? You honestly think those two belong together?"

"They'll have to figure that out for themselves," Raylene said. "But I do think she's self-confident enough to give him a run for his money. Walter needs a challenge."

"Meaning I'm a wimp," Sarah said, looking disgruntled.

"You were a wimp," Raylene concurred without hesitation. "And now you're not. You are the woman you were meant to be—strong, confident, comfortable in your own skin. Watching the transformation has been amazing. You're amazing!"

Sarah's expression brightened at her words, but then Raylene realized the change had nothing to do with her. Travis opened the kitchen door and at the sight of him, Sarah practically glowed with happiness. It was that way whenever he dropped by, which was most nights and weekends. For a man who lived blocks away, he was underfoot a lot.

"Hey," he said in his low, sexy drawl, his gaze on his fiancée. Raylene might as well not have been in the room.

"Hey," Sarah said, equally oblivious to the fact that they had company.

"I'll just go and check on the kids now," Raylene said, backing out of the kitchen. "Don't let the casserole burn."

She shook her head as she left. She doubted they'd heard a word. It was a toss-up whether her friends or dinner would go up in flames first.

CHAPTER SIX

The following Saturday the kids had gone to the ball field with Sarah and Travis, and Raylene was alone in the house, when Carter's truck pulled up out front. Two teenagers climbed out. Raylene guessed these were Carter's sisters. The girl who appeared older wore the sulky, bored expression of someone who wanted to be anywhere else but here. The other teen was gazing around with frank curiosity as her brother led the way to the front door.

Filled with a mix of anticipation and annoyance, Raylene held it open as they approached.

"I wasn't expecting to see you today," she said, her tone light but chiding.

The younger girl frowned at Carter. "You didn't call to say we were coming or to see if she'd be home? What is wrong with you? That is so rude." She grinned at Raylene. "You have to make allowances for him. Our parents did try to teach him some manners. Honest."

Raylene smiled. "I'm sure they did. Do you suppose he'll remember to introduce us? I'm Raylene."

"And I'm Mandy," the young teen replied. "Sourpuss here is Carrie."

"That's no way to talk about your sister," Carter scolded.

"Oh, come on," Mandy protested. "She's been cranky all day."

"I can wait in the truck if you find my company so objectionable," Carrie snapped, then glanced apologetically at Raylene. "Sorry. You shouldn't have to listen to our family squabbles."

"I don't mind," Raylene said, feeling an unexpected sense of camaraderie for this girl who'd lost her parents just when she was entering the vulnerable teenage years and needed them the most. "Come on inside, *all* of you."

"I wanted the girls to see the garden and to check to see if it needs watering or weeding," Carter told her. "I hope that's okay. We won't stay long."

"Of course it's okay. How about some lemonade or sweet tea before you go outside again?" Raylene asked. "Even for June, it's miserably hot today. And I baked sugar cookies yesterday."

"Sounds good to me," Mandy said eagerly. "Nobody bakes at our house. Carrie used to, but then she discovered that cookies have …" She lowered her voice to an exaggerated whisper and added, *"Calories!"*

Carter nodded sadly. "It's true. That was the day our source of home-baked cookies died."

Raylene watched Carrie's expression. Even though her brother and sister were obviously teasing, the barbs clearly hit home. Carrie looked as if she might cry. Again, Raylene felt an unexpected connection to her.

"Well, consider me your new source for cookies," Raylene told them. "I bake two or three times a week. Travis grabs a handful every time he passes through the kitchen, which he seems to find excuses to do a dozen times while he's here every day. He's like some kind of bottomless pit when it comes to sweets. I can't tell you how much Sarah and I envy him."

Interest flickered in Carrie's eyes. "Are you talking about Travis McDonald, the guy on the radio?"

Raylene nodded.

"He lives here?" Carrie said, clearly excited by the possibility that she'd stumbled into the home of a local celebrity.

"No, but Sarah does. They're engaged, so he's over here a lot."

"Then you see him all the time?" Carrie persisted.

"Quite a bit," Raylene confirmed.

"Oh, my gosh! He is so sexy on the air. That voice…" She made an elaborate show of fanning herself.

Raylene grinned. "Yeah, he has that effect on me, too."

Carter appeared fascinated by that news. "Okay, I'm a guy. You're going to have to explain it to me. What does Travis McDonald have that, say, I don't?"

Carrie rolled her eyes at the question, but Raylene met his gaze. "Sorry. It's the voice. Not that the package is anything to sneer at, but that deep, slow, sexy drawl is something else."

"Does Sarah know her fiancé gets you all charged up?" he asked.

To Raylene's regret he sounded more curious than jealous. "It took a while, but I think she's gotten used to women swooning every time he opens his mouth," she said.

"Do you think we could meet him sometime?" Mandy asked.

Carter regarded her as if she was a traitor. "Not you, too?"

"Hey, I'm a girl, too," Mandy said, then regarded Raylene hopefully. "Is he coming by today?"

Raylene nodded. "He and Sarah should be back soon. They take the kids out for pizza after they play T-ball, but they usually get Tommy and Libby back here for their naps."

Carrie regarded Carter hopefully. "Can we stay?" She turned to Raylene. "Would you mind?"

"It's fine with me," Raylene told her as she took glasses from the cupboard and poured lemonade for everyone. She opened a tin of freshly baked cookies and put them on a plate. Mandy and Carter reached for them eagerly, but Carrie ignored them and went to the back door to look out at the garden. After a minute, she turned, an expression of shock on her face. "Carter, you did that? You planted all those flowers?"

He winked at Raylene. "I had a lot of guidance."

"Can we go check it out?" Mandy asked, joining her sister at the door.

"You *may*," Carter said, subtly correcting her.

Mandy stuck out her tongue. "*May* we?"

"You may, if you'll get the hose and water everything while you're out there," Carter said. He turned to Raylene. "It needs it, right?"

"It does, and I would appreciate it," Raylene said, then almost regretted giving permission when she was left alone with Carter, who was studying her with what was becoming an increasingly unnerving look of fascination.

"Thanks for not slamming the door in my face," he said.

She bit back a smile. "Unlike you, I remembered the manners I was taught. And I'm sure you knew I'd never slam the door if you turned up here with your sisters, especially with all my lovely flowers out there drooping from the heat."

"I was hoping," he admitted with an unrepentant grin.

"They're lovely girls."

"You can say that even after Carrie walked in here with an attitude?"

"She's sixteen, right? It comes with the territory. Believe me, I remember that stage all too well."

"She'll be sixteen in a few months, but I get what you're

saying. Does that mean Mandy's sunny disposition will vanish and she'll be transformed into an impossible little diva in another year or so?" He looked shaken by the thought.

"More than likely," Raylene confirmed.

"Gee, something to look forward to."

"They're at a tough age to have lost their parents," Raylene said sympathetically. "It's an especially hard time for a girl not to have a mother."

"And, believe me, I'm a poor substitute. I encourage them to talk to me about anything, but sometimes they have questions I don't have any idea how to answer."

Raylene hesitated, then thought of the lost, lonely and scared look she thought she'd seen in Carrie's eyes. "Bring them by here anytime," she told Carter. "I'd be happy to listen, at least. And I won't offer advice on anything important without talking it over with you."

He seemed startled by the offer. "You'd do that for a couple of girls you just met?"

"If it would help, of course."

"Amazing," he said, half to himself.

"Don't nominate me for sainthood. As you can imagine, I love having company."

He held her gaze. "Even me?"

She forced herself not to look away, even though the intensity in his eyes was unsettling. "Surprisingly, yes."

His expression brightened. "Then we're definitely making progress."

"Carter," she began, a warning note in her tone. Before she could continue, Tommy came bursting into the house, Libby right on his heels.

"Ray-ween, I hit the ball way far away and ran all the way around the bases today," Tommy announced excitedly. "Daddy came and he saw me, and Travis said I was the best player on the team. He didn't say it loud, though, 'cause he didn't want the other kids to feel bad."

Raylene knelt down to give him a hug. "Wow, what a great day! Congratulations!"

"I had pizza," Libby said, then added sorrowfully, "but I couldn't hit the ball. It was too fast."

Libby wasn't officially on the team, but then the whole activity was geared toward kids who were too young to play officially. Travis always made sure even Libby got a turn at bat, despite the groans of the slightly older kids.

"Next time," Raylene assured her. "You'll learn. In fact, I bet your daddy or Travis will practice with you this week."

As Sarah and Travis walked into the kitchen, Sarah's eyebrows rose when she spotted Carter. "Back again, I see."

"He brought his sisters by to water the garden," Raylene told her. "They're out back now giving it a good soaking." She winked at Travis. "They're going to be very glad to meet you. They're huge fans."

Sarah rolled her eyes. "Naturally. He attracts females of all ages."

As if to prove the point, Libby held out her arms to Travis. "Up?" she pleaded.

Travis scooped her up and tickled her. "Nap time, kiddo."

"No nap," Libby said, her little chin set stubbornly. "Me and you hit the ball."

"Later," Travis promised. "You could use a nap, too, Tommy. Let's go."

"While you put Libby and Tommy down, I'll get your fan club to come inside to meet you," Raylene promised. "They'll probably want to touch up their lipstick and comb their hair. Can't meet the town sex symbol without being properly primped up."

Travis shook his head at the amusement in her voice. "You're really enjoying this, aren't you?"

Raylene nodded. "As a matter of fact, I am. I love watching a grown man blush."

Sarah poured her own glass of lemonade, then sat down opposite Carter and studied him over the rim of her glass. "Now you and I have a chance to chat," she said meaningfully. "I get why your sisters wanted to hang out. It's all about Travis. What about you? What's the attraction for you?"

"Sarah!" Raylene chided.

Carter didn't look the slightest bit disconcerted by the question. "Isn't it obvious?"

"You do know she's not going to make it easy for you, don't you?" Sarah asked, as if Raylene weren't sitting right there blushing furiously.

"Easy's not much fun," Carter said, his gaze catching Raylene's. "I've suddenly discovered a fascination for more complicated women."

"If you ask me, you already have enough complicated women in your life," Raylene said. "Weren't you saying not ten minutes ago that you didn't know how to handle Mandy and Carrie?"

"Not the same," he said easily.

"How so?" Sarah queried.

"If I get it right with my sisters, I'll have the satisfaction of knowing I did my best and can send them out into the world. If I get it right with Raylene, something tells me the payoff will be far more rewarding and has the potential to change the rest of my life."

Sarah looked impressed by his response, but it scared Raylene to death. It implied expectations and a future, two things that required guarantees she couldn't possibly make.

"Carter," she protested, "you shouldn't be saying things like that."

"Just calling it the way I see it," he said evenly. "I wouldn't want you to accuse me of not giving you fair warning about my intentions."

"You don't even know me," Raylene said, then reminded him, "And when we met, you didn't even like me."

"I didn't like what happened," he agreed. "You, however, intrigued me. Nothing that's happened since has changed that."

"But that's crazy," Raylene said, feeling a little frantic and overwhelmed.

He held up a hand. "Sorry. I didn't mean to panic you by getting so intense. One thing I learned when my folks died was that things can change too fast and when you least expect it. I've been too busy since then to think much about relationships, but I'm smart enough not to walk away when something looks promising."

"And you think a relationship with a woman who hasn't left the house in two years looks promising?" she asked incredulously. "Is that because you think I can't run away?"

He laughed at the suggestion, which wasn't exactly the reaction she'd been going for.

"I can't say I have a lot of experience with women trying to get away from me," he said. "It's mostly been the other way around."

Carrie and Mandy came back into the house just in time to overhear.

"It's true," Carrie said with an expression of sisterly tolerance. "Women chase him all the time. It's really pitiful. They should have more pride, you know."

"I do know," Raylene said. "I don't think that will be an issue with me."

Carrie studied her, then nodded. "Good for you." She finally spotted Sarah and realized the implication of her presence. "You're Sarah Price, right? If you're home, that must mean Travis is here."

Sarah nodded. "He's with the kids. He should be back any minute."

Carrie stood up a little straighter. Even Mandy, who was clearly more of a tomboy, fluffed her hair in a purely feminine gesture.

"And here he is now," Sarah announced, barely containing a grin as both girls stared at Travis with openmouthed awe.

"Carrie and Mandy Rollins, meet Travis McDonald," Raylene said.

Travis grinned and held out his hand, first to Carrie, then to Mandy. "Nice to meet you, girls."

The tongue-tied girls just stared.

Carter shook his head. "Manners," he muttered.

"*Very* happy to meet you," Carrie murmured, suddenly looking everywhere except at Travis.

"Hi," Mandy said. "You're even hotter than I thought you'd be."

"Amanda Rollins!" Carter scolded.

Mandy gave him a defiant look. "Well, he is."

"Thank you," Travis murmured, his cheeks flushed.

"On that note, I think it's time for us to go," Carter said, standing up. "Come on, girls. I think we've made enough of an impression for one afternoon."

"Don't worry about it," Sarah told him, walking to the door with them. "It happens all the time to Travis."

"And to you," Raylene said. "You have your share of admiring fans."

Sarah cast a pointed look at Carter. "And apparently so do you."

"Gee, it seems as if there's plenty of embarrassment to go around this afternoon," Raylene commented wryly.

His eyes filled with humor, Carter leaned down and pressed a kiss to her cheek. "See you soon. I think next time I'll leave the girls at home."

"Don't," Raylene said with heartfelt urgency. Because as long as he brought chaperones along, there was no chance he'd act on that unexpected glint of desire she'd seen in his eyes.

He met her gaze, his expression knowing. "We'll see."

After they'd gone, Raylene had to steady herself before she could even take the few steps into the living room. No man had left her weak kneed like that in years. Sarah regarded her with amusement.

"Living with you has suddenly gotten very interesting," she said.

"Bite me," Raylene retorted.

Sarah merely laughed. "I hope you'll remember to thank Tommy at the wedding."

"Excuse me?"

"If he hadn't tried to chase after the ice-cream truck that day, who knows how long it would have taken before the two of you crossed paths. You owe my son."

"You actually think what's going on here is some kind of blessing?"

"I do. You haven't looked this rattled or this excited since you came back to town."

"Maybe I don't want to be rattled or excited," Raylene grumbled.

"Doesn't matter. Fate doesn't always wait around until you're ready. It's time to start living again, sweet pea."

"This has nothing to do with fate," Raylene declared emphatically.

"Kismet? Destiny?"

"Insanity," Raylene corrected. "The man thinks he's falling for a woman who's locked away in some emotional prison and it's his job to save her."

"Very romantic, if you ask me."

"No, it's nuts," Raylene insisted.

And maybe, if she were being totally honest, just a little bit romantic.

Carter had been on patrol all morning on the opposite side of the county from Serenity, mostly driving up and down the streets of some of the new developments that were being built. It seemed a shame to see so much rural land being gobbled up by cookie cutter houses, but the region was growing. He supposed there was no way to stop progress.

When his cell phone rang, he was surprised to hear Mayor Lewis's voice.

"Son, do you have time for a break?" Howard asked. "There's something I'd like to discuss with you. It's important."

"It shouldn't be a problem. Let me check in with dispatch. Where'd you want to meet?"

"Wharton's is as good a place as any, if that's convenient for you. I'll go now and get us a table."

"Can I call you back on this number if there's a problem?" Carter asked.

"You do that. Otherwise, I'll see you when you get here. No rush. There's always someone around I can talk to."

Carter cleared the break with Gayle, then drove to Serenity. Since it was close to lunchtime, most of the parking spaces in front of Wharton's were occupied, so he parked over on Azalea near the radio station. As he passed the studio with its view of the town green, he waved at Sarah, who was still on the air. She gave him a thumbs-up. A couple of other people he recognized gave him knowing looks, as if they were in on some secret he wasn't yet privy to.

When he walked into Wharton's, the men sitting with the mayor immediately got up, shook his hand as Howard introduced him, then moved to another table.

"You didn't invite me over here for a casual chat, did you?" he asked Howard, who had a discernible glint in his eyes.

"Nope. I did tell you it was important, didn't I?"

That part had slipped Carter's mind. Maybe he'd just mistakenly assumed that everything was important to Howard. "What's going on?"

"Haven't seen you at any of our town meetings, so I'm guessing you don't pay a lot of attention to local politics, is that right?" Howard asked.

"I've read the local paper, but that's about it. The move over here came up pretty quickly. I've been busy settling into my job and getting my sisters settled in school. I wanted to be sure they met some kids their own age before school let out for the summer."

"As it should be," Howard said. "You may not know just how much this town has grown recently. Development in the county's taken off, too."

"Now, *that* I do know," Carter said. "I was just patrolling out at the Oak Haven and Willow Creek developments. Once those houses sell, it wouldn't surprise me if the county doesn't need another new elementary school at least."

"Already being discussed," Howard confirmed. "And here in town, we've been talking about wanting to start our own police department. The sheriff's going to have his hands full with all the outlying areas, and we want a department that's accountable to the folks right here in town."

"Makes sense," Carter said. He knew firsthand that the

sheriff's department was stretched thin trying to cover an increasingly populated region. So far, there'd been no local tax dollars allocated to add new deputies. His own job had been created because the county had gotten federal stimulus money to add an extra deputy.

"What would you think about taking on the job of chief and building the police department here from the ground up?" Howard asked.

Carter sat back in shock. "You're considering me for the job? Why? I barely know my way around the region."

Howard leaned forward. "Here's the way I see it. You're young. You're energetic. And you're sensitive. I liked what I saw and what I heard about the incident with Tommy Price. You didn't just go through the motions. You cared about what happened to that boy."

"And I also jumped to conclusions and misjudged Raylene," Carter reminded him.

"The way I hear it, you've apologized. I admire a man who can admit his mistakes, who doesn't pretend to be perfect. It's a good quality to have in a leader. You'll listen, and I'll bet you won't be leaping to any more conclusions."

"You really think I'm the right man for this job?" Carter asked, still incredulous that a relative stranger would be the town's choice.

"I do," Howard said emphatically. "And I'm not alone. The sheriff and I have talked and he backs up my thoughts about this. So do most of the council. Tom McDonald's our town manager and you'd be reporting to him, so the two of you need to talk some more. You should spend some time thinking about how you'd see a police force being created, what kind of staff you'd need, the kind of equipment. Tom has a rough idea of our budget. You two can sit down and compare notes, hash out the details. That is, if you're interested."

Carter didn't have to think about it for long. "I'm interested," he said at once.

Starting a department would be a challenge. While it would probably entail a lot more paperwork than he'd prefer, it might also give him more regular hours, which would give him more time with Carrie and Mandy. As safe as the area was, he still hadn't been looking forward to leaving them at home alone when he had the night-shift rotation.

Howard nodded with satisfaction, then looked Carter directly in the eye. "One thing you should know. We're going to want a decent commitment from you. If you have any reason to think you're going to want to leave for a bigger police force anytime soon, then we should call this off now."

"I understand. And I'm sure you're aware that I left a bigger police force to come here. I have no desire to go back. My younger sister won't graduate for another four years, and I intend for it to be from Serenity High School."

"Good to know. I'll tell Tom to expect your call. I'll get him working on the details of an offer, and we'll see if we can't move this along. Council will have to approve your deal and a budget for the department before we can go forward, but I don't anticipate any problems. The sheriff will work with us on a timetable."

"Thank you for thinking of me, Mayor Lewis."

"Call me Howard. I'm looking forward to working with you, son."

Carter walked slowly back to his cruiser. When he neared the radio station, Sarah was off the air. She'd apparently been in the studio and had seen him, though, because she popped her head out the door.

"Did you say yes?" she asked.

He regarded her innocently. "To what?"

"The chief's job. I know Howard was going to talk to you about it."

"Now, how did you know a thing like that?"

She gave him a pitying look. "You really haven't been here long, have you? Small town, active grapevine. Grace Wharton knows everything, and now that I'm on the air here, I'm the first person she likes to tell."

"So all of Serenity will know about me maybe taking the job of Serenity police chief by tomorrow morning when you go back on the air?"

"I'd say sooner than that. It's lunch hour at Wharton's. Grace has probably told most folks already that you and Howard were huddled together over coffee."

"Are there any secrets in a place like this?"

"Not for long," Sarah said. Her expression sobered. "Which is why if you're not serious about Raylene, you should probably back off. The word's already out that you've been hanging around. It'll embarrass her if it turns out you're playing some kind of game."

He frowned at the suggestion. "Why would I be playing games?"

"You wouldn't be the first man who couldn't resist a challenge."

"I'm not interested because she's a challenge," he said. "You're selling her short."

"Not me," Sarah said. "I know Raylene. I know how amazing she is."

"And I'm just starting to figure that out." His gaze steady, he gave her a warning. "Keep an eye on me, if you feel the need to, but don't make the same mistake I did with Raylene and jump to conclusions. It would be a disservice to Raylene and to me."

To his surprise, she beamed at him. "Good answer. You dropping by later to share your news?"

"If the Serenity grapevine is so hot, what makes you think she hasn't already heard?"

"She probably has, but I'm sure she'd like to hear the details straight from the horse's mouth."

"Then I'll be sure to drop by on my way home."

In fact, he thought, it would be the perfect ending to a very surprising day.

CHAPTER SEVEN

Raylene had baked three batches of cookies that afternoon, rather than the single batch of chocolate chip she usually made at midweek. She knew it was probably ridiculous to be baking extras just in case Carter came by, but she hadn't been able to stop herself. She'd even lined an extra tin with foil, then packed it with an assortment of not only chocolate-chip cookies, but oatmeal raisin and sugar cookies as well.

After she'd closed the lid, she shook her head. Was she just a little smitten, after all? It had been a very long time since she'd been tempted to make a sweet gesture to impress a man. Her attempts to please Paul with special desserts or gourmet meals had never had the desired effect. Most of the time he'd found some way to demean her best efforts and make her feel like an idiot for even trying.

Ironically, the result had been that she'd tried harder. She owned more cookbooks than most women accumulated in a lifetime. She experimented constantly with new recipes. Now she had an appreciative crowd at the dinner table each evening. Even Tommy seemed to love her cooking almost as much as he liked hot dogs and pizza.

Tonight she was making an easy beef Stroganoff recipe.

The meat had been simmering in a slow cooker most of the day. There was enough to feed an army.

When Sarah walked in the door, she sniffed the air appreciatively. "Stroganoff?"

Raylene nodded.

"Perfect. There's bound to be enough for company."

"Company? Is Annie coming over and bringing the kids? Not that the baby is eating real food yet, but Trevor can eat his own weight. He's exactly like Ty was when we were kids."

"He can, indeed, but they're not coming over." Sarah's eyes glinted with mischief. "This is guy company."

"Travis isn't company."

"No, he isn't, but Carter is."

Raylene's gaze narrowed. "What makes you think Carter's coming by? Did you invite him? I told you not to interfere in this."

"No interfering," Sarah swore. "I saw him earlier. He has news he wants to share."

"Tell me," Raylene commanded.

"Not me. It's his news."

"Since when have you ever kept hot-off-the-presses news to yourself? It's not in your genetic makeup."

"I'm reforming," Sarah said airily. "When he gets here, why don't you tell him to invite his sisters over, too. We should celebrate."

"Celebrate what?"

Sarah merely grinned. "I'm going to take the kids for a walk before dinner. That'll give you time alone with Carter when he arrives."

"And what if I don't want time alone with Carter?" Raylene demanded, trying to keep a frantic note out of her voice. Of course, the problem was that she did want to spend time with him. She just didn't think it wise.

Sarah shook her head sorrowfully. "Then I'll tell Dr. Mc-Daniels you really do have a screw loose."

Raylene scowled at her. "You are not amusing."

"Not trying to be. Hiding inside is one thing. You can't help that. Ignoring a hot man who's definitely interested in you would be flat-out wrong."

"I don't think he's going to let me ignore him," Raylene said, then groaned when the doorbell rang. "My gentleman caller, I assume."

Sarah grinned. "That would be my guess. I'll let him in, then take the kids and scram. Dinner in an hour?"

"If you say so," Raylene grumbled. "I hope he can at least make a salad."

She heard Sarah and Carter exchanging a few words, and then he was in the kitchen. Even though she'd known he was on his way in, seeing him was still a shock to her system. The man could probably thaw a roast with one of those searing looks he tended to give her. As it was, her blood sizzled in ways it hadn't in a very long time. The reaction was troubling because she wasn't entirely sure, when push came to shove, if she'd be able to respond to a man's touch ever again. That was just one more thing to worry about, when she already had her hands full dealing with therapy.

Before he could say a word, she moved a bowl in his direction, then pointed to the raw vegetables she'd assembled. "You're on salad duty," she told him. "And if you want to invite Carrie and Mandy, then you'll need to make a big one."

He blinked at the order. "Am I invited for dinner?"

"Sarah says you are. She thinks the girls should come, too. Something about a celebration." She finally dared to meet his gaze. "What's that about? She wouldn't tell me."

He chuckled. "That must have killed her."

Raylene couldn't stop her own grin. "More than likely.

She says she took the kids for a walk to give us time alone, but I think it's because she was terrified she was going to spill the beans."

"Time alone, huh?"

He seemed a little too intrigued by the thought. Raylene frowned at him. "Don't be getting any ideas, buster. She thought you had something to tell me."

"I do, as a matter of fact. Let me call the house and tell Carrie and Mandy to ride their bikes over, then I'll tell you."

"Do they know?"

He shook his head and gestured to his uniform. "I haven't been home yet. I came straight here when I went off duty."

"Then wait until they get here and tell us all at once," she suggested. "And in the meantime you need to get busy on that salad."

Carter eyed the vegetables with dismay. "Not my area of expertise. Maybe you should wait and teach the girls."

Raylene put her hands on her hips. "You can't even make a salad?"

He looked sheepish. "Sorry, no."

"That is just pitiful."

"Tell me about it. I hadn't planned on being what amounts to a single dad."

"What does that have to do with anything? You eat, don't you? What were you doing for meals before your folks died?"

"I went to restaurants or threw myself on my mom's mercy," he admitted, then added with a grin, "And then there were those women who were trying to impress me."

She shook her head. "Well, that's about to change. As soon as you've called the girls, we'll start with the basics."

"Were you a drill sergeant in another life?" he grumbled.

"Could have been," she said. "The important thing now

is that you're in my kitchen, so you do what I say." She liked the feeling of power that idea gave her.

"I thought this was Sarah's house."

"The kitchen is all mine," she corrected. "It works out nicely."

Carter made the call to his sisters, then hung up with obvious reluctance. "They'll be here in fifteen minutes. Are you sure you don't want to wait for them to make the salad?"

"Now you're just being pathetic," she said, handing him the head of lettuce. "Tear off the leaves and put them in the colander."

"The what?"

She held up the metal strainer. "This," she said. "Once you've torn up enough lettuce—small pieces, by the way— then rinse it and shake off as much excess water as you can."

"Why not just buy the bags of already prepared salad?"

"Because I like the old-fashioned way."

"Who would have guessed," he muttered with a dramatic air of resignation.

Raylene had to bite back a smile as he tore the lettuce into small pieces, a frown of concentration on his brow. There was something utterly charming about seeing a big, strong cop, still wearing his gun, in fact, looking so completely out of his element.

When Raylene assured him he had enough lettuce, he ran water over it, then shook the colander a bit too energetically. Lettuce flew everywhere. Fortunately, enough was left to make the salad. He dumped it triumphantly into the bowl.

"Now what?" he asked.

"Now you chop the peppers, tomatoes and green onions and add those. See what I mean? It's pretty basic stuff. Even a beginner can make a salad."

He glanced over the ingredients she'd assembled. "I don't see any dressing."

"Because you're going to make it."

"You're kidding me! Companies spend millions making all sorts of perfectly good bottled dressing, and you want me to start from scratch?"

She patted his shoulder. "If succeeding with the lettuce gave you a thrill, just wait till you've made your own dressing. You'll feel like an accomplished cook."

"I think we should save one triumph for Carrie and Mandy," he argued.

"Okay, we'll see."

"What's for dinner, anyway?"

"Beef Stroganoff."

His eyes widened with surprise and unmistakable pleasure. "You actually made beef Stroganoff? On a regular weeknight, not even for a special occasion?"

"It's an easy recipe, and there are always leftovers for another night."

"Easy?" he repeated skeptically.

"You just dump a few things into a slow cooker and let it simmer for most of the day, then add a few more things, boil the noddles and it's done."

"Do chefs know about this? They always make it sound very complicated. I watch the Food Channel sometimes, hoping something will sink in and I'll wake up knowing how to cook."

She raised a brow at that revelation. "And yet you still don't cook."

"Because it all sounds too complicated."

"You can read, right?"

"Of course."

"And follow directions?"

He gave her an impish look. "That's a little trickier. I am a guy, after all."

She shook her head. "These are directions, not orders. They're a way to get from point A to point B," she said, then slapped her forehead. "Of course, guys never ask for directions, do they?"

"We are adapting to the idea of a GPS system," he told her. "That's technology, so it's acceptable."

"Good grief!"

Carter laughed at her reaction. "I'm really not quite as inept as you're probably thinking about now." He gestured to the cutting board. "See, all chopped and diced."

"Very good," she praised. "Now toss them with the lettuce." When he looked as if he might take the bowl and toss the ingredients into the air, she held the bowl in place and handed him the salad tongs. "Gently."

Just then Carrie and Mandy walked into the kitchen and stared.

"Carter's fixing the salad?" Carrie said, looking stunned. "Are you sure you want to do that? We'll probably die."

He scowled at her. "And you're going to make the dressing from scratch."

"Now I *know* we're going to die," Mandy said.

Carter frowned, then turned to Raylene. "Make her do something, too."

Raylene grinned. "You can make the noodles for the Stroganoff." When Mandy looked uncertain, she said, "Boil water, dump in the noodles and stir them. You can handle it."

A half hour later, dinner was on the table, Sarah and the kids were back, Travis had arrived and they were all seated at the larger table in the dining room, which the girls had helpfully set.

Raylene looked around and nearly had to blink back tears.

This was what she'd imagined her life being—a family and friends gathered around for a meal she'd prepared. After all this time, after she'd pretty much given up on the dream, here it was.

And yet it wasn't quite real, because the family, at least, wasn't hers.

Carter stashed the girls' bikes in the back of his truck for the drive home. In the car the girls were bubbling with excitement. Some of their enthusiasm was over the prospect of Carter's new job, but mostly it was about the fabulous meal and their part in getting it ready.

"We actually cooked tonight," Mandy said triumphantly.

"You boiled water," Carrie scoffed. "I actually made a salad dressing from scratch."

"Let's not forget my contribution," Carter said. "The salad was awesome, if I do say so myself. Carrie, what did you think of the Stroganoff?"

"It was good," she said, avoiding his gaze in the rearview mirror.

"How would she know? She ate one bite," Mandy reported. "I thought it was amazing, and Raylene says it's really easy to make. She said she'd teach me if I want to come by after school one day or maybe when school lets out next week. Is that okay, Carter?"

"If she invited you, I'm sure she meant it. Just call her to make sure when it's convenient."

"How come she can't leave the house?" Carrie asked quietly. "That's so sad."

"I don't know the whole story," Carter admitted. "I do know she's trying to get over her phobia, though."

"Is that what it is, a phobia?" Carrie persisted. "Like a fear of spiders or of flying?"

"That's the way I understand it," he told her. "She has panic attacks if she tries to go outside."

"Even in the yard?" Mandy asked.

Carter nodded.

"That's why you planted the garden," Carrie guessed, her expression lighting up with sudden understanding. "So she'd be able to see something beautiful from the kitchen. You're pretty awesome, big brother."

"Keep that in mind next time you disagree with something I'm telling you to do."

"Not the same thing," Carrie said, then fell silent.

As they pulled into the driveway at home, Mandy jumped out immediately, but Carrie hung back to walk in with Carter. He sensed there was something on her mind, so he deliberately slowed his pace.

"Everything okay?" he asked eventually.

She paused and looked up at him. "You like Raylene, right?"

"I do," he admitted, seeing little point in denying the obvious.

"Does it bother you that she's kind of messed up with this phobia thing?"

He frowned at the question. He had a feeling his answer was vitally important for some reason he couldn't quite fathom. "It bothers me for her sake," he said. "I hate to see anyone missing out on so much of life."

"But you don't think she's weird because she needs a shrink?"

"Of course not," he said. "She's getting help that she needs to get better." He met Carrie's troubled gaze. "Why? Does it bother you that she's seeing a psychologist?"

"No. I guess I just never knew anyone who needed that kind of help before, at least not anyone who talked about it."

Carter knew there was more on her mind, but he had no idea how to dig deeper to unearth the real problem. Still, he knew he needed to try. "You're not afraid your friends will freak out if they find out I'm seeing Raylene, are you?"

She scowled at the question. "Like I would care what anyone else in this town thinks!" she said indignantly. "Don't you know me at all?"

"Then what's this about, Carrie? Something's obviously on your mind."

For a brief instant, he thought she was going to open up and tell him, but then her expression shut down.

"Nothing's on my mind," she claimed, and flounced off, leaving him to stare after her and wonder how he'd blown the opportunity.

Carter glanced skyward. "Mom, Dad, I could use a little guidance here."

Unfortunately, there were no heavenly messages suddenly written on the clear night sky. As he had been for two years now, he was left to cope on his own.

Walter had canceled two appointments with Rory Sue to look at houses. Unfortunately, they both knew it wasn't due to his busy schedule, as he'd claimed. The woman rattled him. He knew instinctively that she was ready and willing to have some kind of fling, but for all of his many flaws, he was a pretty monogamous guy. Once he and Sarah had gotten together in college, that had been it for him. Cheating had never once crossed his mind, not even when his marriage had been falling apart. Since the divorce, he hadn't met anyone half as intriguing as his ex-wife.

Even though he'd been telling himself for days now that he was due to cut loose and have a relationship that was completely free of strings, he couldn't see it happening. And, though he was about as sensitive as a fence post, he'd seen something in Rory Sue that told him she wasn't half as care-free as she wanted everyone to think. She was lonely and vulnerable and reaching out for any connection that might make her feel better, even temporarily. He didn't want to take advantage of that.

He was still sitting in the office at the radio station a few minutes after canceling their latest appointment, when the door opened and Rory Sue walked in. This time, she was attired for work in a dress made of some kind of clingy fab-ric that hugged every generous curve, but at least covered most of them.

"You're avoiding me," she accused as she sat down on the edge of his desk.

Her bare calf, which tapered to a shapely ankle and a pair of sexy, high-heeled sandals, was unnervingly close as she swung it back and forth. Watching it was like falling under the spell of a clock pendulum.

"What's the problem?" she asked when he couldn't seem to find his tongue.

Walter swallowed hard. "No problem. Really."

Rory Sue gave him a knowing look. "I scare you, don't I?"

The blunt question, which unfortunately hit the mark, rattled him even more. No man was ever going to admit to being scared of a woman.

"Absolutely not," he said at once. "I've been swamped at work. That's all."

"And yet here you sit, all alone and looking bored to tears," she said, then grinned. "At least until I walked in."

"Just taking a five-minute breather," he insisted, ignoring the comment about his reaction to her arrival.

"And then what? Aren't most of your potential advertisers

at home with their families by now? Does it work out well when you interrupt their evenings?"

"I have paperwork to do," he claimed, aware that he probably sounded a little desperate for excuses.

"And yet there are no papers or files piled up on your desk," she said.

Walter sighed and gave up the battle. "Okay, you got me. I was thinking about grabbing a burger and going back to the motel." He scowled at her. "Alone, in case you were getting any ideas."

She laughed. "As intriguing as an evening at the Serenity Inn with you sounds, right this second I'm much more interested in selling you a house."

He regarded her skeptically. "Really?"

"Yes, really," she said seriously. "Come on, super stud, let's find a place for you to live. Then we can discuss what lies ahead for you and me."

Because it was better than spending another boring evening on his own, Walter walked out with her. "Just so we're clear, this is strictly business."

"Of course it is," she said at once, then met his gaze. "Until it isn't."

"Why do you do that?" he asked.

"What? Flirt?"

"Practically throw yourself at a man you barely know," he corrected. "You're a gorgeous woman. You're obviously well educated. You have a great sense of humor. I can't imagine that men don't fall all over themselves asking you out."

"You didn't."

"Because you never gave me a chance."

"What is so wrong about a woman taking the initiative?"

"It's not wrong exactly," he said, choosing his words carefully. "It just makes you seem desperate. That's not an attractive quality."

"Are you saying women need to sit back and wait around until some man notices them? That's a waste of time. I see a man who intrigues me, I let him know it."

He regarded her with frustration. "And how's that been working for you?"

"Up until you, not all that badly, as a matter of fact," she said with a touch of defiance.

Walter smiled despite himself. "Look, I'm hardly an expert. My marriage certainly fell apart mostly because I was clueless about how a woman ought to be treated, but I do know one thing. Relationships are all about achieving an optimum balance of power."

Rory Sue gave him a disbelieving look. "Meaning, I suppose, that the man is superior and everything has to be on his terms."

"Of course not." He *had* learned that lesson.

"Okay, let's say I stop right here, turn around and kiss the daylights out of you," Rory Sue suggested. "Who has the power then?"

Walter swallowed hard, his gaze suddenly locked on her lips. "You do," he said.

"And you object to that on principle? Because a man should take the initiative when it comes to sex?"

"Not always," he said, suddenly unable to think of anything except hauling her back to the inn and into his bed. He didn't like how easily she could throw him off of the moral high ground. He sucked in a deep breath and forced himself to concentrate on counting backward from a hundred. When he felt more in control, he finally looked her way again and caught her smug expression. She knew exactly the kind of effect she was having on him and she was enjoying every minute of it.

"Tell me about the first house we're going to see," he said, his tone brusque.

"It has three bedrooms," she said slowly and dramatically, amusement in her eyes. She lowered her voice to a sexy purr. "And the most amazing Jacuzzi tub you've ever seen in the master bathroom."

She managed to imbue the description with enough innuendo that Walter flushed.

"Rory Sue, this has to stop," he commanded. "If you expect me to look at houses with you, you can't be talking about bedrooms and tubs."

She laughed then. "You don't want me to mention bedrooms or bathrooms?"

"No. I'll find 'em on my own."

"You scared I'm going to seduce you in one of them, Walter?"

He stared at her. He'd never met anyone quite like her before. He held her gaze.

"Truthfully?" he responded, losing the fight with his conscience. "I'm thinking we're not going to make it to any of those bedrooms tonight. How fast can you get to the Serenity Inn?"

"Really?" Her face lit up. "Well, hallelujah!"

That was pretty much his reaction, as well. Tomorrow would be soon enough to figure out just how big a mistake he was making.

CHAPTER EIGHT

Raylene had been on medication for a couple of weeks now, but she was no closer to stepping across the threshold at the house than she had been before starting treatment. She'd been so sure she'd at least be able to go back out on the patio by now, but she still couldn't make herself do it. She regarded Dr. McDaniels with frustration after yet another failed attempt just to step outside the front door.

"I'm not getting any better," she said as she hovered inside the door, palms sweating and heart racing.

Dr. McDaniels gave her an unrelenting look. "Maybe you need to take a leap of faith here."

"Meaning?"

"Look around, Raylene. There's no danger in sight. I'm right here with you. Take a deep breath and take that first step. Don't stand here thinking about all the times you've failed. Just do it."

Raylene regarded her incredulously. "Don't you think I want to?"

The doctor's gaze remained steady. "I don't know. Do you?"

Angered that the psychologist questioned her determination, Raylene stepped outside almost without realizing she was doing it, then turned to give Dr. McDaniels a defiant look. The older woman was grinning at her.

"There now. That wasn't so impossible, after all, was it?" she said.

Raylene blinked, then felt a swell of triumph. Emboldened, she took a few more steps, until she was standing in the middle of the sidewalk. The sensation of being outside actually made her feel giddy with relief. Maybe she could do this. Right this second, she almost felt as if she could walk around the block. Maybe even all the way into town.

But then the sound of an approaching car had her tensing. Once again, her heart raced, and the door to the house seemed a million miles away.

As if she sensed Raylene's sudden fear or simply recognized the first signs of an oncoming panic attack, Dr. McDaniels moved to her side. "Deep, slow breaths," she reminded her.

The car drove past, and Raylene felt the tension in her shoulders ease.

"Great job, Raylene, but I think that's enough for today," the doctor told her, leading the way back inside.

"How long were we out there?" Raylene asked.

"About two minutes."

"That's all?" she said, disappointed.

"Come on now," the doctor scolded. "This is a little like dieting. You have to remember that you didn't get to this point overnight. Turning it around isn't going to happen overnight, either. That's two minutes longer than you've been out there before."

The psychologist studied her intently. "I sense more frustration than usual today. Is there some reason you're suddenly so anxious to get better?"

Raylene thought about Carter and what it might be like

to go on an actual date with him. She'd never really dated all that much. Oh, she'd been out with guys in a group back in high school. She'd even had a steady boyfriend she'd hung out with for a bit during her junior year, but then she'd met Paul.

Because he'd been in medical school and she had transferred to a strict private boarding school, their dates had been rushed, mostly squeezed in between his classes. Occasionally they'd gone on study dates, when his attention had been focused on books, not her. They'd married soon after her graduation from high school.

With everything moving so quickly, there had been no lingering glances over romantic dinners or intense conversations after a fabulous movie. She couldn't even imagine what it would feel like to be courted the old-fashioned way, but lately she desperately wanted to experience it. She credited Carter for stirring that desire.

"I think I'm just tired of staring at the same walls," she said, not ready to reveal that her sudden rush had anything to do with a man.

"They weren't closing in on you when we started," the doctor said, proving that she was intuitive. "You seemed relatively content with your sheltered life. It made you feel safe."

"True," Raylene conceded.

"What's changed?"

Raylene hesitated, then said, "The truth is that I've met someone interesting. He's been by a few times. I can't help wondering what it would be like to go out with him."

"Has he been pressuring you to do that?"

"No. Oh, he asked once, but he seems to understand the way things are right now."

"Wanting to leave the house, especially to go on a date, seems like progress to me," Dr. McDaniels said, looking surprisingly encouraged. "Could you have imagined feeling this way a few months ago, or even a few weeks ago?"

"Not at all," Raylene said. "I was content to stay right here, but I have to say that I don't see how feeling restless the way I do now can possibly be a good thing."

"It means you're going to be more highly motivated," the doctor told her. "Frankly, I'd prefer it if you were suddenly this anxious to get better strictly for yourself, but if wanting this so you can be with someone else helps, I can work with that."

"Maybe I could take a different medication or a stronger dose," Raylene suggested.

"No, we're going to give this one a little more time. Just think about what you accomplished today. I know it must seem like you're progressing at a snail's pace, but you are progressing. We need to talk some more, too."

"About what?" Raylene asked wearily. "We've already talked my marriage to death. There's nothing more to say."

"Apparently there is, because you're still locked in this house. Next time, we'll see if we can figure out what else is going on. In the meantime, I'd like you to go out for two minutes every day."

Raylene regarded her with dismay. "Without you?"

"You don't need me. You already know you can do it. If it helps to reassure you, have Sarah or someone else go with you, but I don't want you backsliding between my visits. Think of it as learning a new skill. The more you practice, the faster you'll improve."

Raylene sighed. "Okay, fine." She walked to the door with Dr. McDaniels but, despite her earlier success, she couldn't seem to make herself step onto the stoop as she said goodbye. It was as if there was an invisible wall in front of her. She simply couldn't summon the courage to break through it, not even when she watched in frustration as the doctor merely stepped casually outside and walked to her car. Watching how easy it was for her nearly made Raylene weep. Her earlier sense of triumph disintegrated.

The phone rang as she closed the door, but she tried to compose herself before answering.

"Hey," Carter said. "You busy? Has Dr. McDaniels left yet?"

"Since when do you keep track of my appointments with the shrink?" she asked testily.

"You mentioned it when I called last night," he said carefully. "Are you okay, Raylene?"

"Of course I'm not okay. Haven't you heard, I'm agoraphobic?" she said, unable to control the bitterness in her voice.

"I'm coming over," he said at once.

"Don't," she said, already regretting snapping at him. Who knew what she'd do or say if he was here when she was in this crummy mood.

Unfortunately, he'd already hung up. She sighed. This was one of those times when she really did wish she could leave the house. Simply pretending she wasn't home was hardly an option. He'd know better and, being a cop, he probably wouldn't hesitate to break down a door if he thought there was something wrong.

When the doorbell rang a few minutes later, she resigned herself to seeing him.

"The door's open," she called out.

Carter stepped inside, frowning. "You shouldn't do that," he said. "I could have been anyone."

"I saw your cruiser pull into the driveway," she said defensively. "Even though I'd told you not to come."

"You sounded upset."

"A wise man would have picked up on my lousy mood and run for the hills."

"Well, it sounded to me as if you needed company."

"Which just proves you're not as perceptive as you think you are."

Instead of walking right back out the door, which many men would have done, he regarded her with amusement. "Still trying to run me off?"

She sighed. "It's not going to work, is it?"

He settled onto the sofa beside her. "Nope, at least not until you tell me what happened to bring on this mood."

"I thought today was going to be the day," she admitted.

"The day for what?"

"When I walked through the doorway and back out into the world."

He nodded with sudden understanding. "And that didn't happen."

"Actually, it did. I was outside for two whole minutes."

His expression brightened. "Then why do you sound so discouraged? That sounds like progress to me."

"I suppose."

"Is the doctor discouraged?"

She shook her head.

"She's the expert," he reminded her. "Maybe you should let her be the judge of whether you're making the right kind of progress."

She frowned at him. "Don't be all rational and reasonable. Men do that all the time, when women just want sympathy."

He looked undaunted by the accusation. In fact, he draped an arm over her shoulder and drew her back against his chest. "Hey, I can do sympathy. If you want to cry on my shoulder, be my guest. Just try not to get the uniform too damp. I have to go back to work eventually."

She chuckled despite herself. "I'd hate to send you out of here all soggy to sit in an air-conditioned cruiser. You'd probably wind up with pneumonia, and I'd have this whole boatload of guilt on top of everything else."

"Then let's just sit here like this for a minute," he suggested, his arm still resting lightly in place.

For a moment Raylene let herself surrender to the comfort he was offering, but then his arm started to feel as if it was imprisoning her. Even though she knew rationally that all he was offering was comfort and that she could break free of his grasp whenever she wanted, she felt herself starting to hyperventilate.

Carter heard her first gasp and released her at once, his expression filled with concern. "Are you okay?" he asked.

The genuine worry in his eyes reassured her, but still she moved away until there was distance between them. She was shaking, but when he reached out to put his hand over hers, she jerked away.

He regarded her with understandable confusion. "Raylene, what just happened here?" he asked quietly.

Feeling like an idiot, she couldn't bring herself to meet his gaze. "I panicked," she admitted.

"Because I had my arm around you?" he asked, sounding bewildered. Then understanding apparently dawned. "Is this about your marriage? Did you have some kind of flashback to the abuse?"

Tears welling up in her eyes, she nodded. She couldn't tell, though, if the reaction was to the awful memories or because Carter had understood. She'd never envisioned anyone realizing how powerless she had felt, and he didn't even know the whole story.

"Maybe you should tell me about your marriage," he coaxed gently.

She automatically shook her head. "I really don't want to talk about it."

"I can understand not wanting to relive bad memories, but I need to know so I won't inadvertently do something else to upset you."

She didn't want to think about all that ugliness. She wanted it to stay in the past, but it obviously couldn't be shut away like that. It was very much in this room right now. And Carter was right. If they were going to have any kind of chance, he needed to know about her past.

When she didn't answer, Carter took the initiative. "He hurt you, didn't he?" he asked quietly, his voice tight with anger. "A lot."

She nodded.

"How bad did it get?"

"Really bad."

Carter looked as if he wanted to punch something, but he didn't. Instead, his touch oh so gentle, he covered her hand with his. He just rested it on hers, offering comfort, but giving her the easy option of pulling away. "I'm sorry."

His calm voice and compassionate tone seemed to unleash a torrent of words. She described the fights that began for no reason, the arguments that quickly escalated to violence, the unpredictability of it all, and the way it had eventually cut her off from the rest of the world.

"Most of the time I think I've put it behind me, but just now..." Her voice trailed off.

"My arm around you reminded you of him pinning you down," he guessed.

"It just came over me out of the blue. I...I hadn't felt like that since I moved in here. Suddenly all I could think about was how strong he'd been and how powerless it had made me feel," she admitted. "I think that was worse than him hitting me, feeling as if there was nothing I could do to fight back."

"You know that I would never hurt you, right?"

"In my head, I know that, or at least I want to believe it."

"But after what you've gone through, you can't be sure you can trust me or any other man," he concluded.

She regarded him with a teary gaze. "You see what a mess I am? And your life is complicated enough. You should leave and never look back."

He smiled at that. "Too late," he said.

"It's not," she insisted. "You could walk away now and there'd be no harm, no foul. You could just chalk it up as one of those things. I wouldn't blame you."

"That would suggest I'm a quitter," he said. "I'm not. How about you?"

"It would be easier if I were. It *was* easier when I thought things would never have to change."

"Life is all about change and moving forward."

"Even when it's terrifying?"

"I think maybe that's when it's most important of all," he said. He stood up. "Look, I really hate to leave you like this, but I need to get back on duty. Will you be okay? Should I call Sarah or someone else?"

"I'm fine. Go. Protect the world."

He started toward the door, then turned back. "I really wish I'd been there to protect you," he said softly. And then he was gone.

Raylene reached for a pillow and hugged it to her. Amazingly, just hearing those almost wistful, heartfelt words made her feel more cherished than she had been in years.

Carter wanted to break things. Seeing the terror in Raylene's eyes, the look of utter devastation on her face when she'd gone back in time for just one heartbeat into the dark world of her marriage, made him sick to his stomach.

He'd dealt with his share of domestic violence cases in Columbia, even a couple right here in Serenity. He'd hauled men into jail, left women battered both physically and emotionally. While each case had mattered, none had cut him as deeply as imagining it happening to Raylene.

The first chance he got that evening, he got on the computer at headquarters and pulled up the records. Typically there was only a handful of calls—and no arrests—before the one that had sent Paul Hammond to jail and Raylene into the hospital with a miscarriage. Right now the man was locked behind bars, which was a good thing, because Carter felt an overwhelming desire to teach him a few lessons about picking on someone weaker and more vulnerable.

The bad news, though, was that the man's sentence—way too short to begin with, in Carter's opinion—was already running out. With time off for good behavior, he could be back on the streets in a matter of months, if not weeks. Carter wondered if Raylene knew that. He doubted it. It would be a while before the court would have to notify her of Paul's impending release.

When Carter went off duty, he drove over to the radio station where Travis was still on the air. The door was locked, so he tapped on the studio window to get his attention. Travis held up a finger to indicate he'd be there in a minute, then put on another song and came to open the door.

"Is it okay that I'm here?" Carter asked.

"Sure. I'll set up a few commercial-free music packages and we can talk." He studied Carter. "Something on your mind?"

"I'll get into it after you've taken care of business."

Travis nodded. When the song ended, he hit the button for the microphone and chatted intimately with his audience, no doubt making every woman out there head for bed thinking she was on his mind.

When the next set of music was on, he turned back to Carter. "You want something to drink?" He gestured through a window in the studio to the antique red Coca-Cola cooler in the lobby. "That's filled with soda. Sorry I don't have anything stronger. You look as if you've had a tough day."

"I've had better," Carter admitted, waving off the offer of a soda.

"Then what's up?"

Carter filled him in on the incident at the house earlier and told him what he'd found in the police records. "I assume you know about her background."

Travis nodded. "Sarah filled me in."

"Does she know that sick SOB is getting out of jail in the not-too-distant future?"

Travis sat up straighter, his jaw set angrily. "How soon?"

"Hard to say. I'll check that out in the morning, but I'd say by the end of summer at the latest."

"Damn!"

"My sentiment exactly," Carter said. "Do you think she knows?"

Travis shook his head. "I know she doesn't. Anytime he's mentioned, which isn't all that often, all she says is how thankful she is he's locked up."

"We need to prepare her," Carter said. "And we need to figure out how to protect her in case he comes out of prison with a chip on his shoulder."

Travis frowned. "You're really worried about this, aren't you? You don't think he'll have sense enough to stay the hell away? No man in his right mind would come out of jail and then do something likely to land him right back behind bars."

Carter lifted a brow. "He didn't have sense enough not

to beat her in the first place, did he? Men like that rarely learn their lesson behind bars. They just come out angrier than ever."

"Okay, what can I do?"

"For now just alert Sarah to what's going on. I'll dig around, see what kind of timetable we're looking at. Then we can decide how to break the news to Raylene. Sarah might have some ideas about that."

"What about protection? Do you have a plan for that?" Travis asked.

"Leave that to me," Carter said, his tone grim. Because if Paul Hammond wanted to get to Raylene, he'd have to go through Carter first.

Raylene opened the door late one afternoon to find Carrie on her doorstep, her expression uncertain.

"Is it okay that I'm here?"

"Of course it is. Did you come by for a cooking lesson?"

The teen shook her head. "I just wanted to visit, if it's okay."

"Come on in the kitchen. I'll get us something to drink. Would you like some cookies?"

"Just some water," Carrie said.

"I thought all kids were starving by the time they got out of school," Raylene said.

Carrie shrugged. "Not me."

Raylene regarded her quizzically, not really clear why Carrie had dropped in. She had a feeling, though, that it would come out when the girl was ready to talk and not before.

"It's such a nice day, it would be great to sit outside and have our drinks, but you know I can't do that, right?" she asked instead.

Carrie nodded. "How long have you been this way?"

"A couple of years now."

"And you can't go out at all? What if you get sick and need to see a doctor?"

"Thankfully I haven't had to find out," Raylene said. "And my psychologist comes here." She studied the teen. "You knew I was seeing someone about the panic disorder, didn't you?"

"Carter told me." She hesitated, then asked, "Is it hard? I mean, telling someone everything that's going on in your head?"

"Sometimes," Raylene admitted. "But it's the only way she can help me."

"I don't know if I could do that," Carrie said. "You know, just spill my guts to a stranger."

Raylene bit back a smile. "Actually a lot of people find it easier to talk to a complete stranger. They don't judge you. Besides, Dr. McDaniels is trained to listen and to ask the right kinds of questions. Sometimes I find myself saying things before I even realize they were on my mind."

"I wish I had someone I could talk to like that," Carrie said wistfully. "Carter tries, but he's a guy."

"If something's bothering you, you could talk to me," Raylene suggested.

For a split second Carrie looked hopeful, but then her face fell. "But you'd have to tell Carter."

"I would if it was something serious," she conceded. "But I'd do my best to keep whatever you say strictly confidential."

"But a shrink, somebody I pay, they'd have to keep it to themselves, right?"

"I'm not sure," Raylene admitted. "Carter's your guardian. In that case, even a psychologist might have to tell him if it was something he needed to know." She reached across the table and covered Carrie's tightly clenched fist. "What's this about, sweetie? Whatever it is, don't keep it bottled up inside. If you don't want to tell me or Carter, then I can arrange for you to see Dr. McDaniels."

"But Carter would have to know that, too," Carrie said, sounding defeated. Suddenly she started to cry. "Everything's such a mess, and I don't know how to fix it."

Raylene gathered the teen into her arms and held her. "Whatever's going on, I know it must seem overwhelming, but there's not a problem in the world that can't be solved. You just have to ask for help. You know your brother would do anything he possibly can to make sure you're happy."

"I know," she said with a sniff. She took the tissue Raylene held out to her and wiped her nose. "But he's trying so hard to take care of me and Mandy. He even gave up his job to move here because he thought it would be better for us to grow up in a small town."

She hesitated, then blurted, "But it's not better, it's worse. I'm miserable. My whole life is spinning out of control. I hate school. I miss my friends. I miss Mom and Dad. I miss going to the mall and hanging out." She regarded Raylene with watery eyes. "And I sound like a selfish brat, when I know it's not easy for Carter or Mandy, either."

"You're not being selfish," Raylene told her. "You're just trying to adjust to something that would be very difficult for anyone. Losing a parent is never easy. I still haven't entirely gotten over my dad's death. I can't begin to imagine what it would have been like to lose both parents at once, especially at your age."

"Still, I need to suck it up," Carrie said. "I can't dump all this on my brother when he's doing the best he can."

"I think you'd be surprised by how much of this he'd understand," Raylene told her. "He's a pretty intuitive, compassionate man."

Carrie looked surprised by her assessment. "Carter? He's usually clueless."

"Well, in my experience, he's figured some things out without me having to say a word. I'm willing to bet he has some idea of how you're feeling, too. Talk to him, Carrie. Give him a chance to help."

"Maybe," Carrie said. She hesitated, then asked, "Do you have to tell him I barged in here today?"

"Not if you don't want me to," Raylene said. "And you didn't barge in. You have a standing invitation. I do think, though, that you ought to tell him yourself that you dropped by. Keeping secrets, even little ones like this, can create problems."

"I suppose," Carrie said, her expression doubtful. Eventually, she nodded. "Okay, I'll tell him I stopped by to visit, but that's all."

"Good. That way I can send some lasagna home with you for dinner."

Carrie gave her a knowing look. "Are you trying to win my brother by cooking for him?"

Raylene laughed. "No. I just love to cook, and I always make way too much. If you like the lasagna, let me know, and I'll teach you how to make it yourself."

Carrie immediately shook her head. "It's too fattening for me, but I know Mandy and Carter will love it. They eat like pigs."

It wasn't the first time Raylene had gotten a nagging feeling that Carrie might have an eating disorder. At first she'd told herself that because of her experience years ago with Annie, she was overreacting, but now, especially in light of their earlier conversation about seeing a psychologist, she had to wonder. Maybe Carrie had even recognized herself that she had a problem that went beyond her dissatisfaction with her life in Serenity. The compassion Raylene had felt earlier was now tinged with a sense of urgency.

"There's nothing wrong with having a healthy appetite," Raylene said casually, hoping to make her point without putting Carrie on the defensive. "Too many young women start obsessing about weight when they don't need to."

"Yeah, Carter gets on my case about that," Carrie admitted openly. "He just doesn't know what it's like for girls, though."

"But I have some idea," Raylene told her. "So does my friend Annie."

"The one who's married to the ballplayer, Ty Townsend?"

Raylene nodded. "Did you know that she had a severe problem with anorexia when she was about your age?"

Carrie looked skeptical. "Really?"

"She did," Raylene said, then added bluntly, "It almost killed her."

Carrie looked alarmed for just an instant, but then her expression closed down. "You're just saying that to scare me."

"No," Raylene said emphatically. "You can talk to her yourself. Her heart quit, and she ended up in the hospital. It was touch-and-go for a few days. I was there the night she collapsed. It was pretty awful."

Looking shaken, Carrie immediately stood up. "I have to go home," she said.

"Wait. Let me get that lasagna," Raylene said, but Carrie had already gone.

Obviously talking about Annie had upset her even more than the conversation about her dissatisfaction with her life. Raylene found the entire exchange upsetting. She didn't want to be an alarmist, but Annie's experience had proved that anorexia wasn't something that could be ignored for long. She knew, though, that for Carter to believe her, she'd need more evidence, perhaps even a situation in which he could see Carrie's behavior and judge it for himself.

School would be out soon, and the Fourth of July holiday was just a few weeks away. Usually it was Ronnie and Dana Sue, along with Annie and Ty, who hosted a barbecue after the town's annual parade. Since Raylene couldn't go, maybe she'd explain the situation to Annie and they could move the barbecue here. If nothing else, it would throw Carrie and Annie together. If Carrie was in trouble, Annie would pick up on it right away.

And then Annie and Raylene together would have to find a way to help Carter deal with the problem before it went spinning out of control and quite literally destroyed his sister's life.

CHAPTER NINE

Carter's day had gone from bad to worse. After a fairly routine morning, he'd started the afternoon dealing with a fatal crash on one of the rural roads outside of town. A teenager going too fast on his way home from school had missed a curve, hit a tree and died on the scene.

Every time he handled a call like that, he felt an urgent need to rush home and check on Carrie and Mandy. He knew they were both sick of his lectures about driving too fast, but he felt the lesson had to be repeated if it was ever to sink in. Thankfully, neither of them had a license yet, but it was only a matter of time.

After facing the boy's parents to tell them what had happened, he went back to the station where he found a voicemail message from the prison saying that Paul Hammond's release was tentatively scheduled for August. There seemed to be little chance that it would be postponed. He'd been a model citizen, the caller reported, using his time in prison to provide medical care for other inmates. As Carter saw it, that could be good news or bad. If it proved he'd learned his lesson, great, but it was just as likely that he'd simply manipulated the system to look favorably on an earlier release.

By the time Carter finally wrapped up for the day and walked into the house, all he wanted to do was take a hot shower, order in some food and relax. Instead, he found Carrie and Mandy in the middle of an argument that escalated into tears and doors slamming. Just what he needed.

Sighing, he followed Mandy to her room and tapped on the door. "Go away," she mumbled tearfully.

"Not an option," he said, and walked in.

She sat up and made room for him on the side of her bed. "I thought you were Carrie."

"My hair's shorter," he joked.

That drew a faint smile.

"So what's going on with you two?" he asked.

"She's just being a pain, that's all," Mandy said, snuggling against his side and leaning her head on his shoulder. "Raylene left a message about having lasagna for us, so I rode my bike over to get it, and Carrie freaked out."

"Why?"

Mandy shrugged. "I have no idea. Anyway, she said she wouldn't eat it if it were the last meal on earth. Like I care whether she eats or not." She regarded him hopefully. "You and me, we can have it, though, right? It looks really good. Raylene says it just needs to be heated in the oven for a half hour or so. I can do that, while you change. She even gave me garlic bread to go with it."

"Sounds good to me. You go and do that. I'll see if I can figure out what's going on with Carrie."

"It's a waste of time, if you ask me," Mandy said.

"Trying to keep the two of you happy is never a waste of my time," Carter chided. It was just a challenge.

He crossed the hall and tapped on Carrie's door. She didn't even bother to answer. He opened it and walked in to find her with her face buried in a pillow and her shoulders still shaking with sobs. He sat down on the edge of the bed.

"Go away," she said, her voice muffled.

"You know that never works with me," he chided. "What's going on? Why were you and Mandy fighting about lasagna, of all things?"

"It wasn't about lasagna," Carrie said, sitting up and turning to him with an indignant expression. "Is that what she told you?"

"What's your version?"

"It was about her sneaking off to Raylene's house just to check up on me."

Carter frowned. "To check up on you? Were you over there?"

She flushed at the question. Apparently she hadn't realized how revealing her comment had been. "I stopped by," she said defensively. "But I'm sure *she* told you that."

"She who? Mandy? She didn't mention it."

"No, Raylene," Carrie said impatiently. "She probably told you every word I said."

"I haven't spoken to Raylene all day, but something tells me I need to."

Carrie flushed and grabbed his arm. "No, don't," she pleaded. "She promised she wouldn't tell you anything, and I guess she didn't. I'm sorry I accused her of being a blabbermouth."

Carter regarded her with bewilderment. "Carrie, what's going on? What did you and Raylene talk about?"

"Just stuff," she said evasively. "She told me to tell you, so it's not like she's going behind your back or keeping stuff from you."

"What is it she thinks you should tell me?"

She hesitated, her expression miserable. "That my life

sucks," she admitted in a small voice. She gave him an apologetic look. "I'm sorry, Carter. Really, really sorry. I know you didn't want to wind up stuck with me and Mandy, and I know you're trying, but I hate everything about this boring town and the people here and my whole, stupid life."

Carter felt as if the wind had been knocked out of him. He'd known she wasn't happy about the move, but he'd figured she would adjust. Teenagers had a tendency to overdramatize everything, so he probably hadn't taken her frequent complaints seriously enough.

"I'm sorry," he said. "How can we make this better for you?"

She looked at him hopefully. "Move back to Columbia," she suggested.

He shook his head. "Other than that."

"You won't even consider it?"

"No, this is our home now. I'm going to start a police department for Serenity. I've made a commitment to the town, and I take that seriously."

"I know," she said, looking defeated. "I thought maybe you'd consider it before, but I knew it was too late now."

"Meaning?"

"Before, it was like you just had this job with the sheriff's department, no big deal. Now you're going to be chief of your own department, and that's really cool. And there's Raylene, and I know you like her. You have everything you want right here. But what do I have? Nothing. Not even any friends."

"You'll make friends here," he said. "It just takes a little time in a new school." Despite his very deep reservations, he held out the promise of something he knew she wanted. "Maybe you can even find a summer job, so you can save up for a car."

For a fleeting instant, her eyes lit up. "You'd let me have my own car?"

"By the time you've saved enough money, I think you'll be ready for it," he said.

"In other words, it'll take forever," she said, looking defeated. "My life sucks."

She did, in fact, look so unhappy that he couldn't help feeling a certain amount of pity for her. Even if the move had been for the best, it must have been hell being uprooted from the home and neighborhood she'd always known and the friends she'd had since grade school.

"Why don't we go to Columbia this weekend," he suggested impulsively. "We can get rooms at a hotel with a pool and you can invite some of your friends over. We'll see a movie, too. You and Mandy can pick it. I'll even suffer through a chick flick, if that's what you want."

She giggled at that, and for just a minute she reminded him of the carefree girl she'd been before they'd lost their folks.

"Okay," she said grudgingly. "Can we eat all the candy in the minibar?"

"At those prices?" he said with exaggerated horror, then grinned. "What the heck! Go for it. Just this once."

She threw her arms around him then. "You're the best big brother in the entire world."

"I try," he said.

Her expression immediately sobered. "I know you do, and I promise not to be a pain all the time."

"You're not a pain all the time," he told her with a grin.

"But when I am, I'm a big one," she said.

"True."

She laughed.

"Come downstairs and have dinner," he said. "If Raylene

sent it over, it's bound to be better than anything we could order."

For a minute, he thought the mention of the lasagna was going to start another argument, but instead she nodded. "I'll be right there."

Carter left her room feeling as if he'd negotiated a very tricky and temporary truce between two warring factions. He hoped dinner went smoothly, because he wasn't sure he had sufficient energy in reserve to go another round.

And he still had to come up with some way to tell Raylene that she had less than two months before her ex-husband was going to be released from prison.

Raylene decided the best way to handle her suspicions that Carrie might have an eating disorder would be to get the Sweet Magnolias on the case. The day after Carrie's visit, she started making the calls midmorning and had everything lined up for a margarita night by lunchtime.

When Sarah arrived home in the afternoon, she brought all the ingredients for the margaritas, along with everything Raylene had requested to make a new burrito recipe.

"I think we're getting to the point that guacamole isn't enough to counteract the effects of all that tequila," she told Sarah. "We need real food."

"Works for me," Sarah said. "So, what's going on? Why the call for an emergency gathering?"

"I'll explain tonight. In the meantime, though, I need to see how you'd feel about hosting the Fourth of July barbecue here this year."

Sarah looked startled by the suggestion. "But Dana Sue and Ronnie have always had it. Don't you think their feelings will be hurt if we steal it away from them?" Her expression immediately fell. "Sorry. I know you miss out every year, so of course we should have it here this time."

"Honestly, it's not about me," Raylene told her. "I had a very disturbing conversation with Carrie Rollins this afternoon. I think she could be anorexic, or at least she might be on the verge of developing an eating disorder. I want an opportunity for Annie and Dana Sue especially to observe her behavior to see if I'm right."

Sarah regarded her worriedly. "Shouldn't you just mention it to Carter and let him take it from there? He might not appreciate your meddling."

"I would, but it's a pretty serious thing to say about someone. I want to be sure. He's got a lot to handle as it is. There's no point in upsetting him if it turns out I'm overreacting."

"Unfortunately, I don't think you're likely to overreact about something like this. You and I were there with Annie. We both still feel a certain amount of guilt for not jumping in sooner to tell Dana Sue what we thought was happening."

"We were kids," Raylene said. "We didn't go running to parents to tattle on our friends. And just about everyone we knew was dieting, so for a long time it didn't seem as if Annie's behavior was unique or out of control."

"Still, we should have spoken up when we did realize what was happening," Sarah said. "If Annie had died..." She shuddered, much as Raylene did when the same thought occurred to her.

"She didn't die, thank God," Raylene said fiercely. "But it certainly taught us all a valuable lesson about not ignoring possible eating disorders."

"You're right," Sarah agreed. "Are you sure you can handle all this by yourself on the Fourth? Travis and I will be at the radio station all morning covering the parade."

"Not a problem. I'm sure some of the others will pitch in

to set things up in the backyard. I'll just have to cook and coordinate everything."

"Maybe you'll be able to come onto the patio by then," Sarah suggested, her expression optimistic. "These little two-minute forays have gone pretty well. In another couple of weeks, who knows how long you'll be able to stay outside."

"Don't get your hopes up," Raylene said, though her own optimism had grown with each step she'd taken back into the outside world. "But, like you said, who knows? Maybe I'm due for a minimiracle."

That's certainly what it was going to take for her to spend a whole evening on the patio. Still, this barbecue wasn't about her. Right now she needed to focus on Carrie and what she needed.

As soon as Raylene described her fears about Carrie Rollins, all of the Sweet Magnolias were immediately on board with moving the Fourth of July event to Sarah's house.

Dana Sue seemed especially upset by the possibility that Carrie was anorexic. Annie moved to her mother's side.

"I'm right here, Mom. Fit as a fiddle," Annie told her.

Dana Sue squeezed her hand. "But you almost weren't. Just look at all you would have missed—being married to Ty, raising his son, having Meg, your career as a sports-injury therapist and fitness instructor."

"It's not as if the world couldn't live without another fitness instructor," Annie said half-jokingly.

"Stop it," Maddie chimed in. "You provide an important service to a lot of women who need help staying fit. They might complain bitterly while they're exercising, but all of the women you work with at the club leave there feeling better about themselves."

"I know that," Annie conceded. "I suppose I'm trying

to diminish it out of guilt. I was out on maternity leave for months. I felt as if I'd abandoned them. Some of them worked with Elliott, but a lot of them just quit. I failed them."

"If they quit, it was their choice," Maddie reminded her. "You didn't even stay away half as long as we were expecting you to. You couldn't wait to get back to work."

"Yes, she was anxious to get that gorgeous body of hers back into shape right away," Sarah said. "Of course, Ty's so taken with her shapeliness, she'll probably end up pregnant again!"

Annie rolled her eyes. "Let's try to concentrate on Carrie, okay? Do you think I should sit her down and have a talk with her?"

Raylene shook her head. "I thought about that, but it's not our place to charge in to the rescue. If we decide there's a problem, I'll tell Carter and then offer to have you or Dana Sue talk to Carrie or set up something with Dr. McDaniels. Carter will have to take it from there, unless he wants more help from us. Agreed?"

Annie frowned. "What if he's in denial? If Carrie's like I was, she's probably pretty good at covering up what's going on. And if he asks her directly, she'll only lie. I did."

Dana Sue nodded. "Then we have to gang up on him and *insist* he get help for Carrie. If we honestly believe there's a problem, we can't just turn it over to him and walk away. I can't, in good conscience, do that. Not when I know the possible consequences of doing nothing. I had to almost lose Annie before I realized just how deep my own denial was."

"Carter will get her help," Raylene said confidently. "He takes his responsibility as her big brother and guardian very seriously."

Helen had been quiet most of the evening, but she'd been studying Raylene with a penetrating gaze. "Mind telling me how this turned into your problem? Last time I was over here, this was a man who was threatening to have you charged with child neglect."

"Times have changed," Sarah said, grinning. "Haven't they, Raylene?"

Raylene blushed furiously. "We're getting along okay now."

"He's kissed her," Sarah confided.

"Sarah!" Raylene protested, her cheeks heating.

"Well, we're your friends," Sarah retorted. "We all care about what's going on in your life, especially the fact that you have a very sexy guy who's hot for you."

Helen continued to look troubled. "Are you really ready to have a man in your life?"

"Honestly, I don't know," Raylene admitted. "But he doesn't seem to be going away. His persistence is actually kind of sweet, to say nothing of flattering."

"And he understands the situation? Not just that you can't go out, but why?" Helen persisted.

"Even I don't know why," Raylene said irritably.

"Of course you do," Helen said. "It all goes back to Paul Hammond."

"That's probably too simplistic," Raylene said. "Paul's certainly part of it. Anyway, I'm trying to sort it all out with Dr. McDaniels."

"Maybe you should see how that goes before you add in a distraction like Carter," Helen advised.

Sarah turned on her. "Why are you being such a downer? I think Carter's the best thing that's happened to Raylene in a long time. You should see how she glows when he's around."

"That's terrific," Helen conceded. "I'm just concerned that he—or any man—might start out thinking he can deal with a woman in Raylene's situation, but then realize all the ramifications." Helen shrugged. "I don't want to see Raylene get hurt."

"You're assuming she's not going to get better," Sarah said. "I believe she will. She's been making progress. Tell them, Raylene."

When Raylene remained silent, Sarah added, "She's been going outside every day."

Helen looked mildly impressed. "That's great, but—"

"Okay, stop it, you two," Raylene ordered. "It's not as if Carter and I are having a serious relationship. Right now we seem to be enjoying each other's company. That's it."

"You're getting involved with his family," Helen said. "That sounds serious to me."

"We're *all* getting involved with Carrie," Raylene corrected.

Helen frowned. "Still, you can see my point," she said, looking to Maddie and Dana Sue for support.

"Raylene is a grown woman," Maddie said. "I'm sure she understands the risks."

"Better than most," Raylene said quietly. After all, none of the other women in this room had had their hearts broken quite the way hers had been. If she could open hers again, she saw it as a testament to the spirit of hope that still lived deep inside her.

Walter ate the salad that Raylene had prepared for him. He was actually starting to like what he'd always thought of as rabbit food. He enjoyed the company even more, though she'd been getting on his nerves today with all her questions about Rory Sue. He was tired of being on the defensive, so he turned the tables on her.

"I hear you had another one of those margarita-night things here last night. Why didn't you include Rory Sue?"

Raylene frowned at the question. "She's never been a Sweet Magnolia."

"Is it like some kind of secret society that requires a long social pedigree?"

"Of course not."

"An engraved invitation?"

"Don't be ridiculous."

"Then why not ask her?"

"I don't make the rules," she said defensively.

"There are rules?"

"You know what I mean. It was started by Maddie, Dana Sue and Helen, then they included Jeanette because she works with them at the spa. They asked Annie because she was Dana Sue's daughter and Maddie's daughter-in-law. She brought me and Sarah along. It's not some big, formal organization, for pity's sake. It's just a bunch of friends who get together to talk about their lives."

"Seems to me Rory Sue could use some friends like that."

Raylene frowned at his persistence. "You're awfully protective of her all of a sudden. Has this thing between you gotten serious?"

"No. I just feel bad because she's living back here now and she's lonely."

Raylene studied him intently. "Do you think that's the only reason she's latched onto you, because she's lonely?"

He shrugged. "Could be." He was pretty sure he wasn't the kind of man Rory Sue was used to dating.

When he met Raylene's gaze, she was staring at him incredulously. "Do you not have any idea what a catch you are, Walter? You're handsome. You're turning into a great dad." She gave him a pointed look. "That's still a work in progress, of course."

"Of course," he said wryly, amused by her determination to remind him that he had a long way to go before he'd qualify for father of the year in her book.

She merely frowned at him. "Please tell me that you don't believe you were a better catch when you stood to inherit your family's cotton mill."

"Let's face it," he said. "Selling ads for a radio station in Serenity is never going to be financially rewarding."

"There are more important things," she said at once. "You know that, Walter. You stayed here because of your kids, so I know your values aren't entirely screwed up. Did Rory Sue say something to make you question your decision to stay in Serenity?"

"No, but she's grown up with a pretty big sense of entitlement. Money matters to her."

"Then she can earn her own," Raylene retorted. "And if she's that shallow, you don't want her anyway. Cut her loose."

Walter smiled at her indignation. "Slow down. I'm just thinking out loud here, trying to anticipate some of the pitfalls in this relationship."

"So there is a relationship?" she said triumphantly.

"There's...*something*," he said eventually. "I don't know that I have a name for it."

"Well, figure it out before it goes too far and you wind up getting hurt."

"You don't think I'll be the one hurting her?"

"Honestly, no. Rory Sue's a lot like her mother. She's a barracuda when it comes to men. Despite all the many reasons I had to hate you when you were married to Sarah, at heart you're a decent guy. I've come to appreciate your better qualities. It might be a stretch to expect Rory Sue to see them."

"Need I remind you that you're the one who put this whole thing into motion?"

"I expected you to have a fling, not to get all tied up in knots over her. I'm afraid I misjudged your fling capacity."

Walter chuckled. "Yeah, I have a feeling I missed the boat on that, too."

Raylene's gaze narrowed. "Please tell me you're not in love with her."

"I slept with her once. Even I know that's not love."

"Then what is it?"

"When I come up with a definition, I'll let you know. In the meantime, as a favor to me, try to reach out to her. Maybe invite her over for this shindig on the Fourth. That's not just for Sweet Magnolias, is it?"

"No. I can do that, if you're sure you want me to."

"Why wouldn't I want you to? It was my idea."

"Have you considered how much fun it will be to have me and Sarah putting the relationship under a microscope?"

"I'll just consider it penance for all the mistakes I've ever made, especially since I know you'll both keep your opinions to yourselves."

"In what universe?" Raylene retorted.

Walter sighed. "I can always hope."

And if it gave Rory Sue the opportunity to find a few friends she could count on, any grief he had to put up with would be worth it. Maybe, though, what he was really doing was putting her to the test. If Rory Sue's life was both busy and fulfilling, would she still have any room in it for him?

Just asking himself a question like that came as a shock to Walter. After all the hits he'd taken about destroying Sarah's self-confidence, it was startling to realize the impact the divorce had apparently had on his.

CHAPTER TEN

With the Fourth of July picnic rapidly approaching, Raylene decided it was time to really push herself to take bigger strides to overcome her panic over leaving the house. She'd been strong enough to survive her marriage—surely she could stay outside longer than a couple of minutes without falling apart!

What if, she asked herself, she'd been cutting the excursions so short because she was afraid of humiliating herself in front of someone? Even though the psychologist and Sarah were definitely on her side and understood her problem, that didn't mean she wanted to be embarrassed by coming unglued.

When she really thought about her slow progress, she decided that going toward the street was probably a bad idea, as well. Out there lay too much uncertainty. Anyone could happen by.

Maybe she ought to be trying to get to the more secluded patio. For a brief time she'd felt safe out there. Maybe that goal would be easier to conquer, and she'd be able to surprise everyone by joining them out there on the Fourth.

She sighed. So many *maybes* and uncertainties. The only way she'd ever know for sure would be to try.

She waited until an afternoon when she was alone. Sarah was still at work, and Laurie had taken the kids to the park. Walter had come for lunch and gone. No one else was expected.

For fifteen minutes—she watched each minute tick by on the clock over the stove—she sat at the kitchen table and did all the relaxation exercises Dr. McDaniels had taught her.

When she felt calm and in control, she went to the door and opened it, then put her hand on the screen door and drew in a deep breath. She thought about how much she wanted to keep a close eye on Carrie at the party, something she wouldn't be able to do if she was stuck inside the house. That goal got her to take her first step outside.

"I can do this," she murmured to herself as she took a few more steps. "It's perfectly safe out here. I only have to stay for two minutes, if that's all I can do. I don't have to stay if it doesn't feel right."

She walked to the edge of the garden, then paused and glanced around. There wasn't a soul in sight. The sun was bright, the sky clear. It couldn't have been a more perfect day to venture outside. The brightly colored flowers in her garden—the flowers she'd never touched—were beckoning. She bent down and pulled a couple of stray weeds, feeling a sense of accomplishment even over mastering such a small task.

Glancing at her watch, she realized she'd only been outside for a minute, maybe two. So far, though, so good. Maybe she could sit for a minute and enjoy the breeze and fresh air.

Heart pounding, she crossed to the patio itself. As she neared one of the comfortably cushioned chairs, she broke into a cold sweat. In an instant, she was hyperventilating so badly, she thought she might pass out, but she managed to get a death grip on the back of a chair and steadied herself.

She closed her eyes and tried to breathe evenly, consciously trying to calm her nerves.

And then she heard a sound, no more than the rustle of leaves in a breeze, she thought, but it was enough to terrify her. Panic, never far away, crawled up the back of her throat. She stood where she was, frozen in place, tears streaming down her face. The kitchen—her safe haven—seemed a thousand miles away. No matter how hard she tried, she couldn't seem to take the first step to get there.

She glanced over at that wonderful garden that Carter had created for her, tried to take comfort in the colorful flowers, but she couldn't seem to focus. She was shaking too badly, her eyesight blurred by tears.

Then she heard him, Carter calling her name. She tried to answer and couldn't. He came around the side of the house and took in the situation with a glance.

"Well, look at you," he said lightly, moving slowly toward her as if fearing he'd startle her. He approached her as carefully as someone trying to gentle a spooked horse. "Did you decide to take a walk on your own?"

Unable to speak, she merely nodded.

"Ready to go back inside?"

She nodded even more vehemently.

"Take my hand then," he said gently. "We'll go in together, unless you'd rather I just sit out here with you."

She shook her head, glancing desperately toward the house.

"Okay, then," he said quietly, still holding out his hand. "We'll go inside."

It took what seemed like an eternity for her to release her grip on the chair and take his hand. The warmth of his skin did what nothing else had. It reassured her. She clung to him. His hand became her lifeline.

"It's only a few steps," he told her. "We can count them as we go. One."

She stepped forward haltingly, slowed by an inability—or unwillingness—to open her eyes for more than a second at a time, as if that would shut out the fear.

"That's good," he said soothingly. "Now another. Two."

It was five endless steps in all, but she did it by concentrating on the sound of his voice and his commands and not thinking at all about the terrible panic that had her in its grip.

Once inside, she collapsed into a chair, sobs racking her body. "I thought I could do it. I thought it would be okay," she whispered in a choked voice, unable to look at him. She'd never felt more humiliated.

He brought her a tall glass of iced sweet tea, then sat across from her. "Stop beating yourself up. You tried. That's what counts. And tomorrow will be better."

She shook her head. "I don't believe that. It's always going to be like this." She lifted her gaze to his. "You can't imagine what it's like."

"No, I can't," he agreed. "But the fact that you tried, that's what counts. It tells me how brave you are, how badly you want to conquer this disorder or phobia or whatever it is."

"Brave?" she scoffed, an almost hysterical note in her voice. "I took a few steps into my own backyard, no more than I'd been taking every day for a couple of weeks now with Dr. McDaniels and Sarah. Today, though, I fell completely apart. If you hadn't come along, there's no telling how long I might have stayed there, completely frozen. I thought my heart was going to pound right out of my chest. I couldn't breathe."

He ignored her interpretation and spun his own. "But you did this all on your own," he reminded her. "I think it was amazing."

"Then you have very low standards."

He smiled at that. "And you're way too hard on yourself. So, why today? And why without Dr. McDaniels?"

She explained her earlier thoughts. "I got to thinking that maybe the reason I was making such slow progress was that I was afraid of being humiliated in front of someone, that maybe I'd do better on my own. And the Fourth of July picnic is coming up, and I wanted so badly to be out here with everyone else. It just seemed like the right time to push myself." She didn't mention her concerns about Carrie, her need to be available to her in a way she couldn't be if she remained housebound. She gave him a bleak look. "Maybe there is no right time."

He studied her for a minute, then asked, "Are you pushing yourself so hard all of a sudden because of me? I know that probably sounds egotistical, but I don't want to be the one putting added pressure on you."

Once again, he'd surprised her with his perceptiveness. "In a way," she admitted. "Sooner or later, you're going to get bored to tears by me never being able to go anywhere. You'll lose interest, and who could blame you?"

"I don't see myself losing interest anytime soon," he told her. "I keep coming back, don't I?"

"So far," she conceded. It suddenly dawned on her that his arrival today, which had been timely under the circumstances, was unexpected. "Is there some reason you dropped by in the middle of your shift? You're not upset because Carrie and Mandy dropped in here the other day, are you? Because I'd told them to come by anytime."

He shook his head. "No, I appreciate the fact that you're willing to spend time with them. They need a woman they can talk to, Carrie especially. As you know, she's having a tough time, and it's worse now that school is out. She doesn't seem to have made any friends at all, so she's hanging around the house, bored to tears."

Raylene regarded him with surprise. "She told you how she's been feeling?"

He nodded. "She admitted that she's miserable. I should have seen it myself. I'm taking them to Columbia this weekend. I hope that will help, but we can't run over there every time she starts feeling homesick."

"Who says?" Raylene countered. "If going back helps, you need to do it as often as you can. Columbia's not that far."

"The problem is that it's usually worse for her afterward," he said. "She's happy for a couple of days talking about who she saw and everything we did, but then she crashes right back down again. Even though she tries to hide it most of the time, I can see how angry she is about being here. This is the first time, though, that she's opened up to me. I have a feeling I have you to thank for that."

"I didn't do anything other than encourage her to tell you what was on her mind."

"I appreciate that. She needs to know we're in this together, that we're all making adjustments."

Raylene hesitated, then once again asked, "If you aren't here now because of Carrie or Mandy, what did bring you by?"

Her question, though an obvious one, seemed to unnerve him. He waved it off.

"This isn't the best time to get into it. It can wait."

"Tell me," she insisted.

He continued to hesitate.

"Carter, you're making me nervous. Is there a problem?" A thought suddenly struck her. "Did you come by to tell me it's best if we don't go on seeing each other?"

"Absolutely not," he said with such heartfelt emotion she

couldn't possibly doubt him. "I've already told you that I'm drawn to you, that I want to be with you."

Since him dumping her before they'd really had half a chance to get to know each other was just about the worst thing she could think of, anything else was bound to pale by comparison. "What then?" she pressed.

"It's about your ex-husband."

She regarded him blankly. "Paul? What about him?"

"There's something you need to know."

At his dire tone, a sense of dread settled in her stomach. "What?"

"He's due to get out of prison sometime in August. I thought you should be prepared."

Raylene's world, which had barely steadied itself on its axis after her unfortunate excursion outside, began spinning again. "No," she whispered. "That can't be."

"I'm afraid it's true. I checked it out myself after you told me about him. I wanted to see if you were likely to be in danger anytime soon."

She started to tremble and couldn't seem to stop. "No," she whispered again. "No, no, no."

Carter moved to her side, then paused. "Is it okay?" he asked tentatively.

Raylene nodded, and he pulled her into his arms. She tried to relax, to let herself feel the comfort and reassurance he was offering, but the fear was more powerful. She couldn't stop shaking.

"It's going to be okay," Carter promised. "He won't get near you, not if I have to convince the sheriff to put twenty-four-hour security around this house."

"No," she said fiercely, pulling away. "I can't rely on other people. This isn't your problem. And the sheriff doesn't have that kind of manpower." She groaned as another thought struck her. "I can't put Sarah and the kids in danger. I'll need to move out."

"Raylene, don't get ahead of yourself."

"But you said he's getting out in August. I have to make plans. I have to handle Paul on my own, and I need to be able to protect myself."

Carter regarded her with dismay. "What are you suggesting?"

Her mind made up, she looked at him with a steady gaze. "I want you to teach me how to use a gun."

"Absolutely not," Carter said at once, his expression grim.

"Carter, I have to do this my way."

He raked his hand through his hair. "Come on, Raylene. Have you ever even fired a gun before?"

"No, but that's why you'll teach me."

"How?" he asked reasonably. "It's not as if I can take you to the gun range."

Raylene faltered at that. "I have to learn," she insisted. "It's the only thing that makes sense."

"Do you honestly think you could shoot a man?" he asked.

She thought of the way Paul had mistreated her, the night that he'd in essence killed their baby. "Any man?" she said softly. "No." Then she met his gaze evenly. "But I could shoot Paul Hammond," she said with conviction.

Despite her fierce certainty, Carter shook his head. "You might be able to pull the trigger," he told her. "But you'd never be able to live with the consequences. I know you, sweetheart. Even after everything that man did to you, it would destroy you to take his life. That kind of violence or revenge just isn't in you."

"What about justice?" she asked, her voice pleading. "That's what it would be, you know. My life is the way it is because of him. Maybe if he was gone once and for all, I'd finally be able to live in peace. The court system obviously didn't care about that when they gave him such a light sentence."

Carter touched her cheek. "I know you want to believe that killing him would let you live a normal life again, and maybe it's even true, but there are better ways to handle this. Let me go and see him. I'll find out what his plans are, what his frame of mind is. For all we know, he's going to relocate to Alaska."

"He hates cold weather," she said automatically.

Carter frowned at the glib comment. "My point is that we need to know if he has a plan for the rest of his life. We can go from there."

Raylene nodded reluctantly. "But we're not ruling out the gun."

"Not entirely," he agreed, though with obvious reluctance.

She met his gaze. "Thank you for giving me some time to get used to the idea that he's going to be free. Now I have time to figure out what's best."

Carter regarded her with alarm. "But you won't do anything hasty, right? Promise me, we'll work this out together. Please don't make me regret telling you."

Ironically the panic she'd felt outside earlier, the fear she'd felt when Carter had told her the news, all of that had faded now. What she was left with was a cold emptiness inside, and the kind of grim determination she'd never expected to experience. Paul Hammond wouldn't terrorize her again, not ever. No matter what she had to do to stop him.

Carter walked away from Raylene with a sick feeling in the pit of his stomach. He'd seen something in her eyes that had terrified him. Though he admired her for wanting to face down her ex-husband, he knew without a doubt that such a confrontation was bound to turn out badly. She was no match for a bully who'd likely let his resentment fester during a jail term.

Once again, he contacted Travis and filled him in. "I didn't like what I heard in her voice. If I don't take the initiative here and deal with Hammond myself, there's no telling what Raylene might do."

"How can I help?"

"I can circulate the word with all the deputies in the area, but as thin as we're spread, it's going to take more men to make sure Hammond doesn't get near her again."

"I'll make some calls," Travis said at once. "How about I get Cal Maddox, Ronnie Sullivan, Erik Whitney and my cousin Tom over to my place later tonight? I'm sure we can put together a plan to keep her safe."

"That would be great. Around eight?"

"Make it nine. Erik works at Sullivan's, but he should be able to break free by then."

"Aren't you on the air tonight?"

"I'll ask Bill to stick around and cover for me."

"Look, Travis, I don't know what your timetable is for the wedding, but you might think about having Sarah and the kids move in with you sooner rather than later, at least until this is resolved," Carter told him. "I'm going to do anything I can think of to make sure Paul Hammond never sets foot in Serenity, but you don't want to take any chances that they could get in his way."

"Done," Travis said at once. "But that will leave Raylene there all alone. She'll be a sitting duck."

"She wants a damn gun," Carter said, still shuddering at the thought.

"I suppose I can understand that," Travis said. "She should be able to protect herself."

"Come on. You know Raylene as well as I do. If she even shot the man in the toe, she'd be riddled with guilt forever."

"You have a point. Okay, we'll thrash all this out tonight."

"Thanks, Travis. I owe you."

Once he'd gotten off the phone with Travis, Carter radioed the sheriff and told him what was going on. "Can you free me to take a trip to the prison? Shouldn't take more than a couple of hours."

"I'll cover for you myself," the sheriff promised. "Tell that SOB to stay the hell out of my county, you hear."

"That's the plan," Carter confirmed.

But two hours later, he walked away from the prison with a certainty that Paul Hammond wasn't going to make things easy. He was still seething with barely contained anger at the woman he blamed for ruining his career and putting him behind bars.

And there wasn't a doubt in Carter's mind that given half a chance, he'd want to finish the job he'd started the last time he'd beaten her. Behind the smooth facade, Carter had seen a man who was coldly calculating revenge.

Raylene had the local paper spread out on the kitchen table and was circling ads for places for rent when Sarah came home from work.

"What are you doing?" Sarah demanded, looking over her shoulder.

"Finding my own place to live," Raylene told her,

Sarah sat down at the kitchen table and regarded her with dismay. "What brought this on? I thought you planned to buy this house from me once Travis and I are married. I've been counting on that."

"I still want to do that, but I can't stay here right now." She filled Sarah in on the news Carter had shared about

Paul's impending release from prison. It was six to eight weeks away, but she explained that she had to start making her plans now. "I won't stay here and risk putting you and the kids in danger."

"But you said Carter's going to deal with him," Sarah said. "I can't imagine he'll set foot in Serenity once Carter has a come-to-Jesus talk with him."

"I'm not taking any chances," Raylene argued, her jaw set stubbornly.

"Let's think this through," Sarah pleaded. "We'll get everybody together and talk about what's best."

"It's not a group decision," Raylene retorted. "It's mine, and I've made it."

"Well, you're not moving out tomorrow, no matter what, so put that paper down and let's fix dinner. I always think better on a full stomach."

Raylene recognized a stalling tactic when she saw one, but she folded the newspaper and put it aside.

"Is everything all set for the picnic on the Fourth?" Sarah asked, deliberately changing the topic.

With everything that had happened that afternoon, Raylene had pushed the barbecue completely out of her head. "I think so. Dana Sue insisted on bringing the fried chicken and ribs. I'm making the salads. Erik's doing the burgers and the pies. Maddie said she'd find red, white and blue paper plates and napkins. Ronnie's in charge of getting sparklers for the kids and making sure they don't set themselves on fire."

"And Annie?"

"To be honest, I think she's having a little trouble juggling work and dealing with Trevor and a new baby on her own with Ty on the road. I didn't give her an assignment."

"She'll be furious if she thinks you let her off the hook because she can't cope," Sarah said. She closed her eyes and sighed. "I remember what it was like for me when I had Tommy and Libby so close together. I know exactly what she's going through, but every time I offer to pitch in, she bites my head off."

"I'll have her pick up some soda or something. And I'll make sure she knows her most important assignment is to pay attention to what's going on with Carrie," Raylene said.

"Have you heard from Carrie since she dropped by?"

"Not a word. Maybe she had a lot of studying to do for finals, but school's been out for a week now, and she hasn't been by again. She may be embarrassed about having revealed so much. I'm glad this picnic's coming up so soon. I don't want to take too long to figure out if she really is in trouble. At least Carter told me that she's been talking to him about how miserable she's been here. That's a start."

She hesitated, then met Sarah's gaze. "There's something else you should know."

"Yes?"

"I tried to make myself go onto the patio earlier today. Carter found me out there. I was a total basket case."

Sarah's eyes lit up with excitement. "But you were on the patio? That's fantastic."

"Did you miss the part about me being a basket case?"

"I don't care. A basket case who's actually outside completely on her own after all these months is still fantastic!"

"You're way too easily impressed," Raylene said.

"Wait till you tell Dr. McDaniels. I'll bet she's impressed, too."

Raylene studied her. "You really think it was that great, even though Carter found me pretty much unglued?"

"I think it was amazing, and so should you. You should be proud, Raylene. You left this house without me or Dr. McDaniels! Whoo-hoo!"

Raylene grinned at her enthusiasm. "I guess it was kind of cool."

"Better than cool. Awesome!"

"Okay, you can settle down now," Raylene said dryly. "I didn't walk on water."

"No, but you walked on bricks," Sarah replied. "In my book that's, what, half a dozen steps in the right direction."

Raylene tried to view it through Sarah's eyes. Maybe it had been a little bit of a triumph, after all. The all-important questions, though, were whether she could make herself do it again and how long it would take before being outside started to seem like second nature, especially now that she knew Paul could be a more immediate threat.

CHAPTER ELEVEN

Carter was surprised to find Walter Price among those at Travis's place when he arrived that night. He hadn't realized that Sarah's ex-husband would be tight with her current fiancé. He supposed in a small town it would be hard for the two men to avoid each other.

"I spend a lot of time at the house with the kids," Walter explained when they were officially introduced. "Raylene's been a good friend to me. When Travis told me what was going on, I wanted to help."

Carter nodded. "We can use all the help we can get."

Cal Maddox, Ronnie Sullivan and Tom McDonald nodded agreement. "Whatever you need," Ronnie said, his expression grim. "That man will not get anywhere near Raylene on our watch."

"Amen," Erik added, walking in the door in time to overhear Ronnie's comment.

"We should speak to Elliott Cruz, too," Cal said. "Maddie says he was at The Corner Spa the day Raylene turned up all battered and bruised. He really took it to heart. He didn't even know Raylene at the time, but he was ready to charge off and beat the guy to a pulp. Plus, he's a solid block of muscle. I imagine any man encountering him would think twice about doing anything when he's around."

Carter was relieved to know there were so many men he could count on. "We should definitely include him, then."

Travis handed out beers all around, then looked at Carter. "Did you go to the prison?"

Immediately sobering, Carter nodded. "We're dealing with one angry man. He blames Raylene for all of it. He says he'd never have wound up in prison if she hadn't lied about everything that happened. He still claims she took a tumble down the steps at their house to get all those bruises. He says that's probably why she lost the baby, too, that it had nothing to do with him."

"Typical," Ronnie said grimly. "Men like that rarely believe they've done anything wrong. I ran across a few when I was working construction. They'd get a few beers in them, lose their tempers and take it out on their wives or girlfriends just because they were handy. What I never got was why the women put up with it."

"For one reason or another, they don't think they have a choice," Carter said, citing some of the things he'd been told during his police academy training. "Usually there's a lot of psychological abuse that goes along with the physical abuse. The women are isolated, convinced somehow it's their fault, that if only they were more perfect, their men wouldn't resort to hitting them."

Walter seemed to be squirming uncomfortably as Carter talked. Carter turned to him. "Everything okay?"

"I'm just thinking how close I came to being one of those men," he said very quietly. He turned to Ronnie. "You know what I was like when Sarah first left me. I never laid a hand on her and I'd like to believe I never would have, but I was filled with all this rage. And Lord knows I'd made her feel like she was to blame for all the misery in my life. Thank goodness, she was smart enough to leave when she did. I finally got a grip and faced the fact that most of the problems in my life were my own. I never want to be that domineering, controlling kind of man again."

"Well, you certainly won't get away with it with Rory Sue," Ronnie said, lightening the moment. "If that girl is anything at all like her mama, you'll dance to her tune, or not at all."

Walter chuckled. "I've noticed that. We seem to be at odds most of the time over who's in charge. Doesn't matter if we're talking pizza or sex."

"Now, *those* are the kind of discussions that can liven up a marriage," Ronnie said. "Dana Sue and I have had our share."

As the laughter died down, Carter said, "Let's get back to Paul Hammond. I'll be notified the minute he walks through the gates at the prison. I'll make sure there's an active restraining order in place and that he knows about it. Not that it'll be worth the paper it's written on, if he wants to get his revenge. I keep hoping he'll come to his senses and see that being free is more important than getting even, but I'm not counting on it."

Carter sighed just thinking about how many women were injured, even killed, despite having a restraining order on file. He was convinced it would be useless in this situation, too. If Paul was determined to make Raylene pay for what he perceived as her deliberate betrayal, he'd just do it.

"Beyond the restraining order, we need to do everything we can to be sure Raylene's never in that house alone and that somebody's always nearby keeping an eye on things," he added.

"I'm in," Cal said at once.

"Me, too," Ronnie said.

"I'm already over there several times a week," Walter added. "No reason for that to change. I'll just hang out a little longer, make sure things are quiet."

Tom McDonald's expression had turned thoughtful. "As you well know, Carter, we don't have our own police force in place yet, but we do have a public-works crew. Let me see if I can coordinate with them and anyone else I can think of from the utility companies in the area to see if we can't find a lot of work that needs to be done on that street. At least I might be able to add some extra eyes and ears for a couple of weeks when the time comes. We've got enough advance notice that I may be able to get this in place."

Carter was astonished by the show of support.

"You all are amazing," he said. "Thank you. You're going above and beyond."

"Hey, we look out for our own around here," Cal told him. "And, believe me, in one way or another the Sweet Magnolias require a lot of looking after."

Ronnie smirked. "Please tell me you have not ever said that to them. These women of ours think they can take perfectly good care of themselves."

"And they can," Cal said hurriedly. "Doesn't mean they don't wander into trouble they can't handle from time to time. I think they appreciate that they always have backup."

Erik shook his head ruefully. "Well, I for one have never heard Helen admit they need it. Remember her stalker? She thought she could take him down single-handedly. Almost got herself killed trying to prove it."

Carter shuddered. "Please tell her not to give Raylene any ideas."

"You really don't want me telling Helen anything," Erik said. "She'll do exactly the opposite."

"That's true," Ronnie confirmed. "Helen's a stubborn one."

Carter sat back and listened as these men talked with clear-eyed vision about the strong, ornery women in their lives. He'd never run across a group of men more obviously devoted to their spouses, flaws and all. For the first time in his life, he was envious of the solid marriages they had. With responsibility for Mandy and Carrie still very fresh, he thought it would be a while before he could risk having that kind of relationship with anyone. And yet here he was, already involved enough with Raylene that he felt this overwhelming need to make sure she was safe.

"You know," he said eventually, "when I first heard people talk about the Sweet Magnolias and how deep their friendship ran, I was skeptical. Seemed to me there's always some fussing and feuding when a bunch of women get together."

The other men groaned at the comment and Carter winced. "Okay, so it sounds sexist. The point is that I'm seeing them in a whole new light now. There's a rare kind of loyalty at work, isn't there? And it extends to you guys, too."

"It does," Ronnie confirmed. "And now that you're with Raylene, you're a part of it."

Walter studied him with a narrowed gaze. "You are with Raylene, right? This isn't just some macho need to protect her just because it's what cops do? You really do care?" The genuine note of concern in his voice proved how deep his own caring for Raylene ran.

"I care," Carter confirmed. He was far more certain of that than he was of his readiness to act on his feelings…or Raylene's ability to handle the kind of relationship he might someday want.

The Fourth of July dawned with a hard rain that left the ground steaming the second it ended and the sun came out.

By the time the parade started, the skies were blue and the streets had dried off, though there were still enough puddles that most of the kids in town had managed to get soaked along the sides of the parade route down Azalea Drive and onto Main Street.

Carter stood on the town green with Carrie and Mandy to watch their first big event since coming to Serenity. Carter had heard people talking about how much the residents of Serenity loved their holidays, and they were about to see that firsthand.

"This is so lame," Carrie grumbled as a ragtag group of veterans marched by, some in uniform, some out, waving small American flags.

"It's not lame," Mandy said indignantly. "Those men fought for our country."

Carrie flushed at the criticism. "I know that. If we were in Columbia, though, they'd all be wearing uniforms and marching in time to the music."

"Who cares what they're wearing?" Mandy retorted. "Look how proud they are. And look at how everybody's clapping for them. I think it's awesome. Show some respect."

Standing behind them, Carter sighed. He'd hoped the parade and the town's Fourth of July celebration might help Carrie to see the advantages of living in a small town where events like this brought people together as a community. Instead, it seemed she was going to judge everything in comparison to Columbia, and Serenity was going to come up short. He hoped to heaven her attitude improved before they walked over to Sarah's for the barbecue. Otherwise it was going to be a long afternoon.

"Oh, look," Mandy exclaimed. "Tommy and Libby are on the float for the radio station. Don't they look adorable?"

Even Carrie smiled when she saw them sitting in a rep-lica of the station's studio, wearing headsets the way their mom and Travis did. Walter sat nearby operating the con-trols, though he was more likely there to keep them from tumbling off the flat-bed trailer. Country music filled the air as the float went by. When they spotted their mom in the real station studio, they nearly fell off their chairs wav-ing. Walter snagged them and sat them back where they belonged.

"You have to admit they looked pretty cute," Carter said to Carrie.

She frowned at him, but there was a twinkle in her eye. "Okay, yes," she admitted grudgingly.

There were another half-dozen floats from local businesses, a marching band from the high school and several antique cars before the parade finally wound down.

"Can we check out the booths on the green before we go to Sarah's?" Mandy asked Carter. At his nod, she tugged on her sister's arm. "Come on. I saw some really cool jewelry when we were walking over here."

"Don't take too long," Carter told them. "I promised I'd help get the grill going for the hamburgers."

"You can go ahead. We know the way," Mandy told him. "We'll be there in a half hour. I promise."

Pleased to see that Carrie was at least willing to go along with her sister, he nodded. "Thirty minutes," he warned. "I don't want to have to come looking for you."

He watched the two of them walk off toward the booths, Mandy skipping along excitedly and chattering a mile a min-ute, while Carrie walked more sedately behind her. At least her mood had improved slightly since returning from their weekend in Columbia, but he didn't trust it to last. Maybe all teenage girls had mercurial mood swings, but Carrie's seemed to him to be off the charts.

At Sarah's, he found a few of the men already in the yard. Raylene was in the kitchen supervising what looked to him like barely organized chaos. She spared a grin for him before giving several other guests their marching orders.

When everyone except her had cleared out of the kitchen, she motioned for him to come in. "Or are you afraid I'm going to put you to work, too?"

He dropped a kiss on her flushed cheek. "You don't scare me," he said.

"I probably should. There's a lot to be done before we can eat."

"Tell me, and I'll help. I checked in with Erik and he doesn't need me to help with the burgers yet, so I'm all yours for the moment."

She shook her head. "Erik's never going to need your help with the burgers. The man is a control freak when it comes to his grill or a kitchen. I swear, if Dana Sue didn't own Sullivan's, he probably wouldn't let her in the kitchen there, either. I heard stories about Helen pitching in over there before she and Erik got married that made me wonder how they ever made it down the aisle. Can you imagine Helen letting anyone boss her around?"

"I don't know her all that well, but no."

"Well, Erik did it, and lived to tell the story. I think it's the only place in their lives he dares to pull rank."

Carter studied Raylene as she talked. Her hair was scooped up in a casual ponytail that made her look about eighteen. Her cheeks were pink and her eyes sparkling. "You're in a good mood today," he observed.

"It's a holiday and the house is overflowing with company.

What's not to love?" Suddenly her expression sobered. "It's probably the last one I'll get to spend here like this."

He frowned at her words. "You're not still considering getting your own place, are you?"

"I have to, and you know why." When he started to speak, she held up a hand. "Let's not talk about this now."

"Okay, but we will discuss it," he said firmly. "I have my reasons why it's important for you to stay right here. Promise me you won't make any final decisions until we've talked."

"I can do that much," she agreed. She shoved a huge bowl of potato salad at him. "Take this outside. There's a big table for the food on the patio. You'll see."

He hesitated. "Is everyone going to be eating outside?"

"Don't frown like that. Some people will stay outside and some will come in here to be in the air-conditioning. I'm not going to be stuck in here all alone, if that's what you're thinking."

"Have you been outside since the other day?"

She frowned at the question. "A couple of times with Dr. McDaniels," she said tersely.

"And?"

"No meltdowns, but I'm not taking any chances today."

Carter backed off. "Just checking," he said. "Be sure you save a seat for me."

"I'll make sure there are places for you and the girls," she assured him. "Annie's in the living room holding them now. She's always said she doesn't give two hoots about the theory that women glow in hot weather, that she just sweats. Of course, since that argument made her look like a wuss, she says she's staying in today because it's too hot out there for the baby."

"Is anyone buying that?"

"No, but they're humoring her because Ty's not here to wait on her himself. At last count, she had two glasses of lemonade and three of sweet tea on the table beside her, along with an entire bowl of her mother's guacamole. Frankly, I think spicy food like that is a really bad idea when she's still nursing the baby, but there's no stopping her from eating it. Meg will probably wind up with terrible heartburn."

Carter hesitated, struck by something that hadn't occurred to him before. "With Ty on the road so much with the team, was he able to get back when Meg was born?"

"The team flew him home the second Annie went into labor. He made it with just minutes to spare."

"That's good," Carter said. "I know I'd want to be there for the birth of my child."

She regarded him with surprise. "Really? A lot of men would prefer to sit in the waiting room with a box of cigars."

"Well, I'm not one of them. I had to deliver a baby once when the mom wasn't going to make it to the hospital. I don't recommend giving birth in the backseat of a car, but it was still pretty amazing. I definitely want to be there when my own kids arrive in the world."

She regarded him thoughtfully. "So raising Carrie and Mandy hasn't scared you away from wanting to be a parent?"

"Not so far," he said. "Now let me get this potato salad outside and I'll be back to see what else needs to go out."

"I think that's it," Raylene told him. "I'm just going to fill a couple more pitchers with ice and sweet tea."

"Then I'll get those and let Erik know it's time to put those burgers on the grill."

He spotted Carrie and Mandy in the backyard when he set the potato salad on the table, spoke to Erik and offered to help with the grilling, only to be told once more that his help wasn't needed. He went back to get the tea from Raylene.

"Tell me what you want to eat and I'll fill a plate for you," he said.

"You'd better take Annie's order first," she told him. "Travis is heading this way. I'll send the tea out with him."

He walked into the living room and found Annie seated in a comfortable oversize chair. She did have her daughter cuddled in her arms, so he supposed there was a case to be made that she had her priorities in order and wasn't totally slacking off.

"Hey, little mama, what can I get you to eat?" he asked.

She grinned at him. "I just sent my mother out for fried chicken and potato salad, but now I'm thinking about ribs."

"I'll bring some in," he promised. "Anything else? I saw what looked like some excellent corn on the cob out there."

"Perfect."

"You sure that's it?"

"I have to pace myself. I know there's peach pie, ice cream and Mom's bread pudding for dessert."

Carter's mouth immediately watered. "I may have to start with those."

Outside, he put together a plate for Annie, delivered that, then filled two more for himself and Raylene. He glanced over and saw his sisters were deep in conversation with Travis and Sarah at one of the tables that had been set up under a tent on the lawn. At least Mandy was talking. Carrie seemed to be gazing at Travis with the rapt expression of a love-struck fan.

He went back inside and handed a plate to Raylene.

"Where are the girls?" she asked.

"With Travis and Sarah. I don't think we're going to tear them away."

Raylene looked oddly disappointed.

"Did you want to spend some time with them for some reason?" he asked.

"No, it's fine. I just wanted to be sure they didn't feel like outsiders."

"As long as Travis is in the vicinity, I think they're very happily occupied," Carter told her.

He and Raylene took their meals into the living room and joined Annie. People came and went for the rest of the afternoon and into the early evening.

"Is everybody going to see the fireworks?" Ronnie asked, standing in the doorway just before dusk.

"Not me," Annie said. "I need to take Meg home and get her to bed. Even though she sleeps like a rock, I'm afraid the noise of the fireworks will be too much for her. Where's Trevor? Can you take him with you, Dad?"

"Will do," Ronnie said. "Carter, you coming?"

"No, I'm going to hang out here and help with cleanup."

"You don't have to do that," Raylene told him. "Don't you want to see your first Fourth of July fireworks in Serenity?"

"Carrie and Mandy can tell me all about it," he said. "I'm staying. I don't want Sarah and Travis to come back to a major cleanup job."

"Actually, pretty much everything's inside," Ronnie told him. "The leftovers have been wrapped up and put away in the fridge."

Raylene gave Carter an amused look. "Frankly I think those leftovers are the real attraction. Since no one at his house cooks, I think he's hoping he can steal them for home."

"Maybe the leftover pie," he agreed unrepentantly.

"As if," Ronnie said. "That apple pie was the first thing to go."

Carter sighed dramatically. "Just my luck. I'll have to settle for some fried chicken."

Annie's expression brightened. "There's more fried chicken?"

"If you eat it, you'll explode," Raylene told her. "I've watched what you packed away this afternoon. It's little wonder you can barely move. You're stuffed."

"Hey, I'm enjoying food while I can. Once I stop nursing, I'll be back to eating miniportions again."

Though she sounded as if she was joking, Carter thought Ronnie looked alarmed.

"Annie," Ronnie began, but she looked at him and he fell silent. Carter couldn't imagine what the aborted exchange was about.

Annie struggled awkwardly to her feet with the baby. "If I don't walk home now, I'll never do it."

"I could drop you by the house," Ronnie offered at once.

"No, the walk will do me good." She kissed his cheek. "Stop fretting, Dad. I'm fine. Just look out for Trevor."

After everyone had gone, Carter checked to make sure the kitchen was in good shape, then came back to settle beside Raylene.

"Did I sense some tension between Annie and Ronnie?" he asked.

Raylene nodded. "Any time the subject of food comes up, there's tension between them. Annie was anorexic in her teens. Ronnie and Dana Sue were divorced then, and he wasn't living in town. When Annie collapsed and nearly died, he came back. I don't think he's ever really gotten over the shock of finding her in such bad shape. The one good thing that came out of it was that he and Dana Sue got back together."

Carter frowned. "Annie really came that close to dying? I didn't realize anorexia could be so serious."

"Oh, it's serious, all right. I was there the night Annie collapsed. Sarah and I both were. I've never been so scared in my life. It was a huge wake-up call to both of us about just how dangerous an eating disorder could be."

Carter stood up and began to pace. He thought about how many times he'd seen Carrie eating like a bird, mostly just shoving food around on her plate. Surely, though, it hadn't gone that far. She was a little on the thin side, but he'd chalked that up to fashion. Most girls her age seemed too darn skinny to him.

"Carter, are you okay?"

"I was thinking about Carrie." He met her gaze. "She worries me."

"Me, too," Raylene said, startling him.

He hesitated, then asked, "You think she has a problem with food, too?"

"It's crossed my mind. Frankly, that's one reason I wanted everyone to come here today. I wanted Annie and Dana Sue, in particular, to keep an eye on Carrie and see if they thought my suspicions were correct before I said anything to you."

"And then Carrie stayed outside," he guessed, realizing now why she'd looked so disappointed.

"Yes, I hadn't counted on that. I certainly didn't want to spoil things and make a big deal about getting her to come in here. It won't help if she thinks she's under a microscope."

"I know. She overreacts every time I say anything at all to her about eating," he said. "What the hell am I supposed to do to be sure if there's a problem?"

"We'll try my plan again. You all can come to dinner one night this week. I'll just have Annie over. Believe me, if there's a problem, she'll recognize the signs."

He stopped pacing and sat back down beside her. "Let's not think about Carrie right now," he suggested. "If we turn on the TV, we can watch the Boston Pops or the celebration on the National Mall in Washington and have our own Fourth of July celebration right here."

And if the evening progressed the way he wanted it to, they might even have their own fireworks!

CHAPTER TWELVE

Though Raylene was relieved to have Carter acknowledge an awareness of Carrie's disturbing attitude toward food, she was now anxious for an entirely different reason. She'd seen the glint of desire in his eyes right before he'd settled next to her on the sofa. She knew what that look meant. And though she was as attracted as he was, all the reasons not to move forward and complicate their relationship even more kept spinning around in her head, leaving her a little dizzy.

When he put his arm behind her on the sofa, she froze. But when he didn't actually drape it across her shoulders, she allowed herself to relax. Every once in a while, his fingers brushed idly across her bare shoulder, sending shivers dancing across her flesh. Good shivers...at least so far.

She turned toward him, and found his gaze on her.

"I really want to kiss you," he said quietly. "But I don't want to freak you out."

She closed her eyes against the tide of longing that washed over her. "I want that, too," she admitted eventually, daring to meet his gaze. "But I don't know if it's a good idea."

"Because of what happened the last time I touched you?"

"No, actually because I think this is leading toward a complication that neither of us really need."

"It's just a kiss," he said.

Her lips twitched at the sweet innocence behind those words. Surely he had to know better.

"Not if you do it right," she said. "Carter, there have been sparks between us since we met, some good, some not so good. If you kiss me, we're both going to want more. I'm not sure I'm ready for that, and I don't think you are, either."

"Oh, I'm ready."

He said it so fervently, she laughed. "Well, when you put it that way, so am I, but come on. Are either of us in any position to take this to the next level?" She ticked off all the strikes against them. "You have two young girls who're counting on you. One of them might have an eating disorder. I'm agoraphobic, most likely because I can't cope with the way my ex-husband abused me. I'm just now starting to make a little progress toward getting better and now that same man is about to get out of prison. That scares me to death. For all I know, it could make me regress, and then I'll be worse off than before. None of that is exactly conducive to starting a normal, carefree relationship, which is the way a good relationship should start."

"Carefree's great, but it's not terribly realistic, is it?" he asked. "Everyone has problems, Raylene."

"But ours are huge," she insisted.

He sat back with a sigh. "You're being very rational about this."

"Somebody needs to be."

"Usually I'm the one who starts thinking with my head," he admitted. "Especially since Carrie and Mandy became my responsibility. I haven't let myself get carried away by what I wanted in a long time. Heck, I haven't even let myself want anything—or anyone—in a long time."

Despite her words of caution, Raylene was pleased by the admission. "I really get to you?"

He smiled. "Yes, you really get to me." His gaze narrowed. "You're not ruling this out forever, right?"

"*This* being a relationship?"

He nodded.

She hesitated. She wanted to think a time would come when both of their lives would be less complicated, but she couldn't guarantee it. "I don't know," she said honestly. "None of these problems—especially mine—have quick fixes. That much is clear."

"I'll take that as a maybe." He looked into her eyes. "I know the timing sucks for a lot of reasons, but I think we could have something pretty amazing going on here. I like spending time with you."

Raylene wanted to believe that, too, but those reasons she'd enumerated were all stacked against them. With her ex-husband possibly poised to come back into her life with a vengeance, with Carter's sister facing a possible eating disorder, to say nothing of a boatload of unhappiness, how could either of them even begin to think about the future?

"You don't look very happy," Sarah said when she arrived home from the fireworks later that night and found Raylene sitting in the dark all alone. While Travis took the kids in to put them to bed, Sarah switched on a couple of lamps and took a closer look. "You've been crying! What did Carter do?"

"He wanted to kiss me, and I blew him off."

Sarah looked bewildered. "Why?"

"I'm wondering about that myself right now. He's a decent, wonderful, caring guy, and he really seems to like me."

"Isn't that all good?"

"Right up until I add in all the things that make both of us a bad bet for a relationship."

"You're talking about Paul getting out of prison," Sarah concluded.

"And my awful marriage. I didn't walk away from that without scars, Sarah. The ones I have run pretty deep. I'm not sure I'll ever be able to have a normal relationship with a man again. Every time Carter touches me, I get jumpy, and not always in a good way."

"But *sometimes* in a good way, right?"

Raylene smiled. "Definitely sometimes."

"You just need time to be sure you can trust him," Sarah concluded. "Even I can see that, but talk it over with Dr. McDaniels when you see her. I'll bet I'm right."

"I'll bet you are, too, but what if it never happens? What if I lead Carter on for a few weeks or months with the hope that things will get better, and they don't?"

"He's a grown man. I'm sure he understands the situation. He'll deal."

"But by then, it would more than likely break my heart to let him go."

"Are you feeling all that great about sending him home tonight?" Sarah asked wryly.

"No, but you know what I mean. It will hurt a thousand times worse if I let myself fall in love with him and we can't make it work. Plus, I haven't even mentioned the complications in his life. What about Carrie? He needs to be able to focus on her problems right now."

"All very valid points," Sarah conceded. "But I'll tell you what a very wise friend—that would be you—told me when

I was questioning whether Travis and I could make it. Love flat out doesn't come without risks and complications, but it's worth it. Because when it works, there's nothing more amazing. To not even try for that brass ring when it's right within your grasp, that would be wrong. In a way, it will be letting Paul win."

That, of course, was the most persuasive argument she possibly could have offered. No matter what happened down the road, Raylene vowed she would do absolutely nothing in any way that would let Paul have even the tiniest bit of control over the rest of her life. Whatever strength it required, she would find some way to keep that promise to herself.

Fortunately Carter was working the evening shift this week because that allowed him to hang around the house until Carrie and Mandy finally dragged themselves out of bed on the day after the holiday. He couldn't recall the last time he'd allowed himself to linger in bed as late as those two did.

Of course, lately he hadn't slept all that well, either. Last night he hadn't been able to stop thinking about the conversation he'd had with Raylene about Carrie's eating patterns. He didn't want to think his sister was in trouble, but he couldn't deny it was possible. The upcoming dinner with Raylene and Annie would tell the story, but like any good cop, he wanted to start assembling his own evidence.

When Carrie eventually wandered into the kitchen, she paused when she saw him, her ever-ready scowl settling into place. "What are you doing here?"

"Hanging out," he said, determinedly keeping his own tone light. "My shift doesn't start until three today. What are your plans?"

She shrugged. "Mandy wants to go swimming. I don't

know, though. I don't like going out in public in a bathing suit."

"Why on earth not?" he asked, then realized that when they'd been in Columbia and her friends had been over to swim in the hotel pool, Carrie had stayed on the sidelines wearing a cover-up over her suit. Was this a symptom of the messed-up body image that often came along with eating disorders? He'd read about that in the middle of the night when he'd gone online, determined to get up to speed on anorexia.

"I need to lose a couple of pounds before I'll look good enough to wear that bathing suit I bought," she said, confirming his fear.

"Don't be ridiculous," he snapped without thinking. Obviously if there was a problem, it wouldn't be solved by him yelling at her. He'd vowed to handle her with compassion and try his best to understand what was going on in her head.

"Carrie, you look great in anything you wear," he said more gently.

"You're just saying that because you think you're supposed to," she said, dismissing the comment as biased.

"No, I watched the way those boys were looking at you when we were in Columbia. Made me want to strangle every one of them," he said with feeling. That had been true.

She almost smiled at his words, but then shrugged off his observation. "They're just boys. If a girl's got boobs, they look."

Now *he* had to smother a smile at the accuracy of her assessment. "Possibly," he admitted. Then, struggling to keep his tone even, he asked, "What did you have to eat over at Raylene's yesterday? Did you try the fried chicken? I'd love to get Dana Sue's recipe."

"And we'll all die from clogged arteries," she retorted.

"Then you didn't even taste it?"

She shook her head.

"How about the ribs? If Erik would teach me how to make the sauce, I could probably master those. We'd have to buy a big grill, though, one of those fancy gas grills."

She frowned at him. "What is this? Are you on food patrol all of a sudden?"

"I was just asking," he said. "I hate to think you missed out on all the fabulous food that everyone worked so hard preparing. You must have at least tried the apple pie."

"Desserts aren't my thing," she said, already backing out of the room. "I need to go up and get dressed."

She practically ran out of the kitchen. A moment later, Mandy came in. She immediately filled a bowl with cereal, then doused it with milk. Carter was relieved to see that there was nothing wrong with *her* appetite.

He hesitated, then asked, "Did your sister eat anything yesterday?" He knew he was asking her to breach some kind of sisterly oath of silence, but this was too important.

Mandy shrugged. "I'm not her keeper."

"But you are observant, Amanda. This is important. Did she eat?"

Mandy frowned at his sharp tone. "Not when I was around," she admitted. "What's going on?"

"I'm just concerned that her dieting is getting out of hand."

Mandy obviously grasped immediately what he was suggesting. Her eyes widened. "You mean like anorexia or something? We learned about that in health class. It can be really dangerous."

"Exactly."

Mandy set down her spoon and met his gaze. "Are you really worried, Carter?"

He nodded.

"I thought maybe she was just going through a phase or

something," she said, her own expression now filled with alarm. "What should we do?"

He patted her hand. "You don't have to do anything, except keep your eyes open and let me know if she's eating or not. I'll handle this. And don't worry. We're going to make sure she's okay."

A couple of hours later, though, he realized he might have made things worse. He came out of his room wearing his uniform to hear Mandy and Carrie in the middle of a shouting match in the kitchen.

"Hey, what's going on in here?" he demanded, joining them.

"Squirt here is trying to tell me what to do," Carrie said, her cheeks flushed with indignation.

"I just fixed her a sandwich and told her to eat it," Mandy said.

"I don't want a sandwich," Carrie snapped.

"Well, if you don't eat, you're going to die," Mandy snapped right back, then burst into tears and ran from the room.

Carrie stared after her, a shocked expression on her face. "Why would she think I'm going to die?"

Carter sighed. "Because I told her I was worried about you not eating."

"Gee, thanks," she said. "I'm watching my weight, that's all. She might want to give some thought to the way she eats, because if she's not careful she'll be big as a house by the time she's my age."

Carter frowned at her. "Don't you dare suggest to Mandy that she needs to go on a diet. She's perfectly fine."

"But I'm not?" Despite her indignant tone, she looked genuinely hurt.

"You're beautiful," he said honestly. "But if you lose any

more weight, you'll be gaunt, rather than fashionably thin. If you don't see how beautiful you are when you look in the mirror, then maybe that's something we need to deal with."

"Now you're saying I'm crazy?"

Carter was so far out of his league, he didn't even begin to know the rules. "You're not crazy. But you may need to talk to someone to figure all this out."

"What? Does Raylene get a two-for-one special if she drags me along to her shrink?"

Carter merely stared at her until she flushed.

"Sorry," she murmured.

"I think we had this conversation before, but in case you've forgotten, there's absolutely nothing wrong with asking for help," Carter told her. "Raylene is very brave to be trying to face her problems. I admire her. I'd feel the same way about anyone who does whatever it takes to get better."

"But there's nothing wrong with me!" Carrie all but shouted at him, than ran from the room, up the stairs and into her bedroom, slamming doors in her wake.

Carter sighed. Well, he'd certainly made a mess of things so far. He could just imagine how well it would go over if he suddenly suggested having dinner at Raylene's. That little experiment was going to have to remain on hold, at least until things calmed down. He just hoped by then, it wouldn't be too late. Maybe he was the one who should see Dr. McDaniels to figure out how he'd managed to let things spin so far out of control.

Raylene called first thing in the morning and left a voicemail message for Dr. McDaniels canceling her appointment. She was therefore stunned when she answered the door that afternoon and found the psychologist on the stoop.

"I canceled today's appointment," Raylene said testily. "Didn't you get the message?"

"I did, but the good part about having you stuck here in the house is that I knew where to find you."

Raylene scowled. "Was that supposed to be funny?"

"No, actually it was just an observation. Most people who cancel their appointments with me do it when they need to see me the most. I can't always track them down." She leveled a look into Raylene's eyes. "Are you going to send me away?"

Raylene heaved a sigh at the daring note in her voice. "No, you can come in," she conceded grudgingly.

"Thank you," Dr. McDaniels replied solemnly. She took a seat in a chair, then waited for Raylene to sit. "What happened that made you want to avoid me?"

"I just don't think we're going to make any more progress," Raylene said, thinking of her disastrous outing to the patio a few days earlier. She'd managed a couple of trips outside since then, but they hadn't lasted long.

"Is that because you went outside on your own and had a panic attack?" the psychologist asked. "I hope not, because we've been outside together since that happened. You were just fine."

Raylene regarded her with dismay. "You found out about what happened on the patio?"

"I ran into Annie. She told me. I'm surprised you didn't mention it yourself."

"I was trying not to make a big deal out of it."

"Then that's not the only reason you called to cancel today's appointment?"

Raylene hesitated. She knew it was much more than that one incident. This was all about Paul and his upcoming release. "My ex-husband may be getting out of prison soon."

"So you're justifiably scared," Dr. McDaniels said. "Notice that I said *justifiably*."

"The only place I've felt safe while he was *in* jail was inside this house. How can I possibly go outside, when he could show up any second?"

"There's a restraining order?"

"If there isn't, there will be. I have someone checking to make sure of that." She met the doctor's gaze. "You and I both know it won't mean anything, not if he really wants to come after me."

"Then you need to be prepared."

"I want to learn to shoot a gun," Raylene told her.

Not even Dr. McDaniels, who was trained to keep her reactions neutral, was able to cover her surprise. "That's your solution?"

"I can't think of another one. I have to be able to protect myself. I won't feel powerless, not again."

"What about having a gun in the house with children? That seems like a bad idea to me."

Raylene hesitated. This was the hardest part of her decision, facing a future that didn't include Sarah and the kids. "I'm going to move."

"How?" Dr. McDaniels asked simply. "You haven't been able to leave the house for months and months. To move, you'll not only have to step outside, you'll have to get in a car and go someplace entirely new, someplace that's bound to feel less safe and secure."

"Maybe you can drug me and someone will carry me," she said, only half-facetiously.

"That's one way," the doctor acknowledged, though it didn't sound as if she'd go along with it. "Of course, it might be better for you to take your stance right here."

"Not if it's going to put Sarah and her kids in danger," Raylene said flatly. "That's not an option."

"What do your friends have to say about this?"

"They're all against it," she admitted. "Carter says he has a plan to protect me, but *I* need to do this. No one seems to understand how important it is to me to stand up to Paul once and for all."

"Well, I can certainly understand that. I even admire your determination." She held Raylene's gaze. "But there's nothing wrong with standing up to Paul and having plenty of backup nearby. We're talking about a man who's beaten you more than once. No one, I don't care how strong they are, would take chances with someone like that on their own. Even armed police officers or soldiers work with partners, and they're trained to face danger."

"I suppose," Raylene said, seeing her point.

"There's something else to consider," Dr. McDaniels told her. "When friends want to help, sometimes it's important to let them, as much for their sakes as for your own. It's not a sign of weakness."

She waited until Raylene met her gaze. "Your friend Carter, for instance. He's a policeman. You might not have known him when Paul was abusing you, but I imagine he feels pretty awful that he wasn't there back then."

Raylene nodded. "He's said that."

"Don't you think he wants to be here for you now?"

"But protecting me is not his responsibility."

"He apparently thinks it is."

Raylene knew that was true. Carter clearly felt involved in keeping her safe. She knew all about the big meeting he and the other men had held over at Travis's. Though he hadn't told her all the details of their plan, she knew there was one.

"If anyone got hurt because of me, I'd never forgive myself," she said.

"And if you got hurt because they did nothing, they'd never forgive themselves," Dr. McDaniels countered. "Protecting each other is what friends do, Raylene. It seems to me you have some very good ones. Best of all, you have at least one who actually knows how to defend you and keep you safe. I'd rather see any gun in his hand than in yours."

There was no doubt that Dr. McDaniels had a valid point about that. When Raylene was being totally rational, she knew that without adequate training there was a better-than-even chance she'd wind up accidentally shooting herself rather than Paul.

Dr. McDaniels stood up. "Will you think about what I've said?"

"Of course."

"And will you be ready to get back on track and go outside when I come back later in the week? I think it's time to reexamine our goals."

Raylene regarded her with suspicion. "Meaning what?"

"You told me you used to like to garden. You also told me about the garden that Carter planted for you. Who's been tending to that?"

"He's been by a couple of times. So have his sisters."

"Wouldn't you like to take care of it yourself?"

"Did you miss the part about me falling apart last time I was out there?"

The doctor shrugged it off. "It was a setback. Don't let it be an excuse to stop trying. When I come back, we're going to spend a half hour out there watering and weeding, whatever it needs. Then you're going to keep it up on your own."

Raylene wanted to believe it was possible, but she hesitated. "I'm not sure I'll be able to do that."

"The only way to know is to try," the doctor said easily. "I can be pretty persuasive when I put my mind to it."

Raylene smiled. "Yes, I've seen that firsthand. You got me to let you in here today without even half trying. Who knows what you can get me to do if you're determined."

The psychologist chuckled at her resigned tone. "You know we started down this path to your recovery because you were finally motivated. There's nothing to prevent us from finishing, because I'm the one who's motivated. I believe you're going to get better, Raylene. It's not until we both give up that the battle's lost."

Raylene smiled at her determination and optimism. "I see why Annie likes you so much."

"There were plenty of times she hated me, too," the doctor said candidly. "All that matters, though, is that she got well."

"Can I ask you a question that isn't about me?"

"Of course."

"If I happen to know a teenage girl who could be anorexic, what should I do?"

The doctor's gaze immediately filled with concern. "Do her parents know?"

"Her parents are dead. Her older brother's her guardian, and he suspects, too."

"Do you think she's ready to admit she has a problem?"

Raylene shook her head. "I thought maybe she was, a couple of weeks ago. She was asking me what it was like to see a psychologist, but then she backed off. Since then, she's been avoiding me when she can."

"Can you contact her?"

"I can try," she said, though Carrie had avoided her prior calls.

"Then try," the psychologist said. "Push her to get help, gently, of course, and make sure her brother knows not to wait too long before insisting on getting her help if she doesn't do it willingly."

"Thanks. I'll do that. Does she need to get into a program at the hospital, the way Annie did? Or can she just work with you?"

"I won't be able to answer that until I see her."

"Okay, then. I'll do what I can to get her to see you." In fact, maybe she could kill two birds with one stone, by seeking Carrie's help with her own recovery. Perhaps if they worked side by side in the garden, if Carrie saw that seeing Dr. McDaniels had helped her, Carrie would not only feel comfortable enough to confide in her again, but feel hopeful about what seeing a doctor could accomplish.

"Whatever you do, don't wait too long," Dr. McDaniels advised. "You remember what it was like for Annie."

"I know," Raylene said. "That's why I'm so scared for this girl."

And for Carter, who'd never be able to forgive himself if anything happened to his sister when he could have done something to prevent it.

CHAPTER THIRTEEN

Rory Sue stood defiantly in the middle of the office at the radio station, hands on hips, eyes flashing. Her posture and the drape of her dress made her look like some kind of goddess, Walter thought. A very angry goddess. He had to admit the sight was impressive.

"You are not putting this off one more minute, Walter Price. I found the perfect house for you, and you keep making excuses not to see it. What is your problem?"

Walter wished he could explain it. At first he'd avoided all the appointments Rory Sue tried to schedule because he hadn't wanted to give in yet again to the kind of reckless passion she stirred up in him. Lately, though, it was something else. He hadn't been able to put a name to it.

When he remained silent, she heaved a sigh and sat down in a swivel chair and propelled herself across the room until they were sitting knee to knee. He wanted to back away because he couldn't think straight when she was that close, but there was no place to go.

"Talk to me," she said, her voice gentler and less demanding. "I thought we were getting close. That night we spent together was amazing, but you've been avoiding being alone with me ever since."

"I took you to the Fourth of July picnic," he reminded her, recalling the shock on Sarah's face when the two of them had arrived together. Apparently Raylene hadn't bothered to mention the invitation to her. Though it had posed an awkward moment, it was probably better that she hadn't been given a chance to nix the idea.

Rory Sue didn't seem to be impressed with his gesture. She rolled her eyes. "And then you spent the entire day as far away from me as you could possibly get. Is that because of the way Sarah reacted? She's your *ex-wife*, for goodness' sakes. Her opinion shouldn't count anymore."

"It's not about that. I wanted you to spend time with Sarah, Raylene and Annie. You need friends."

She regarded him incredulously. "You were treating the barbecue like some kind of grown-up playdate?"

He winced at the accusation. It sounded stupid when she put it that way. In fact, it sounded patronizing. "Sorry. I was trying to help. You've said before that you don't have a lot of friends, particularly women friends."

"So you figured you needed to rush in and fix that? I don't need a knight in shining armor, Walter. I just want someone I connect with emotionally and physically." She studied him thoughtfully. "Or was this another way to avoid spending time with me yourself? Did you decide you're not interested, after all?"

"Of course not," he said, regretting it the instant the words left his lips, because of the way her expression immediately brightened. He sighed. "I was just trying to help. That's all."

"Okay, maybe I get that you meant well that day, but what about since then? Why have you been avoiding me? You can tell me if you've changed your mind about the house, or even about me, for that matter." She gave him a wicked grin. "But I don't think I'm the problem."

"Actually you are," he said, deciding he had no choice but to be candid. His excuses were only making a mess of things.

She backed away so fast, she nearly tilted over. "Me?" she said, looking hurt. "What did I do?"

Walter took a deep breath, then said, "You've stirred up some feelings in me that I really don't want to have."

"You don't want to have sex? Mind-blowing sex, I might add."

He allowed himself a grin at her incredulous expression. "No, I definitely want to have sex. I just don't want it to matter quite so much."

In fact, if he had to put a name to his behavior, it would be fear. He was terrified he was getting in too deep way too fast, just the way he had with Sarah. He suspected if he and Sarah had had time to think things through, a lot of their decisions would have been different. Not that Sarah was impulsive or free-spirited like Rory Sue. They were opposites, in fact, but he was still the same guy who got sex and love all tangled up in his head and thought it all should be forever.

Rory Sue looked bewildered. "I thought we were just having a casual fling."

"You see, that's the thing," he said. "I don't do casual flings. I get involved. It's the way I was brought up."

"And you never once rebelled? You never figured out you can sleep with someone just for fun?"

"Apparently not." Respect for women had been ingrained in him. It was ironic, really, given the lack of respect his parents and, ultimately, he had shown for Sarah.

It looked as if understanding was beginning to dawn for Rory Sue, because there was a faint hint of the same panic he felt in her eyes.

"And you think you're getting too emotionally involved with me?" she said, as if trying to be clear.

"Afraid so."

"I see," she said slowly. "But what does that have to do with looking at houses?"

"Remember how anxious I was to get out of that last place you showed me?"

"Sure. I thought you just hated the wallpaper. It was a little freaky."

He grinned as he recalled the formal, dark brown, flocked wallpaper that made every room look closed in and depressing. "I did, but despite that, I kept imagining the two of us living there. I could practically see you in the kitchen cooking dinner when I got home from work."

"Then your imagination definitely needs to be reined in," she said with a shudder. "I don't cook, at least not anything that can't be nuked."

He chuckled at her horrified expression. "Yes, I've gathered that, which just shows how delusional I can be."

"Now, if you were getting any wild ideas about me in the bedroom, that would be different," she teased.

"Believe me, I could envision us in there, too, and in that big old tub in the bathroom, and pretty much everywhere I looked."

"I think I'm beginning to see the problem," she told him, amusement lurking in her eyes. "How about this? Today I'll just wait in the car. You can walk through the house all by yourself."

"I don't think that's going to solve anything," he said. "You're still going to be in my head." In fact, she was in his head so much and so vividly, he couldn't sleep.

"Well, we need to figure out something, because this house

is perfect for you. In fact, if it weren't so perfect for you, I'd buy it myself."

He stared at her. "That is the last thing you should have said. Now I really will envision you in every room. Maybe you should just buy it. If you have your own place and I can think about you there, maybe I won't see you in every room of the houses you're showing me."

"Even I know that's wishful thinking," she said. Her tone turned brisk. "Come on, Walter, suck it up. Focus on Tommy and Libby. You want them to have a great place, don't you? They have to be sick to death of visiting you at the Serenity Inn. There's no room to play there, and this house has an amazing backyard. It even has an old tire swing hanging from a tree and room enough for Libby to practice T-ball."

"Tommy's the one—" he started to say, but she cut him off with a sharp look that reminded him a lot of both Sarah and Raylene.

"Haven't you noticed yet that your daughter is determined to please you?" she asked with a touch of impatience. "Even I, without a single maternal bone in my body, can see she's dying to get better at T-ball so you'll notice her."

All of her arguments—about Tommy and Libby and about the house—made sense. This place did sound ideal for his family. He stood up. "Let's go," he said grimly. "You'll stay in the car."

"If that's what it takes," she agreed.

What the heck! It might work.

At least until he got to the bedrooms.

When Carter stopped by Wharton's for a burger in the middle of his shift, Grace was so busy, she barely spared him a glance, much less her usual chatty greeting.

"Cheeseburger, fries and regular iced tea?" she said as she passed by with an armload of meals for another table.

"That'll do," Carter said, relieved that he hadn't had his heart set on something else. Clearly she was distracted and out of patience.

By the time she returned with his meal, the pace had settled down a bit and she took time to look him over.

"You look about worn out," she said. "Busy day? I haven't heard about any trouble."

"And you would know, wouldn't you?" he teased. "No, it's been quiet. I just have a lot on my mind."

"Those sisters of yours probably give you quite a time, don't they?" she said, squeezing into the booth opposite him, her expression compassionate. "Every teenager in town comes through here at one time or another during the week, so I know them all."

Something in her voice suggested to Carter that there was more on her mind. "The girls haven't given you any kind of a problem, have they?" He couldn't help thinking about kids who turned to shoplifting as a cry for attention or just for a lark.

"Heavens, no! Not the way you mean," she said, obviously guessing his meaning at once. "I have noticed that the older girl—Carrie, isn't it?—she doesn't eat much. I probably wouldn't pay any attention, but after what happened with Annie all those years ago, I'm more alert to that kind of thing with the teenage girls who come in here regularly. Just thought you should know."

"I appreciate you taking an interest," Carter told her.

"You know, I could use some extra help in here this summer, if she's looking for something to do to earn a little money. I could maybe keep an eye on her at the same time. Maybe she'll open up to me."

Carter regarded her with gratitude. "That's a very generous offer, Grace. I appreciate it. I'll mention it to Carrie."

"You do that," Grace said, standing up. "Now eat your burger before it gets cold. I have customers who are starting to look a little antsy. Better see what they need."

Carter chewed his burger thoughtfully. He didn't know yet just how serious Carrie's problem might be, but it seemed if she was in trouble, they couldn't be living in a better, more caring place. He doubted his sister would think much of all the well-meant meddling, but he did. It reassured him that he'd made the right decision moving here.

After having a houseful of people on the Fourth of July and an appointment with Dr. McDaniels the day before, the peace and quiet the next day were making Raylene a little stir-crazy. With Sarah, Travis and the kids all out of the house on an overnight trip to Myrtle Beach, the silence felt oppressive. Worse, she hadn't heard a word from Carter. The fact that it mattered after all those rational arguments she'd given him for not moving their relationship to the next level really annoyed her.

On top of that, ever since she'd heard the news about Paul, she'd been jumpier than ever. He might not be out of prison yet, but he might as well be for the way her nerves were shot. The slightest noise rattled her.

Earlier she'd tried going to bed, but she hadn't been able to settle down, so she'd pulled on an old robe and gone back into the living room. She'd turned on every light, fixed herself a glass of wine and found a book she hoped would be so dull it would knock her right out. None of that had worked, either.

It was closing in on midnight when the doorbell rang, scaring her so badly she knocked over what was left of her wine.

She crossed the living room slowly, regretting that there

was no peephole to indicate who was on the other side of the door.

"Who's there?" she called out, trying not to let her voice shake.

"Carter."

She threw open the door and had to resist the desire to throw herself straight into his arms. He looked so solid and reassuring in his uniform, and way too sexy for this hour of the night.

"You're on duty," she said, stepping aside to let him in.

"Just got off," he responded. "I was driving past and saw every light in the house on. I thought there might be a problem."

She regarded him sheepishly. "Sarah and Travis took the kids to Myrtle Beach. I got jumpy."

"Why didn't you call me?"

"And say what, that I'm too chicken to be left alone in the house at my age?"

"Or just that you wouldn't mind some company," he said. "That would be enough to get me over here."

"But this way I didn't have to humiliate myself by saying a word," she said.

He shook his head. "That pride of yours is going to get you in trouble one of these days." He spotted the wineglass on its side. "Did the drink help?"

"Most of it's on the floor," she told him. "But what I did drink didn't do a thing to mellow me out."

"How about a cup of chamomile tea? My mother used to swear by that."

"I think there's some in the kitchen," she said, leading the way. "My mother was a warm-milk person, but to be honest, I'm pretty sure she laced it with booze."

"We could go that route, too," he said, but Raylene shook her head.

She found the tea bags for him, while he put water on to boil.

"Are you wide awake just because you're alone in the house, or do you have something on your mind?" he asked as he poured boiling water over the tea bag, then handed her the cup.

"Mostly Paul," she said.

"Want to talk about it?"

"Then I'll never get to sleep. Tell me about your day, instead." She sat across from him and sipped her tea, while he drank a beer he'd snagged from the refrigerator. She liked that he'd started to feel comfortable here, that he knew his way around. There was an intimacy to his actions that somehow warmed her. She could envision a future of nights just like this.

When he told her about his fight with Carrie, and then Grace's observations and her offer to give Carrie a job, Raylene smiled.

"Grace means well, but do you really think a girl with food issues is going to want to work waiting on tables?"

"Probably not, but don't you think it's better than having her sit around at home all summer? She needs to do something, make some friends, maybe even earn her own money so she can feel a little independent. Don't you think that might help with her self-confidence?"

Raylene thought about it. "I hadn't looked at it that way. It might. Anyway, it should be her decision, not mine. Carrie might love the idea. Just don't be too disappointed if she doesn't." She hesitated, then added, "If she doesn't, I might have an idea of my own."

"Oh?"

"Dr. McDaniels is encouraging me to spend more time in the garden. She's going to stay out there with me on her next visit, but after that she thinks I should try doing it on my own. I was thinking it might be easier if I got someone to help me work out there. I thought of Carrie—that is, if you don't think Mandy would feel left out. She could always come along."

"I'll handle Mandy." Carter's lips curved. "This isn't really about a summer job at all, is it? You're hoping Carrie might open up to you."

She nodded. "Maybe it's crazy to think that something so simple would form a bond between us, but I thought it was worth a try."

"It definitely is," Carter agreed. "I like the idea of her spending time here with you."

"Well, don't push this idea on her, either. Tell her about Grace's offer and mine, but give her the option of choosing." She yawned before she could stop herself.

Carter chuckled. "Getting sleepy?"

"I think I am. You being here helped to relax me."

"Why don't you curl up on the sofa. I'll stick around till you fall asleep."

"You don't have to do that. I'm sure you want to get home to the girls."

"They're fine. I called and checked on them right before I stopped here." He winked at her. "Besides, since I won't be getting into your bed anytime soon, this will be the next best thing."

Raylene suddenly wanted more. Maybe she wasn't ready for an all-out affair, but just having him nearby wasn't enough.

"How about you sit on the sofa with me?" she suggested, then added tentatively, "I think I'd like to fall asleep in your arms." As an innocent teenager, she'd imagined the joy and intimacy of that, but her reality had been very different. Most nights she'd lain awake, terrified that Paul would wake and force himself on her. There was never any tenderness in their relationship, not even when they were making love.

Carter looked momentarily surprised by her suggestion, then grinned. "Works for me."

"I'm not asking too much of you, am I?" she asked worriedly. "It's not as if that's going to lead to something more, not tonight anyway."

"I'll let you know if something's too much," he promised. "This seems like the perfect next step."

He sat at the end of the sofa and Raylene rested her head on his shoulder. His arms came around her oh so carefully, surrounding her with his warmth. Something in his relaxed embrace reassured her that she could get free if she wanted to. After a few hesitant moments, she felt the last of the night's tension flowing out of her.

When her eyes eventually drifted closed, for the first time ever she felt a hundred percent safe in a man's arms.

Carter's arms had fallen asleep and his legs were cramped, but he couldn't bring himself to move. Holding Raylene meant too much to shatter the intimacy by trying to get more comfortable. His heart ached with the understanding of just how much faith she'd put in him by letting him be this close.

She stirred. Her eyes opened slightly, then blinked.

"Carter? You're still here?" She sat up straight, looking suddenly disconcerted as she realized sun was streaming in the windows. "It's morning. You were here all night?"

"I didn't want to leave you alone. Besides, you seemed so comfortable, I didn't want to risk waking you."

"What about you? Did you sleep at all?"

"A little," he said, but he didn't meet her eyes.

"Meaning you closed your eyes for about five seconds," she guessed. "You should go home and get some real sleep before you go back on duty."

"To be honest, I never sleep all that well during the day. I'll just drink plenty of coffee today. I'll be fine."

She stood up. "Let me put the coffee on and then take a quick shower. After that, I can fix you a decent breakfast."

"I should go home and check on things."

"Will the girls be up at this hour? It's barely seven."

"No," he admitted. "They're slugs once school is out. They won't be up for hours."

"Then please stay."

It sounded so important to her—and he wanted so badly to grab every minute he could to be with her—he didn't resist. "Okay, but let me get the coffee started while you get dressed." He risked looking directly at her. "You are planning to get dressed, right?"

She smiled at the question. "You scared I'm going to come back in here wearing some kind of sexy negligee?"

"Actually, I'm already a little turned on just by you in that robe. I keep trying to imagine what's under it."

"I think maybe I'd better not answer that," she said in a way that hinted she might be wearing very little. She tightened the belt self-consciously.

Just his luck, he thought. He'd been holding a half-dressed woman in his arms all night long and he hadn't done a thing about it. Maybe he had some saintly attributes, after all.

"I don't suppose you want some company in the shower?" he asked, a hopeful note in his voice.

She laughed. "Nice try, but we agreed to keep things casual and friendly."

"There's nothing friendlier than showering together," he retorted.

"What am I going to do with you?" she murmured.

"Nothing, apparently," he said with not entirely exaggerated dismay.

He watched her walk out of the room, hips swaying provocatively. He wondered if she was deliberately taunting him, but he doubted it. Because of her past, he thought she'd be very careful about risking him making a move for which she wasn't entirely ready. He couldn't help wondering, though, if he was crazy for thinking that she'd ever be ready for the kind of relationship he was wanting more and more every time he saw her.

With her cheeks still pink every time she thought about the heat in Carter's eyes and the desire she'd heard in his voice, Raylene had to resist the urge to dress in the most sedate outfit in her closet. Not that she had all that many. Her preferences had always run to clothes that emphasized her curves without being slutty. Lately, though, she'd been living in the same old jeans—designer label though they were—and whatever blouse she grabbed out of her closet. Now that she was living on the modest income awarded to her by the court from Paul's savings, she was embarrassed to think how casually she'd thrown away money on expensive clothes.

Today she took the time to find a pair of linen slacks and a pale pink sleeveless shell that had cost more than her current monthly income. She even added a touch of lipstick and fluffed her hair before going back downstairs to join Carter.

He studied her intently when she walked into the kitchen. "You look different."

"Different how?"

"Lady of the manor?" he suggested, his expression quizzical. "Like someone in that fancy magazine, what's it called, *Town and Country*."

"Do you spend a lot of time looking at *Town and Country*?" she asked, amused.

"No, but my mother did. I think she secretly aspired to be one of those women who went to polo matches and lived on a country estate."

"Mine certainly did," Raylene admitted. "She wasn't happy being in Serenity. I think she got all caught up in the romance when she met my dad. It helped that her parents hated him. She was obviously in her rebellious phase and nothing would do but marrying him. Then reality set in. It was kind of sad for both of them, I think. My dad was a great guy and smart enough to know he could never make her completely happy."

"Is that how you wound up with a guy like Paul Hammond? You decided to go for someone the opposite of your dad, the kind of man your mom should have married?"

"I never thought of it that way, but you're right. I met him at my debutante ball. My mother and her parents were very impressed with his family connections and the fact that he was going to be a doctor. It didn't seem to bother them that he was older and that I was way too young to be making such a huge commitment. I was a little in awe of the life he could offer me." She met Carter's gaze. "Pretty shallow, huh?"

"I'd say pretty normal for a girl who was, what? Seventeen?"

"Sixteen, when we first met. We married as soon as I graduated from high school. I'd barely turned eighteen."

"How long before the problems started?"

"If I'm being honest, they started before the wedding, but I was too naive to realize that the way he wanted to control me wasn't about love. It was about power and jealousy. If he called and I wasn't there, he flipped out. He'd accuse me of cheating on him. I actually thought it was amazing that he loved me that much."

"And no one in your family spotted the warning signs?"

"He hid them around my family. He was always the perfect gentleman, totally solicitous with them. They thought he was wonderful. And I loved him so much, I didn't want them to know about this dark side that popped up from time to time, so I never said a word against him. Later, when things were really bad, my mother refused to believe it."

Carter shook his head. "So you had no one on your side?"

"I think maybe my father would have been, but I didn't want to tell him. Maybe I just couldn't bear the thought that he might side with my mother. I would have been so disillusioned if he had." She shook her head at how mixed up everything had been back then. "And then my dad died, and I was relieved that I'd never burdened him with my problems. He died thinking I was happily settled with someone who'd always take care of me."

"What about Sarah or Annie?"

"I'd pretty much ended my friendship with them when I left for private school. In retrospect, I know I could have gone to them at any time. They certainly didn't hesitate to help when I finally did turn to them, but for a long time I was too embarrassed to admit to anyone what a terrible mistake I'd made."

"That's pretty common," Carter said. "Men who are abusive like to isolate their wives or girlfriends, make them think they're the cause of all the problems."

Raylene nodded. "Before I started seeing Dr. McDaniels, when I thought I could conquer all my problems on my own, I read a lot of books and a ton of articles online. I could see myself practically on every page. That was when I finally stopped feeling so alone and downright stupid."

"I'm so sorry you went through all that," Carter said. "You didn't deserve it."

"No, I didn't," Raylene agreed. "But for way too long I thought I did. I thought it was payback for being young and foolish and, let's face it, a little greedy. I wanted what Paul could offer me—the big house, the fancy clothes, the expensive car. It's taken a long time to adjust my thinking. Not only did I have to accept that no matter how selfish and immature I was, I didn't deserve to be abused, but I had to grow up and realize that none of those material things matter."

"Tough lessons," he said.

"They were for me." She met his gaze. "Carrie and Mandy are so lucky to have grown up with someone like you in their lives. They know how a decent man behaves. They won't settle for less."

Carter flushed at the compliment. "Don't make me into any kind of hero, Raylene. I've made plenty of mistakes."

"Not the kind that count," she said with certainty. "Even if you weren't wearing that uniform, I'd know you were one of the good guys. It's in everything you do, in the way you care about them and about everyone else. I knew it that day you brought Tommy home. Even though I could feel your anger radiating at me for letting him slip away, what I saw was how much you cared about that little boy."

He held her gaze. "We've come a long way since then," he said quietly.

"I know, and I'm really glad about that," she said. "I just wish I knew if we'll ever be able to go any further."

"We will," Carter said firmly. "Count on it. I certainly intend to."

Raylene wanted so badly to believe he was right, but about

a million doubts crowded in, shouting so loudly she couldn't ignore them. Maybe a few years ago, before Paul, she could have had more faith. As it was, though, she'd long since stopped believing in fairy tales and happily-ever-afters.

CHAPTER FOURTEEN

When Carter got home at nine o'clock, both of his sisters were sitting in the living room waiting for him. Their dour expressions reminded him of the way his parents had greeted him when he'd missed curfew.

"Where were you?" Carrie demanded. "You stayed out all night, and don't even think about denying it with some phony story about going out for coffee or breakfast or something. You're still in your uniform."

"Yeah, what if we'd needed you?" Mandy said, though she didn't look half as upset as Carrie did.

"You both know you can reach me at any time on my cell phone," Carter responded. "Did something happen? You're usually not up this early."

"We were worried!" Carrie practically shouted, a hysterical note in her voice. "We even called the dispatcher this morning when we realized you'd never come home. Gayle said she had no idea where you were. Apparently you didn't bother to clock out."

He ignored the accusation about clocking out. He'd deal with that at the station.

"If you were looking for me, why didn't you try my cell

phone?" he asked reasonably. "Do either of you even remember that I called here just as I was going off duty? You told me everything was fine. I even told you I was going to stop by Raylene's. You could have called there if you were worried."

"And interrupt your big late-night date?" Carrie said sarcastically. "That wouldn't be cool."

"It wasn't a date," Carter said. "I was just checking on her."

"All night?" Carrie retorted. "Yeah, right."

He narrowed his gaze and studied his sisters. "What's really going on here? You knew where I was. You knew how to reach me. Why the overreaction? Were you scared about being in the house alone? Usually you can't wait for me to let you hang out here alone so you can order pizza and watch movies half the night, because I wouldn't let you do that in Columbia."

Carrie looked at him as if he were denser than dirt. "No, you idiot, we're scared you're going to pick her over us." As soon as she'd blurted that out, she looked even more miserable, as if she hadn't meant for him to know how scared they were that he might abandon them.

"You can't be serious," he said, even though it was obvious that she was. "Come on, Carrie. You know that's never going to happen. You're my sisters. We're a team. What put such a crazy idea into your heads? I would never choose anyone over you."

"You've never stayed out all night before," Mandy whispered, looking shaken, though less so than her sister. "That must mean Raylene's different, that she's more important than us."

"No one is more important than the two of you," he said fiercely. "I thought you knew that. It's just that Raylene is the first woman in a while who's actually mattered. I have no idea where it's going to go, but I want to find out. That does not mean, though, that I will ever choose her over you. That's simply not how family works, not ours, anyway."

"You chose her last night," Carrie said stubbornly. "That's got to mean there was sex involved."

Once again, the direction of the conversation caught him off guard. "Excuse me? You do not get to ask me if I'm having sex."

"You'll ask us, I bet," Carrie retorted. "Assuming you ever let us date."

"You can absolutely count on me asking, because you're not even sixteen," he said. "I'm more than ten years older than you and I'm responsible for you. I get to make those kinds of decisions for myself. You don't, not for a long, long time."

"How long?" Mandy asked, her expression a mix of curiosity and impishness.

"Until you're at least thirty," he said, as he had many times before. He was dead serious, but he doubted he could pull it off. He'd be happy if he could at least get them through high school before they took such a huge step.

One at a time, he held their gazes, then said, "And if there comes a time when you're considering having sex, you talk to me first. I get to meet the guy. You use protection."

Carrie moaned. "We'll be virgins forever if we have to drag every guy over here before we sleep with him."

Now it was Carter's turn to groan, though he tried not to do it aloud. "There won't be that many guys. Period." He noted that the girls were still in their pj's. "Were you both down here all night waiting for me? Seriously?"

They avoided looking at each other for a full minute, then Mandy grinned. "No, but you should have seen the guilty expression on your face when you walked in and saw us here."

"Then you weren't really worried?"

"Yes, we were," Carrie insisted. "But we didn't actually

lose sleep over it. We just freaked out when we came down here this morning and realized you'd never come home. We didn't know what it meant. Then we got to talking about what would happen if you decided to marry Raylene, and she didn't want us around."

The workings of their minds were going to be the death of him. "You had to know better," he said.

"Well, we thought she liked us, but you never know," Carrie said. "Some women want a man all to themselves." She met his gaze. "So, if sex wasn't involved, why did you stay there all night?"

"It definitely wasn't about sex," he repeated firmly. "Raylene was having a tough time last night, and I sat with her until she fell asleep."

Carrie, of course, looked immediately skeptical. "Which was when? Fifteen minutes before you got here?"

"No, not exactly."

"So you did sleep with her," she accused.

"None of your business," he repeated. "The point is that I'm here now, and frankly I could use a shower and a nap."

"What about breakfast?" Carrie asked. "It's the most important meal of the day. Isn't that what you're always telling me?"

"Had it," he said.

"Oh," Mandy said, looking wistful.

"What?" he asked.

"I wanted to go to Wharton's for pancakes. I figured if we piled on enough guilt, you'd take us."

He turned to Carrie. "And you?"

"I wouldn't mind a pancake," she said.

He was so stunned by the admission, he immediately nodded, "Okay, then. Pancakes at Wharton's. Be ready to go in fifteen minutes." He turned to Carrie. "That reminds me.

Grace says she has a job opening for the rest of the summer, if you're interested."

"Waiting on tables?" she asked, making a face. "I don't know. It doesn't sound like much fun."

"It's not supposed to be fun. It's a job. It's a busy place. I imagine the tips are decent, but it's up to you. You might get to know some more people, too. And if you aren't interested in that, Raylene brought up an alternative. I'll let her tell you about that."

"I'll take whichever job she doesn't want," Mandy piped up.

Carrie frowned at her. "Stay out of it, squirt." She turned back to Carter. "Do I have to decide today?"

"Of course not. Talk to Grace when we get there. She can tell you what the job entails. Then you can call Raylene or go over there. After that, make a decision."

"If you don't want the job at Wharton's, I do," Mandy said eagerly. "I could save up for some really cool clothes for school next fall."

"Back off," Carrie said. "Carter says Grace offered the job to me. You're still a kid. No one's going to hire you."

"I'm just saying, if you don't want it—" Mandy began, only to have her sister cut her off.

"I'll probably take it," Carrie said, though Carter could tell her heart wasn't in it. She was just trying to keep Mandy from getting it.

"Okay, fine," Mandy said huffily. "It's all yours."

When Carrie stalked out of the room, Mandy turned to Carter with a wide grin. "Reverse psychology," she said. "You should try it sometime. Not on me, though. On her."

He laughed. "I'll keep that in mind."

Apparently there were quite a few lessons he could learn from the women in his life. If they didn't drive him into an early grave.

★ ★ ★

An hour later Carter noted that despite her earlier enthusiasm for going out for breakfast, Carrie had merely dissected her pancake and pushed the resulting pieces around on her plate. She gave him a look that dared him to make something of it. He was so relieved that she'd actually talked to Grace about the part-time job at Wharton's that he kept silent about her failure to eat.

"What do the two of you have planned for the rest of the day?" he asked as they headed for the car.

"Would you mind if I went over to see Raylene?" Mandy asked. "I was going to volunteer to weed her garden since she can't do it."

"That would be very thoughtful," Carter told her. "What about you, Carrie? Do you have plans?"

"I might as well tag along with Mandy," she said casually. "I should see what kind of job she had in mind before I give Grace my final answer."

"Good idea. Call Raylene and make sure she's not busy." He was struck by a sudden thought. "You two aren't planning to cross-examine her about last night, are you?"

"Not me," Mandy said.

Carrie was not as quick to respond. "Only if the subject comes up," she said.

"Try to make sure it doesn't come up," he told her. He handed her his cell phone. "Her number's on speed dial. Give her a call. If she says it's okay for you to come over, I'll drop you on my way home."

"Speed dial, huh?" Carrie gave him a knowing look.

"Do not make too much out of that. Everyone I ever call is on speed dial. I can't remember phone numbers."

"It's sad that you're so old and decrepit that you can't remember stuff," Mandy teased.

Carter shook his head. "You two are determined to give me grief today, aren't you?"

"Pretty much," Mandy said happily, then fell silent when Carrie got Raylene on the phone.

"It's okay? You're sure?" She grinned. "Okay, we're on our way."

She handed the phone back to Carter. "It's fine with her. You don't have to take us. We can just walk or ride our bikes over."

"We're already in the car," he said. "I'll drop you off."

Carrie grinned at her sister. "I knew it. He's not about to miss a chance to get one more glimpse of her this morning."

"Whatever," Carter said.

Carrie laughed. "You hate it when I say that."

"Because when you say it, it's annoying," he told her.

"Well, guess what," she retorted. "That goes double for you."

As soon as he pulled into the driveway at Raylene's, the girls bolted from the car. He debated following them, but decided in the mood they were in, that would be way too telling. He settled for waving to Raylene as she held the door open for the girls.

As soon as they were out of sight, he dialed her number. "Watch out," he warned. "Something tells me those two are on a mission."

"Oh?" she said. "Explain."

He could hear Carrie's voice in the background. "That's Carter, isn't it? Tell him to butt out."

Raylene laughed.

"You won't find this so amusing when they start cross-examining you about whether we slept together last night," he warned.

"Uh-oh," she murmured, though there was still amuse-ment threading through her voice.

"Uh-oh, indeed. If they get to be too nosy, send 'em home."

"Not to worry. It's all under control," she assured him.

"That's what you think. Talk to you later."

"Bye."

He hung up with a sinking feeling in his gut that he'd just made a terrible mistake by leaving Raylene to the mercy of his two overly inquisitive sisters. She was skittish enough as it was.

"Carter's never stayed out all night with a woman before," Carrie announced as Raylene poured them all glasses of sweet tea. "At least not since he's had us to look out for."

"Were you frightened about being at home alone?" Raylene asked, refusing to rise to the obvious bait.

"No way," Mandy said. "Carter's worked the night shift before and we've been by ourselves. In Columbia, he'd make the housekeeper stay, but now that we're here and we're older, he says it's okay as long as we don't have anyone over."

"And do you follow that rule?" Raylene asked, knowing full well how many times she, Annie and Sarah had broken it. It was the nature of teens to test their boundaries.

"Never," Mandy said solemnly, though there was a twin-kle in her eyes. "Mostly because we don't know that many kids well enough to invite them over yet."

Carrie interrupted. "My point was—" she began with ob-vious frustration.

Raylene covered her hand. "I know what your point was. You aren't happy that he was here with me."

Carrie frowned. "It's not that exactly. It's just that Carter takes his responsibilities very seriously, so for him to stay here all night, it had to mean something."

"Like what?"

"That you're special," Carrie said. "Do you feel the same way about him? Because I wouldn't want him to get hurt, if you're just having an affair or something."

Raylene might have laughed if Carrie hadn't looked so earnest. The girl really was worried that her big brother might be in over his head. "What exactly did Carter tell you about last night?" she asked eventually.

"That you were having a rough time and he stuck around to make sure you were okay." She looked directly into Raylene's eyes. "I figured he said that because he didn't want to admit he was having sex. It's kind of a touchy subject in our house."

Raylene could imagine. The idea of Carter discussing his sex life with his sisters was pretty much beyond her imaginative capabilities.

"No, he said that because it was the truth," she told Carrie. Carrie looked vaguely disappointed. "Really?"

"Honest to goodness."

"That's kind of a shame," Carrie said. "Don't guys his age want to have sex all the time? The guys I know certainly do."

"I can't speak for most guys, or even for your brother," Raylene told her. "What matters is that you don't ever let yourself get talked into doing something you're not ready to do."

"Yeah, Carter says that, too," Mandy chimed in.

"How old were you the first time you had sex?" Carrie asked, throwing Raylene yet again with her uncensored directness.

"I may not be the best example in the world," Raylene

said. "I was eighteen, but I was also married. As it turns out, that was a huge mistake."

"Why?" Mandy wanted to know.

"Because I was much too young to make a decision that important. I didn't have enough experience to have good judgment about someone I was supposed to spend the rest of my life with."

"So you got a divorce," Carrie said. "Lots of people get divorced."

Raylene didn't know how much she should reveal about her marriage to two impressionable young girls. It was possible, though, that she could turn it into a cautionary tale without revealing too much detail.

"My situation was more complicated than most," she said. "My husband turned out to be abusive."

Carrie's eyes widened. "He hit you?"

Raylene nodded. "And maybe if I'd been a little older when I met him, I would have recognized the signs that he wasn't a good guy and I would never have been in that situation. I like to think so, anyway."

"What signs?" Carrie asked.

"He was controlling and extremely jealous. I was so naive, I thought that showed how much he loved me."

Carrie fell silent, but Mandy had tears in her eyes when she asked, "He's not ever going to hit you again, is he?"

"No," Raylene said adamantly.

"Carter won't let him, that's for sure," Mandy declared.

"No, he won't," Raylene agreed. Her faith was as strong as Mandy's when it came to that. "Now, why don't you go check out the garden and see how bad the weeds have gotten."

"Okay," Mandy said eagerly.

After she'd gone, Carrie finally met Raylene's gaze. "He's

the reason you don't go outside, isn't he? Your ex-husband, I mean. You're scared he'll come back?"

Raylene nodded. "That's certainly part of the problem." She saw no reason to mention that he was in prison now, but about to be released.

"Do you think you'll ever stop being afraid?"

"I'm working on it," she told her.

Carrie hesitated, then said, "I get scared sometimes, too."

"Of what?"

"That something will happen to Carter. If it did, what would happen to me and Mandy?"

"Your brother's not going to let anything happen that would take him away from you," Raylene said, trying to reassure her.

Unfortunately, they both knew that fate sometimes overrode the very best of intentions, which was all the more reason for his sisters to know there were other people in their lives they could count on.

Raylene met Carrie's worried gaze. "Did Carter mention I might have a job for you?"

She nodded.

"It's not much, but I could really use some help to maintain the garden."

"Mandy and I are willing to help with that for free," Carrie said at once.

"But this would be more than that," Raylene explained. "The psychologist wants me to spend more time outside. I was thinking that would be easier if someone were here with me."

Carrie looked puzzled. "You want to hire me to be like a companion or something?"

"I'm not sure I have an actual job description, but the

hours would be flexible, so you could still spend time with your friends."

"And it would help you to get better?"

"I hope so."

Carrie's expression turned thoughtful. "That would make my brother happy, and it would be cool if you could go shopping with me and Mandy sometime or out to dinner with all of us."

"Let's be careful not to make the goals too ambitious," Raylene cautioned.

"Still, helping you would be doing something that really matters," Carrie said. "That's way better than just waiting on tables."

"You might earn more at Wharton's," Raylene said.

Carrie looked out the window, then turned back to her. "But I like it here. I'll take the job."

Raylene smiled. "I'm glad. How about starting tomorrow?" she suggested, then added impulsively, "You can come over when Dr. McDaniels is here, so you'll know what she's expecting from me."

Carrie stilled. "You want me to be here when the shrink comes?"

Raylene could hear the distrust in her voice and backed down at once. "I thought it might be helpful," she said, "but it's fine if you'd rather start another time."

Carrie immediately looked relieved. "What time does she leave?"

"Around two o'clock."

"I'll be here at two-thirty."

"Perfect," Raylene said, grateful that she'd dodged an inadvertent complication. But Carrie's skittishness when it came to the psychologist told her just how frightened the girl really was that her eating habits weren't normal and that someone with expertise might call her on it.

Carter's impromptu meeting with Tom McDonald to discuss the new Serenity police department took most of the afternoon. He'd actually stopped by the town manager's office just to check on his progress with finding ways to put some Public Works employees on the scene in Raylene's neighborhood, but the conversation had evolved into a planning session.

"I'd like to take a proposal to the council by the end of the month. Do you think you can have something ready in writing by then?" Tom asked.

"I can, but don't you think you need to work out the parameters for the chief's job and decide if I'm the right man to fill it first?"

"Let me tell you something about the politics around here. Howard may not technically be a strong mayor in terms of the way Serenity's government is set up, but he usually gets his way. He wants you for the job, so you can consider it yours. You have my backing, too. The council approved the position and the salary at their last meeting."

He jotted down a figure and passed it to Carter. "It's probably not what you're worth, but it's more than you'll make as a deputy with the sheriff's department."

"It seems fair," Carter said. And the three-year contract would give him both the kind of job security and regular hours that mattered to him. Starting a department from scratch would be challenging, too.

"Are you saying yes?" Tom asked.

"I'm saying yes," he confirmed.

"Then work out your schedule with the sheriff, so he's not left in the lurch, and give me a starting date." A worried expression crossed his face. "Or do you want to stay in uniform and on duty with the sheriff's department until this situation with Raylene's ex-husband is resolved?"

It told Carter a lot about his new boss that he would think of something like that. "I'd like to stay on there, either until Paul's gone for good or we have this department up and running. I'll give you as much of my spare time as I can to put together the department. Frankly, the sooner our own force is in place, the better I'll like it."

"How about we pay you hourly for the time you put in until you come on board full-time?"

"That'll work."

"Just so you know, the public-works guys and the local utility crews will do whatever they can to pitch in when the time comes. Some of them knew Raylene in high school. They were furious when I told them she might be in danger from an ex-husband."

Carter worried about untrained men getting too enthusiastic about protecting Raylene. That could be as dangerous as whatever crazy thing Paul decided to try. "You don't think they'll get carried away, do you? Maybe take the law into their own hands? The last thing we need is a bunch of vigilantes taking over."

"You'll meet with them and set the rules," Tom said at once. "They're good men. They just want to help."

Carter nodded. "I'll schedule a meeting as soon as I have a clear idea of the timetable for Hammond's release. You'll be able to get them in place on short notice?"

"I can have them there within twenty-four hours. Will that work?"

"It should."

Having extra eyes keeping close tabs on Raylene's house

might not prevent Paul from getting into the area, but it should go a long way toward keeping him from getting anywhere near Raylene.

After spending a couple of hours in the yard, Carrie and Mandy came back into the house looking hot, tired and bedraggled just as Walter arrived unexpectedly for a late-afternoon visit. They regarded him warily.

"You were at the picnic," Carrie said, her gaze narrowed suspiciously. "I thought you were with Rory Sue."

"I was," he said, looking amused.

"Then why are you here now?" Carrie pressed.

Raylene stepped in before Carrie could continue grilling him. It seemed she had potential as an investigative reporter, but she probably needed to channel the skill in a different direction. "He's Tommy and Libby's dad, remember? He stops by a lot to see his kids."

"Oh, yeah," Carrie said, but she still looked suspicious.

"I think I'll see if they're up from their naps," Walter said, backing out of the kitchen.

"Does Carter know he comes by here?" Carrie asked, still determined to protect her brother's interests.

"I think so. Walter and I are just friends," Raylene reassured her. "Now, how about some iced tea? Or would you prefer lemonade? There are cookies, too. I baked oatmeal raisin while you all were weeding for me."

"Just water for me," Carrie said.

"But you barely touched your sandwich at lunchtime," Raylene said. "You must be starved by now."

Carrie immediately frowned. "You're not going to start on me, too, are you?"

"Why shouldn't she?" Mandy demanded. "Anyone can see that you're not eating right."

"Because it's none of her business," Carrie snapped at her sister. "I'm going home. You stay here, if you want to."

Raylene stepped in front of her, then shot a warning look toward Mandy. She'd practically been handed the perfect opportunity to discuss eating disorders, but it was about to blow up in her face.

"Please don't go," she said to Carrie. "I didn't mean to upset you. I told you the other day about what happened to Annie. I probably worry too much when I see someone your age not eating."

Carrie didn't look pacified by the apology, but she did sit down. She even took a cookie off the plate. She broke it into at least a dozen tiny pieces on her napkin, then forced down one of them. It took an obvious effort, which spoke volumes about her attitude toward food.

"I don't know why everyone's so freaked just because I don't want to eat a bunch of stuff that's bad for me," she muttered.

"You don't eat at all," Mandy blurted.

"I'd eat if I were hungry," Carrie said, turning to Raylene for support. "Isn't that the way it's supposed to be? Food is fuel for your body. You don't need more until you're running on empty."

Raylene shook her head. "That's only true up to a point. Sometimes, for whatever reason, people can't sense when their body needs more fuel. That's when there's trouble."

"I'm never hungry," Carrie said. "So what's the point of eating a bunch of extra calories?"

"Because your body needs some calories every day in order to function properly," Raylene said. "Without the proper nutrients, your kidneys and other organs can get all out of whack before you even realize what's happening."

"Is that what happened to Annie?" Mandy asked.

Raylene nodded, her gaze on Carrie. She looked intrigued despite her declaration that she was just fine.

"How old was she?" Mandy asked.

"Just sixteen. She collapsed at a sleepover."

"Maybe she was just faint from hunger," Carrie suggested hopefully.

"No. Her heart failed. She nearly died," Raylene said, determined not to sugarcoat what had happened.

"Then she must not have been very strong to begin with," Carrie said, looking for some explanation that would separate her from Annie and the path that had nearly led to her death.

"Because over time she'd put her body through hell by not getting the proper nutrients," Raylene said, refusing to back down from the bleak picture.

"Well, she obviously lived and got better," Carrie said. "She just had a baby. She must be fine."

"She got better because she got help," Raylene said. "But only after it was almost too late. You're a smart girl, Carrie. You don't want to wait that long."

"But I'm not anorexic," Carrie insisted, her tone belligerent. She glared at Raylene and at Mandy. "I'm not! And if it's going to be like this every time I come over here, you can forget your stupid job."

This time when she stood up, she didn't give either of them a chance to persuade her to stay. She ran from the house.

Mandy heaved a sigh. "I'd better go after her."

"Maybe she needs a little time alone to think about all this," Raylene suggested, but Mandy shook her head.

"We made a pact when Mom and Dad died. We stick together, even if one of us says we want to be alone."

Raylene smiled at the show of unity. "Then, go. If you need anything, give me a call." She would call Carrie herself later and try to make peace. She hated that the teenager had thrown the job back in her face. She'd been counting on that time to win Carrie's confidence.

Mandy regarded her worriedly. "You're not mad that we wanted to know what's going on with you and Carter, are you?"

"I could never be mad that you care so much about your brother."

"He's a really cool guy," she told Raylene earnestly.

"I know that," Raylene said.

Mandy hesitated, then asked, "Do you think you'll marry him? You'd be like our big sister, then."

"It's way too soon to even consider something like that," Raylene told her, but the wistful expression on Mandy's face got to her. "How about you just consider me a friend. And we'll stay friends no matter what happens between Carter and me."

Mandy's expression brightened. "Really?"

"It's a promise."

"Cool," the teen said, and threw her arms around Raylene for a fierce hug. "Bye."

"Bye, sweetie."

Raylene watched from the window as Mandy ran down the street after her sister. With each passing day, it seemed she was getting to be more emotionally entangled with the entire Rollins family, whether she was ready for it or not.

CHAPTER FIFTEEN

Raylene was just putting the pitcher of tea back into the refrigerator, when Walter walked into the kitchen.

"Do you have any idea what you're doing with those girls?" he asked, his expression filled with concern.

"Being a friend to them," she responded, unable to keep a defensive note out of her voice. "What's wrong with that? And, by the way, why were you eavesdropping? My relationship with Carter's sisters is none of your business."

"I wasn't eavesdropping, at least not on purpose. The kids are watching a video. I came to get cookies for them."

"Cookies will spoil their supper," Raylene said, mostly just to be contrary because she was annoyed by Walter's observation. It was two hours till dinner and one cookie each would hardly matter.

Walter merely lifted a brow, picked up two cookies and left the room. Unfortunately, he wasn't gone long.

"Shouldn't you stay in there with the kids?" she asked testily. She wasn't sure she could face another inquisition this afternoon, especially from someone who knew her well enough to see right through her. If even a man as insensitive as Walter recognized that getting entangled in Carrie's problems posed a risk, maybe she should be thinking twice about it. She just wanted so badly to find a way to prove to Carter—and even to herself—that she could play an important role in his family. Lately that hope was what kept her going.

Unfortunately Walter wasn't fazed by her attempt to discourage his meddling. "Laurie's with Tommy and Libby," he reminded her with exaggerated patience. "They won't get into any mischief. I'm more concerned about you."

"Why?"

"Because you're getting too involved with those girls and their problems. What's going to happen when things don't work out with their brother?"

"Why wouldn't things work out?" she demanded irritably, though it was a question she'd asked herself more than once.

"Because you won't let them," Walter said, taking her by surprise with his insight. "I saw you with him at the barbecue. It's obvious you're crazy about him, but you were pushing him away, as if you had no right to grab on to any happiness that comes your way."

"The same way you were pushing Rory Sue away?" she inquired, hoping to redirect the conversation. "For the same reason, I might add."

"That's entirely different," he said, disagreeing with her. "For once in my life I'm trying not to rush into something for all the wrong reasons."

"Maybe that's what I'm doing, too," she suggested. "After all, I could be afraid that I'm only attracted to Carter because he's the first man to come along since my marriage who's shown an interest in me."

"Oh, I do believe you're scared," he said. "And who could blame you? It's not as if your marriage to Paul was any kind of picnic. It's natural for you to be skittish. But I think your fear runs a lot deeper than just thinking that the attraction is superficial. I don't think you're anywhere close to being ready for a real relationship, and you know it. But that's what Carter wants, isn't it? The real deal?"

She couldn't deny that. "Look, I'm working through my issues, okay?" she told him. "I'm getting more comfortable with Carter every time I see him." At least she hoped that was true. She wanted it to be, because the attraction ran deep. So did her respect for him. She didn't want her problems standing in the way of a real relationship.

Walter obviously wasn't satisfied with her response. "How comfortable?" he pressed. "Enough to have an honest-to-goodness, long-lasting relationship with him, because if that's not where this is heading, then you shouldn't get too involved with those girls."

"I don't know," she admitted. "Why are you pushing this? What does it matter to you if I mess this up?"

"I'm worried about you getting hurt. I'm even worried about a couple of teens who've obviously lost too many people they cared about. Carter may know your history. He may have the patience of a saint, but if you send mixed signals long enough, he may get tired of it and walk away. Then where will you be? Especially if you've gone and fallen in love with him."

"I'm a big girl. I can handle a broken heart."

Walter looked skeptical. "Okay, let's say I believe that. Can you handle breaking his heart? Or hurting his sisters? What if they've learned to count on you?"

"Are you saying I need to back off?" she asked, her heart sinking at the thought. That reaction, as much as anything, told her she needed to fight for the future she was just starting to envision.

"That pretty much goes against the popular wisdom

around here," she told Walter. "Everyone else thinks it's time for me to start living again."

"I'm all for you starting to live. Getting out of this house would be a fantastic start. Rushing into a relationship might be asking too much of yourself. I just want you to be sure you can handle all the consequences."

Raylene knew deep inside that he had some valid points, but as she studied him intently, she realized something else. "You know something, Walter? I don't think we've been talking about me at all. I think you're scared spitless that you're getting too involved with Rory Sue and that one of *you* is going to get hurt."

To her surprise, he didn't deny it.

"Guilty," he admitted.

"What's the problem? She seems very taken with you."

"She's nothing like Sarah. And contrary to what all of you probably think, she's a lot more vulnerable than she lets on. There's a good chance I'll let her down. That's what I do. I was a lousy husband to Sarah, and I'm just finally getting a grip on being a halfway-decent father. It's probably way too soon for me to try to figure out how to have a mature relationship with another woman."

"If you're thinking that clearly, it obviously means you're making progress," Raylene told him. "Stop selling yourself short." She waited, thinking about the situation. "Or are you really worried that Rory Sue's just playing a game, and you don't want to put your heart at risk?"

"Damned if I know," he admitted. "It could go either way. It's just too soon to tell, which is why I've been trying to put some space between us." He shrugged. "Rory Sue's not much interested in space. She wants what she wants when she wants it."

"Just like her mama," Raylene said, smiling at the thought

of Walter trying to hold a determined Rory Sue at bay. "Mary Vaughn went after Ronnie Sullivan more than once despite all the odds against her. I suppose that kind of determination could be flattering."

"No, it's terrifying," Walter said. "I'm a man. It would be very easy to give in. The woman is amazing. But I'm trying to use my brain here, not my...well, you know."

Raylene laughed. "Yes, I do know, and I admire your restraint." She met his gaze. "Not to change the subject too much, but how's the hunt for a house going? Once you find something, you could stop seeing Rory Sue altogether if that's what you really want."

"I found one, as a matter of fact. Rory Sue said it was perfect, and she was right. I put in an offer. We should know something tonight."

"Congratulations! The kids are going to be so excited."

"I know. I can't wait until I can take them to pick out whatever they want for their rooms."

"Is Rory Sue going to help with that?" she asked.

"Probably. She does know where the best stores are."

"Really?" she said, amused. "And you haven't been in every furniture store in the region to sell advertising for the radio station?"

He frowned at the question. "What's your point?"

"She's becoming every bit as involved in your life as Carter and his family are in mine. I'd say the danger signs are posted for both of us."

But as clear as she was on the dangers that lay ahead, she wondered if she, any more than Walter, would heed them.

Carter drove up just as Walter was leaving. He exited his sheriff's cruiser with a take-out bag in hand.

"I came with dinner," he told Raylene. "Can I stay? I figured you deserved a respite from cooking after dealing with my sisters today."

"Your timing's great. I was going to start cooking any minute," she said, aware that the mere sight of him had stirred up her senses. Given the conversation she'd just had with Walter, it was disturbing. Maybe she really should think things through carefully before she allowed herself to get any more involved in his life. He and his sisters represented the unattained dream she'd envisioned for herself, a ready-made family. She finally dared to meet his gaze.

"I hope Sarah and Travis like Chinese food," he said. "I brought enough for them, too."

"That's very thoughtful of you," she said. "Travis will probably just grab a quick bite. He has his show to do tonight."

"Then maybe we should leave everything in the to-go containers. He can take whatever he wants with him."

"Perfect," she said, then studied him. "Aren't you still on duty? Can you really take a break?"

"Dispatch can reach me." He patted the radio and cell phone at his hip. "And I gave Gayle this number, too. It's fine. I have some news I wanted to share." He leaned down and kissed her cheek. "And I just wanted to see you, make sure you survived an entire day with Carrie and Mandy."

Raylene sighed. "We do need to talk about that," she admitted. "Let's go in the kitchen. We have a little while before Sarah and Travis will be here."

Carter frowned as he followed her. "Was there a problem? They didn't bug you about me staying over here last night, did they?"

"That wasn't the problem." She told him about the discussion she'd had with Carrie. "She got extremely defensive. I might have made matters worse by pushing so hard.

She'd agreed to take the job here, but now I'm not so sure she'll be back."

Carter sighed. "I'm glad you spoke up. I've been on her case lately, too. She needs to know we're paying attention."

"But she must have felt as if we were all ganging up on her. Mandy chimed in, as well. I'm not sure all that pressure at once is good."

"Isn't that exactly the way those interventions work?" he said.

"But those are usually handled by professionals," Raylene said. "A psychologist would have known what to do when Carrie fought back. They might have been able to stop her from taking off."

Carter's expression turned grim. "She left?"

Raylene nodded. "Mandy went after her. I should have done it. That's what a responsible adult would have done."

"Come on. There were extenuating circumstances," he said. "To say nothing of the fact that helping my sister is my job, not yours."

"But you don't upset a kid and then let another kid deal with the fallout," she said with self-derision. "I tried calling earlier, but Carrie wouldn't take my call. Mandy said she'd shut herself in her room."

Carter muttered a curse and immediately stood up. "I'd better get over there and check on things. A rain check on dinner, okay? I guess that news of mine will have to wait, too."

"Do you want to take the Chinese food home with you? The girls would probably like it."

"I don't think walking in the door with food right now is a good idea." He gave her a frustrated look. "What's it going to take to fix this? I'm at a loss."

"Do you want to talk to Dr. McDaniels? I'm sure she'd

be happy to give you some ideas. She'll be here tomorrow at one. You could drop by, say, around one-thirty."

He nodded. "I might do that." He leaned down and kissed her again, just a quick brush of his lips across hers. "Thanks for caring."

He paused in the doorway. "It means the world to me that you care about what's going on with Carrie. The past couple of years have been tough. I've been totally out of my depth with everything that's happened since my folks died." He gave her a lopsided grin. "Who knows? Maybe with a little help from you I'll figure out this parenthood thing, after all."

When Dr. McDaniels arrived for their session, Raylene immediately filled her in on what had been going on with Carrie. "I told Carter he could stop by to speak with you, if that's okay. He'll be here at one-thirty."

To her surprise, the psychologist frowned.

"Is it a problem?" Raylene asked, puzzled by her reaction. "Would you rather not speak to him? Did I violate some code of ethics or something?"

"It's not that," Dr. McDaniels said. "I'm happy to help. What worries me is that you're putting your own situation on the back burner to deal with his sister's problems."

"But this is important," Raylene said.

"So is your recovery."

"I'm not skipping a session," Raylene argued. "At least not all of it. We have a few more minutes before Carter will be here."

"Not long enough to spend the time in the garden that we'd planned," the doctor said. "Are you sure you didn't intentionally plan it that way?"

Raylene shook her head. "That never even crossed my mind, I swear it. In fact, I'd even offered Carrie a job spending time out there with me. The rest of this kind of came to a head after that. I saw how worried Carter was, and it seemed this would be the perfect chance for him to speak to you. The offer to let him use part of my time with you was impulsive. I'm sorry if it was the wrong thing to do."

Dr. McDaniels didn't look entirely convinced, but she nodded. "Okay, then, let's see what we can accomplish before he gets here. In fact, why don't we try going outside to wait for him. We'll spend time in the garden next time."

"Okay," Raylene said. Maybe on some subconscious level she had hoped to put off an extended period outside, but maybe it was better this way. She'd have to just do it, ready or not.

She led the way to the door and grasped the handle.

"Deep breath," Dr. McDaniels encouraged. "Don't think about what's next. Just open the door. Concentrate on the fact that it's a beautiful summer day. You've been doing this a lot lately. It's nothing new."

Raylene released the latch on the door and pushed it open. So far, so good. Her palms weren't sweating. Her breathing was steady. All she had to do was take a step and she'd be outside. It should be second nature by now, but there was always that one instant, just before she took the first step, when she wondered if she'd be able to do it.

She counted slowly, tried to time her breaths to a nice even rhythm and took that next step. Then a few more.

"There, that wasn't so hard, was it?" the psychologist asked.

"I haven't fallen apart yet, if that's what you're asking."

"Then keep going. Let's cross the grass so you can wait for Carter to turn in to the driveway. Think about how pleased he'll be to have you waiting for him. It's only a few more feet. No big deal. And you'll still be close to the house. I'm right here with you. You're perfectly safe."

Raylene swallowed hard, but she took the first step onto the grass. She couldn't help glancing back toward the house to make sure she hadn't strayed too far away from her sanctuary. Dr. McDaniels nodded encouragement.

"You're doing great," she told Raylene. "What kind of car does Carter drive?"

"A pickup," Raylene responded, her breath catching. "A silver one." Suddenly she couldn't seem to get another breath. Her chest heaved. It felt as if her heart was going to pound right through her ribs. She hadn't had a setback like this in days. Angry with herself, she forced herself to take slow, deep breaths until her breathing steadied and her heartbeat slowed.

"You're just fine," the doctor soothed. "You heard the sound of Carter's truck, that's all. See, here he is, turning in to the driveway right now."

Carter stepped out of the truck, amazement on his face, as if he'd caught her turning somersaults down the block. "Well, look at you," he said, grinning as he had on the day he'd discovered her on the patio. "Going for a walk, are you?"

She frowned at the hopeful note in his voice. "Hardly."

Even so, he looked thrilled, as if he'd been waiting for a moment like this since the day they'd met. As he came around the car, a part of her wanted to run to him, but the panic stirred yet again, then took over. She was rooted in place, hyperventilating, close to passing out.

Dr. McDaniels obviously recognized the symptoms, because she moved in close and took Raylene's arm. She must have given Carter a subtle nod, too, because he was immediately beside her, as well. They half walked, half carried her back to the house. It wasn't more than twenty feet or so, but it seemed like miles. The psychologist murmured soothing words until they were safely inside. Raylene nearly collapsed with relief.

Carter went for water while Dr. McDaniels continued to talk to her. Slowly, Raylene's breathing returned to normal. The panic receded and her pulse rate slowed.

"You did great," the doctor said as Raylene sipped the water, her face flushed with embarrassment.

"You call that great? What happened? I'd been getting better. I should be past these attacks by now."

"There will be days like this, Raylene."

"Forever?" she asked plaintively.

"Not forever," the psychologist assured her. "Think about what you have accomplished, not about today's minor little setback."

"It's not enough," Raylene said despondently. What counted was getting well enough to have a normal life, a full life with Carter. Being able to be there for Carrie and Mandy the way she should be, not sitting on the sidelines, but truly involved in their lives. Maybe even kids down the road. Not a life where success was measured by stepping a few feet outside of her own front door.

She gathered the few bits of her composure remaining and stood. "I'll leave the two of you alone to talk. I'll be in the kitchen if you need me."

She saw the dismay on the psychologist's face and the worry on Carter's, but she had nothing to say that would reassure either one of them. In fact, she didn't even have words to reassure herself.

"You should go to her," Carter said, his gaze following Raylene. He'd never seen her look so defeated, not even after he'd found her in a similar state in the backyard.

Dr. McDaniels shook her head. "She won't hear anything I have to say right now. Besides, she's very anxious for the two of us to talk about your sister. Tell me what's going on with her."

Carter shook off his worries about Raylene and described everything he and others had been noticing about Carrie's behavior. "I'm really scared for her, but she denies there's a problem and I have no idea what to do next."

"You know she needs help," the doctor said. "That's a great first step. I'd like to speak to her myself. Do you think she'd agree to come to my office?"

"Not willingly," he said grimly. "But I could make it happen."

"What about the nutritionist at the hospital? Would Carrie see her willingly? Maybe you could suggest that you know she's been worried about her weight and that the nutritionist is someone who could help her develop a sensible eating plan."

"She'll see right through that. Right now she's touchy about any mention of food."

"What about insisting she get a physical for school with a general practitioner? I'd like to see some kind of clinical evaluation so we know where her health stands. If she really is anorexic, more than likely there will be evidence of it."

"Again, she's so sensitive to every suggestion even remotely related to her health, she'll probably balk at that, too."

"Okay, then, here's where tough parenting is required. You may have to insist. It probably doesn't matter which of those steps you take first, as long as you take one of them."

"That's it? There's no other way?" he asked.

"You won't like the alternative any better, and neither will she," the doctor said, her expression grim. "I'd recommend that you put her into the hospital or a residential-treatment program to be evaluated. If a teen is simply in denial, usually the first mention of a hospital or treatment facility is enough to get them to start taking the situation seriously. She may be angry, but you're the responsible adult. You can't let anger or tears sway you from doing what needs to be done."

Carter closed his eyes, trying to envision Carrie's reaction to being committed somewhere for treatment. He wasn't sure he could do that. He was too afraid she'd feel as if he'd betrayed her.

"I'd like to make an appointment for her with you," he said. "The first opening you have."

"Tomorrow morning at ten," she said at once.

"We'll be there."

"I'll want to talk to her alone," she told him.

"Not a problem. But I'll be just outside the door in case she decides to try to bolt."

"She's going to be furious with you."

"I can handle that, as long as she gets well."

Dr. McDaniels regarded him with concern. "I know she's your sister, not your child, but it's awfully hard to see anyone you love look at you as if they hate you. Be prepared for that. Maybe you should talk to Ronnie or Dana Sue Sullivan and see how they coped with that when Annie was in treatment."

"I'll do that. I can deal with hard. It's just as difficult to watch her wasting away and not have any idea how to help," he said, grimly determined to get them both through whatever lay ahead.

"I'll want to have some sessions with you and her sister, as well. Family counseling is an important part of the recovery from anorexia, if that's what we're dealing with."

"Whatever you need. It'll probably be good for Mandy, too. I think they've both dealt with a lot since we lost our parents. I've done the best I could, but I'm sure there's a lot they've kept bottled up inside."

"Grief could be a big part of Carrie's behavior," she said. "If it is, we'll find better coping mechanisms."

Carter nodded, relieved to have someone with real expertise on his side. "I'll see you in the morning then. Do you want to see Raylene before you go, or is it okay if I spend a few minutes with her?"

"I think she probably needs you more than she does me right now," Dr. McDaniels said. "Tell her I'll be back day after tomorrow at the regular time."

Carter nodded and walked her to the door. When she was gone, he drew a deep breath and braced himself for seeing Raylene. He knew she'd probably spent the past half hour beating up on herself over falling apart. It was what she did. She set her expectations too high, then berated herself for failing.

When he went into the kitchen, he found her sitting at the table, her cheeks tracked with dried tears, her gaze distant.

"You doing okay?" he asked, though he could see that she wasn't.

She merely shrugged.

"I had a good talk with Dr. McDaniels. She's terrific. I'm going to take Carrie to see her tomorrow."

A flicker of interest stirred in her expression before she shut down again. "I'm sure that will help."

"Raylene, about what happened earlier—"

"I don't want to talk about that," she said, her cheeks flushing. "It was humiliating."

"No," he said adamantly. "It was brave. Every time you step outside, you're fighting a fear I can't even begin to imagine."

"You face down worse fears every day when you go to work," she said. "I'm practically scared of my own shadow. It's crazy. *I'm* crazy."

"Don't you dare say that," he said furiously. "You have a treatable panic disorder. You're going to get better."

She regarded him with a bleak expression. "What if I don't? What if this is the rest of my life, shut up in this house?"

"Then we'll deal with it," he said.

"Not we," she said adamantly. "It's my problem."

"Sorry, it doesn't work that way. You and me, we're friends, no matter what else happens. Friends stick together. If you have a problem, I'm right here with you."

"But you have Carrie to worry about," she protested. "You don't need to take on my situation, too."

He held her gaze. "Yes, I do," he said solemnly.

There was a faint flicker of hope in her eyes, but it faded. "But, Carter—"

"No arguments," he said. "I'm not walking away from you. You can push all you like, but I'm staying."

A smile touched her lips. "Maybe," she began softly, "maybe you're the crazy one."

He grinned. "Could be, but that's just the way it is."

He stood up. "I need to get to work. Are you going to be okay?"

"Laurie and the kids will be back soon, and I think Sarah's coming home early. I'll be fine."

He leaned down and touched his lips to hers. This time, though, a casual kiss wasn't enough. He lingered and when she didn't pull away, he deepened the kiss, tasting and savoring until he heard a low moan in the back of her throat.

He pulled away, then met her gaze. "*That's* worth fighting for, don't you think?"

She touched her fingers to her lips, which had curved finally into a full-fledged smile. "It just might be."

He left then, feeling more optimistic than he had in weeks, not just about his sister's future, but his own.

CHAPTER SIXTEEN

Raylene had a bad night wondering if she was ever going to get better. Nothing Dr. McDaniels, Carter or even Sarah had said to her had reassured her that she was making real progress. For every step forward she'd taken, literally, it seemed she'd taken another one back. She tossed and turned most of the night and eventually wandered into the kitchen well before dawn, probably looking as frazzled and out of sorts as she felt. Sarah was already there having coffee before heading to the radio station.

"You look like hell," Sarah commented cheerfully. When Raylene merely scowled and poured herself a cup of coffee, Sarah winced. "Okay, definitely not in a good mood."

"Sorry. I didn't get much sleep."

"Because of what we talked about last night, the way your session with Dr. McDaniels went?"

Raylene nodded. "But, please, leave it alone. I don't feel like rehashing it this morning."

Sarah opened her mouth, then shut it again.

Raylene smiled. "Thank you."

"If I didn't have to get to work, I'd make you talk about this some more."

"Go. Entertain. Laugh. Have a good day."

Sarah paused. "You will be okay, right? Should I send someone over to cheer you up?"

"No," Raylene said firmly. She needed to work through this on her own. She'd felt a few glorious glimmers of hope about the future recently. She had to figure out how to cling to those, rather than sinking into despair over her failures.

But despite what she'd told Sarah about wanting to be alone with her thoughts, a few hours later she opened the door and found Carter on the doorstep. She had a feeling his arrival wasn't a coincidence.

"Sarah called me earlier," he said. "She said you might be over here freaking out. What's that about?"

"Just more of the same old, same old," she said, dismissing it. "Do you have time for something to drink? Coffee? Tea? Tell me about Carrie. Did she have her session with Dr. McDaniels this morning?" Though she was genuinely interested, she hoped asking about Carrie would redirect the conversation away from her. "How did Carrie react when you told her she had an appointment to see a shrink?"

Carter rolled his eyes. "I'm sure you can imagine. First, she threw a tantrum and refused to go. Then, when I didn't budge, she turned on the waterworks and pleaded with me not to make her go."

"How'd you cope with that?"

"Thankfully I was prepared. Mostly, I tuned her out, even though the tears were killing me. I felt like the worst kind of big brother ever for forcing her to do this."

"But you had to know in your heart you were being the *best* kind of big brother."

"I tried to remember that, but it was hard with tears streaming down her cheeks. I really, really hate it when people cry, especially when I'm responsible."

"Ultimately, though, you got her to go?"

He nodded. "By then she was sulking and not speaking to me at all. The look she gave me when she walked into the office came pretty close to breaking my heart."

"Any idea how the session went? Did Carrie say anything afterward? Or did you speak to Dr. McDaniels?"

"I have a follow-up with Dr. McDaniels tomorrow. We all do, in fact. I guess I'll find out more then. Carrie's still not speaking to me. She's freezing out Mandy, too. The doc says that's normal. Right now, Carrie obviously thinks we've all ganged up on her. We're the enemy."

"I'm so sorry."

"Me, too, but it has to be this way. Even I can see that. It's better than sending her to the hospital or a treatment center. I tried to make her see that, but she told me there was nothing wrong with her, that I was just being mean and freaking out over nothing."

He looked so miserable that Raylene found herself moving closer to him on the sofa. She reached out and touched his cheek. It was the first time she'd let herself initiate any contact. She saw surprise register in his eyes.

"It's going to get better," she assured him. "There may be some rough patches. There certainly were with Annie. I can remember back then Ty was just about the only one who could get through to her. Everyone else was her enemy, even Ronnie, and she adored her dad. It just about killed him to be tough with her. Maybe you could talk to him sometime, and see how he dealt with her anger."

"Believe me, I will speak to him. I need to be reminded that we will get through this. It helps to see how close Annie and her family are, even after all they went through. That gives me hope."

Raylene squeezed his hand. "I'm just coming to realize

how important hope is," she said. In fact, even though it was hard won, hope was just about the only thing that got her through some difficult days. Maybe if she tried hard enough, she wouldn't lose it now.

Carter checked at least once a week with the prison to see if there was anything new on Paul Hammond's possible release date in August. Though officials had promised to alert him before any release occurred, he wasn't inclined to take chances. Parole hearings could be delayed or moved up. While he wouldn't mind the former one bit, he wasn't about to risk having the date come up faster than he was anticipating.

In the meantime, he'd been doing more research into Hammond's background. Today he'd driven over to Charleston on his day off, left the girls to shop at a mall and done a little investigating around the hospital where Hammond had worked as an orthopedic surgeon. What he'd discovered had alarmed him even more.

It seemed Raylene hadn't been his first victim, just the only one he'd married and the only one who'd reported him to police. Most of the women he spoke with thought she'd been incredibly brave, though some had openly declared it to be social suicide.

"She'll never be welcome back in Charleston, not by that crowd," one of the nurses said candidly. "In that social world, wives either suffer in silence or they leave. They don't create a scandal. Their attitude is pretty disgusting, if you ask me. It means the men just keep getting away with it."

Carter agreed. He couldn't imagine a world where anyone turned a blind eye to abuse. "What about Hammond? Will he be welcomed back?"

"Not here," the nurse said fiercely. "And I can't think of

a woman who'd let him treat her or allow him to touch her kids. The men might stick by him." She shrugged. "If it were up to me, he'd lose his license to practice, but I don't know what the medical board will decide."

Though Carter wanted Hammond to lose everything, he worried that if Hammond wasn't welcomed back into that same world with open arms, it would fuel his rage against Raylene.

By the time he picked up the girls a couple of hours later, Carter was more concerned than ever about the danger Hammond might pose.

"How come you're so quiet?" Mandy asked, giving him a questioning look as she climbed into the front passenger seat.

"I just have a lot on my mind," he said. "How was your shopping trip? You don't seem to have a lot of bags. Does that mean my credit card didn't get a workout?"

"Carrie wouldn't shop," Mandy said with disgust.

"I don't need any clothes," Carrie countered, settling into the backseat.

Her sour, defensive tone was the same one with which Carter was becoming all too familiar. She'd been this way ever since she'd started seeing Dr. McDaniels. Clearly, she hadn't yet forgiven him for making her continue to go. So far she'd been refusing to go to Raylene's as well, obviously counting her among the enemies. He'd hoped the outing to Charleston would help, but it obviously hadn't.

"Now, *that* has to be a first," he said, his voice determinedly cheerful. "I thought you were dying to shop where the clothes have some style. Isn't that what you've been telling me?"

"I just don't want anything," she said.

"She says everything makes her look fat," Mandy said, turning around and giving her sister a defiant look.

Carter's gaze shot to Carrie in the rearview mirror. "What's that about, Carrie?"

"I never said that," she said, casting a murderous look at Mandy. "I said I *felt* fat today. I ate too much at breakfast."

All Carter recalled her eating was a half piece of toast and a bite of scrambled eggs. It was more than she usually touched, true, but hardly enough to cause her to feel full, much less fat.

Still, he refrained from responding. In their session this week, Dr. McDaniels had suggested he keep a close eye on Carrie and report to her, but not to be the bad guy by challenging her over every meal. She'd said the time would come for that, once the nutritionist became involved. That was scheduled for this week, though she hadn't mentioned it to Carrie yet.

"Okay, let's talk about something else," Carter suggested. "How about stopping to see a movie before we head back?"

"That'd be cool," Mandy said eagerly.

"I don't feel like it," Carrie said, clearly determined to be a spoilsport about everything.

"We could go sightseeing," he suggested, giving Mandy a pleading look in the hope that she wouldn't argue. "The last time you girls were in Charleston, Mom and Dad brought you. You were pretty young."

"I was old enough," Carrie said. "It's boring."

Carter felt his last nerve close to snapping. "Okay, since you haven't liked any of my suggestions, what would you like to do, Carrie?"

"We might as well go home," she mumbled.

"No," Mandy protested. "We're here. I want to do something fun. Come on, Carter. Just because old sourpuss is in a bad mood, it shouldn't spoil the day for the rest of us. Let's at least go to the market downtown where the vendors have all that cool stuff. We can probably find someplace to eat, too."

"Works for me," he said, silently agreeing with her that to give in to Carrie's mood would be sending the wrong message. She'd just have to get it together and deal.

He wove through the crowded streets until he finally found a parking place.

"I'll stay in the car," Carrie announced.

He turned and frowned at her. "No, you won't. I can't make you enjoy yourself, but you *will* come with us."

"You've turned into nothing but a big bully," she accused. "I wish Mom and Dad were still here." And then she burst into tears.

Before he could think of what to say, Mandy scrambled out of the front passenger seat and jumped into the back to hug her sister. "I miss them, too," she whispered, burying her face in Carrie's shoulder.

They sat like that for a while until Carrie's sobs quieted. When they separated, Carter handed her a fistful of tissues.

"Feel better?" he asked gently.

She nodded, her expression chagrined. "I'm sorry I've been such a pain all day."

"Nothing new," Mandy taunted, poking her in the ribs with an elbow.

A smile finally broke through on Carrie's face. "You'll pay for that, squirt. You have to use your allowance to buy me the first thing I see that I want."

"Okay," Mandy said agreeably. She grabbed Carrie's hand and dragged her out of the car.

Carter watched as they started toward the market, then sighed. Was he ever going to figure out how to deal with two teenage girls and their mood swings, much less Carrie's eating disorder? His appreciation for what parents everywhere had to cope with had increased a hundredfold since his parents' deaths.

He glanced skyward. "Forgive me," he murmured, hoping his folks could hear. "I apologize for every moment of grief I ever gave you."

And then he went to catch up with his sisters.

Raylene listened as Carter described Carrie's outburst earlier in the day. He'd left the girls at home watching a video, then dropped by to see her to bring her a pair of earrings he'd picked up from a jewelry vendor.

"The girls told me they'd go with your eyes," he said of the lapis stones.

Raylene chuckled at the admission that the girls had made the choice. "Did you even have any idea what color my eyes are?" she teased.

"Sure, blue," he said.

"Which can cover anything from gray-blue to turquoise or dark blue," she said.

His gaze narrowed. "Is the eye-color thing a test of some kind?"

"Maybe."

"Well, all I know is that when I used to look into your eyes I'd see nothing but sadness, and now I see a whole range of emotions."

"Such as?"

"Right now I see laughter lurking in there. Sometimes there's joy, sometimes annoyance..." He grinned. "And when you're not censoring yourself, I see desire. Or maybe that's just my ego playing tricks on me."

She hesitated, not sure she was willing to have this discussion. "It's true," she finally admitted. "I want you, Carter, at least a part of me does."

"And the rest?"

Now that the door had been opened, she might as well

be completely honest. "The rest of me is scared of wanting you too much."

His mouth curved. "Is there such a thing?"

"Typical male," she accused, then explained, "Wanting something—someone—this much is new to me."

"You were obviously in love with your husband at one time."

"I was a teenager with stars in my eyes. Believe me, that feeling died in a hurry. This is different. It feels real and full of possibilities."

"You're being very careful to avoid putting a label on it," he noted.

She grinned. "Yes, I am." Because if she called it what she thought it was—love—the stakes of getting it wrong would increase a thousandfold.

He studied her intently. "Is this really about the emotions, or is it about the intimacy?" he asked.

"Both," she conceded. "Don't you remember what happened a few weeks ago when you put your arm around me?"

He waved off the incident. "I took you by surprise, that's all. I've kissed you since then and you were fine with it. In fact, I'd say it went very well."

"Very well," she agreed.

"And just the other day, you reached out to me. It's obvious, to me anyway, that you're starting to trust me not to do anything you don't want me to do."

"I do trust you," she said. "But I can't predict when all those ingrained fears are likely to kick in. What if it happens at the wrong moment? Talk about a mood killer."

He studied her intently, then asked, "Do you feel as if I'm pressuring you for sex?"

"No, absolutely not. You've been wonderful. You've been

incredibly patient, but come on, Carter. Every man expects to have sex sooner or later with the woman he's seeing."

"*Hopes* for," he corrected. "And I do want you, but there's no rush, Raylene. When it comes to that, you're in charge of the timetable."

Raylene regarded him with a sense of wonder. "Do you have any idea how amazing you are?"

His lips twitched. "Maybe I'm one of those fully evolved men you women are always hoping to find."

"You are," she concurred. "I'm so lucky you came into my life."

He shook his head. "I'm the lucky one." He hesitated, then asked, "Can I tell you something?"

She nodded. "Of course. Anything."

"I used to basically roar through life, dating any woman who appealed to me, never thinking for a minute about the next day or the next week, much less the future. I didn't have the patience to stay with any woman for long. I got bored pretty easily."

"In other words, you were a typical bachelor," she said.

"Pretty much," he agreed. "And then my folks died. Not only was that devastating and a huge wake-up call that life doesn't last forever, but I suddenly had this huge responsibility. It was overwhelming."

"But you've coped with it," she said. "You've adapted and changed your life to do what's best for your sisters."

He shook his head. "You're wrong. I didn't adapt all that well, to be honest. At least not at first. I was resentful. I was furious with God for taking my parents and leaving me to figure out how to relate in a totally new way to Carrie and Mandy. I was impatient with them, even though I knew they were grieving. I was barely getting from one day to the next.

I was scared all the time that I'd mess things up. Still am. But now I'm here. That helped, just settling in this town."

He looked into her eyes. "And then I met you."

"A blessing or a curse?" she asked, her heart in her throat.

"How can you even ask that? You're the biggest blessing in my life. You've grounded me. You've provided backup when I need it."

He hesitated, then traced the curve of her cheek with a touch so gentle, so filled with yearning, that it nearly brought her to tears.

His gaze locked with hers. "You've taught me patience, which is pretty darn close to a miracle in my book."

"I've done all that?" she asked, incredulous.

"And more," he said. "Because of you, I have a lot more faith that I'm going to get through what's going on with Carrie, that she will get healthy again."

His hand still rested against her cheek, his gaze held steady. "So, if you need time, you've got it, because I know with every fiber of my being that you're worth it."

Walter had been communicating with Rory Sue by e-mail and through voice messages. He was very proud of the way he'd managed to avoid any tempting face-to-face contact with her for a couple of weeks now.

Unfortunately, if the goal had been to get her out of his head, it had failed abysmally. She was there 24–7, taunting him like one of those mythical Sirens who supposedly lured ships to crash against rocky cliffs. She was certainly playing havoc with his resolve.

He was sitting alone in Rosalina's, alone with yet another pizza and a beer, when Sarah slid into the booth opposite him. "This is just downright pitiful," she said, regarding him with a knowing expression.

"What?" he asked defensively.

"You in here all alone when you know you'd rather be on a date with Rory Sue." Before he could reply, she went on. "I'm not a big fan of hers, but even I can see the sparks between you two. Why aren't you doing anything about it?"

He gave her an odd look. "It feels really weird to be discussing my love life, or lack thereof, with my ex-wife."

"Oh, get over yourself. We used to be friends, too, when you weren't so busy being hateful to me."

He smiled at her newfound ability to call things as she saw them. "You've changed."

"I certainly hope so. Now, tell me why you're here all alone instead of with her."

"Because of you, to be honest."

She looked taken aback by the claim. "Come on. We've been over for a very long time."

He grinned. "But our marriage left a lasting impression," he said. "I blew it big-time with you. I've been sort of hoping not to do that again."

She looked confused. "So your plan is to, what? Avoid all women?"

"Heaven forbid," he said. "No, I'm just trying not to rush into anything the way I did with you. I fell head over heels the day we met and never looked back."

"It went both ways, you know."

He nodded. "And look how that turned out."

She gave his hand a sympathetic squeeze. "The problem isn't that we fell in love, Walter. It's that we didn't try hard enough to make it last. Honestly, it's sort of sweet the way you give your heart so easily, instead of running scared the way a lot of men do. Now you just have to learn to work through the rough patches." She grinned, then added, "And maybe avoid your parents."

He laughed. "I'm thinking that last one is the critical point."

"So, give Rory Sue a call. Just because you get involved with her doesn't mean you have to rush straight into marriage. Take your time."

"Why do you sound as if there's some urgency to this?"

"Because if I know one thing about Rory Sue, it's that she's not a patient woman. If you keep her at arm's length for too long, she'll find some other man who won't."

"Then it wasn't meant to be, was it?"

She sighed at his obstinance. "Is that what you're doing, testing her? Because if it is, you're going to lose, Walter. And it won't be because she doesn't care for you. It'll be because she believes you don't love her. Playing games is a waste of time. Only immature fools do it." She met his gaze. "Except when it came to me, you're no fool."

She walked away to rejoin Travis across the room, leaving him with plenty to think about. But, instead of thinking, he grabbed his cell phone and dialed.

"Hey, Rory Sue," he said, brightening at the welcome he heard in her voice. "You interested in meeting me at Rosalina's? I'll have the pizza and beer waiting."

"I have a better idea," she said at once. "Why don't you bring it over here. My folks are out of town with the baby. We'll have the whole house to ourselves."

His head wanted to refuse, but this time, with Sarah's words echoing, he went with his heart. "I'll be right there."

He just prayed he wouldn't regret it in the morning.

CHAPTER SEVENTEEN

In an effort to keep busy, Raylene tackled the job she most hated in the kitchen, cleaning out the refrigerator. Too many leftovers got ignored until they turned into something unidentifiable. Wrinkling her nose, she was tossing the contents of yet another disposable container when there was a tentative knock on the kitchen door. When she opened it, she found Mandy outside, her face streaked with tears.

"Can I come in?" she asked, her voice hoarse from crying.

At Raylene's nod, she all but threw herself into Raylene's arms.

"Carrie won't even speak to me," she said between great, gulping sobs. "We promised to stick together and now she thinks I've betrayed her. I'm her sister and she hates me!"

"She doesn't hate you," Raylene soothed, urging her into a chair. She pulled her own chair close and held on tightly to Mandy's hands as she looked into her eyes. "Right now she's mad at the world. She doesn't want to admit she has an eating disorder, so she's blaming everyone else because she has to see a psychologist. You do know this is the very best thing for her, right?"

"I guess," Mandy said with a sniff. "It's just that we've al-

ways been a team, just the two of us, even before Mom and
Dad died. Carter was gone, but we had each other's backs,
you know?"

"I never had a sister or brother, so I don't know firsthand,
but I always had Sarah and Annie. It was a little bit like that
with the three of us. We stuck up for each other. And when
I was in trouble, even though it had been a long time since
we'd been in touch, they were still the ones I turned to. I
knew I could count on them."

"So you get it," Mandy said. "Why doesn't Carrie see she
can count on me? Instead, it's like I don't even exist for her
anymore."

"That's temporary, I promise," Raylene consoled her.
"Carrie will get her feet back under her. She'll figure out
that you and Carter were both doing what's best for her. She'll
forgive you, and then things will go back to being the way
they used to be between you."

Mandy heaved a sigh. "I hope so." She regarded Raylene
with a wistful expression. "Do you think I could work in
your garden for a while? I know Carrie was supposed to help
you, but I need something to do, and gardening makes me
feel better. I've already yanked out pretty much everything
I could in ours at home."

"Gardening always made me feel better, too," Raylene
said. "Go on out there and weed to your heart's content. Be
careful not to stay outside too long, though. It's a scorcher
today. Take some bottled water with you."

"I'll be careful," Mandy promised, looking happier already.
"Are you sure you don't want to help? It's not far and I'd be
right there with you."

Raylene hesitated. She had been out twice now with Dr.
McDaniels, and it had gone well both times. Did she dare risk
it with Mandy? What if she had a meltdown? If she at least

tried, though, it would be another step toward her recovery. And Mandy obviously needed the company.

She took a deep breath, then said, "You know, I think I will come with you. Let me get us a couple of drinks and I'll be right out."

Mandy's expression brightened. "Really? You'll come?"

"I'm going to give it my best shot."

"Cool. Do I need to do anything, you know, to make it easier?"

Raylene smiled at her eagerness to help. "No. Just having you here should help." Her expression sobered. "Mandy, if I start hyperventilating or having one of my panic attacks, will you be okay? I don't want to scare you to death."

Mandy straightened. "Just tell me what to do."

"Take my hand and help me back inside. That's all. I'll be fine."

"Got it," Mandy said confidently and bounded outside, as if the prospect of Raylene having a panic attack was no big deal.

Raylene grabbed two bottled waters and followed her onto the patio, albeit more slowly. She joined Mandy at the edge of the garden, kneeling on the warm ground and carefully pulling the nearby weeds. The sun soaking into her shoulders felt wonderful. The air was steamy, but filled with the heady scent of roses.

Beside her, Mandy was quiet, concentrating on pulling weeds, not flowers. Even though she worked quickly, it was evident how careful she was being not to harm the flowers.

Even though Raylene felt the familiar comfort of nurturing such beautiful plants, she envied Mandy the ability to lose herself in the simple task. A part of Raylene kept waiting for the first wave of panic to hit. When it didn't, even after a half hour, she told herself that staying any longer would be pushing her luck.

She stood up, eyeing what she'd accomplished with satisfaction. Mandy's efforts were even more impressive.

"You're really good at this," she told the young teenager.

Mandy looked skeptical. "It's not exactly rocket science. I'm just yanking weeds. No big deal."

"Any job is worth doing well," Raylene reminded her. "Be proud of what you do, whether it's weeding a garden or schoolwork or rocket science. I'm going in to start dinner. Laurie will be home soon with Tommy and Libby. Would you like to stay?"

Mandy's expression brightened. "Can I?"

"If it's okay with Carter, of course you can."

"I'll call him as soon as I come inside and wash up. I need a little while longer to finish." Suddenly she beamed at Raylene. "You stayed out here almost as long as me!"

Raylene grinned back at her. "I know. Pretty cool, huh?"

Back inside, she started on dinner preparations. She put together a casserole of mac and cheese with bits of onion and browned hamburger. She cringed at the thought of all the cholesterol involved, but it was the kind of comfort food kids Mandy's age still loved. With a salad, she could pretend the meal was reasonably healthy.

She'd just put the casserole into the oven to bake, when Mandy came into the house with a piece of trailing vine in her hand and a worried expression on her face. "I pulled this out, but then I realized it has these amazingly sweet little flowers on it. Is it a weed or not?"

Raylene stared at the honeysuckle with a bemused expression. She'd never noticed any in the yard before, not when she'd visited Sarah as a kid and not since she'd been back. It was usually hard to miss because it could take over in no time.

Honeysuckle had been the bane of her existence in Charleston, left over from the home's previous owner, and coming back no matter how many times she thought she'd rid the garden of the last of it. Its sweet scent and tenacity had eventually overcome her distaste for the disorder it created.

"It's honeysuckle," she told Mandy. "I have no idea where it came from. I've never seen it in the yard before."

"Blame me," Carter said, walking into the kitchen in time to overhear.

She stared at him incredulously. "You planted it? Who does that?"

He shrugged. "You talked about it being in your garden in Charleston, and then I happened to find some growing over the fence in our yard. Even though you acted like it was this huge annoyance, I thought I'd heard something in your voice. I thought maybe you actually liked the battle."

She was stunned that he'd gotten that from the one occasion when she'd mentioned her garden. It was just more evidence of what a wonder he was…a man who actually listened to the details of a conversation. "I think maybe I did like the battle," she admitted.

He gave her a sheepish look. "I had this crazy idea that if honeysuckle started taking over out back, you wouldn't be able to stand it, that you'd run out there and yank it out yourself."

Mandy was staring at both of them as if they'd gone a little crazy. "So, do I leave it in, or pull it out? There's more. It's way in back along the fence."

Raylene met Carter's gaze. He looked so hopeful, as if he'd given her more than an uncontrollable vine, as if he'd provided the lure to get her out of the house once and for all. It was a lot to expect from honeysuckle.

Then, again, perhaps there was a lesson to be learned from the plant's tenacity.

"Leave it," she said softly.

Maybe one of these days, it could do what nothing else had. If so, she'd never again regard it as a nuisance. Instead, it would become her summer miracle.

Carter watched Carrie's expression as Dr. McDaniels introduced her to the nutritionist. The woman was young and a little offbeat in a way that should have appealed to his sister, but as understanding dawned about the reason for the woman's presence, Carrie grew increasingly sullen. She turned to him.

"You knew about this, didn't you?" she accused. "You knew they were going to blindside me like this."

He nodded.

"Why didn't you warn me?" she demanded, a deep sense of betrayal in her voice.

"We both know that would have been a bad idea," he responded quietly. "You would have refused to come."

"Yes, I would have," she said, her voice rising in anger. "Because I don't need some stranger monitoring every bite of food I put into my mouth."

Carter held her gaze. "Yes, you do."

Dr. McDaniels had allowed the exchange to run its course before stepping in. "Carrie, I know that deep down you know you need someone to help you develop a healthier eating pattern. You've turned food into an enemy. If that behavior keeps up, it will make you very ill."

"And I'll die," Carrie said flatly. "Yeah, I've heard it before."

The nutritionist sat down beside her. "And what? You don't believe that's a possibility?"

"Maybe I *want* to die!" Carrie retorted, shocking Carter so badly he felt himself turning numb.

The two professionals, however, took her angry words in stride.

"Because then you'd be with your mom and dad, right?" Dr. McDaniels asked gently.

Tears flowed down Carrie's cheeks as she nodded.

Carter had never felt so helpless in his life. He looked to the psychologist to see if it would be okay for him to speak. At her nod, he hunkered down in front of his sister. Because she was almost sixteen and mostly behaved in a mature way, he sometimes forgot that she was still a young girl who'd lost her mom and dad and was still struggling to find her way.

"Carrie, do you know how awful it would be for me and Mandy if we lost you?" he said, holding tight to her ice-cold hands and willing her to absorb his warmth and to feel the love he felt for her.

"You don't want me or Mandy," she said. "We messed up your life."

"You *changed* my life," he amended. "You didn't mess it up. It's so much better because the two of you are with me. I don't think I'd realized just how much I missed being with family until you and Mandy came to live with me. Nothing matters more to me than your happiness and Mandy's. It kills me to think you're so unhappy that you'd rather die than be with us."

"But we're a lot of trouble," she argued. "Especially me."

"Which is why we're here. Do you think if I didn't care about you, I'd be insisting on this therapy? You have such an amazing, bright future ahead of you. I want you to get better and experience every minute of it. I want to be there when you graduate from college, and I want to dance at your wedding, and then come to the inaugural ball when you get to be president!"

She stared at him incredulously, then to his delight, she giggled. The sound was something he'd almost forgotten.

"I think you can cross that last one off your list," she said, then whispered, "But I do want you to dance with me at my wedding."

"Then you need to believe that Dr. McDaniels and the nutritionist are going to help make sure that happens," he told her. "Will you please, please listen to them, instead of fighting them every step of the way?"

She blinked back a fresh batch of tears. "You won't give up on me?"

"Never," he said fiercely. "You, me and Mandy, we're a team. I know it was always just the two of you, but I'm here now, and I am always on your side. If one of us is in trouble, the other two will be there. That's the way it works. I promise."

She threw herself off the chair and into his arms. "I love you, Carter."

She felt so fragile and thin in his arms, he was almost scared to hug her too tightly, but he did. She needed to feel the strength of his love, to believe in it. Right now, it was all he had to give her.

Because Carrie's recovery was at such a critical stage, Carter knew he needed to monitor every meal. He couldn't rely on Mandy to do it. He didn't want her in the position of becoming a tattletale against her sister. Even though Carrie now seemed to grasp that the program was meant to help her, she still had more than a few moments when she rebelled angrily against being watched so closely.

After taking a couple of days off so he could keep a closer eye on his sister, he finally managed to make a quick stop at Raylene's to fill her in on what was going on. "If I don't get by here as much, it's not because I don't want to," he assured her.

"It's just that right now Carrie needs you," she said, her voice filled with understanding, though her expression had turned bleak as he talked. "If there's anything I can do, let me know."

"I think we need to handle this as a family," he said, and watched as a light died in Raylene's eyes.

"Of course," she murmured.

He knew at once that he should have chosen his words more carefully, but he didn't have time now to explain. Even as they sat there, he could feel her pulling away from him without moving an inch. Frustrated and torn, he struggled with the decision that had brought him over here.

"Let me explain. Carrie's in a real crisis, Raylene. It's even worse than I thought." When Carrie had even hinted that she wanted to die, it had terrified him. He felt he had to be there every minute until he knew with a hundred percent certainty that she was on a path to a full recovery and not sinking into a despair that could take her away from him forever.

"Carter, believe me, I get that," she said.

"I'll call you so much, you'll probably get sick of hearing from me," he promised, knowing it was small consolation for the visits that they'd both come to count on.

She regarded him doubtfully.

Aware that he was running out right when he needed to stay and reassure her that this was only temporary, he glanced at his watch and knew he had no choice. He was on duty in a half hour.

"Look, I have to run, but I'll speak to you later." He kissed her thoroughly, well aware that there was a hint of sadness and desperation in the way she kissed him back. He looked into her eyes. "This isn't forever."

"I know," she said, but she didn't look as if she believed it. "It's probably for the best."

He stopped in midstride and turned to face her. "What does that mean?"

"Carrie has a hard road ahead of her. Naturally she deserves your attention. You don't need the kind of complication that I'd bring into your life. Maybe we should just admit that and move on."

He stared at her incredulously. "You want to break up?"

"Oh, Carter," she said sorrowfully. "We've never really been together."

"Hold on a minute! Why are you saying this now? What's happened?" He raked his hand through his hair in frustration. "Dammit, I know I've said this all wrong." He glanced at his watch again and muttered another curse. "I can't argue with you about this now, but I will be back. You and me, we are *not* over!"

But as he looked back, he saw that his words had had absolutely no impact. She looked resigned to the idea that their relationship had come to an end. If he'd had even one more minute to spare, he would have gone back and tried to reason with her, but there was no time.

And, if he were being truthful, there was also very little hope that he would succeed.

"You broke up with Carter," Sarah echoed, a stunned note in her voice.

Raylene nodded. "It was for the best. He can't deal with me and my issues right now. He has to focus on his sister."

"Ever heard of multitasking?" Sarah demanded. "In today's world, most of us can do it. I bet Carter is an excellent multitasker. Look how well he's handling being a deputy and working with Tom to get the Serenity police force to become a reality."

"This is different," Raylene said stubbornly. "Besides, those are just two more critical things besides Carrie that he has on his plate. He doesn't need one more. And I need to focus on my own recovery. After that..." She shrugged.

"After that what?"

"Maybe we can try again," Raylene said.

"I don't get it. You're getting better. You're out in the yard almost every day now. You and Mandy are getting close. Think what this will do to her."

"She'll still be welcome here anytime."

"And do you honestly think she'll want to come if she finds out you've dumped her brother? You've become a real support system for her, and now you're letting her down."

Raylene hadn't looked at it that way. In fact, she hadn't really thought about anything other than the overwhelmed expression on Carter's face when he'd stopped by. She'd thought letting him off the hook was an unselfish gesture. And he was the one who'd turned down her offer of help, who'd said they needed to handle it as a family. He'd shut her out.

"You really think I've made a mistake, don't you?" she asked Sarah.

"Oh, yeah. You have this perfectly wonderful, caring man in your life and you blow him off and somehow twist that around so you're doing him a favor? I don't think so. And if you don't believe me, let's get the Sweet Magnolias over here and see what they have to say."

"I thought I was letting him go so he could do what he needed to do to support Carrie. I thought it was a generous gesture."

"A generous gesture would be supporting him, standing

by him, listening to him when he needs to vent," Sarah retorted. "Who's he supposed to count on now?"

Raylene winced. "When you put it that way, I feel like an idiot."

"Then apologize the first chance you get," Sarah advised. "In the meantime, I'm calling Annie and the others. I want reinforcements in case you get cold feet and start thinking about not making that call."

An hour later the house was filled with Sweet Magnolias, strong opinions and even stronger margaritas.

To Raylene's dismay all of them agreed with Sarah that she'd made an impulsive decision she was going to regret.

"If I were you, I'd call him first thing in the morning and tell him you're sorry, that you didn't mean it," Annie said.

As Annie spoke, she cradled baby Meg in her arms. Even though Meg was nearly six months old, Annie had refused to leave her at home with Trevor and the sitter. Jeanette had brought along her baby boy as well. All these babies were reminding Raylene of yet another thing she'd lost. Now, according to every one of these women, she was on the verge of losing Carter as well.

Listening to them, she'd grown defensive all over again. She turned to Annie. "You walked away from Ty when you found out about Dee-Dee and the baby," Raylene reminded her.

Annie regarded her incredulously. "Surely you're not comparing the two situations. Ty betrayed me. I didn't leave so he could focus on his new little family. I left because I was spitting mad that he'd been cheating on me. All Carter wanted was a little time to help his sister. For that, you dumped him."

Raylene sighed. "He's the one who shut me out. I offered to help."

"He chose his words poorly," Annie scoffed. "He didn't mean he didn't want your help."

Raylene looked around at the others. "You all really think I blew it?"

"I certainly do," Sarah said emphatically.

"Me, too," Annie said.

Raylene turned to Maddie, Helen, Dana Sue and Jeanette. All were older and, perhaps, a bit wiser. "Any help from the rest of you?"

"Sorry, sweetie, but no," Dana Sue said. "It's not that I think you were being selfish. I don't think that was your intention at all. I think you were a little overly sensitive when he made that comment and that you really thought you were giving Carter an out he needed."

"But it was kind of presumptuous," Jeanette chimed in. "He didn't ask for an out. He's a grown man. If he'd wanted to call it quits, he'd have done that, instead of just asking for a little leeway during a difficult time."

"Exactly," Maddie said.

Only Helen, so far, had remained silent. Raylene focused on her. "Any thoughts?"

"I think maybe we've all been concentrating so hard on how Carter will take this and how unfair it is to him, we've missed the point," Helen said.

Maddie groaned. "Here it comes. We're going to get the totally rational, analytical interpretation now."

Helen scowled at Maddie over the rim of her margarita glass. "Go suck an egg," she said cheerfully. "As I was saying, maybe we've all been missing the fact that Raylene did this because it's what's best for her."

She turned her intense gaze on Raylene. "Is it? Is there some reason, besides what we've been discussing, that you want to end the relationship? Did this just happen to give you the perfect excuse?"

Raylene sat back, stunned by the question. Could Helen be right? Had the whole idea of a relationship with Carter gotten to be too much? Had she started feeling the pressure of trying to get back to a normal life for his sake? Maybe so.

When she remained silent, Helen gave her a sympathetic look. "I thought so," she said, no trace of triumph in her voice. "You obviously need time just as badly as he does, though for different reasons."

All six women in the room started talking at once, arguing the validity of Helen's analysis. The noise was giving Raylene a headache. Since they were so busy debating with each other, she slipped from the room, retreating to the kitchen.

No sooner had she flipped on the light than there was a tap on the door that scared her half to death. She saw Carter standing there. Even with only the glow of moonlight illuminating him, she could see how exhausted he looked. Right this second, despite everything that had happened earlier, she was surprisingly glad to see him.

"I saw you had company, so I came around back, hoping to catch you alone for a second," he said. "I won't stay."

"It's okay. They're in there debating just how insane I was for breaking up with you," she admitted, her expression rueful.

He looked startled at first, then amused. "Any consensus?"

She met his gaze. "My opinion's the only one that counts."

"And?"

"I still think it was the right decision, but I don't think I was entirely honest with you. Could we talk about it some more, when you have some time?"

"Then you're not closing the door on us, after all?" he asked hopefully.

"I'm leaving it ajar," she confirmed. "Just a crack."

He gave a nod of satisfaction. "That'll do for now." He pressed a quick kiss to her cheek. "I'll be by again first chance I get."

"I'm sure I'll be here," she said wryly.

After he'd gone, she leaned against the door and sighed. The fact that he'd come over, even braved dealing with a houseful of Sweet Magnolias to try to make things right, told her just how deep his commitment to her ran.

Now, as Helen had guessed, Raylene needed to determine if hers was strong enough to withstand all the odds against them or if she'd been the one who'd been looking for an easy way out of a relationship she wanted, but was too scared to fight for.

CHAPTER EIGHTEEN

It was nearly a week before Carter found time in his schedule to plan a visit to Raylene. He called every chance he got, relieved to find that their conversations, though brief, were as friendly as they'd always been. Whatever had been going on with her the other day seemed to have passed, or she was getting better at disguising her feelings.

On Friday, he was working an early shift, which meant he got off midafternoon. Carrie was working at Wharton's, which she'd opted to do after her falling-out with Raylene. Mandy had gone swimming at a friend's house. He had at least a couple of hours to himself before he needed to be home to supervise dinner.

He took time to shower and put on jeans and a freshly ironed shirt before going to see Raylene. He even used a bit of the aftershave Mandy had given him for his birthday, then rolled his eyes at his own behavior. He was acting like a kid going on his first date, trying to make a good impression. Surely he and Raylene were past that stage. He was pretty sure the issue at this point wasn't whether they cared, but whether it was enough to overcome all the obstacles each of them were facing.

As proof that his efforts had been a bit over the top, Raylene sniffed the air when he walked into the kitchen, then smiled knowingly.

"Are you trying to impress someone?" she asked.

"You, as a matter of fact."

"Well, consider my socks knocked off," she said lightly. "Can I get you something to drink?"

He glanced at her bare feet with the very sexy red toenails and grinned. "Boy, I must be good."

"As if you didn't know that," she said. "A drink? Did you want something?"

"Sweet tea will do," he said.

She poured two glasses. "Shall we sit in here or in the living room?" She took a deep breath, then said, "Or we could sit on the patio. Thanks to Mandy's company I've been out there every day recently."

Carter regarded her with surprise. "She didn't say a word."

"I think she's become very protective of me and she understands from Dr. McDaniels that pressure doesn't help. You counting on my improvement would add pressure."

"Would you rather stay in, then?"

"I actually think I'd like to show off. Let's go outside."

"Can I sit next to you on the glider?" he asked hopefully.

"If you want to," she said, then arched a brow. "Are you hoping to take advantage of me, Carter?"

He studied her expression, startled by her teasing. "You're in a very odd mood this afternoon. Did your session with Dr. McDaniels go especially well today?"

She shook her head. "About the same."

"Was there some other news?"

"Nope. I just woke up feeling particularly cheerful, and nothing's happened so far to ruin my mood."

He grinned. "I sense a warning in there."

"Not at all."

She stepped confidently outside and took a seat on the glider. Carter hesitated, then sat down right beside her. "Okay?"

"Sure."

He considered just going with this unexpected mood of hers and seeing where the afternoon took them, but he wasn't the kind of man who liked putting off confrontations when they were inevitable. "I thought we should talk about what happened the other day," he said eventually.

"We probably should," she agreed, then met his gaze. "I'm really sorry if it seemed that I was dumping you just to get even with you. I really did understand why you needed to pull back so you'd have more time for Carrie. The truth is, I thought I needed some space for myself to focus on my own recovery without the pressure of wanting to be normal for you."

Carter had suspected—maybe even hoped—it was something like that. "I can understand why you might have been feeling rushed, but I swear I never meant to put pressure on you."

"You haven't," she said candidly. "I've been putting it on myself, partly because I worry that you're too good to be true."

"Me? In what way?"

"You've been incredibly patient. Most men aren't. I worry that you'll get tired of it."

"Never."

"There's more," she told him. "I think I magnify every failure because it means I'm no closer to the goal of being the kind of woman who's right for you."

"But you *are* right for me," he protested.

"Not the way I am now," she insisted stubbornly. "Come

on. You already have Carrie to worry about. It's not fair to ask you to take on my problems, too."

"But look at how much better you are already," he said, gesturing around at the garden to remind her of how far she'd come, quite literally.

"The fact that I can sit outside with you is enough?" she asked skeptically.

He reached for her, then pulled back. "Don't you know how much I count on you? That's what matters."

"But when it came to Carrie, you said you needed to handle it as a family."

He sighed. He'd known that off-the-cuff comment was going to come back to bite him in the butt. "I never meant to shut you out or to imply that we don't need you."

"But that's how I felt, excluded and unable to contribute anything to Carrie's recovery."

"I'm sorry."

"It's so frustrating to me not to be able to be there for her, to be there for all of you."

"But you have been there for all of us," he said, mystified by her determination to minimize her role in their lives. "Right now, this time you're spending with Mandy is as good for her as it apparently has been for you. With so much attention focused on Carrie, it would be easy for Mandy to feel neglected. That's one less thing I need to worry about right now. Can't you see how you've stepped in and taken up the slack?"

She seemed startled by his analysis. "Really?"

"Absolutely. Mandy needs a woman in her life right now, not that anyone can replace her mother, but just to give her a woman's perspective on things. You're providing that. I know you'd do the same for Carrie, if she weren't being so stubborn."

"I just feel as if I should be doing more, that you need a real partner."

"And I feel as if I have one," he said firmly.

"But Carrie needs the kind of attention I can't give her because I can't meet her on her own turf. She hasn't been back over here since that day we fought. She won't take my calls." She held up a hand when he would have interrupted. "And that's okay. She feels what she feels. But anyone else would have been able to go directly to her by now and make things right. Don't you see? I'm the grown-up. It's up to me to fix this and I can't do it because I'm locked away in this house."

"All I see is that you're beating yourself up for something that's not your fault. Carrie's not your responsibility. She's my problem, not yours."

Raylene looked as if he'd slapped her. He knew at once that he'd said exactly the wrong thing...again. This time, though, he rushed to correct his mistake.

"I didn't mean that the way it sounded, as if you aren't important. You are."

"I understood exactly what you were saying," she said. "And you confirmed my point, that you have to protect poor Raylene from having to deal with the tough stuff."

"I did not say that," he said, thoroughly frustrated at having the conversation veer wildly offtrack again.

"You might as well have. I think you should go now."

"We're not finished talking about this."

"I am," she said quietly, standing up. "I'm sorry, Carter. My instincts were right. We're not good for each other right now. Maybe that will change down the road, but right now, it's best if we go our separate ways and deal with our own problems."

"Dammit all, Raylene, this is crazy," he protested.

"Haven't you heard? I *am* crazy."

"Oh, for Pete's sake, you are not crazy," he said impatiently. "No one, least of all me, thinks that. You are, however, the most stubborn, ornery woman with whom I've ever crossed paths."

"How flattering," she said sarcastically.

He was so outraged that things between them were going to end like this that he impulsively pulled her into his arms and kissed her. Normally he would never have grabbed her like that, but he was too far past frustrated to think straight.

She went perfectly still for the space of a heartbeat, clearly shocked by the kiss, then she started to struggle. The instant he realized that the whimper in her throat was fear, not pleasure, he released her and muttered a curse directed at himself. He dragged a hand through his hair as he looked into her panicked eyes. Though he wanted to reach for her, he kept his arms at his sides.

"I'm so sorry," he said, his tone filled with self-disgust. "I didn't stop to think what a sudden move like that would do to you. I was just trying to get through to you how much I care about you."

Though she'd wrapped her arms around herself to stop herself from shaking, she nodded. "I know that." She met his gaze, her expression filled with weariness. "Can you see now why this is never going to work? I can't even respond to a kiss the way I should."

"Don't say never," he pleaded. "I'll give you time, if that's what you want, but don't say you'll never be ready to try again."

"Carter, it's hopeless," she said, sounding utterly defeated.

"I refuse to accept that."

Her lips curved slightly. "Now who's being stubborn?"

He managed to pull a carefree grin from somewhere deep inside. "Which makes us a perfect match, if you ask me."

He walked her to the door, then waited until she'd stepped inside. "I'll be in touch, Raylene. We're not over."

But as he walked slowly back to his car, thinking about just how badly the afternoon had gone, he couldn't help wondering if he wasn't deluding himself.

Raylene was a wreck. She hadn't slept a wink all night, so she was in no mood to spend an hour with Dr. McDaniels rehashing her marriage or even talking about the mess her relationship with Carter was in.

For just one second when he'd kissed her the day before, she'd let herself feel all the emotion and desperation that he'd poured into that kiss. She'd experienced once-familiar sensations...joy, yearning, passion. Oh, how she wanted all that! It had felt almost within her grasp.

And then fear had crowded out all those normal responses. It wasn't Carter, the man she trusted, holding her. It was another man, whose grasp had been meant to intimidate and hurt. God, was she never going to get past what Paul had done to her?

"You look exhausted," Dr. McDaniels said when she arrived. "Is everything okay?"

"In my life?" Raylene asked bitterly. "Please. Nothing is okay."

"Tell me about it," the psychologist suggested in the patient, cajoling tone that scraped Raylene's last nerve.

"Why bother?"

"Because if we don't get to the bottom of things, you're not going to get better."

"I am better," Raylene contradicted, choosing to focus on her recent strides for a change. Maybe she'd come as far as she could.

The doctor lifted a brow. "You're content to sit on the patio? That's not the life you told me you wanted."

Raylene sighed. "No, it's not," she agreed.

"Okay, then. Let's get busy. We'll try a new approach today," Dr. McDaniels suggested. "There's something we've never really discussed. Why don't you tell me about your mother."

"How very Freudian," Raylene responded. "Are we going to start blaming everything that's gone wrong in my life on my parents now? Come on. We both know Paul is responsible for this mess."

"He's certainly responsible for the abuse," the psychologist agreed. "But maybe not for how you've handled it."

Despite her doubts, Raylene couldn't help being intrigued by the theory. "Meaning?"

"First, humor me. Tell me about your mother. You've mentioned she wasn't supportive when you told her about the abuse, but before that. Was she a good mother? A loving person you could turn to with your problems?"

Raylene had to stop and actually think about the questions. All she could recall was how bitterly her mother had complained for years about being stuck in a nothing little town like Serenity. Compared to Dana Sue, who'd welcomed all of Annie's friends with warmth, Raylene's mother hadn't much wanted anyone around. She'd deliberately isolated herself from most people in town.

"Not really," she said slowly. "She was fairly self-absorbed. She was miserable with my dad, who was a great guy whose only flaw as far as I could see was that he wouldn't give in and move to Charleston. My mother hated it here."

"Why didn't they divorce?"

"To be honest, I have no idea," Raylene admitted. "I'm sure they'd have been happier if they had."

"You never asked your mother about that? Or your dad?"

"No, I think I was always too scared that they *would* get a divorce. I loved my dad. I was afraid if my mother left him, I'd have to go with her to Charleston."

"And yet, in the end, that's exactly where you did go."

Raylene had never looked at it like that, as if she'd chosen the path her mother wanted but couldn't have. Ironically, it had been her decision to marry Paul and live in Charleston that had finally allowed her mother to get her way. Her father had agreed to retire and move there, as well. He'd wanted to be there for the grandchildren he'd hoped would come along someday.

"What was it like growing up with a mother who made it so plain she didn't want to be here, who diminished a world where I assume you were happy?"

Raylene thought back to her childhood. What she remembered most was the tension. It never ended. She could barely recall a time when she'd heard her parents teasing each other or laughing. Instead, there'd been either cold silence or heated fighting. She'd walked on eggshells around them, trying not to make things worse. The only times she'd relaxed had been when she was at school or with Sarah and Annie.

"It was scary," Raylene said. "I never knew what to expect. The only time I can remember being really happy was when my dad would take me places. We went to Myrtle Beach once and to Walt Disney World another time."

Dr. McDaniels, usually so good at maintaining a neutral facade, looked startled. "Just you and your dad? Your mother didn't go?"

Even Raylene was surprised when she realized the oddity of what she'd said. "No, she didn't go with us."

"What about trips to see your grandparents? Did she go on those?"

"My grandparents usually came here," she recalled, beginning to see a pattern she'd never even noticed as a child.

"Raylene, is it possible your mother was agoraphobic?"

The significance of the question stunned her, but even as the words registered, she knew it was entirely possible based on what she'd learned about the panic disorder. Other than maybe her first couple of years in school, when her mother had walked with her to kindergarten and first grade, she couldn't recall a single occasion when they'd gone anywhere together, not to Wharton's, or dinner, or a movie. Nowhere.

"Oh my God," she whispered. "You could be right."

"And if I am, then doesn't it make sense that when confronted with a situation like your abuse, you've reacted in a way that seemed perfectly normal and familiar to you? You shut yourself inside."

"But she did move to Charleston," Raylene said.

"Did she start going out once she was there?"

"Some," Raylene recalled. "Not so much at first, but after a while, yes."

"Then perhaps, because she was finally where she thought she belonged, she stopped punishing your father by closing herself off from the world."

Raylene tried to sort through what the doctor was saying. "So in her case, it might not have been about fear?"

"I can't say with certainty, since I've never spoken to her, but sometimes it doesn't matter how the pattern starts— from a history of abuse like yours or in some sort of passive-aggressive attempt to hurt someone, which is what I suspect your mother might have done. In the end, the result is the same. You stay inside for a day or a week, then longer until it becomes a way of life. You're locked away from the world and you can't break the cycle without help of some kind."

Though Raylene was blown away by what they'd discovered, she regarded Dr. McDaniels with bewilderment. "How does knowing this help? I doubt I'm going to spring up from this chair and run into downtown Serenity."

Dr. McDaniels allowed herself a smile. "You could try. Who knows what might happen."

"Seriously, I don't see what difference it makes that we've figured this out," Raylene said, her momentary excitement now lost to reality.

"Do you think your mother would come over here to participate in a session?"

"I doubt it."

"Not even if she understood how important it is? I could speak to her myself and explain what's happening."

"I don't know if I want to see her," Raylene admitted. "I haven't forgiven her for not listening when I told her about Paul. Maybe if she had, things wouldn't have gotten as bad as they did."

"All the more reason to have her come. You need to clear the air." She met Raylene's gaze. "May I call her?"

"I guess," she said reluctantly.

"Good. I'm proud of you. We've had a real breakthrough here today."

Raylene understood why the doctor sounded so excited, but she felt no differently than she had before the so-called breakthrough. What she needed was a miracle. Because if one didn't come along soon, she was going to lose the one person who might be able to give her the life she'd always dreamed of.

Carter hated the idea of using his sisters to worm his way back into Raylene's life, but since Carrie's situation was part of the problem, he convinced himself she could also be part of the solution.

That night after dinner, before the girls cleared the table, he regarded them hopefully. "I need a favor," he said.

"Anything, you know that," Mandy said at once.

"Sure," Carrie said, though with more reserve.

"I'd like to have dinner with Raylene tomorrow night," he began.

Carrie immediately brightened, probably because she thought it meant he wouldn't be spying on her. "Go for it. We don't mind."

"I meant all of us," he said. "It's really important."

"It's okay with me," Mandy said. "I like Raylene. I'm over there almost every day anyway. I'll just hang around till you come."

Carrie's expression turned sullen. "You two go ahead. I'm not interested. I don't want to eat out in public with everyone staring at me."

"We won't be in public. We'll be at Raylene's."

"Same difference," Carrie insisted. "I'll stay here."

"It's all of us, or none of us," Carter told her.

"Because you don't trust me to eat on my own," Carrie said sourly.

"That's part of it, yes," he confirmed, unwilling to sugarcoat it for her. "We're still in the tough-love phase of all this."

"You said part of it," Carrie said, expressing a faint hint of the curiosity he'd counted on. "What's the rest?"

He searched for the right words. "Raylene's been feeling left out. She's really worried about you, Carrie. You haven't been over to visit recently and I've been here with you. I think it's important that we all let her know she matters to us."

Carrie looked even more suspicious. "She dumped you, didn't she?"

"I wouldn't put it that way," Carter said, his pride still a little wounded by the fact that it had been exactly that way.

"Have you been seeing her?" Carrie persisted. "I mean, since I started with Dr. McDaniels?"

"Not as often as I had been before and not at all for the past few days."

"Because she dumped you," Carrie concluded.

"We agreed we needed some space," he said, trying to spin it.

"That doesn't make sense," Mandy said. "If you're giving each other space, then why would you want to drag us over there to dinner?"

"Because, you dope, we're his intermediaries," Carrie said, her expression knowing. "He knows she won't throw us out, no matter how mad she is at him."

God save him from teens who understood too much. "It's not just that," he insisted. "I want her to feel as if she's a real part of our family." He met Carrie's gaze. "And I know she wants to make amends for what happened the last time you were over there. It's killing her that she can't come to you to apologize and that you won't take her calls. You've deliberately shut her out because you know there's nothing she can do about it."

Carrie turned pink with embarrassment. "I didn't mean to make her worry."

"I know, but that's what adults do when it comes to kids they love. We worry."

Mandy's eyes brightened. "Do you want to marry her?"

His stomach flipped over at the mention of marriage. "It's way too soon to be talking about anything like that," he said emphatically. "But I don't want to slam the door on any possibilities."

"And that's going to happen if we don't go over there and make nice," Carrie concluded.

His gaze narrowed at her choice of words. "Are you still upset with Raylene?"

"Sure I am," she said with a touch of defiance. "I'm still mad because she was in my face about my eating. It was none of her business." She sighed and backed down with another of her whirlwind mood changes. "But I wasn't trying to pay her back or anything. I don't want her to feel bad."

"You do understand that she only said something because she cares, right?"

"I guess so," Carrie said.

Carter was starting to wonder if this was a bad idea, after all. The last thing he needed if he was to get things back on track was to take Carrie over there in a belligerent frame of mind. "If we do decide to go, you're going to give her another chance, right? You'll be on good behavior?"

"Anything to keep from messing up your love life," she said sarcastically. "But if the subject of food comes up, I am out of there. I'll follow all the rules so you won't have any reason to complain about my eating in front of her, but you have to promise not to sit there and stare at me or my plate."

"We're going to take dinner," he said. "Food's bound to come up."

"You know what I mean," Carrie retorted.

"Okay, I promise we won't make an issue out of your eating," he said.

Carrie looked doubtful, but she grudgingly conceded, "Then I'm in."

"Me, too," Mandy said with more enthusiasm.

Carter sighed. Despite getting the agreement he'd wanted from both of them, he had a feeling this dinner idea of his had disaster written all over it.

CHAPTER NINETEEN

Raylene watched without comment as Carrie picked at her meal. She'd been surprised earlier when Carter and the girls had appeared at the door carrying an elaborate take-out meal from Sullivan's.

"Dana Sue said we have all your favorites," he'd said, giving her an appealing grin. "Will that get us in?"

Despite all her best intentions to keep some distance between them, she seemed to be incapable of turning him away, especially with Carrie and Mandy looking on. This was, after all, what she'd been hoping for, a chance to make amends with Carrie. She'd let them in.

With Carter overseeing the transfer of the food from take-out containers to plates, she and the girls had set the table.

"Carter misses you," Mandy confided, then got an elbow in the ribs from her big sister.

"You're not supposed to say stuff like that," Carrie told her. "It's like giving information to the enemy or something."

Mandy had looked confused. "But Raylene's not the enemy. She's Carter's girlfriend. At least he wants her to be, and we're supposed to be helping. Isn't that the whole point of being here?"

Thoroughly embarrassed and unwilling to be the center of an argument between the sisters, Raylene had ended the discussion by telling them to go in the kitchen and help Carter with the food. "I'll finish up in here."

Now they were all seated around the dining-room table making stilted conversation. And she couldn't seem to keep herself from watching the way Carrie pushed her food around on her plate. Despite the teen's sessions with Dr. McDaniels, it seemed she was still exhibiting textbook anorexic behavior. Very little of that food was making its way into her mouth. Carter, however, seemed to be oblivious to it.

Torn between ignoring the behavior and trying to make him see that Carrie was still in trouble, she finally opted for what she hoped would be a bit of subtle probing that might also catch his attention. Even as she spoke, she knew she was testing the very tentative truce established between her and Carrie. She felt she had no choice. It was more important to act responsibly than to be the good guy.

"Carrie, don't you like meat loaf?" Raylene asked. "Sullivan's has a reputation for making the best in the entire region. It's always been my favorite comfort food, along with their garlic mashed potatoes."

"It's okay," Carrie said with a shrug. "I'm just not hungry."

She shot a look at Carter that Raylene couldn't interpret.

Unwilling to let the subject go, she tried another approach, trying to reach the girl on some level. "You'd probably rather be out with your friends on a Saturday night," she suggested.

"It's not that," Mandy piped up as if to make up for her sister's lack of responsiveness. "Carrie doesn't like to eat in front of people. She's self-conscious."

Carrie's head snapped around as she glared at her little sister. "You and Carter promised we wouldn't talk about my eating tonight," she said, her voice shrill. "You promised! I should have known you wouldn't keep your promise."

Mandy turned pale, her expression miserable. "I'm sorry. I just didn't want Raylene to think you were being rude."

"Raylene knows what's going on," Carrie said. "It's practically because of her that I have to see a shrink."

"Hold on," Carter said, scowling at her. "You know that's not true. You're in therapy because it's what you need right now."

Carrie looked to be near tears. Obviously frustrated at hearing her brother deflect any blame from Raylene, she whirled on Mandy. "I'm sick of you criticizing what I eat. Maybe you should consider sticking to a few carrots and lettuce leaves before you blow up like a blimp," Carrie said, casting a meaningful look at the two slices of meat loaf and the mound of mashed potatoes on Mandy's plate.

When Carter opened his mouth to scold her, Carrie snapped, "Oh, forget it. I am so out of here."

She stood up and ran from the room. Carter turned to Raylene with an apologetic look. "I need to go after her."

Raylene felt the salty sting of tears in her eyes. "This is my fault. I'll go."

He hesitated. "But—"

"She's still in the house," Raylene told him. "I didn't hear the door. If she's gone, I'll tell you, and you can go after her."

She found Carrie in the living room, huddled in a corner of the sofa, tears streaming down her face.

"I'm sorry," Raylene said, sitting down beside her. "I pushed you, and I shouldn't have. I know this is a sensitive topic and that you're getting help. I should have left it alone."

Carrie seemed surprised by her admission. "Why didn't you?" she asked.

"I told you before about Annie. What I didn't tell you was

how many times I saw her do exactly what you were doing tonight, just pushing her food around, pretending to eat, and I did nothing. The night she collapsed, I felt as if it was all my fault for not doing more to make sure someone knew she was in trouble. Sarah felt the same way. So did Ty and the rest of her friends. I can't begin to tell you how scary it was for all of us sitting at the hospital waiting to hear whether she was going to be okay."

"So when you see me not eating, it pushes all those buttons," Carrie concluded, looking less angry. "I guess I can see why."

"It would break my heart if something happened to you," Raylene told her honestly. "Especially if I could have prevented it."

"But Carter knows. And I'm seeing Dr. McDaniels. I get that what I've been doing is wrong. I've even figured out why it was happening and I'm really trying to fix it." She regarded Raylene with an earnest expression. "Honest."

"I know that, and I am so proud of you for trying."

Carrie looked away. "It's really hard," she said in a small voice. "Harder than I ever thought it would be. And I hate that everyone's watching me all the time."

"Annie hated that, too, but it all gets easier. You'll see. And once the eating pattern really starts to change, the trust will come back. People won't watch as much."

"I don't know," Carrie said skeptically. "I saw how Dana Sue watched Annie at the barbecue, even after all this time."

"I suppose it's a worry that never entirely goes away, but that feeling that you're under a microscope will get better. I promise. And you'll start to feel like your old self, the way you did before your parents died."

"You think so?" she asked, a faint glimmer of hope in her eyes.

"You've been around Annie," Raylene said. "What do you think? Doesn't she seem perfectly fine now?"

Carrie nodded. "She seems okay."

"She *is* okay. It's still a struggle for her from time to time, but that's why she sees Dr. McDaniels whenever she feels herself slipping. She's smart enough to recognize the signs and ask for the help she needs."

Carrie sighed. "I don't know if I want to see a shrink forever."

Raylene risked giving her a hug. "Then you'll try even harder to get well, won't you?"

Carrie's lips curved slightly. "I guess it is up to me, isn't it?"

Raylene nodded. "Pretty much." She hesitated, then said, "You know, I'd really love it if you'd come by sometime with Mandy and work in the garden with us. Every time I'm out there I feel as if I'm getting stronger. Maybe you'd find it healing, as well. Or maybe you'd just enjoy being there with us. I miss talking to you."

Carrie looked surprised. "Really?"

"You're a wonderful girl, and since you're working at Wharton's, I'll bet you know everything that's going on in town. You can keep me up to date on all the local gossip."

Carrie brightened. "I could definitely do that."

"Great." She gave her a hug. "Now, how about it? Do you feel like going back in to dinner?"

"I guess," Carrie said, though with obvious reluctance.

"Come on. It won't be that bad. I promise not to say another word about your eating all night."

"And you'll tell Carter to back off when he starts trying to push dessert on me?"

Raylene nodded. "Mostly because if you're not going to eat Dana Sue's bread pudding, then I get your share."

Carrie looked startled. "It's that good?"

"It's amazing," she confirmed.

"Then maybe I'll at least have a bite."

Raylene gave her another squeeze. "Bet you'll have two."

To her relief, Carrie laughed. "I hope you and Carter get back together."

"He actually told you we broke up?" Raylene asked.

"He said you dumped him," Carrie said. "That's why we're here. He figured you'd never send me and Mandy away. He'd get a free pass to spend time with you, at least this once."

"Your brother is a very sneaky man," Raylene concluded.

"Tell me about it."

Sneaky or not, Raylene couldn't help admiring his tactics. His determination not to allow things between them to end was sweet. Annoying, but sweet.

Though the rest of the evening with Raylene and the girls had gone smoothly enough, Carter left with the distinct impression that he hadn't succeeded in proving to Raylene that they could make their relationship work.

Unfortunately, for the next couple of weeks there was virtually no time to press whatever tiny advantage he might have gained that night. In addition to his regular shifts with the sheriff's department, Carter had almost daily meetings with Tom as they prepared to make their budget proposal to the council for the new Serenity police department. Without adequate funding, it was simply impractical to move forward. He'd made that clear to Tom, who expressed confidence that they'd win the needed approval.

"This is Howard Lewis's pet project," Tom reminded him. "It's going to pass. I guarantee we'll have the funds in place, and you'll have a fully operational department by the first of the year."

Carter couldn't deny the excitement he felt at the thought.

Though dealing with all the paperwork and financial issues had been tedious, he'd loved the challenge of putting the proposal together. The only thing he worried about was whether or not he'd start to hate spending so much time in an office once things were up and running.

As if he'd read Carter's mind, Tom studied him with a knowing expression. "You thinking about how you'll miss being on the street?"

"As a matter of fact, I am. I got into police work to make a difference. I can't do that from behind a desk."

Tom grinned. "Well, here's where the joy of a small department comes in. You'll still be out there on the street. You saw how tight the scheduling is going to be with the staff we can afford. I imagine you'll be backup most days and on the streets more than you ever imagined."

Relieved, Carter nodded. "I hadn't looked at it that way. That'll be good."

"To change the subject, what's happening with Paul Hammond these days? Any word?"

"I checked this morning. His hearing was delayed. I'm not sure why, but it's pushed any possibility for release into September at the earliest."

"Doesn't Raylene have an opportunity to speak at the parole hearing?" Tom asked, then winced. "But, of course, she can't."

"She is sending over a video. Helen arranged for it. At least she'll be on record reminding the parole board what he's done to her life. Helen's asking the judge in the original case to issue a restraining order, so that will be in place the second he's released."

"Any chance it will have the desired effect?" Tom asked.

"I'm not taking any chances," Carter said grimly.

"Then I'll alert my people and the various utilities that

the work we talked about may need to be pushed back until September."

"Is that going to cause any problems?"

"Not a one. Everyone I spoke to is committed to providing extra eyes and ears on that street once he's out. Hammond won't slip into that neighborhood without us knowing about it."

Carter wished he felt as if those efforts would be enough. The days would be covered, but nights were something else. Travis had promised to be in the house most nights after he got off the air at the radio station. Walter would hang around as often as possible, too. And Carter planned to be on the street out front.

But he knew better than most that someone determined to wreak havoc could often find a way to do it, despite all the well-intentioned efforts in the world.

Raylene started shaking when Helen told her that the parole board had granted Paul's release. It was mid-September, and his release date was scheduled for the end of the month.

"I'm so sorry," Helen said, her frustration plain. She'd never liked losing, especially when it was something this important. "We did everything possible to convince them to hold him longer. I even asked for another delay, but his lawyer fought me. Carter testified that Paul still represented a threat to you, but Paul was good. I'll give him that. He made a compelling case that he'd learned his lesson and reformed. He said all the right words. And sitting up there in his Armani suit, he looked every inch the perfect gentleman. He managed to get a few respected character witnesses to testify on his behalf, too, and that went a long way to convincing the parole panel to let him go."

"Yeah, he's very good at getting the world to see what

he wants them to see," Raylene said. "And the good-old-boys' network is still alive and thriving. I imagine his daddy was able to find plenty of cronies willing to step up for his golden boy."

"I tried my best to provoke him into showing his true colors, but he was cool, calm and collected," Helen said. "Heck, even I would have had a hard time turning him down after hearing all he did to help his fellow inmates. It was quite a performance. I would have been ready to nominate him for sainthood myself, if I didn't know what a violent bully is hidden beneath that smooth facade."

Raylene gave her a resigned look. "Thanks for trying. I'm ready for him."

Helen immediately looked alarmed. "Meaning what?"

"Don't worry about me, that's all."

"Raylene, you didn't get your hands on a gun the way you were talking about, did you?"

"Stop," Raylene said. "Don't ask questions, especially when you don't really want to know the answers."

It had been surprisingly easy to get the gun that was now locked away in a metal box on the top shelf in her closet. There were plenty of unscrupulous dealers on the Internet who didn't care about the law. Even if that gun was never loaded or out of the box, she felt better knowing she had it. It evened the playing field between her and Paul, at least a little. He'd never expect her to fight back, any more than he'd expected her to turn him in, in the first place.

"Does Carter know about this?" Helen asked, looking distraught as she drew her own conclusions from Raylene's evasiveness.

"Of course not," she said. "If he knew anything, he'd have to arrest me, more than likely. I don't want him to be in that position. You, either, so leave it alone, Helen. I have to handle this my way."

"Raylene, do you even know how to fire a gun?"

Raylene forced the most innocent expression she could manage. "Who said anything about a gun? Certainly not me."

Helen regarded her with frustration. "This is nuts. And what about the kids? What if they find it, Tommy especially? Have you even considered the danger you're putting them in?"

"Which is exactly why I've told Sarah they need to move over and stay with Travis the second Paul's released. I begged her to move up the wedding, too, but she's determined not to do that until her father can be here."

"Carter's counting on Travis staying here," Helen protested.

"Well, he won't be," Raylene said stubbornly. "He needs to look out for Sarah, Tommy and Libby. I want them all where they'll be safe. I'm not his problem."

"But you are his friend," Helen said, then waved off her own argument. "Okay, forget Travis. I suppose we can get Ronnie, Cal and Erik to alternate nights staying here. It goes without saying that Carter will be nearby."

Raylene was horrified by the idea of putting her friends in harm's way. "Absolutely not. This is my responsibility."

"Not in this town," Helen said. "And not when you're a Sweet Magnolia. Your problem is our problem, and that's just the way it is. Deal with it. Heck, if it comes down to it, I spent my share of hours on a shooting range. I'll take a turn staying here."

Now it was Raylene's turn to be horrified. "Helen, do I need to remind you that you have a daughter? You are not risking your life for me. Period. I suppose I can't stop a bunch of stubborn, macho men from feeling the need to protect me, but I draw the line at you sitting here holding a weapon."

"But I'm highly motivated," Helen protested. "Men like Paul Hammond need to be taken down. The court system did a lousy job in his case, and I hate when that happens."

"But you know better than most that you don't get to go all vigilante because of it," Raylene argued. "No, you are not taking one minute of guard duty over here. This is my fight. I don't want to involve anyone else."

"Well, you'll have to fight that out with Carter," Helen said, then grinned. "Good luck with that, by the way."

Raylene grimaced. She knew the conversation wasn't going to go even half as smoothly as her attempt to break up with him, and that had pretty much been a waste of breath.

Rory Sue flipped her hair back in a gesture that was all female. Usually she did it just to drive Walter wild, but today she was clearly exasperated and probably just trying to get her windblown hair out of her face.

"Please say that again," she demanded, frowning at Walter. "Surely I can't have heard you correctly."

"I'm going to be hanging out at Raylene's for the next couple of weeks," he repeated patiently. He'd explained before about the impending release of Raylene's ex-husband, but only after Raylene had put her foot down about Sarah and the kids moving over to stay with Travis had he decided it was up to him to stay at the house to protect her. Carter had his own family to watch over.

Unfortunately, Rory Sue didn't seem to be taking the news any better than Raylene had.

"No way," she said emphatically. "No boyfriend of mine is going to live with another woman."

"While I suppose I should be flattered by the show of jealousy, you know perfectly well you have nothing to worry about," Walter said. "Raylene and I are just friends."

She held his gaze as if trying to decide whether to debate the point, then nodded. "Okay, then neither of you will mind if I move in there with you," she said decisively.

"Absolutely not," Walter said. "I can't be worrying about two of you if that nutcase shows up."

"You won't have to worry about me," Rory Sue said. "I'll bring along Granddad's shotgun."

Walter groaned. "Your grandfather has a shotgun?"

"Well, of course he does. He hunts. He started taking me with him when I was around ten. I was a little freaked by the idea of him killing Bambi, but I can handle a shotgun just about as well as he can."

Despite her boastful claim, he still thought it was a bad idea. He shook his head.

"Carter will never go for it," he told her. "He doesn't want to involve any more civilians than absolutely necessary."

"Well, if you're staying there, then my staying there is absolutely necessary," she said, her chin set defiantly.

"Why?" he asked. He had the feeling it went beyond jealousy.

She looked as if she couldn't believe he even needed to ask. "Because the thought of losing you to some creep like Raylene's ex-husband is simply unacceptable."

He smiled at that. No one had ever worried about him like that. Other than maybe his mother, but she'd been a little overzealous on that score. "Rory Sue, believe it or not, I can take care of myself. Want to go to the gun range so I can prove it? If I win, you give up this crazy idea, okay?"

"You actually think you're a better shot than I am?" she asked incredulously.

"Honey, I hate to burst your liberated bubble, but I know I am."

An hour later, he'd proved it.

"Well, damn," she murmured as she studied his target with several clean shots directly through the heart or close enough to do serious damage.

"Sorry."

She grinned at him. "Don't be. I'm still not letting you go to Raylene's alone, though."

"Raylene—"

"Sorry. My decision's final," she said. "Now, all of this has made me a little hot. Let's go back to your place."

"My place still doesn't have any furniture," he reminded her. They'd closed on it earlier in the day. He'd originally planned to have furniture delivered on Saturday, but given this business with Raylene, he'd put it off.

"It has a bed," she told him with a grin. "I had it delivered right after the closing. I went by and put brand-new sheets on it myself."

Yet again she'd caught him off guard. "Well, now, aren't you efficient?"

She winked at him as she sashayed past. "I certainly aim to please."

That, of course, was part of the problem, Walter thought, even as he followed her from the gun range. She pleased him in ways he'd never imagined. Part of it was the fact that she was never predictable. He'd spent so much of his life doing exactly what was expected of him. Discovering that he could be spontaneous had been a revelation to him.

But that cautious side of his nature that still overwhelmed him from time to time warned that it might be hard to live with unpredictability over the long haul.

Still, as he cast an appreciative glance over the woman seated next to him, that was a worry for another day. Tonight, spontaneity held a lot of allure.

CHAPTER TWENTY

Because of Sarah, the kids, a babysitter and Travis, the house had always been filled with people coming and going, but even after they'd all moved over to Travis's, the place was a nonstop circus. Raylene knew exactly what was going on. Everyone she knew was taking shifts—planned or otherwise—to be sure she was never in the house alone. Though she appreciated the gesture, it was getting on her nerves.

When Walter showed up and announced both he and Rory Sue were moving in for the duration, she lost it. It had been bad enough when Walter had insisted he was going to stay with her, but nothing she'd said had dissuaded him. The thought of dealing with Rory Sue for the foreseeable future as well was just too much.

"Are you totally out of your mind?" she demanded. "Rory Sue and I don't get along that well on a good day."

"Then now's the perfect time for the two of you to get better acquainted," Walter replied cheerfully, his expression unyielding.

"Why would she even agree to do this?" she asked, bewildered.

"Mostly to protect her turf," Walter admitted. He held up

a hand to prevent her protest. "I know there's nothing going on between you and me, but she doesn't buy it."

"She doesn't trust you? That should tell you something. A relationship without trust is, well…" She tried to think of an appropriate description. "It's basically nonexistent. You might as well call it quits, throw in the towel—"

Again, he held up his hand, this time to pause the tirade. "I get the picture. I don't think I'm the one she's worried about. I think she's afraid you'll suddenly find me irresistible and that I, a mere mortal man, will succumb to your wiles."

"As if," Raylene muttered, then met his determined gaze. "Okay, fine. Heaven forbid that I cause a rift between the two of you. How long is this supposed to go on?"

"As long as necessary," he said.

"You do realize this could be the answer to my prayers, don't you? Rory Sue will probably make me so insane, I'll be thrilled to walk out the front door and never look back."

Walter laughed.

Raylene regarded him with a grim expression. "I'm not joking."

In fact, nothing about this entire situation was even remotely amusing. If she weren't quite so terrified of Paul showing up, she really would kick every one of her self-appointed protectors to the curb.

Carter stood aside as Walter and Rory Sue carted several pieces of luggage into Raylene's. It grated on his nerves that protecting her inside the house had been relegated to Walter, of all people. Unfortunately, with things the way they were at home with Carrie, Carter knew he couldn't do it. Raylene wouldn't have let him if he'd tried. She'd made that clear when he'd broached the possibility. His place was with his sisters. She'd also insisted that he keep both of the girls away from her house for the foreseeable future.

"I don't like this," he muttered as Rory Sue and Walter headed for Tommy and Libby's room to settle in.

"I'm not exactly overjoyed about it myself," Raylene said. "You're the one who insisted I needed bodyguards."

"These are not the ones I had in mind," he said in frustration.

"Well, Travis needs to be with Sarah and the kids."

He met her gaze. "At least you've stopped telling me that you don't need anyone. I suppose I should be grateful for small favors."

She frowned. "I'm not stupid. I know Paul better than anyone. Sooner or later, he will turn up here to get even or at least to tell me how I've ruined his life."

Carter studied her. There was no mistaking the underlying tension in her voice. It hadn't been there yesterday or even earlier in the day today. Something had happened to shake her bravado in the face of Paul's release.

"What happened, Raylene? Don't even try to tell me it was nothing. I can tell from your tone that you didn't just wake up this morning and decide to be agreeable."

She looked flustered that he was able to read her so well.

"Don't you dare hold back," he said when she remained stubbornly silent.

"I don't really know if it's anything," she admitted eventually. "I've had some calls, hang-ups. The number was blocked. It's probably just kids or someone who's dialing a wrong number, but it has creeped me out a little bit."

Carter's stomach clenched, but he tried to stay calm and matter-of-fact. "I'll have a trace put on your line, but if it is Paul and he's just hanging up, they may not be able to catch the number. You'd have to keep him on the line for a while." He met her gaze. "Could you try to engage him in conversation?"

"You mean just start talking as if I know it's him, and keep the line open?"

Carter nodded.

"If it means catching him before something happens, I'll do it."

Carter hesitated. "You know we're not going to be able to arrest him just because he's calling you, right? So far it doesn't even rise to the level of harassment. We really need him to come over here and violate the restraining order. If he so much as steps onto your property, it will also violate the conditions of his parole. Then we can get him locked up again. This time he'll have a good long stay behind bars."

Raylene sighed with evident frustration. "No wonder so many battered wives lose faith in the system. They have to be attacked before they can get any kind of justice."

Carter was no less frustrated. He'd seen too many instances where abusive husbands had gone right back home and beaten the daylights out of their wives before anyone could legally intervene. The hands of the police were often tied until too late, just as Raylene had said. Threats alone or past history weren't enough to offer the kind of protection these women needed. Even in a place like Serenity, where the local sheriff's department was more than willing to step in, there wasn't enough manpower to do round-the-clock surveillance. Despite that, he was determined that Raylene wouldn't wind up as one of those sad statistics. At least, thanks to Tom, there were extra people on the street during the day to keep an eye out for the arrival of any strangers. Even the neighbors had been alerted.

He squeezed her hand. "We'll get him, Raylene. He's not going to lay a hand on you ever again."

She met his gaze. "I almost wish he'd try. This time I think I could fight back."

He heard the grim note in her voice and almost regretted that he couldn't grant her that chance. He didn't want Paul getting close enough to do her any harm at all, not even a scratch.

"If he does turn up, I can always hold him and let you land a few punches before we cart him off," he offered instead.

She gave him a tired smile. "Now, would that be fair? I want to get to him when it's a fair fight."

"I understand the sentiment, but he's bigger and obviously a lot meaner. Unless you've been taking self-defense lessons I don't know about, it will never be a fair fight." He leveled a look into her eyes. "And forget about using a gun to shoot him."

She immediately looked dismayed. "Helen told you," she said, her tone flat.

"And I found the gun last time I was over here. It's gone."

"Dammit, Carter, you had no right to do that."

"It was unlicensed, Raylene. More important, you don't know how to use it. I couldn't take a chance Paul would grab it and turn it on you." He held her shoulders and looked into her eyes. "I'm not losing you like that. Understand? Keeping you alive and safe is my number-one priority right now."

Her defiant expression faded. "I just wanted to know I could protect myself."

"That wasn't the way."

"What if Paul comes over here with a weapon?" she asked.

"Did he ever use a weapon of any kind against you? Did he own a gun?"

She shook her head. "No, he only used his fists. A stab wound or a bullet would have been way too hard to explain in the emergency room."

"Then I doubt that's changed." He knew she was scared and frustrated, but she'd never admit it, at least not the fear. "You need a distraction. We have no idea how long it might be before he'll decide to show up. How about fixing some dinner? I'm starved."

She gave him a wry look. "Do you usually ask your subjects to cook for you when you're on a stakeout?"

Carter laughed. "No, I usually take along bad coffee and a peanut butter and jelly sandwich or a bag of doughnuts. I thought this time maybe I could throw myself on your mercy."

"Fine. I'll cook." She gave him an impish look as she walked into the kitchen. "Should I have Rory Sue bring the meal out to your car?"

"No, I'll eat at the table like the rest of you civilized folks."

She'd opened the freezer door, but she turned at his response. "I thought you were on official guard duty here tonight."

"I am."

"Shouldn't you be outside watching for the bad guy?"

"I have a couple of other guys doing that for now. I'm working inside."

She closed the refrigerator without selecting anything. "Carter, do you think Paul's going to show up tonight? Is that why there are extra people watching the house?"

"Just a gut instinct," he said. "Nothing concrete. Don't freak out on me now. We've got it covered."

Before she could respond, the phone rang. Raylene jumped, then looked embarrassed as she reached for it. He noticed her hand was shaking.

After a moment, she drew herself up. "Paul, I know it's you. Say something. I imagine you're still furious with me for turning you in, so why not just say what's on your mind?

Rant and rave and get it out of your system. I'm actually surprised you didn't use your phone privileges in prison to call me and tell me what an awful person I am."

She blinked, then sighed and hung up. "He didn't say a word, but I know it was him. I just know it."

Carter crossed the kitchen and touched a finger to her chin. "You did good."

"I was shaking like a leaf," she admitted, then grinned. "But I did it anyway. That's something."

He heard the note of pride in her voice after the small triumph. He realized then just how much self-respect Paul Hammond had stolen from her. If he'd been able to put his hands on the man in that instant, he would have made him pay.

Going through the motions of making spaghetti and meatballs and a salad kept Raylene sane through what seemed like an endless evening. Each time the phone rang, she jumped. Except for the one hang-up, the calls were mostly from people checking on her. Tired of saying the same thing over and over—that she was fine and nothing was happening—she finally told Walter to answer.

Rory Sue regarded her with sympathy. "It's getting old already, isn't it?"

Surprised by the understanding, Raylene nodded. "I'm not crazy about waiting or about being the center of attention."

"Not even in Carter's universe?" Rory Sue asked.

"What do you mean?"

Rory Sue regarded her with disbelief. "Come on, Raylene. It's obvious the man is crazy about you. He watches you like he'll never get enough of you. And every time the phone rings, I swear it looks as if he's ready to draw his gun and kill whoever's on the other end of the line. I'm a little surprised he hasn't shot the phone."

"He's just doing his job," Raylene said, though she knew it was more than that. The connection between them was powerful. One of these days, she hoped their lives would be less complicated and they could truly explore those feelings.

Right now Carter was outside checking in with whomever he had watching the house. The plan was to send them home, and he'd take over out there. Raylene had argued futilely that he should be going home himself to get some sleep before he went back on duty in the morning.

"I'll get by with enough caffeine," he said. "It won't be the first time I've pulled an all-nighter."

"But have you had to go out the next day and put your life on the line?" she'd countered to no avail. The man was stubborn as a mule.

She glanced over at Rory Sue and saw a frown on her face. "What's wrong?"

"I thought maybe, since I'm going to be staying here, we could try to be friends," Rory Sue said. "Instead, when I asked about Carter, you blew me off. You wouldn't have done that with Sarah or Annie."

Raylene smiled despite the tension in the air. "You'd be surprised how often I've told them exactly the same thing," she admitted. "Things between Carter and me are complicated, so I minimize the relationship."

"Self-protection in case it doesn't work out," Rory Sue guessed.

"Exactly. I can't lose something if I don't let myself admit I've ever had it."

"That's kind of crazy, isn't it?" Rory Sue said, looking bewildered by the concept. "Besides, what's so complicated that you can't work it out? Look at me and Walter. Nobody would have predicted the two of us being together, but we are. At least we're working at it, because we think it's worth it. Don't you think Carter's worth it?"

"Of course he is," Raylene said at once. "He's amazing."

"And you're as hot for him as he is for you. I can see it in your eyes."

"Sometimes it's still not that simple."

"But great sex along with friendship is a pretty good basis for a relationship. That's what I have going with Walter that I never had before. We don't just have sex, we really talk. It's taken me my whole life to figure out how important that is. Before, I was all about the chemistry."

"I'd say that's a sign of maturity," Raylene said.

"So what about Carter? He looks like the kind of man who could set off all sorts of fireworks."

Raylene really wasn't comfortable with the direction of the conversation. She knew Rory Sue was reaching out, but the topic was simply too intimate. She didn't especially want to admit that she and Carter hadn't made it anywhere near a bed yet.

"I'm really happy if you and Walter have found something special," she said instead. "Now, if you'll excuse me, I need to try to get some sleep."

Rory Sue looked startled by the abrupt announcement. "Did I say something wrong? That's another thing I'm lousy at, knowing the boundaries, especially with other women. My mom had the same problem."

"Don't worry about it. I really am tired."

Rory Sue looked disappointed, but just then Walter came out of the kitchen, and her eyes brightened. Raylene was no longer even a blip on her radar.

Raylene went into her room, changed into her nightgown and slid between the sheets. When the phone rang, she almost left it for Walter, but decided at the last second to grab it. Her nerves tensed in that first instant after she'd said hello, as she waited for nothing more than silence in response.

Instead, Carter asked, "You all tucked in?"

"Carter Rollins, are you sitting out there in the dark spying on me?" she teased.

"Thinking about you in there stripping off your clothes helps to keep me awake," he told her. "Are you naked? Please tell me you're naked. That ought to be good for a couple of hours of sleeplessness, at least."

She laughed and snuggled down under the covers. "Stark naked," she fibbed. Anything for the cause, she thought, allowing herself a delicious shiver at his sharply indrawn breath.

"Ah, there it is," he said softly. "The image that's going to get me through the night."

"Has it been quiet out there?"

"Too quiet," he said. "It's a little spooky. If it weren't so dangerous, I'd try to convince you to come out here and protect me from the goblins of the night."

"Under the circumstances, that might be counterproductive."

"Yeah, I know. One of these days, though, this is going to be behind us, Carrie's going to be better, and you and I are going to have our chance. I believe that with all my heart, Raylene. I'm going to fight to make sure it happens."

"Our chance to do what?" she pressed, needing to hear the sweet promise of his words.

"Be together in that very bed where you are right now. We'll be all tangled together after a night of making love, and we'll talk about our hopes and dreams, and then we'll make them come true. Every one of them, Raylene."

She sighed at the lovely thought. "I wish—" she began.

"We'll have that," he said firmly, interrupting her. "Believe it. Now, get some sleep. I'll see you in the morning."

"Good night, Carter."

"Night, Raylene."

She disconnected the call and put the phone back on the nightstand, then curled up with her pillow. It was a very poor substitute for the man outside, but it would have to do for now.

The pattern established the first night after Paul's release went on for more than a week, with only the personnel changing. Walter, Rory Sue and Carter were the only constants. Raylene was increasingly dismayed by the lack of a resolution.

As for Carter, how much longer could he go on getting little to no sleep beyond the occasional nap in the afternoons between his shift at the sheriff's department and his arrival at her house for the night? She was worried by the lines of tension on his face, the exhaustion in his eyes, to say nothing of the fact that he seemed to be neglecting Carrie and Mandy. He flatly refused, though, to turn the night watch over to anyone else. Finally Raylene reached her limit. She started making phone calls.

Her first one to Ronnie got a promise that he'd take over surveillance outside the house that night. Her next four, to friends of Paul's, were designed to try to rattle his cage and provoke him into taking action, if that was what he had in mind.

When Carter showed up that night and found Ronnie parked in his truck right in front of the house, he stormed inside.

"Ronnie says you called him and asked him to take over," he said, pacing up and down the living room as he dragged his hand through his already mussed hair. "Why would you do that? Don't you trust me to do the job?"

"You know it's not that," she said patiently. "Your sisters need some attention. Plus, you're wiped out. You need a decent night's sleep."

"Well, I certainly won't get it at home worrying myself sick about you and what's happening over here."

She'd anticipated that response. "Which is why you're staying here tonight. I've arranged for Carrie and Mandy to stay with friends from school for a couple of days so you won't have to worry about them." Before he could argue, she added, "I've spoken to the parents who'll be looking out for Carrie. They understand the situation. They'll make sure she eats and will report back if there's a problem."

"Well, you've just thought of every damn thing, haven't you?"

With the words ground out like that, it didn't sound like a compliment, but she forced a smile, anyway. "I certainly tried to. I knew it was the only way you'd agree to stay here."

He stopped pacing to stare at her as if the significance of that part had previously escaped him. "Here?"

"In my bed, in fact."

His eyes lit up, but she held up her hand. "I'll sleep on the sofa."

"Like hell you will. You'll be right in Paul's path if he breaks in."

"I thought the idea of having Ronnie outside was to keep Paul from getting inside."

"It is, but you never know what could happen to change the best theory. I won't have you right smack inside the front door. If this is going to work, you'll have to sleep with me."

Raylene finally grasped the flaw in her plan. She should

have foreseen it. "That's not going to work for me, Carter. You know that." Even to her ears, her tone sounded wistful.

"It'll work," he said grimly. "Even if we have to put pillows down the middle of the bed or hang a blanket between the two sides. I want you where I can reach out and touch you."

An image from an old movie came to her. "You'd do that?"

"If that's what it takes. Though I have to admit, I'd sleep a whole lot better if we could at least snuggle."

"I don't know," she whispered, as drawn by the idea as he was.

"We could try it and see how it goes," he suggested, longing in his eyes.

That's what did it, finally. If he'd been pushing for more, she might have been able to deny him, but to see the yearning just to be close, how could she turn her back on that? A very big part of her had been longing for the same thing, but not daring to believe it was possible.

"We'll give it a try," she said, making up her mind.

His gaze met hers then, and held. Then, a faint smile on his lips, he nodded.

Raylene felt as if she'd granted him a birthday wish and a miracle all rolled into one. Now she could only pray she wouldn't let him down.

Raylene owned one pair of flannel pajamas for the rare winter nights when she couldn't seem to get warm. She found them in her dresser drawer, put them on, then took a deep breath and emerged in her bedroom.

Carter was lying on top of the covers, still wearing his jeans and a formfitting white T-shirt but no shoes or socks.

"Are you planning to sleep like that?" she asked just as his lips curved into a smile as he surveyed the loose-fitting flannel pj's.

"I should ask you the same thing," he commented. "I hate to tell you, sweet pea, but those are more provocative than any nightie I've ever seen."

She frowned as she looked down. "These? Why? I'm practically covered from neck to toe."

"I know. It sparks my imagination." He grinned wickedly. "I have a very vivid imagination. Come on over here and climb into bed."

She regarded him warily, but she did cross the room and sit gingerly on her side of the bed.

"You won't get much sleep sitting up," he murmured, amusement threading through his voice. "Settle down here next to me. I promise I won't touch you unless you want me to."

She hesitated. Her gaze sought his. "I might want you to," she admitted. "But it might not go very well."

"Only one way to find out," he said. "The first second I do something that scares you, all you have to do is push me away or say no. I promise, you're in charge here."

Reassured, she stretched out next to him, keeping several inches between them. Even so, she could feel his heat radiating toward her. All that solid strength beckoned to her. She rolled onto her side and dared to rest her hand on his rock-solid abs. She could feel them tighten under her touch.

"What kind of workouts do you do?" she asked, a little awed and a lot intrigued.

"Weights, resistance machines, that kind of thing," he said, sounding slightly breathless.

She hesitated, then asked, "Would you mind taking off your shirt?"

He grinned at the request. "My pleasure. You want to do it for me?"

Raylene gave it a moment's thought, then reached for the

hem of his shirt and tugged it over his head. She knew what he'd done. He'd left the act to her so she had total control over whether that shirt stayed or went. Even as her knuckles skimmed over bare flesh, she felt the kind of yearning she hadn't felt in years. She could feel her body coming alive, tightening and moistening in all the right places.

"What would you think about taking off your top?" Carter asked solemnly. "Seems to me you shouldn't be the only one with a view."

She froze, then reminded herself this was Carter, not Paul. There would be no cruel comments about the inadequacy of her chest, no rough handling that caused more pain than pleasure. She told herself she could do this.

Slowly she reached for the buttons. Once she'd undone the first one, she hurried with fumbling fingers to finish the rest. Carter's avid gaze never left her.

"May I?" he whispered, gently pushing the flannel top aside to reveal her breasts.

To her amazement, he didn't grab as if there was some race to be won. He just looked, his eyes filled with wonder.

"You're beautiful," he said, a hitch in his voice. He stroked a finger down one breast, then gently rubbed the nipple.

Raylene almost cried as desire shot straight through her. It had been so long since she'd felt that kind of tenderness, so long since she'd allowed herself to want a man's touch. Yet Carter's caresses felt right.

She'd never known a man to take such care, to risk a touch, then wait to assure that it was wanted before risking more. She felt her skin heat, felt the return of moistness between her legs, the stirring of her blood. It was such sweet wonder to experience it all again without fear.

Carter met her gaze. "Do you want to stop now?" he asked.

She looked at him as if he was crazy. "Now?" she asked incredulously.

A smile played over his lips. "Just checking."

"No, I want more, Carter. I want it all."

Because for the first time in years, she needed to know what it was truly like to make love. Maybe if she experienced that at long last, it would finally push the bad memories from her head once and for all, replacing them with memories she could cherish.

CHAPTER TWENTY-ONE

Carter woke and rolled over in bed to discover he was alone. He wondered if he'd dreamed that he and Raylene had made love the night before. If so, it had been one helluva dream. She'd surprised him with passion and fire, then fallen asleep in his arms as if she'd finally found shelter from a storm. He knew what an amazing gift she'd given him by placing her trust in him.

Discovering that she'd abandoned him, though, made him wonder if she'd awakened with second thoughts. He knew she still worried that she was too much trouble, especially when he had a kid sister with an eating disorder. He had no idea how to make her see that it was easier for him to face that with her at his side. Words weren't going to be enough. Neither, he knew down deep, was sex.

Feeling refreshed for the first time in what seemed like an eternity, he showered, pulled on the clothes he'd worn over here the night before and went in search of Raylene.

He found her in the kitchen humming to herself and cooking enough food to feed an army.

He glanced at the mound of bacon, the pile of toast and the pan of scrambled eggs she was stirring. There was a pitcher of freshly squeezed orange juice already on the table, along with pots of jam that looked homemade. The table had been set for five.

"Expecting company?" he inquired, stealing a piece of crisp bacon before stealing a kiss. Much as he loved bacon, the kiss—brief though it was—was better.

"Walter and Rory Sue should be in here any minute now, and I called Ronnie on his cell and told him to come in."

Carter stiffened. He opened his mouth to protest, but she waved him off.

"Oh, don't look like that," she scolded. "Erik's taking his place until all those workmen who are filling potholes and checking the power lines show up." She gave him a pointed look. "Who knew this street was in such a sad state of disrepair?"

"Tom's idea," he said succinctly. "The sheriff doesn't have the extra manpower to put surveillance on your place 24–7. I was hoping you wouldn't notice."

"I'm neither blind nor stupid," she told him, then touched his cheek in a gesture apparently meant to take the sting out of her words. "Thank you. Tom may have come up with the idea, but I know you're the one who insisted there had to be a plan."

Carter studied her flushed cheeks and bright eyes. "Not to change the subject, but about last night," he began.

She cut him off. "I don't want to talk about last night, Carter. It was wonderful." She blushed as she met his gaze. "Amazing, in fact. Let's not spoil what happened by trying to analyze it."

He regarded her incredulously. "Since when does a woman not want to talk about intimacy?"

"Just consider me a rare breed of female. I'd like to let the experience speak for itself."

He didn't buy it for a second. "Is it that, or are you hoping to pretend it didn't happen, or maybe that it didn't mean anything?"

"There you go, discussing," she said with exasperation. "Leave it alone, Carter. I mean it."

He sighed and dropped the subject...for now. He knew, though, that they couldn't avoid it forever. It was too important. And he could see by the fear in her eyes that she understood that, too.

Though little about Raylene's life these days felt even remotely normal, Dr. McDaniels had insisted that they not put their sessions on hold.

"Not after that breakthrough we had about your mother possibly being agoraphobic, too," she told Raylene when she called to say that she'd be over at the regular time. "We have some momentum going here. I don't want to lose it."

When she arrived promptly at one o'clock, she stood on the stoop for a minute looking up and down the block. "Busy street," she noted.

"My unofficial watchdogs," Raylene told her, and explained about Tom's plan to be sure Paul didn't slip into the neighborhood.

As they went inside, the psychologist studied her. "How are you feeling about his release?"

"Scared, angry," Raylene said at once, then sighed. "Mostly scared."

"That's perfectly natural."

Deciding she needed to make a preemptive strike, Raylene looked the doctor directly in the eye. "I don't think it's a good time for me to be trying to go outside. If I was terrified before, just imagine how I'll react now that my fear is actually justified."

Dr. McDaniels shook her head. "Actually, I think it's exactly the right time. If you can face your fear and conquer it under these circumstances, think about how empowering that will feel." She touched Raylene's hand. "You don't have to decide right this second. First, I have some news."

There was an edge in her voice that told Raylene she might be better off not knowing what it was. Unfortunately, she also knew that wasn't an option.

"What news?"

"I spoke to your mother at some length the other day. I finally caught her at home. She hadn't been returning any of the messages I left for her."

"She's not coming," Raylene guessed. She hadn't really expected it, hadn't even been sure she wanted her mother's help, but she had to admit to feeling deflated now.

"No, I'm sorry," Dr. McDaniels said sympathetically. "She says it would be too painful to come to Serenity, that living here was the most miserable time of her life."

"She can't even put that aside to help her daughter," Raylene concluded, her tone flat. "Why am I not surprised? She's probably still furious with me for creating the scandal that sent Paul to prison."

"Actually, she didn't even mention that," Dr. McDaniels said.

"Did she know about his release?"

"She never mentioned Paul at all, and avoided talking about him when I brought him up. What she did say was that coming back here would stir up memories she'd worked too hard to put to rest. I tried to probe a little about those memories, but she refused to go there."

"What about the agoraphobia? Did she admit to that?" Raylene asked.

"As a matter of fact, yes. She wouldn't put a name to it, but she said she'd spent years locked away in the house because she hated being in Serenity. She said she'd had no desire to see anyone or to go anywhere."

"Was it her interpretation that it was fear that kept her inside, or was she punishing my father?"

"She wouldn't say anything more about that, either, but it almost doesn't matter. The point is that she set an example that you've been unconsciously following."

Raylene waited for some sense of relief or maybe even vindication, but all she felt was sorrow. "What a waste," she murmured.

The psychologist's gaze was penetrating. "Are you talking about your mother's life now, or your own?"

Raylene thought about it. "Maybe both," she admitted. "At least she got her life back. I wonder if she's even thought for a second about the fact that she got it because of me and my decision to marry Paul. You could almost say she owes me." She shrugged off the analysis. "Bottom line, she is the way she is. I can't change that."

"Here's something I think you need to recognize," Dr. McDaniels said. "It seems to me that even shut away in this house the way you have been, you've led a fuller, richer life than she had. You have the support of countless friends. You have a man who clearly adores you."

At the mention of Carter, Raylene hesitated, then blurted, "I slept with Carter night before last."

The psychologist didn't even try to hide her surprise, or her pleasure. "Good for you. The breakthroughs seem to be coming fast and furious these days."

"You think so?" Raylene asked skeptically. Of course, sleeping with Carter had been huge, but it seemed to her that nothing else had changed. She couldn't see how knowing her mom had been agoraphobic had really changed anything, either.

"It certainly seems that way to me. A few short weeks ago, you couldn't even bear for Carter to put his arm around you. I certainly consider making love an important breakthrough."

Raylene acknowledged that initial skittish reaction months ago was a far cry from what she'd felt the other night. She'd felt safe, at least when she'd allowed herself to believe that what they had could last. She'd had a delicious taste of normalcy, and it had made her want more.

Suddenly more determined than ever not to let Paul ruin her progress, she met Dr. McDaniels's gaze. "Let's go outside. I've missed being on the patio the past few days."

"Good for you."

A few minutes later, taking a seat under an umbrella that shaded them from the sun, she sighed. "It doesn't seem like much."

"Think about where you were when we first started these sessions."

"But I want to be able to do things other women do. I don't want to be half a person. That's not fair to Carter."

"Has Carter complained about your limitations?"

She shook her head. "But, come on, his patience can't last forever."

"Maybe it can," the psychologist said. "Who are you to decide what he can handle?"

"Okay, then maybe I'm the one who can't handle it," Raylene retorted. "If I'm going to have a real relationship, a meaningful one, then I want to bring all of me to it. Right now I'm just a bundle of fears and insecurities."

"That's a little harsh, don't you think?"

"It's how I feel."

"Okay, let's talk about that," the doctor said, her tone annoyingly reasonable. "What's out there in the world that you want and can't have?"

"A normal life."

"Be more specific."

"I'd like to have a job," she said, thinking of old dreams when she'd wanted something more than to be Paul's wife and lead a life of leisure. Ironically, she'd learned to hate that role during her marriage. It was even worse now that it had been forced on her by her fears.

"And if Carter and I were to have kids, I'd want to be able to walk with them on their first day of school, see their plays and holiday programs, go to their ball games," she continued. "I want to go to the movies with my husband, walk into town for ice cream, take part in all of the town's holiday festivals."

"How badly do you want all that?"

"More than I'd ever realized," she said wistfully.

"Good," Dr. McDaniels said. "Then let's try to make sure you get it." She stood up and beckoned to Raylene. "Let's go."

Raylene froze. "Now?"

"No time like the present," the doctor confirmed. "The patio has started to feel safe. Let's see if we can't make the rest of the world feel that way, too."

Raylene stood, but her knees nearly buckled. "What exactly do you want to do?"

"I thought we'd go for a little walk. Just out to the mailbox, maybe even a few feet down the street."

Raylene thought about how close that was, just a few hundred feet or so. It might as well have been across town. She had to fight panic even before they rounded the side of the house.

"You can do this," Dr. McDaniels assured her. "I'm going to be right beside you, just the way I was when we went outside to meet Carter that day. This will be only a little farther. You're going to be perfectly safe. You already know that there are people out there to protect you. There's no risk of Paul getting to you."

It all sounded perfectly rational and sane, but that was the problem. Nothing about her responses were sane or rational. Eventually, though, she nodded. If she truly wanted that normal life she'd described, she had to do this. And if she could do it now, when her fears were nearly overwhelming, it would be a huge triumph, proof that she would conquer the agoraphobia.

As they reached the front yard, the psychologist paused. "You don't have to rush," she told her. "Take your time. One step, then another, at your own pace. You know the drill."

On an intellectual level, it seemed crazy to Raylene that she had to be coached in order to walk down a sidewalk to the mailbox at the curb, but emotionally the distance seemed like miles, miles that were fraught with more unseen obstacles than she could count.

She stepped onto the sidewalk with a small measure of confidence, then waited for the sweaty palms and shortness of breath to kick in. To her surprise, that didn't happen this time. Maybe because the weeks of small victories in the garden had given her confidence, perhaps because the medicine was finally doing its job, she had no idea which. She was simply grateful for the respite from panic.

She took one more step, then another. When the mailman turned the corner, then paused to put the mail into the box, she even managed a jaunty, casual wave.

But the second he'd walked on and she'd retrieved the mail, the sense of triumph she'd experienced faded and suddenly she couldn't breathe. She stopped where she was, her throat closing up. She regarded Dr. McDaniels with dismay, unable to squeeze out a single word.

"It's okay," the doctor soothed. "You're fine. You're in a safe place, and I'm with you. Just stand here and take a deep breath and try to relax."

Raylene clutched at her throat. All of the old, terrifying sensations washed over her.

"Can't breathe," she choked out.

"Yes, you can," Dr. McDaniels insisted. She put a comforting hand on Raylene's shoulder and gave it a squeeze. "Give it a minute. In and out, just like we practiced. Not too fast, or you'll hyperventilate."

Closing her eyes, Raylene concentrated on taking measured breaths until they started to come naturally. In what was probably less than a minute, though it felt like much longer, she felt calmer. She was able to move forward, back to the house, back to safety.

As shaken as she'd been, she allowed herself a small moment of triumph. She'd been to the mailbox and back! It was such a short distance, but the victory seemed huge.

But even that walk, as amazing as it had been, had left her miles and miles away from the freedom of having her life back.

Sarah burst through the front door at midafternoon, scaring Raylene half to death.

"What on earth?" she murmured, when her friend embraced her and danced her around.

"Lynn called me at the station," Sarah said gleefully. "She said she saw you at the mailbox!"

"It wasn't worthy of an announcement on the midday news," Raylene said, then grinned. "But it was pretty cool. I only panicked once. Then I did the breathing exercises, and it got better just the way Dr. McDaniels had said it would. I just have to consciously take control of my breathing. I can almost imagine doing it on my own." She sighed. "But that seems like it could take forever."

Sarah was undaunted. "This week the mailbox, next week you'll be sitting in the studio with me at the station or having breakfast at Wharton's or going to Sullivan's with Carter!"

"I think you're being overly ambitious. I still haven't left the yard, Sarah."

"But you will. I can feel it. You're going to put this whole episode behind you."

Raylene studied her exuberant expression. "I wish I shared your faith."

"Oh, come on. Don't be a sourpuss. This is huge. Let's invite everyone over and celebrate."

"You want to celebrate my walk to the mailbox? That's pathetic."

"No. It's a triumph. I can hardly wait to see Carter's face when he finds out."

Raylene was shaking her head before the words were out of Sarah's mouth. "No. No celebration and we're not saying a word to Carter about this. I can't get his hopes up."

Sarah rolled her eyes. "I have a feeling if you didn't want to get his hopes up, maybe you shouldn't have slept with him."

Raylene just stared at her. "How on earth do you know about that?"

"Thin walls and an ex-husband with a big mouth," Sarah said with a grin. "Walter could hardly wait to tell me."

Raylene winced. "He heard us?" She hadn't thought the walls in the house were that thin, or that she and Carter had been that loud. It was embarrassing.

"Not really, but he said you were positively glowing at breakfast yesterday morning. He guessed the rest."

"I'm going to kill Walter," Raylene said grimly.

"Don't be mad. You know how much he adores you. He

only told me because he was so happy for you and knew I would be, too. You're getting your life back, Raylene! I think it's fantastic. So will everyone else. Please, let us celebrate this with you."

She shook her head. "No," she said again, "it won't be much of a life if Paul has his way," Raylene said realistically, ignoring all the rest. What more was there to say about her night with Carter, anyway?

"Something tells me that danger is going to pass, too," Sarah said confidently.

Raylene chuckled at her determined optimism. "You're very cheery today. Is something going on with you?"

"Travis and I have set our wedding date," she admitted. "Finally. I heard from my mom today, and my dad's gotten an okay from his doctor to make the trip."

Raylene hugged her. "That's wonderful!" she said with genuine enthusiasm. "I'm so glad he's better. I know how worried you've been and how much you've wanted him to be here."

"As important as that is, it's just as important that you be able to walk down the aisle as my bridesmaid. And now you can! Talk about perfect timing. When I married Walter, we had such a small ceremony, and none of my friends were there. This time I'm going to be surrounded by everyone I love."

Raylene hated to put a damper on her excitement, but she had to. "Sweetie, walking to the mailbox is a far cry from being able to walk down the aisle of a church with you, much as I would love that. You absolutely cannot count on that."

"Well, I'm going to," Sarah insisted stubbornly. "And I don't care how much pressure it puts on you, I'm telling you here and now that I'm counting on you to be there."

"Oh, sweetie, please don't do that," Raylene begged.

"The wedding's not until November, Thanksgiving week-end, in fact. I figured that would be appropriate because we all have so much to be thankful for this year."

Despite the pressure, Raylene couldn't help being honored that Sarah was so determined that she be a part of her wedding. It was one more reason for her not to allow Paul's release from prison to cause another setback. She had to push through her fears and continue to make progress.

"Look, I've got to run," Sarah said, still bubbling with excitement. "I'll have more details on the wedding later, but I wanted you to be the first to know about it, besides Travis, of course. He's over at the station right now grumbling that if he'd known I was going to insist on him wearing a tuxedo, he wouldn't have pushed so hard to set the date the minute I heard from my mom. I left him with an entire folder of tuxedo styles I'd ripped out of magazines. I need to get back before he calls the whole thing off."

"He'll never do that," Raylene said with certainty. "He's crazy in love with you, and he's been patient for a very long time."

"Yeah, that's what he says," Sarah said happily. "Love you. Talk to you later."

And then, like a tornado blowing through and leaving everything topsy-turvy, she was gone. And Raylene was left to think about all the ways her life was about to change...if only she were brave enough to step outside these four walls.

As September turned into October, Carter had to admit he was starting to freak a little that Paul Hammond hadn't made his move. He'd been so sure it would be swift. Instead, maybe Hammond was relishing the torture Raylene must be feeling as the waiting dragged on.

The work on Raylene's street had mostly been completed.

Tom couldn't justify having crews out there much longer, so the surveillance would be left to him and their friends, since hiring full-time protection was out of the question.

Worse, Carter knew that the longer Paul did nothing, the greater the chance that they'd all be lulled into a false sense of complacency. That's when things could go very, very wrong.

Tired of being in limbo and desperate to get things back to normal, he opted for taking a drive to Charleston. He had no idea where to start looking for the man. He doubted he'd be anywhere near the hospital where he'd lost his privileges to practice. The house he and Raylene had shared had been sold. A parole officer would probably know where to find him, but he might also try to talk Carter out of seeing him.

The only other option he could think of was checking with the man's parents. From what he'd gathered, the scandal had caused the Hammonds huge embarrassment, but they'd defiantly maintained that Raylene was unstable, that she'd imagined everything that had happened. They hadn't been able to explain away the baby she'd miscarried, so they simply didn't mention it. In every conversation, according to Carter's sources and newspaper reports, they proclaimed their son's innocence and extolled him.

Carter found them at home in an imposing house in the historic district. When he told Grant Hammond who he was, the older man almost slammed the door on him until he said he was there on official police business. Good breeding and respect for the law had him hesitating then, but his expression was no more welcoming.

"I need to see your son," Carter told him. "Is he here?"

"If you're on official police business, wouldn't you know that he's not living here?" Hammond asked.

"I didn't ask if he was living here," Carter reminded him,

thankful he'd left himself the loophole. "I asked if he was here now."

"No," his father said flatly. "And I have no idea where he might be, if that was going to be your next question." He frowned at Carter. "And if you're here on behalf of that sniveling ex-wife of his, you can tell her that she'd better stay far away from my son and keep her lies to herself. She's no longer welcome in this town."

Carter was impressed by the parental blindness to the son's flaws. He knew he should let it go, but he couldn't resist asking, "Do you think your son would have cut a deal and spent one minute behind bars if he'd been innocent?"

The older man's bravado crumbled just a bit at the reasonable question. "Just tell her to stay away from us," he repeated.

"Tell your son he needs to do the same. Remind him there's a restraining order that will put him right back in prison if he violates it."

Hammond seemed startled by that. "I'm sure he never wants to set eyes on her again," he said, but he looked as though his confidence had been shaken.

Carter left then, not knowing if his warning would make things better...or worse.

CHAPTER TWENTY-TWO

In mid-October, three weeks after Paul's release from prison, Raylene was slowly starting to feel more secure. The hangups had stopped after the first week. There had been absolutely no attempt to make contact, no overt or even subtle threats. Perhaps Paul had learned his lesson, after all, and would stay out of her life. Certainly if he ever expected to reclaim some semblance of a normal life for himself, that's what he needed to do. Perhaps he'd realized that.

She'd been feeling so reassured, in fact, that she'd actually walked all the way around the block with Dr. McDaniels the day before without a single second of panic. Though she hardly dared to let herself believe it, she thought the worst of her panic disorder was finally behind her. She'd learned to calm herself at the first sign of panic, which meant the incidence of sweaty palms and hyperventilating lasted barely more than a few seconds before she was able to control them.

Each step she took outside filled her with a sense of triumph. Working in the garden had once again become solace for her bruised soul. More important, these small victories filled her with hope that she could reclaim at least some semblance of a normal life.

None of that, however, made her foolhardy. She knew better than to wander anywhere on her own. Despite her most optimistic hopes, she knew her ex-husband was perfectly capable of lying low and then appearing when he was least expected. Carter, in fact, continued to take precautions, though of necessity the daytime crews on the street had moved on. Tom could no longer justify their presence now that the work had been completed. Carter, however, or one of their friends was almost always with her.

His sisters, however, had been told to steer clear unless they visited with him. Raylene missed Carrie and Mandy terribly, but she insisted that they needed to stay out of harm's way.

Since Carter's instructions to the girls had been quite clear, Raylene was surprised late one afternoon when Mandy came through the kitchen and into the backyard in search of her.

"I rang the doorbell, but then I guessed you'd be out here," Mandy said. "I had Carter's key, so I let myself in. Was that okay?"

Raylene regarded her with a mixture of delight and dismay. "Coming through the house was fine, but you know you shouldn't be here, Mandy," she said. "It's not safe."

"But I really missed you," Mandy protested. "I haven't seen you in, like, forever."

"There's a good reason for that," Raylene reminded her. "I know your brother's explained about my ex-husband."

Mandy looked disappointed. "Please, can't I stay? Just for a little while? The garden really could use some work. If I clean out the dead annuals, I could plant some pansies or some chrysanthemums next time I come over."

"That would be lovely," Raylene agreed. Against her better judgment, she finally nodded. "Okay, you can stay, but just for an hour. I'll call your brother and tell him you're here. Maybe he can swing by."

Mandy grimaced. "I was kind of hoping we could talk, just you and me."

"I still need to let him know you're here," Raylene insisted, dialing his number and filling him in. "I've told her she can only stay for an hour."

Carter was silent for so long, she didn't know what to think. "Would you rather I send her home now?"

"No, I suppose it's okay," he said with unmistakable reluctance. "I'll see if the sheriff can send a deputy over to drive by a few times. Even though we're stretched thin. I know he's been trying to keep somebody in the general area most of the day. I'd come myself, but I'm on a call on the west side of the county."

"I really do think Paul got the message," she reassured him. "It's been ages since I had any of those hang-up calls."

"I hope you're right. Don't take any chances, though."

"It's not as if I'm going to wander off," she said wryly. "We'll be fine. I promise."

Carter didn't seem to be a hundred percent reassured, but he hung up with a promise to check in with her as often as he could.

"Is it okay?" Mandy asked when she'd hung up.

"He says you can stay for an hour," Raylene told her. "Why don't I go inside and fix us some sweet tea?"

"Sounds great," Mandy said, already kneeling by the garden and yanking out weeds.

Raylene left her to it, then stepped into the kitchen and immediately halted in her tracks, heart hammering. Panic, which she'd almost convinced herself was a thing of the past, reached out and grabbed her by the throat.

"Hello, Raylene," Paul said quietly.

There was an all-too-familiar fire in his eyes that had her frantically trying to locate the portable phone. Unfortunately, it was on the counter right beside him. Drawing on some last shred of inner strength, she forced herself to face him without blinking. She even managed to steady her nerves. She had to do everything she could to keep him here, in the house and away from Mandy.

"What are you doing here?" she asked, proud of herself for keeping her voice even.

"I thought I owed you a visit so we could catch up," he said. "I know you had people watching the house, but they've been gone for a few days now."

She regarded him with alarm. "How do you know that?"

He looked amused. "I don't exactly drive around in a car with a big sign on it that says ex-prisoner, you know. I'm capable of riding through a town, even one the size of Serenity, without anyone recognizing me. As long as you don't hang around or break any laws, no one gets suspicious. A few quick trips past the house spread out over a couple of weeks told me everything I needed to know."

"You've been coming here despite the restraining order? Do you really want to go back to prison, Paul?"

He shrugged. "It hardly matters. My life is pretty much over, thanks to you."

"No," she argued. "You won an early release. You have a second chance. Go someplace new and start over."

"My life was in Charleston."

"Oh, please, that's hardly the only city in the world. Qualified physicians are needed in all of them. Come on, think about it, Paul. You're too smart to throw everything away like this."

"Charleston is where I had status and prestige," he insisted stubbornly. "At least I did until you deliberately set out to destroy my reputation."

"*You're* the one who destroyed your reputation," she corrected. Surprisingly, her voice didn't quaver. In fact, she felt unexpectedly calm now, despite the very real danger he represented. No matter what, she was going to stand her ground as she'd never dared to before. Somehow over the past two years she'd discovered an inner strength she hadn't possessed during their marriage.

And, she thought with the ferocity of a mother, there was Mandy to protect. She couldn't allow any harm to come to Carter's sister.

"Paul, if you leave right now, before anyone else discovers you're here, you can still have that second chance. I won't say a word if you go and promise never to come back. You can even have your say before you go, if that will make you feel better. You do need to hurry, though, because despite your impression, there are people watching out for me. If they see a strange car outside, they'll come in to check. If they find you here, it's over. You'll have blown your chance at a new life."

"You don't honestly think I parked out front, do you? My car's a couple of blocks away on the town square. I strolled over here like I belonged." His apologetic look was insincere. "Sorry, but I'm not going anywhere. We have unfinished business."

"Let's go into the living room and talk about this," she suggested, needing to get him out of the kitchen. She didn't want him to catch a glimpse of Mandy through the window. If only she'd locked the door behind her on the way in. What if Mandy wondered what was taking her so long and decided to come inside looking for her? She had to get Paul into the other room.

"Here's good," he said.

"No," she said flatly and shot past him, leaving him to follow.

In the living room, she stayed on her feet. Paul was right behind her, looking annoyed. "What are you trying to pull?"

He took an intimidating step toward her, barely banked fury in his eyes. Raylene sucked in a breath and stayed right where she was. If she backed up, it would be an admission of weakness, and she refused to be weak in the face of his anger ever again. Not that she wouldn't have fled out the front door and into the street screaming her head off if she'd thought she could make it. Unfortunately she hadn't had enough lead time to pull that off.

"Stay away from me," she warned. "I mean it, Paul. I'll fight you any way I have to."

Amazingly, it was true. The fear she'd felt during their marriage had been as much about losing what he represented—status, security, love—as it had been about the physical abuse. Now she understood that all of that had been an illusion, anyway. As for the very real pain, she'd survived that, too.

Right now, she knew if she could keep him talking, she could figure out a plan. Though Carter had expressed the hope that the sheriff would find an available deputy to send by, Raylene knew she couldn't count on anyone showing up to rescue her. Most important, it was up to her to protect Mandy at any cost.

Fortunately, thanks to too many years of practice, she knew his likely moves. When he reached for her with a gesture that might have been meant as a caress, but too often turned into a slap, she ducked agilely out of his path. She caught the faint hint of surprise in his eyes.

She thought about what was on the table behind her...a clay bowl that Tommy had made at a craft store for Sarah's birthday, a lamp and a stack of magazines. She pictured their placement, tried to envision the bowl or lamp as a weapon.

The bowl would be easiest to grab, and it was hefty enough to cause some damage.

Despite her earlier determination to stand her ground, she took a step back. This time the glint in Paul's eyes was satisfaction. Obviously he thought he had her on the run, as he had so many times in the past.

"You need to leave," she said again. "I'm not going to let you hurt me, Paul. I'll fight you with every breath I have in me."

"You wouldn't dare," he said, amused. "You certainly never did before. I have to admit that made it less satisfying for me."

Even as he spoke the hateful words, her hand closed around the edge of the bowl. She imagined Tommy's small handprint pressed into the clay, then painted bright blue, his favorite color.

Again, Paul tried to grab her, but her quick move to the side had him lurching forward and past her. She landed a solid blow to the side of his head with the clay bowl, and he went down, sinking like a rag doll with the stuffing knocked out. Not waiting to see if he was going to get back on his feet, she ran screaming from the house.

Just as she emerged, a sheriff's cruiser skidded around the corner, siren blaring, and Mandy came tearing around the side of the house and threw herself into Raylene's arms.

"I heard him," she said, sobbing against Raylene's chest. "The window was open and I heard him. I called Carter."

Raylene held her tightly. "You did exactly the right thing, sweetie. It's okay. We're both okay."

When Deputy Callahan approached, Raylene pointed a shaky hand toward the house. She realized she was still holding Tommy's clay bowl.

"I hit him. He fell. I don't know if he's okay or not," she said, her words running together.

Callahan charged into the house, gun drawn, as another deputy arrived and urged Raylene and Mandy toward his cruiser, then followed Callahan inside.

She and Mandy huddled together in the backseat. Though she was still shaking, Mandy gave her a wavery smile. "No matter how mad Carter is, I'm glad I was here."

"I'm glad you were, too, and that you had the presence of mind to call your brother."

By the time the two deputies emerged with a dazed-looking Paul in handcuffs, Carter pulled to a stop in front of the house, his complexion pale. He barely spared a glance for Paul. Instead, his gaze was riveted on his sister and Raylene.

"You're okay?" he asked in a voice that shook. "Both of you?"

Raylene nodded, suddenly unable to speak. Though she'd emerged from the cruiser at the first sight of Carter, the panic and shock caught up with her. She trembled violently. Mandy held her steady.

"I swear to God I lost ten years off my life when Mandy called," he said, gathering them close. "I hope I never have to go through anything like that again."

"Believe me, I hope so, too," Raylene said fervently, then met his gaze. "Is it really over? For good this time?"

"We'll do everything we can to make sure he's in prison a lot longer this time."

Raylene released a long pent-up sigh. Maybe between the certainty that Paul would be facing a longer prison term and the courage she'd found to face him down, she really could get on with her life now.

Carter had never been so terrified in his life as he had been when Mandy called, crying almost hysterically, to say she thought Paul Hammond was in the house with Raylene. He'd made the call to Dispatch, then taken off in that direction himself. He'd made the drive at a breakneck speed that even with his experience behind the wheel had seemed insane on the winding rural roads.

"What's this?" he asked, removing the object Raylene was clutching in a death grip.

"Tommy made it," she whispered. "It's okay, isn't it? Sarah will kill me if I broke it on Paul's hard head."

"I think Sarah would gladly make the sacrifice if it meant you were safe," he said, smiling as he examined the lopsided little bowl that only a mother could appreciate. "But it's okay. Not a scratch on it."

Leading Raylene and his sister inside, he asked, "Any idea how Paul got inside?"

"That might have been my fault," Mandy said, looking miserable. "I tried the front door when I got here, then I used your key. I might not have locked the door behind me." She lifted her gaze to Raylene. "I'm so sorry. I didn't think."

Carter opened his mouth to yell at her, but Raylene's touch on his hand kept him silent.

"Does it really matter how he got in?" she said gently. "The point is that he's under arrest and gone now."

"I suppose," he conceded, still wishing he could rant and rave at somebody for allowing this to happen after all their careful plans. He supposed his little sister wasn't the best target for his own frustration over not being able to protect Raylene. He vowed that once he had the Serenity police force up and running, he'd do a better job at keeping local residents safe. He'd fight for the resources he'd need, even under extraordinary circumstances such as this.

He gave Mandy's hand a squeeze, then grinned at Raylene. "I think we're due for a celebration, don't you? Why don't we call Carrie and the Sweet Magnolias and get everyone over here."

"Sure," Raylene said eagerly, but then the light in her eyes dimmed just a bit. "Carter, today is a huge milestone, but it doesn't mean I'll be miraculously cured."

"I'm not counting on a miracle. I'm putting my faith in you."

"Oh, Carter," she whispered. "Please don't do that. Not yet."

He refused to be daunted. He knew she was just trying to be realistic, but he wasn't giving up on their future so easily. He knew, even if she didn't, that they had one no matter how long her recovery took.

"I'm not going to argue about this now," he said. "We have too much to be grateful for. You make those calls, and I'll go by Sullivan's and see what kind of party food Dana Sue can throw together in a hurry."

"We could just have hot dogs and burgers," Raylene said.

"Nope, this is a special occasion. Besides, you know Dana Sue will be offended if she's not asked to bring the food. Do you have all the ingredients for margaritas? Helen's going to want to know that."

"We always have those on hand," Raylene told him. "We just don't make them for the men. Margarita nights are for the Sweet Magnolias only."

Carter shook his head at the traditions of these loyal friends. "Fine. I'll pick up beer and wine."

He leaned down and kissed her, lingering long enough to stir up plenty of heat. "Love you," he said, then took off to clock out and put the party plan in motion.

Only when he was sitting in the front seat of his cruiser on his way back to the sheriff's office did he realize what he'd said. *Love you* had come out of his mouth without thought, but he realized it was true. Somewhere along the way he'd fallen in love with Raylene, the kind of love that had kept his parents together through tough times and good, the kind that would get them through, as well.

Now he just had to figure out some way to convince Raylene she had the strength to love him back.

When Raylene emerged from the house and stepped into the backyard without a moment's hesitation, an impromptu cheer went up. She stood where she was, a tray of food in her arms, and what had to be a silly grin spreading across her face. She found Carter in the crowd and saw the hope in his eyes. It would have dazzled her if she hadn't been so scared of letting him down.

She hadn't missed those casually spoken words as he'd been dashing out of the house earlier. He'd kissed her, then said he loved her. Oh, he could have blown it off as something any friend might say to another one at the end of a visit or a call, but she knew better. He'd meant it. She just wasn't sure she was ready to face the implications.

And until she was, she needed to keep a safe distance between them.

It turned out that was easier said than done on a night when it seemed everyone was conspiring to throw the two of them together. There was undeniable magic in the night air, along with the sweet scent of honeysuckle.

It was nearly midnight when everyone began drifting off. Even Carrie and Mandy rode off on their bikes, leaving Raylene alone with Carter.

"Don't you need to spend some time at home with the girls? You've been neglecting them lately, and I know Carrie still needs you," she said, sidestepping him when he reached out to pull her down beside him. She picked up the last of the plates from the party and carried them inside. With an audible sigh over her evasiveness, he followed.

"You're trying to avoid me," he accused gently, standing directly in her path. "Why is that?"

"I told you earlier. We don't know yet what any of this means. I don't want you getting your hopes up or starting to make any kind of plans."

"I know you might still have a rough road ahead, but just think about what you accomplished today. You faced down your abusive ex-husband. That took amazing bravery."

"Knowing Mandy was outside and that I had to protect her gave me the strength I needed to do that."

"Well, I say that makes you remarkable."

"Carter, it doesn't mean there won't be more bad days ahead."

"Can't you just enjoy the moment?" he asked, regarding her with bewilderment.

"It's not the moment that worries me," she said. "It's that look you keep getting in your eyes, as if everything's suddenly all right." She met his gaze. "Plus, you said you loved me," she added, making it sound like an accusation.

He seemed amused. "Shame on me," he said. "What an awful thing to say!"

"I'm trying to make a point here," she said testily. "You only said it after you thought I was well—and that the agoraphobia was somehow magically behind me now that Paul's been dealt with."

He frowned at that. "And you think that means …" He hesitated, looking puzzled. "What do you think it means?"

"You never said the words before, when you thought I was a wreck. It felt like you were holding back, giving yourself an out in case things never improved."

"That's ridiculous! First of all, I never thought you were

a wreck," he said fiercely, holding her gaze until she finally gave a nod of acknowledgment. "And second, it wasn't until this afternoon that I realized how deep my feelings for you run. I should have said it differently. I should have made some big production out of it, I guess. But it came out, because in that moment, I knew it was how I felt. Period. Don't make some big deal out of the fact that today was the first time I'd said it."

"Love is a big deal, Carter. I'm not sure I'm ready for that, especially if it's contingent on me being back to normal."

She'd known for a while now that what she felt for him was powerful. She'd even labeled it love. Acting on it, however, facing all of the implications for their future, she wasn't prepared to go there, not when her life might no longer be on hold. If she once again had a future filled with possibilities, she wanted to explore all of them.

"Then you don't love me?" he asked.

When she hesitated, he might have looked hurt, but instead, he merely nodded. "That's okay. I think you do, but if you're not ready to say the words, I'll wait."

Was that what she'd wanted to hear, that he would sit on the sidelines patiently waiting until she got her feet back under her and knew who she could be again?

"That's not going to work," she told him, struggling with real regret. "You have a family to think about. Concentrate on them. See that Carrie gets well. Don't put one second of your life on hold for me. If I've learned one thing and nothing else over the past couple of years, it's that life is too precious to waste a minute of it. Out of fear, I've wasted far too much."

"And yet you're still willing to waste more," he said. "You're throwing away what I know we could have."

"I'm not throwing it away," she argued. "I'm just not ready for it now, and I can't ask you to wait."

"So, what? Me telling you I love you, being here for you, is going to put some kind of pressure on you?"

"Yes," she said, near tears. The selfish part of her wanted to seize what he was offering, but the unselfish side knew it was only fair to let him go.

Seeing the dismay in his eyes, she tried to explain. "It's been so long since I've even thought I could have a life again. I need time, Carter, time to figure out all the possibilities that might be out there for me. And you need to think about whether you'll feel the same way about me if it turns out that I'm not recovered, after all."

He looked deeply into her eyes. His were filled with hurt and confusion, but he gave her a curt nod, accepting the finality of her decision. "You want time, Raylene, you've got it," he said.

Then, his back stiff with pride, he turned and walked away.

Carter wasn't entirely surprised when his sisters cornered him a few days after the party and demanded to know why they weren't spending time with Raylene or, more specifically, why *he* wasn't, now that the danger of her ex-husband showing up was past.

"You never go over there anymore," Carrie complained. "You just sit around here and watch me eat. Even though Dr. McDaniels has told you herself that I'm doing everything I'm supposed to do, you act like you don't trust me."

"I do trust you," he said. Mostly, anyway. He could tell she'd put on a few pounds, and meals were certainly less stressful. Not only had she started baking again, she'd even fixed a few dinners and eaten her share. That didn't mean his worry had evaporated.

"Then prove it," Carrie challenged. "Have dinner with Raylene. Take her someplace special."

He shook his head. "I'm giving her space. It's what she wanted. She's probably right. It's for the best."

"I don't believe you," Carrie declared. "And it's not best for us. She actually gets us. We like her. Now we can't go over there, either, if the two of you are fighting. We'd feel disloyal to you."

"We're not fighting," he said wearily. *We just aren't speaking.*

Carrie gave him a piercing look. "Was she just some project for you, so you could feel like a big hero or something?"

He regarded her with shock. "Don't be ridiculous."

"Well, what are we supposed to think?" Mandy chimed in. "You're moping around here like you've lost your best friend. It's depressing."

"Well, this is the way it is," Carter told them. "Deal with it."

Unfortunately, judging from the defiant expressions on their faces as they stomped out of the house, they weren't going to deal with it quite the way he'd envisioned.

Raylene opened the front door to find Carrie and Mandy on the doorstep. Her mood brightened at the sight of them.

"Come in," she said eagerly. "What brings you by?"

"We want you to stop fighting with Carter," Carrie said at once in her familiar, blunt way. "He's miserable, and if you don't mind me saying so, you don't look so hot, either."

Raylene bought herself some time by going into the kitchen and pouring the girls glasses of lemonade and bringing out the oatmeal-raisin cookies she'd baked that morning. To her relief, Carrie grabbed one as eagerly as Mandy did.

"Well, aren't you going to say something?" Mandy finally challenged, even as she devoured her second cookie.

"I don't know what to say," Raylene admitted. "Things between your brother and me are very complicated."

"It seems pretty simple to me," Carrie said. "He loves you. You love him. You work it out. At least that's how I thought it was supposed to work. You can't solve anything if you're not even talking."

Raylene tried to make them understand. "Look, you know about this panic thing, right? We've talked about it before. It hasn't just vanished overnight."

"But I thought you were better," Carrie said, her eyes filled with concern. "Aren't you?"

"Actually, I've made some improvement," Raylene admitted. "Quite a bit, in fact. But there will be setbacks. And once I do get completely well, I have to figure out what I want. There will be options I never even considered a few weeks or months ago."

"Why can't Carter be one of those options?" Mandy asked, then added earnestly, "He's a really good guy. You won't do any better."

"Carter's an amazing man," Raylene agreed. "He needs to move on with someone who's ready for a relationship."

"Come on," Carrie protested. "He can't just move on and pick somebody else like he's choosing a cantaloupe. That's not how it works. He's in love with you."

Raylene regarded her with envy. It must be wonderful to be on the threshold of becoming a young adult, when anything seemed possible and love conquered everything. "Sometimes love's just not enough."

Carrie groaned and exchanged an exasperated look with her sister. "I should have known," she muttered. "Grownups are idiots." She turned to Mandy. "Come on. Let's go home and fix this."

Raylene stopped her with a hand on her arm. "Sweetie, I really appreciate that you want to make things right between us, but it's not up to you."

"Well, somebody has to fix it, and it's obviously not going to be the two adults involved," Carrie retorted with disgust.

And then she and Mandy were gone, though not before Mandy had grabbed a fistful of cookies to tide her over on the walk home. As they walked down the sidewalk, she handed one to Carrie, who accepted it without comment and took a bite.

Raylene smiled at the sight, though she felt oddly wistful. A part of her had hoped to have a place in their lives. Carter had even offered her that. Was she the idiot Carrie had called her for saying no? Or did she owe it to Carter, and mostly to herself, to make sure there wasn't something else she wanted more, a life she couldn't possibly have envisioned just a few short weeks ago?

CHAPTER TWENTY-THREE

Walter had grown up as his parents' golden boy. Right up until he'd finally developed a spine, moved away from home and settled in Serenity, he'd done exactly what was expected—except, of course, when he'd married Sarah.

Even then, however, he'd let his folks influence him and get in the middle of his marriage until the divorce had been inevitable. There were days when he could still hear their voices in his head, complaining about this or scolding him about that.

From the day he'd met Rory Sue, he'd tried to imagine his parents' reaction to her unpredictability and untamed exuberance. Tonight, though, as he looked at her sprawled across his bed, her hair like silk on the pillow, her cheeks flushed, a smile on her lips, he realized that his opinion was the only one that mattered. He knew exactly what he wanted, had known it for a while now, but caution had kept him silent.

"Marry me," he blurted before he could analyze it to death.

Rory Sue shot up, dragging a sheet with her, and stared at him. "Excuse me?"

He grinned at her stunned expression. "I asked you to marry me," he repeated quietly. "I love you, Rory Sue. I've made plenty of mistakes in my life, but I know you're not one of them. You're the best thing that's ever happened to me."

Instead of flinging herself into his arms as he'd half expected, she studied him warily. "Why now?"

"Why not now?"

"Maybe you're just feeling left out because Sarah and Travis have set their wedding date for next month and Raylene's getting her life under control and doesn't need you to look out for her anymore."

"Believe me, this has nothing to do with my ex-wife or my friend," he insisted. "I just realized that you and I balance each other perfectly. When I get stuffy and traditional, you yank me right out of that and get me to do something I never dreamed I'd do. I think maybe you need me for the flip side of that. I'll keep you from doing something so crazy you'll wind up in a hospital or in jail."

"Like when you talked me out of going bungee-jumping?" she asked, a twinkle in her eyes.

"That's one example," he said. "And when you talked me into going skinny-dipping in your parents' pool while they were home." That had been at the same time the most terrifying and the most liberating risk he'd ever taken.

She laughed. "I told you they'd never catch us, but you should have seen your face when that light in the house came on. It was priceless."

"I thought for sure Sonny was going to be out there with a shotgun two minutes later," he admitted.

Rory Sue knelt beside him. "You have to admit, it was pretty exhilarating."

"That's one word for it." He looked into her eyes. "I want a lifetime of that, Rory Sue. I want us to do the unexpected for the rest of our days."

"What about all the normal stuff, like having kids?" she

asked. "I don't think I'm anywhere near ready for that. You understand that, right?"

Walter swallowed his disappointment. He'd known for a while now that Rory Sue would probably never be tamed to the point of being a traditional wife and mother. "As much as I would love to have a baby with you, I have Tommy and Libby. It may take me a whole lifetime just to figure out how to be a good dad to the two of them. If those are the only children I have, it's okay. You'll be an amazing stepmother."

She studied him worriedly. "Are you sure you can live with us not having kids of our own?"

"Very sure," he said solemnly. He waited a minute, then asked, "So, what do you think? Want to get married? We could do it skydiving over the Grand Canyon if you want."

She blinked at the suggestion, then started laughing. "You surprise me, Walter Price! If I thought you were serious about that, I'd book us flights to Vegas tomorrow."

He reached into a bedside table and pulled out two plane tickets he'd booked the week before. "Already done."

She looked at the two tickets, then at the confirmation for the skydiving excursion. "Well, I'll be darned."

"So, what's it going to be, Rory Sue?"

Laughing, she threw her arms around his neck. "What time do we leave?"

Hands on her hips, Carrie stood in front of Carter, eyeing him with disgust. "Please tell me you are not going to spend the rest of your life sitting around here drinking beer and pouting. It's been ages since you've done anything besides work and hang out with us. Mandy and I are sick of it."

Carter scowled at her. "I am not pouting. Two-year-olds pout."

"Well, it looks that way to me, and believe me, I know pouting when I see it. I am the queen of pouting."

He grinned despite his sour mood. "I certainly can't deny that."

"So, get a grip and fight for Raylene," she said, her expression serious. "If you sit back and let her spend who knows how long trying to decide what she wants, she might figure out it isn't you."

"Thanks for the vote of confidence," he replied sourly.

Carrie made a face. "Don't mock me. You need to be in her face while she's deciding, so you're one of the options. If you play this right, I still think you can be at the top of the list."

"*I* think you spent too much time last summer watching soap operas or some of those hot new teen shows," he accused. "This is real life. It gets complicated."

"And you don't think soaps are complicated?" she asked incredulously. "I could fill you in on some plots that would make your head spin. The point is, you want Raylene. She loves you. Sure, she has options now, but that doesn't mean you shouldn't be the one she chooses. How's she supposed to figure that out if you're over here sulking?"

"What do you suggest?" he asked, more out of curiosity than from any intention of following her advice. She'd barely turned sixteen, for goodness' sakes. How wise could she be?

"I'm glad you asked," she said, whipping a piece of paper out of her pocket and handing it to him. "Here are a few ideas for starters. Mandy and I agree they all sound pretty romantic, but what do we know? We're kids. We would have asked Raylene for her ideas, but that might have given away the plan."

"The plan?" he repeated, staring at the list of twelve surefire ways to get Raylene's attention. That's what it actually said in capital letters: "TWELVE SUREFIRE WAYS TO GET RAY-

LENE'S ATTENTION." Clearly they'd given the matter a lot of thought and were pretty confident about their scheme.

He scanned the list. Some of it was fairly predictable— sending flowers, taking over her favorite foods as a surprise. Even sending a hundred balloons that said, I Love You, though over the top, was something any man on a mission might try.

It was the twelfth suggestion on the list that caught his attention: "Work in her garden. Don't wear a shirt." He laughed as he read it.

"You honestly think me parading around half-naked is going to do the trick?" he asked.

"You have a halfway-decent body," Carrie said. "All my friends say so."

"It's late October. Haven't you noticed it's starting to get chilly around here?"

She shrugged that off. "There's a warm spell predicted for this weekend, but even if it's freezing, you should do it to prove how serious you are about getting her attention."

"You don't care if I wind up with pneumonia?"

"Not so much," she said cavalierly.

Carter shrugged. He supposed it was worth a shot, though he wasn't convinced that the sight of him showing off his abs was going to override all of Raylene's doubts about the future.

Still, Carrie and Mandy's list got him thinking. If a piece of paper with a few clearly stated objectives could make him view things in a different light, perhaps something similar would work with Raylene.

"I need paper and a pen," he told his sisters.

Carrie's eyes brightened. "You're going to write her a love letter," she said eagerly. "Great idea. We should have thought of that one."

"Not exactly," Carter responded, accepting the pen and

stationery that Mandy had hurriedly provided. He winced at the pink paper, but what the heck? Maybe Raylene was partial to pink.

And if he got the words right, the color of the paper would hardly matter.

Raylene sat at the kitchen table, despondently sipping a glass of lemonade. It was the first pitcher she'd made in a while, but the unexpected arrival of springlike weather in late October had put her in the mood for it. She pursed her lips when she realized she'd forgotten to add sugar. She'd been doing that a lot recently, getting lost in thought and forgetting things. She couldn't seem to focus, not since she'd sent Carter away and then told his sisters that it was over.

She'd been half expecting them to somehow intervene and stir things up, but as the days passed, they hadn't returned, and there'd been no sign of Carter. Obviously, he'd taken her at her word and was going to stay away. What had she expected, that he'd fight for her?

Oddly, now that she was actually able to leave the house every day, at least for a brief walk into town and long enough to do a little paperwork for Travis at the radio station, she realized there was no place she really wanted to be, except with Carter and the girls. All of those big plans she'd hinted to him that she wanted to make for her future seemed unimportant compared to what she'd already found with him.

A full-time job? Maybe even a real career? Sure, it would be nice if she could define herself as something other than an agoraphobic at long last. Volunteer work of some kind? There was nothing to stop her from doing that, even if she were married and working. Travel? Well, what fun would it be to see the country or the world without someone to share the trip?

But even though she was reaching those conclusions on her own—okay, with plenty of helpful prodding from Annie and Sarah—she couldn't bring herself to pick up the phone and call Carter to tell him she'd made a mistake. She'd given him the freedom to move on. Now she had to let him do just that. If the path ultimately led back to her…well, she'd be waiting.

Carrie's declaration calling her an idiot rang in her head. She probably was. In facing down Paul, she'd discovered that she was a fighter, after all. So why wasn't she fighting for this, for the future she knew she wanted? What was stopping her? Fear? Hadn't she had more than enough of letting fear rule her life?

Somehow she had to find the courage—and a plan—for going after what she really wanted.

When Raylene looked outside the next afternoon, to her astonishment she saw Carter working in her garden. Most of the flowers had died back and weeds had taken over since that fateful day when Paul had turned up. She hadn't gotten around to buying any of the fall plants she'd intended to put in. What was left looked sadly neglected.

On this unseasonably warm day, Carter was shirtless and wearing a pair of jeans that fit like a glove. He made her mouth go dry. Then, again, he inspired that reaction pretty much whatever he wore.

She opened the door carefully, but it brought his head snapping around. His gaze met hers and held.

"I'm surprised to see you here," she said.

He gave her a sheepish grin. "It's been brought to my attention that I've been behaving like an idiot."

She laughed at that. "Mine, too. Your sisters, Annie, Sarah—all of them have expressed that at one time or another."

He chuckled, but then his expression sobered. "One of the

things they all have in common is that they're smart. I *have* been acting like an idiot. I'm in love with you and I walked away from that just because you told me to. That's exactly when I should have stuck around to fight."

"So you came over here to fight for me?" she asked, her heart in her throat.

"I did," he said, pulling a pink envelope out of his back pocket. The incongruous sight made her smile. "It's all in here. Read it."

He crossed the yard and handed it to her.

Raylene took the thin envelope and sat down. When she pulled out the single sheet of paper, she saw that it was a list of all the things she'd ever mentioned wanting to do if she got her life back. Beside each one was a promise.

"Whatever job you decide you want, I will support you in that a hundred percent. No matter how time-consuming it is, I'll never complain, as long as you come home to me at the end of the day."

She lifted her gaze to see that he was watching her intently. "Good start," she said softly, fighting tears.

"Keep reading."

"If you want to volunteer or help out in the community, I'll be by your side," he'd written. "We'll both give something back in return for all the blessings in our lives."

She swallowed hard as the words in front of her swam on the page. She tried to keep reading through her tears.

"Wherever you want to travel, I'll do everything I can to make sure the trip is memorable. We'll fill a hundred albums with all our memories so we can look at them again when we're too old to roam."

Now Raylene's tears were flowing freely as she came to the next item on his list.

"We'll have the family you wanted, starting with Carrie

and Mandy and adding all the kids you dreamed of, raising them together with love, through good times and bad, from colic to acne and angst." She smiled at that.

"And last," he'd written, "we'll grow old together and spend our evenings sitting outside with the scent of honeysuckle in the air, holding hands and remembering the wonderful life we built together."

When she looked up, her eyes shimmering with tears, he met her gaze, then held it. She couldn't have looked away even had she wanted to.

"Make that dream with me," he said quietly. "Please don't go off on your own, Raylene. Let's do it together. Marry me."

Raylene's heart swelled at the sincerity she heard in his voice and the words he'd written on that ridiculously feminine stationery. It was all there, her hopes and dreams, the role he wanted to play in the rest of her life. All she had to do was take a few steps away from the house that had been her haven for so long and walk into his arms.

She'd conquered her fears weeks ago, all except this one, reaching for the dream that mattered the most. Now, once more, her heart was in her throat as she stepped off the patio and onto the grass. She walked slowly until she was right in front of him, close enough to feel his heat, near enough to reach up and touch his amazing face.

"I love you," she whispered as she placed her hands on his warm, sun-kissed shoulders. She waited for the faint flicker of fear at the risk of embracing an untested future, but all she felt was yearning and need.

And then she was in his arms...where she felt safer than she ever had in her life.

EPILOGUE

Honeysuckle twined through the specially built arbor in the backyard, the flower's sweet scent filling the air on a clear summer evening. There was even a sprig of the vine in Raylene's bouquet to remind her of the day she'd first realized how thoughtful Carter could be.

She stood just inside the back door and thought about everything that had happened in the past year—Paul going back to prison, her slow but steady conquest of her fears, becoming a godmother to Meg, then standing up as one of Sarah's bridesmaids when Sarah and Travis had married in the fall in a ceremony that had been everything Sarah had dreamed of and deserved.

Now it was Raylene's own turn, a day she'd never thought would come just one brief year ago. She was marrying Carter, and they were going to Bermuda for their honeymoon, her first trip out of the country, just one more step on her path to a perfectly normal life.

"You look amazing," Annie said, straightening the short train on Raylene's simple white dress. "You were made to wear that dress."

Raylene shook her head. "I don't need designer clothes

anymore, or fancy china and silver, or expensive champagne with dinner. I discovered too late how little those things mean. I'm happier than I've ever been with the off-the-rack clothes from my little shop on Main Street, the plain white dishes I found at Crate & Barrel and a pitcher of sweet tea at the end of the day."

"Face it, if you're anything like I am with Travis, you're so besotted with Carter, you don't even notice what you're wearing or eating," Sarah said, radiating contentment. Or maybe the glow came from the secret she'd shared just a few days earlier. She and Travis were expecting their first child.

Sighing with satisfaction at how well things had turned out for all of them, Raylene glanced outside and caught a glimpse of her husband-to-be.

"I am definitely besotted," she admitted.

Sarah followed her gaze outside, then laughed. "Thanks for letting Libby be a flower girl, but I hope you weren't counting on her sticking with the program."

Raylene spotted Libby already tossing rose petals in every direction. When Travis tried to take the basket from her, her face scrunched up. She looked about two seconds from throwing a tantrum. "Maybe it's a sign we should get this show on the road," Raylene said. "What are we waiting for? Where's Walter?"

"Here he comes, right on cue," Sarah said. "I still can't believe you asked my ex-husband to give you away."

"He might have been a lousy husband, but he's been a good friend," Raylene told her. "With my dad gone and my mother still sulking because I gave up what she considered to be the ideal life, who else was there?"

"We could have done it," Annie said.

"You're my matrons of honor," Raylene said. "From the time we were little girls, that was always the plan. Maybe that's why my first marriage was such a disaster, because the two of you weren't there for the wedding."

"I could say the same about mine," Sarah said, her starry-eyed gaze seeking out Travis, who'd hoisted Libby into his arms as a consolation for not letting her toss any more rose petals before the wedding. "With you all as my witnesses last fall, along with all the Sweet Magnolias, I know this marriage will be a keeper."

Raylene grinned. "You don't think your faith in that has just a little bit to do with the man you married?"

Sarah blushed. "Well, sure, Travis does get some of the credit for making me happier than I've ever been." She waved off the conversation and focused her attention on Raylene. "Enough about me. This is *your* day. And just like me, you not only have us, but all the Sweet Magnolias here to give it their blessing. That's some powerful mojo going on."

Raylene blinked. *"Mojo?"*

"Luck, magic, whatever you want to call it," Sarah said. "It's all on your side today." She gestured around the yard. "Take a look. Have you ever known a more loyal group of friends?"

Raylene turned misty-eyed. "The Sweet Magnolias are pretty incomparable."

Maddie, Helen, Dana Sue and Jeanette were all turned in their seats, watching the house, waiting for the start of yet another ceremony that would launch one of their own on a path to a lifetime of happiness.

"They look restless to me," Annie proclaimed, just as Carrie and Mandy burst into the house, their expressions anxious.

"What's taking so long?" Mandy asked, looking lovely and way too grown-up in her junior-bridesmaid dress.

"You're not getting cold feet, are you?" Carrie asked, worry puckering her brow. She tugged at the top of her strapless dress. "If this falls down in the middle of the ceremony, I will have to move to another state."

Raylene grinned. "It's not going to fall down. You look beautiful. You both do. I couldn't be happier that I'm going to be part of your family."

"Then stop dillydallying," Annie said. "Let's get you married. I'm not sure how long Tom can keep Carter calm. He's starting to look as if he's about to come in here and drag you out."

"I'm ready," Raylene said, filled with a kind of confidence and serenity she'd never expected to feel again.

Walter held the door for Sarah, Annie, Mandy and Carrie, then turned to her.

"You look beautiful," he said. "Carter's a lucky man."

"Rory Sue lucked out, too," she told him. "I still can't believe you said your vows in midair. Every time I think about it, I get chills down my spine."

"Me, too," he admitted. "I'm still shocked I didn't black out." He grinned at her. "Thank you for keeping your wedding on the ground."

"That's just who we are," she said, her gaze going to each of the Sweet Magnolias before settling on Carter. "Two normal, everyday people surrounded by friends and with a whole wonderful lifetime of magic ahead."

★ ★ ★ ★ ★

QUESTIONS FOR DISCUSSION

1. Raylene has been severely traumatized by domestic violence and willingly admits that she waited too long to leave her husband. Have you ever known anyone in an abusive situation? How did she, or he, handle it? If it was a friend or family member, did you encourage that person to seek help or offer a safe haven? Were you too quick to judge her or him for not getting out, or did you understand how difficult that might be?

2. What resources are available in your community for victims of domestic violence?

3. What did you think of the refusal by Raylene's mother to acknowledge the abuse? Have you known family members who turned a blind eye to domestic violence? What were their reasons?

4. Raylene's reaction to what she experienced was to hide from the world now that she'd found a safe haven in Sarah's home. Have you ever known anyone who simply hunkers down and hides from the world after any kind of bad news or a trauma? Did it reach the level of agoraphobia, a diagnosed and paralyzing fear of leaving the house?

5. Though Sarah and Annie both encourage Raylene to seek help, neither of them insist on it. Do you think they're being supportive, or are they enabling what has become self-destructive behavior?

6. When Carter meets Raylene under less-than-ideal circumstances, he is quick to judge her. As he learns her

story, he realizes that things are not always as they seem. Have you ever made a judgment of someone's actions that you've come to regret? What were the circumstances?

7. As a police officer, Carter is trained to want to help people. How do you think this tendency plays into his attraction to Raylene? Have you ever known anyone with a knight-in-shining-armor complex who seeks out damsels in distress?

8. Carrie's eating disorder is, in part, a reaction to the deaths of her parents. Have you ever suffered a great personal loss? How did you handle it? Did food play a role, either as a solace—by eating too much—or did you not eat at all? Was this temporary, or did it become a dangerous pattern?

9. When Raylene throws Walter and Rory Sue together, she's well aware that he's a traditional kind of guy and Rory Sue's a flirtatious rebel. It's an immediate case of opposites attracting. Do you think opposite personalities do well together? Or does the attraction burn out? What have your own experiences been like?

10. Throughout this book and the entire SWEET MAGNOLIAS series, friendships have been at the core of the stories. Do you have strong ties to your friends? Are they people you've known since childhood? Since college? From the time you settled in the community? Where you now live, or where your children started school? How did the bonds form? Have they ever been tested? How did that turn out?

Once again, New York Times *and* USA TODAY
bestselling author Sherryl Woods
draws you into a world of friendships, families
and heartfelt emotions.
Look for Dream Mender *wherever books are sold.*

Turn the page for a special sneak peek at
Lilac Lane
by #1 New York Times *bestselling author*
Sherryl Woods
coming soon in mass-market paperback
from MIRA Books.

PROLOGUE

The death of Peter McDonough would have been a blow at any time, but coming as it had on the very day Kiera Malone had finally accepted his proposal of marriage left her reeling. After her first husband, Sean Malone, had abandoned her with three young children, she had vowed never to let another man into her life, much less into her heart. She'd clung to her independence with a fierce protectiveness. She'd made a practice of scaring men away with her tart tongue and bitter demeanor, even knowing as she did so that she was dooming herself to loneliness. Better that than dooming herself and her children to another loss, another mistake.

After the death of his wife, Peter, bless his sweet soul, had waited patiently on the sidelines for Kiera, running his pub in Dublin, supporting her daughter, Moira, in her efforts to make a career of the photography that Kiera herself had thought of as nothing more than a hobby, and making the occasional overture to Kiera.

To Kiera's confusion, not even her best efforts to push him aside and make clear her lack of interest, efforts that had chased off every other man who'd approached her, seemed to dissuade Peter. He took her rebuffs in stride. If anything, his not-so-secret crush had deepened.

More troubling, aside from his thick, curly hair and firm jaw, he had a combination of traits that drew her to him—strength balanced by gentleness, bold determination tempered by patience and a booming laugh that could fill her heart with unexpected lightness. He was, in all respects, a man who knew exactly what he wanted, and he wanted Kiera. She had no idea why.

Moreover, he'd had the support not only of her father, Dillon O'Malley, but of her daughter. Up until then, Moira, like Dillon, had approved of very few of Kiera's choices in life. Yet for once Moira and Kiera's father had conspired to push Kiera and Peter together at every opportunity. Since their approval had been granted so sparingly over the years, she'd been persuaded to be less resistant than usual. What was the harm, after all, when she knew it would come to nothing? Relationships tended to deteriorate over time, even those begun with passion and hope. They ended. At least that was her experience.

But then Moira and Dillon had somehow convinced Kiera to move back to Dublin, where, they'd said, there were more opportunities. They dangled new opportunities like strands of glittering gold, told her any one of them would be an improvement over her dead-end career in a dingy neighborhood pub in a tiny seaside village on the coast north of Dublin where she'd toiled for long hours and low pay for most of her life. Moira had actually had the audacity to scold her for accepting security for her family over any ambitions she might have once had to run a restaurant of her own.

"Where's your confidence and self-respect?" Moira had demanded. "You're a far better waitress and cook than I am.

And you've management skills, as well. Look at how well you've kept our family afloat."

Kiera knew the truth of that. Moira was competent, but her heart wasn't in the restaurant business, not even that Irish pub she was hoping to run with her new husband in Chesapeake Shores, Maryland. Luke O'Brien was the attraction there.

Moira's clever argument took another twist. "After all Peter's done for me, it's only fitting that I not leave him in the lurch when I move to Chesapeake Shores. Come to Dublin, where you'll be making at least twice the tips and have the support of a man who's been nothing short of an angel to me. He'd be the same for you. It could be the sort of partnership your life's been lacking."

Kiera noted with some amusement that Moira hadn't suggested *romance*, a word her daughter knew well would have sent Kiera fleeing in the opposite direction.

"He has his own children to step in and help with the running of the pub," Kiera had protested, even though much of what her daughter said made sense.

The prospect of starting over, though, was a scary business. As harsh and difficult as her life had been, it was a niche in which she felt comfortable. With children to support on her own, she'd stopped taking chances. Moira was exactly right about that. She'd put her family first. Wasn't that what a mother was meant to do? The thought of taking a daring risk now was beyond terrifying and yet, perhaps, just a little intriguing.

"His sons have little interest in the pub, much to Peter's dismay," Moira said. "There will be room for you. Peter will welcome the help and the company. If you ask me, he's been a wee bit lonely since his wife's passing."

Persuaded at last—or perhaps simply worn down—Kiera had made the move, but only after telling Peter very, very firmly that he was not to be having expectations of a personal nature where she was concerned. He'd agreed to her terms, but there'd been a smile on his lips and a spark in his blue eyes that she probably shouldn't have ignored.

And there he'd been, day in and day out for the better part of two years, always with a quick-witted comment that made her laugh or a gesture that softened her heart. And his patience truly had been a revelation to her. He'd done not one single thing to make her feel rushed, to make her put up her well-honed guard. Nor was he one to overindulge in Guinness, a habit that would have sent Kiera running even faster after living with Sean's uncontrolled bouts of drinking and subsequent abusive talk.

And so, eventually, one by one, her defenses fell. She found herself looking forward to their late-night talks after the pub closed, to his interest in her opinions. Maybe most of all, she'd basked in his kind and steady company that made her feel secure as she hadn't since the very earliest days of her marriage to Sean Malone. She'd last felt that way before Sean's drinking had started, before he'd walked out the door of their home for the very last time, leaving her with two sons who were not yet ready to start school and a daughter just home from the hospital.

Because she'd made such a show of rebellion in marrying Sean in the first place, Kiera hadn't allowed herself to go running home to her parents back then. Instead, she'd struggled to make do, surviving on her own, if barely. It was only when her mum lay dying that she'd reconciled with her parents and eventually allowed them back into her life and the lives of her children. Her sons and daughter hadn't even been aware that they had grandparents who might dote on them if given the chance.

Now with all three of her children grown and finding

their own paths—albeit in the case of her sons, a path she wouldn't have chosen, the same one their dad had taken— Kiera had been at loose ends when she made the move back to Dublin. She'd perhaps been more vulnerable than she'd allowed herself to be in years.

She couldn't claim that Peter had taken unfair advantage of that. He'd been too fine a man to do so, but the fact was, she'd finally been ready to reach for a little happiness. Peter had offered the promise of that and more. And exactly as Moira had predicted, his sons were happy enough to have her in their father's life and working by his side at the pub. The future looked bright with the sort of promise of love and stability she'd once dreamed of, but never imagined truly finding.

And, then, on the very day she'd said yes, when she'd opened her heart and allowed Peter to put a ring on her finger, a ring he'd claimed he'd been holding on to for years for just such a glorious day, he'd betrayed her as surely as Sean Malone ever had. He'd suffered a fatal heart attack just hours later, and once again, Kiera was alone and adrift. Abandoned.

Wasn't that just the way of the bloody world? she thought, her protective bitterness returning in spades and her fragile heart once more shattered into pieces.

CHAPTER ONE

Moira O'Brien sat in the kitchen of her grandfather's cozy home by the Chesapeake Bay, a home he shared with Nell O'Brien O'Malley, with whom he'd been reunited only a few short years ago after a lifetime of being separated. The air was rich with the scent of cranberry-orange scones baking in the oven and Irish Breakfast Tea steeping in a treasured antique flowered teapot on the table. Nell had brought it home from Ireland after visiting her grandparents decades ago. She said it had been her Irish grandmother's favorite.

"What should we be doing about our Kiera?" Nell asked them. Though Kiera hadn't even come to Chesapeake Shores for her own father's wedding to Nell or for Moira's wedding to Luke O'Brien on the same day, Nell had always considered her family, embracing her and fretting over her as surely as she did her own children, grandchildren and great-grandchildren. She was the most nurturing person Moira had ever known.

Moira bounced her baby girl on her knee as she considered the problem they'd all been worrying about ever since they'd heard the news about Peter's untimely death right on the heels of the far happier news about his engagement to Kiera.

"Kiera will make her own choices," Dillon said, his tone a

mix of resignation and worry. "I know my daughter all too well. Pushing her to bend in the way we'd like will never work. She'll simply dig in her heels out of pure stubbornness, exactly as she did when she married Sean Malone against my wishes all those years ago. Right now she's probably regretting the very fact that she let us convince her to move to Dublin in the first place. She'll be listening to very little of the advice we offer."

"Well, it's sure that my brothers won't be around to support her," Moira said disdainfully. "She hasn't once mentioned them since Peter died. I doubt they come around at all these days except to ask for a handout."

Nell gave her a disapproving look, but Moira knew she was right. Her brothers were following a little too closely in their father's drunken footsteps. "She belongs here with us," she said emphatically, keeping her gaze steady on her grandfather. "You know I'm right. She needs the kind of family we've found here. A steady dose of the O'Briens will restore her spirits. She wasted years on bitterness and regrets after my dad left. I know she'd say she was working too hard to waste time on love, but the truth is she was too terrified to take a chance that she'd be making another poor choice. We can't allow her to do the same again."

To Moira's surprise, it was Nell who promptly backed her.

"I agree that coming here is exactly what she needs," she said, then reached over to stroke the baby's cheek. "And I think our darling little Kate right here and her need for a grandmother's attention is the very reason Kiera won't fight us on this."

Moira saw the light of near-certain victory spark in her grandfather's eyes and knew Nell had hit on the perfect solution. "You're suggesting I throw myself on her mercy, tell her that I'm in desperate need of help with the baby, even though our Kate is perfectly content in Carrie's day care center," Moira concluded.

"Which has been dreadfully overcrowded since the day it opened," Nell claimed with exaggerated innocence.

"Dreadfully," Dillon confirmed, nodding, his expression astonishingly serious for a man who knew they were bending the truth, if not flat-out breaking it. Nell's great-granddaughter's child care business was flourishing, that much was true, but she had more than enough competent staff to manage it.

"If you think it will take more to persuade her, there's your own husband's pub, which is in dire need of an extra pair of hands," Nell added. "You're far too busy with your photography and your travel to exhibitions to help my grandson out as you once did."

Moira nodded. "True enough. Megan would have me traveling once a month if I'd agree to it. I suspect she's exaggerating a bit, but she tells me she's had to turn down requests for shows, because I won't make myself available as often as she'd like. She's got quite a knack for inducing guilt."

"Exactly, but we can use that to our advantage with Kiera," Nell said. "And my health is far too fragile for me to be spending my spare minutes in the kitchen at the pub keeping a watchful eye on the chef to be sure the menu doesn't stray too far from proper Irish recipes."

"Nell, you've given us a scare or two, but in all honesty, you're about as fragile as a steel beam," Moira replied, but she was laughing at the clever strategy. If she handled the performance convincingly, it would play on all of her mum's weaknesses, most especially on her need to be useful while keeping a firm grip on her independence.

"And you're wickedly devious to boot," she told Nell. "Both traits I admire, I might add."

"I'll thank you for that," Nell said, clearly taking it as the praise Moira had intended. "With a contrary family the size of mine, it's always best to have a few tricks up my sleeve. Sadly, most of them are on to me now."

"Isn't this something we should at least be discussing with Luke?" Dillon asked, inserting a word of caution. "If we intend to push Kiera into a job at his pub, he should be brought on board with our plan."

"Leave Luke to me," Moira said confidently. "I think I can convince him of the advantages of having her here. It would allow him more free time at home with me and Kate. Mum is far more experienced at running a pub than I ever thought of being. Not only was she more competent, but she loved it as I never did. She'll be a true asset."

"Are we agreed, then, that once Luke's given us his blessing, Moira should be the one to make the call?" Dillon asked. "It'll receive a better reception than any suggestion that comes from me. Kiera and I have made our peace, but it's tenuous at best." He studied Moira. "How are your skills at bending the truth without getting caught?"

Moira laughed. "An improvement on yours, and that's a fact."

Luke walked into his house on Beach Lane well after midnight, expecting to find his wife and daughter sound asleep as they usually were. Instead, he opened the door to discover the soft glow of dozens of candles and his wife wearing one of those shimmery gowns that skimmed over her curves and never failed to cause a hitch in his breath in the few seconds before he managed to get it off her.

Suspicion warred with heat, but as usual the heat won. With his gaze locked with hers, he tried to assess the glint in her eyes as he crossed the room and accepted the glass of champagne she held out to him.

"It's been a while since I've had a welcome like this at the end of the day," he murmured, his gaze drifting to the swell of her breast where the gown had dipped low.

"And it's long overdue, it is," Moira said, her voice soft and filled with promise.

She pushed him back against the cushions of the sofa and settled snugly against him. "I've missed our time like this. Haven't you?"

"It's not as if our love life has been lacking," he commented in a choked voice as her hand tugged his T-shirt free and slipped below to caress bare skin.

"Not lacking for sure," she conceded. "But less spontaneous. You can't deny that. With our schedules so demanding, we practically need an appointment to have a moment like this."

"And you've been missing the spontaneity?"

"Old married couples need an occasional spark to liven things up," she said, and managed to say it with a straight face.

As intrigued as he was by where this was heading, Luke couldn't seem to stop the laugh that bubbled up. "Old married couple? Is that how you're thinking of us these days? When did we both turn gray and start hobbling around? In my opinion, we've barely left the honeymoon phase."

She frowned at his teasing. "If you're not interested after I've gone to all this trouble," she huffed in typical Moira fashion. She'd always been too quick to take offense.

He brushed a wayward strand of hair from her cheek. "I am always interested in you," he contradicted. "And will be until the day I die. However, Moira, my love, I know you a bit too well to take this seduction at face value. You have something on your mind. Out with that and then we'll get to the rest of the evening as you've planned it."

She looked as if she wanted to argue, but in the end she sighed and sat back, then took a healthy gulp of her champagne. Since Moira rarely indulged in alcohol, Luke figured whatever she was about to tell him was likely to be something she knew he wasn't going to want to hear.

"It's about my mum," she confessed.

Luke's antenna went on full alert. He and Kiera had called a tentative truce since he'd married her daughter, but they weren't exactly close. And though he sympathized with what she must be going through since Peter McDonough's unexpected and sudden death, he couldn't imagine what that had to do with him.

"I was with Nell and my grandfather earlier," Moira continued.

"So they're involved in this, too?" he asked, his antenna now waving as if there were a dozen signals coming at him all at once, none of them boding well. If his grandmother was involved, there was a very good chance it involved the sort of sneaky meddling that terrified everyone in the family. The only person even better at it was his uncle Mick O'Brien. Thankfully, so far his name hadn't come up.

"Just tell me," he instructed his wife. "What are the three of you conspiring about when it comes to your mother, and what could it possibly have to do with me?"

Moira leaned toward him, her expression earnest. "You know how devastated she was by Peter's death. We think she needs a change of scenery if she's not to go back to her old ways."

"Her old ways?"

"You know, retreating from the world, wallowing in her misery and bitterness," she explained. "I've already heard hints of that when we've spoken. She feels betrayed. The walls are going back up. It happened after my dad left. I can't let her waste the rest of her days being all alone again.

She's still young enough to enjoy a full and happy life, if only she'll allow it."

Luke recalled how impossible Kiera had been when they'd first met in Ireland. The only person topping her in that department had been the woman sitting right here with him, her skin glowing, the strap on her gown sliding provocatively low, and her voice filled with passion, albeit of an entirely different sort than when he'd first walked in the door. What sort of idiot was he to have redirected that passion to this conversation?

"I'm guessing you three have come up with a solution to save her from herself," he said warily.

"We have," Moira said enthusiastically. "We think she needs to come here, to be with us, with all of the O'Briens. She needs to be surrounded by family. It'll show her just how a life is meant to be lived. We'd be setting a good example."

Though Luke desperately wanted to argue, to claim it was a terrible idea to remind Kiera of all the family closeness she'd just lost when Peter died, he couldn't do it. Despite the flare-ups of old family feuds and conflicts, there was healing power in the O'Brien togetherness. He'd experienced it his entire life. And there was healing magic in Chesapeake Shores, as well. He'd have to be hard-hearted to deny that to Moira's mother.

"Fine. She'll come for a visit," he said. "Why would I object to that? When we built our house, we included a guest suite just for such a visit. When you furnished it, I know you did it to your mother's taste, hoping she'd find it comfortable the first time she came. I believe her favorite Irish blessing hangs on a plaque just inside the door."

"She'll find it welcoming, there's no doubt of that," Moira said. "But there's a bit more. We're thinking of something a little longer than a quick visit."

And here it comes, Luke thought, barely containing a sigh. "Tell me."

"I'm going to ask for her help with Kate," Moira began slowly, then added in a rush, "And you're going to give her my old job at the pub." Her smile brightened. "Won't that be grand? With all of her experience, she'll be far more help than I ever was."

He studied the hopeful glint in his wife's eyes and didn't even try to contain the sigh that came. When he didn't immediately speak the emphatic *no* that hovered on his lips, Moira beamed, clearly taking his silence as agreement.

"And you'll talk to Connor about getting her a work visa as your Irish consultant, just as you did for me?" she asked, referring to his cousin, who'd become a first-rate lawyer. "I understand it may be a bit trickier these days with changes in the law, but I have every confidence Connor can manage it."

"I'm a bit surprised you haven't already discussed this with him," Luke said.

"Never before talking to you," she said with a hint of indignation that made him chuckle.

"Then you weren't a hundred percent certain I'd go along with your scheme?"

"Maybe ninety-five percent," she admitted. "You've a stubborn streak that sometimes works against me."

"Pot calling the kettle black," he retorted. "You know you have me twisted around your finger. And what you can't accomplish, Nell can. I'm quite sure she'd have been by first thing tomorrow if you'd put out a distress call."

"But it's not coming to that, is it?" she asked hopefully.

Luke studied his wife closely. "Does it mean so much to you to have her come and stay for longer than a brief visit?"

"I think this change is what she needs. So do Nell and Grandfather. And I owe her, Luke. She gave up everything for my brothers and me. I don't think I realized how hard she worked or how many sacrifices she made until I'd had a taste of working in a pub myself. I used to blame her for not spending more time with us, but now that we have Kate, I can't imagine being away from her as much as my mum was away from us. It must have been hard for her to put work over her children. My brothers may be ungrateful louts, but I'm not."

"No, you're definitely not that," Luke said, though he couldn't help regretting it just a little. Then, again, having Kiera underfoot would be a small price to pay for the joy that Moira had brought into his life. "I'll call Connor in the morning."

Her eyes sparkled. "Seriously? You'll do it?"

"Was there ever any doubt? Now, come here, Moira, my love," he said, beckoning her closer. "Let's not waste this effort you've gone to tonight. I know you think we're somehow going to gain more time to ourselves with this plan of yours, but I have my doubts. I think we need to take full advantage of this bit of spontaneity."

"There will be more chances, I promise," Moira said, launching herself into his arms. "You'll see."

It helped her case that the strap on her gown slid off. After that, Luke could barely think of his own name, much less any arguments he might have wanted to offer.

Moira was thoroughly pleased with her efforts the night before. She might have used a little manipulation to get her way, but she was pretty sure Luke was pleased enough with the reward for his acquiescence.

When there was no response to her tap on the kitchen door at Nell's, she headed for the garden. Sure enough, Nell was on her knees weeding, while her grandfather observed.

She settled into the Adirondack chair next to his. "Shouldn't you be helping?" she asked him.

"Fool woman chased me off," he grumbled. "She claims I don't know a flower from a weed. Now, I ask you, how am I supposed to tell the difference this time of year? They're all just green things poking through the dirt."

Nell glanced up at that. "Wasn't a nursery among your business interests in Ireland?"

"Yes, and others ran it quite successfully," he countered.

Nell turned to Moira. "If he were half as uninvolved in that business as he claims, you'd think by now he'd have let me educate him about the difference," she said tartly. "I think he finds it convenient not to know."

Moira laughed. It was obviously a familiar argument. "Something tells me you're right, Nell. My grandfather has mastered any number of skills over the years. If he's not grasping this one, there's a reason for it."

Nell took off her gardening gloves. When she went to stand up, Moira started to her feet to assist her, only to be waved off.

"The day I can't get up on my own, I'll have to give this up," Nell said. "And since I don't intend to do that until I'm dead and gone, I'll manage."

"At least you got her to take a break for a cup of tea," Dillon said. "I've been trying since I came out here. It's probably stone-cold by now."

Still he poured her a cup and set it on the table beside her chair. "If you'd like a cup, you'll need to run into the house for one," he told Moira.

"Nothing for me. I just dropped Kate off at day care and stopped by here to give you both an update."

"You've talked to Kiera, then?" Nell said.

"No, only to Luke. He's agreed to the plan."

"I've no intention of asking how you persuaded him," her grandfather said. "I'll just accept the outcome as a blessing."

"He's promised to speak to Connor this morning to get him started on the paperwork. Now, if you'll make an airline reservation for Mum, I think we can put our plan in motion," Moira told him.

Dillon nodded at once. "I'll go straight in and do that now, though I'd probably best buy the kind that's refundable just in case she balks," he said. He touched Nell's cheek. "Shall I warm that tea for you?"

"I'm fine with it as it is," she said, covering his fingers with hers and giving them a brief squeeze.

Moira watched the two of them with a catch in her throat. Would she and Luke have that same sort of devotion after so many years? Of course, Nell and Dillon had fallen in love as teenagers, then separated and had families before being reunited. Perhaps that was why they were so grateful for their second chance.

She turned and caught Nell studying her.

"You're pleased by the prospect of having your mother here?" Nell asked. "I know the two of you haven't always had an easy time of it."

"True enough," Moira admitted. "But I think I understand the choices she made a little better now. I want her to finally have some of the happiness she deserves. I think she may find that here. There's a lot to be said for a fresh start."

"Especially in Chesapeake Shores," Nell said.

"Yes, especially in Chesapeake Shores."

Which was why later that very afternoon, as Kate conveniently cried in the background, Moira called her mum and, with a note of desperation in her voice, pleaded for Kiera to come to Chesapeake Shores for an extended visit.

"I don't need to be at loose ends in a strange country,"

Kiera argued. "Peter's children have offered me a place at the pub for as long as I want to stay on. They'll even boost my pay if I'm willing to take on managing it, so they can go blissfully on with their own lives."

"And you're willing to accept their charity?" Moira asked, putting the worst possible spin on what had no doubt been a genuine and well-meant offer that would benefit all of them, including her mother.

Her comment was greeted with silence, which told Moira her mother had considered the very same thing. They were very much alike in questioning the real motive behind any kindness they might feel was undeserved.

"We're your family, not them. You won't be in the way here," Moira said, pressing her tiny advantage. "I truly need the help, and you should spend a little time with your first grandchild. And with me traveling so much lately, Luke could use your presence at the pub. The customers like chatting with someone with an Irish lilt in their voice. It provides a touch of authenticity."

"So I'm to be the Irish window dressing?" Kiera asked, the once-familiar tart sarcasm back in her voice. "How is that an improvement over accepting charity from the McDonoughs?"

"The job here would be much more than that," Moira promised. "This is a family business, and you're family. It would be almost the same as if it were your own restaurant."

"I doubt Luke would see it that way. Wasn't this pub his dream? Besides, it's not as if I can waltz in and take a job in America," Kiera protested. "I know there are laws about that sort of thing."

"Luke's cousin Connor will handle the legalities of a work visa, just as he did for me," Moira assured her. "Focus on spending time with little Kate for now. I can't wait for you to see her in person. She's growing so fast, and she's a handful. You'll probably find her to be a lot like me in that respect."

With the baby's pitiful cries to lend credence to her story, Moira gave a silent fist pump when Kiera reluctantly agreed to take the very flight that Dillon had already booked. As she hung up, Moira gave the baby a noisy kiss that changed tears to smiles.

"Now we've only to find a way to make her stay," she said.

And that, most likely, was going to be a far more difficult task. Kiera might be feeling a bit vulnerable at the moment, but it wouldn't last. And when her fine temper was restored, there could be hell to pay for their manipulation.

Don't miss
Lilac Lane
by #1 New York Times *bestselling author*
Sherryl Woods,
coming soon wherever
MIRA books and ebooks are sold.

www.Harlequin.com